The Library of Literature

Under the General Editorship of
JOHN HENRY RALEIGH & IAN WATT

The Scarlet Letter
A Romance

THE LIBRARY OF LITERATURE

The text of *The Scarlet Letter* is that of the Centenary Edition of the Works of Nathaniel Hawthorne, a publication of the Ohio State University Center for Textual Studies and the Ohio State University Press.

The
Scarlet Letter
A Romance
by
Nathaniel Hawthorne

EDITED

WITH AN INTRODUCTION BY

LARZER ZIFF

University of California
Berkeley

 THE **BOBBS-MERRILL** COMPANY, INC.
A SUBSIDIARY OF HOWARD W. SAMS & CO., INC.
Publishers • INDIANAPOLIS • NEW YORK

Nathaniel Hawthorne, 1804–1864

The Scarlet Letter was first published in 1850

INTRODUCTION

1: Hawthorne's Preparation

In March of 1837, the American Stationers' Company of Boston issued a volume of stories titled *Twice-Told Tales*. The stories were "twice-told" because all had previously appeared, most of them pseudonymously, in that chaos of taste and tastelessness which was the American magazine market of the time. But this was the first major appearance by name of Nathaniel Hawthorne, who, as he reflected some twenty-five years later, was thereby attempting "to open an intercourse with the world."

Twelve years before the publication of the tales, Nathaniel Hawthorne had graduated from provincial Bowdoin College, eighteenth in a class of thirty-eight. For the next twelve years, he had lived principally in his mother's house on Herbert Street in Salem and had there written for magazines and undertaken hack work for publishers. In his room in that house, he had read and reread Spenser, Cervantes, Shakespeare, Bunyan, Fielding, Pope, Boswell, and Johnson, together with the histories of early New England. In his room he had written a Gothic novel of college life, *Fanshawe*, which he published at his own expense in 1828, and which he recalled in shame when he felt its ineptness and immaturity. In his room he had once burned a book-length collection of stories when he became dissatisfied with their imperfections.

Writing of this room in his notebook, Hawthorne said, "And here I sat a long, long time, waiting patiently for the world to know me, and sometimes wondering why it did not know me sooner, or whether it would ever know me at all." At a later date, he told his notebook, "In this dismal chamber fame was won."

While Hawthorne was perfecting his art, the Salem outside

his window was committing itself to an active present. The town's interest was trade; the town's politics were Whig, to ensure a protective tariff on manufacturing and cheap sources of raw goods; the town's religion was becoming liberal, with emphases on benevolence as the key to life and on explanations of evil as the absence of good; and the town's intellectual class was beginning to be attracted by the doctrines advanced by Ralph Waldo Emerson and others in the neighboring town of Concord. But Hawthorne, working, reading, and brooding in his chamber, was unable to accept the ideals that came to be known as Transcendentalism and was distrustful of the commerciality of the Whig Party.

His political difference from the majority of the neighbors of his class was based on the opinion that the Democratic Party with its agrarian Western flavor was more representative of what the United States should be. Early one morning in 1833 he had slipped from his chamber to see the great man Andrew Jackson pass on his way in procession to Boston. What he saw confirmed his taste for Democratic politics. He would have agreed with Emerson's belief that the Democrats had the more noble ideas, and since he did not share Emerson's faith in the power of great men he would not have agreed that the Whigs were the better party because they had the more outstanding statesmen.

Indeed, Hawthorne's closest friends were prominent members of the Democratic Party, among them that undistinguished man Franklin Pierce, and Hawthorne's loyalty to friends and to party was to be rewarded at three stages of his literary career. When, in 1839, Hawthorne became engaged to be married, Pierce and his other friends procured him a position in the Boston Custom House; when, in 1844, his first child arrived and his writing failed to provide an adequate income, he was appointed to the Custom House in his native town; and, in 1853, after Pierce's election to the Presidency, toward which end Hawthorne had contributed a campaign biography, he was appointed United States Consul in Liverpool.

Hawthorne's ideological differences from the majority of his class, however, were not to be explained on the basis of friendship, but, rather, went deeper. While he was far from being a Puritan—since, in his day, if the term had any precise meaning at all it signified a member of the Protestant (usually Congregational) church who held to Calvinism—his interest in the Puritan founders of Massachusetts, among whom his ancestors were numbered, was more than familial. In his study of early New England history, he developed an understanding of and a considerable sympathy for the sturdy seventeenth-century religionists. At the core of the kind of Puritanism that founded Massachusetts was an insistence upon the inescapably imperfect nature of man, and Hawthorne, unlike most of his New England contemporaries then working in literature, held a qualified view of man's perfectibility. If a man were to be saved, the Puritans held, it was because God had predestined him to salvation and would bestow saving grace upon him. While he did not adopt this terminology, Hawthorne, too, distrusted a salvation that could come from outward things, from the doing of good deeds.

The theology of the first generations of Puritans emphasized piety, the possession of divine grace, far more than morality. It acknowledged that all men who possessed piety would behave in a virtuous fashion but did not accept morality as an unqualified indication of piety. Many a hypocrite, the Puritans maintained, could conduct himself morally and, nevertheless, be without grace. When their opponents urged upon them the argument that morality was the only satisfactory indication of piety, that the appearance of a blessed man would match the reality, that, in short, a tree is known by its fruits, the Puritans replied that while others may know a tree by its fruits, the tree knows itself not by its outward show but by its roots. The potential difference between appearance and reality that followed from this belief was a rich suggestion for Hawthorne, one that encouraged his psychological explorations and yet, paradoxically, helped fix in him the belief that the arch sin was to meddle with the soul of another, for this soul was one's divinity or his damnation, his exclusively private identity.

Nathaniel Hawthorne belonged to no Calvinist church, and he was enough of a man of his times to take a more confident view of the individual's ability to improve himself. Nevertheless, he was not comfortable with what he believed to be the blind optimism of the Transcendentalist movement. He could not share the belief that the outward world was plastic, ready to be molded by the individual with moral strength enough to impress his spirit on his surroundings. Nor could he accept the view that the moral spirit which moved man was identical with that which moved nature, so that, finally, the good man and his surroundings were one and the same. He retained enough of the outlook of his ancestors to believe that corruption was a more pervasive and a more dominant element in the world of men than prevailing idealistic theory granted. And while he worked within the broadest assumptions of the Romantic movement and saw nature as an informative symbol of man's moral condition, he did not see it as unqualifiedly virtuous. In even the most sunshiny of the forests in *Twice-Told Tales* there lingered an incipient evil akin to the Satanism that the Puritans believed dominated the wilds.

Accordingly, as Hawthorne moved out from Herbert Street into politics, marriage, and the intellectual currents of his day, he always held back a part of himself. Even while his sister-in-law, Elizabeth Peabody, was at the center of the Transcendentalist group and his wife, Sophia, attempted to draw him in more closely, he remained, watchful and interested, on the periphery. This condition of being never within and yet close enough to analyze reinforced a habit of mind Hawthorne had developed in his room on Herbert Street, that of the observer of a life of which he was not fully a part. It manifested itself in a number of the sketches he had written for magazines, was to continue to be a shaping force in his work through the complex point of view of *The Blithedale Romance* and the development of the character of Holgrave in *The House of the Seven Gables* and that of Kenyon in *The Marble Faun,* and was to control the way in which he reported his Custom House experience in the sketch prefaced to *The Scarlet Letter.*

ii: Hawthorne's Technique

Early biographers exaggerated the solitude of Hawthorne's life in the "dismal chamber," and they have been corrected by those who have pointed out the frequent trips Hawthorne took in this twelve-year period and the friends he had outside of Salem. But it remains clear that these crucial years of study and practice in Salem formed the basis for the uncommitted-observer stance to which his studies of the Puritans gave strength. As he sat in that chamber looking at the world outside and wanting to open an intercourse with it, he matched his yearning for an active role and public acceptance with an insistence that the world meet him halfway and face the realities he perceived behind the façade of life. He developed a corresponding technique for the *Twice-Told Tales,* unfolding his narratives in terms of double explanations: one, the outside view, providing realistic cause and effect, explaining the action in terms of everyday happenings; the other, the chamber view, insisting on psychological and supernatural explanations without which natural explanations became shallow and unimportant. He rarely made the two views mutually exclusive. In the last analysis, he offered the reader not a choice between the two, but an opportunity to accept both, and, as a result, to perceive an inner dimension in the lives of the characters.

This technique carried with it certain habits of style. The most obvious, perhaps, is Hawthorne's fondness for indirectness or seeming evasion when the mythic or supernatural alternatives are introduced. He will tell his reader, with an apologetic smile but a determined glint, that legend has it that such and such happened, or that the townspeople of the day whispered certain rumors, or that an old manuscript that perhaps cannot be trusted asserts an interesting interpretation. To do this successfully, he needed whatever blurring of outlines elapsed time could lend, and he therefore set most of his early stories in the colonial past. But the blurring of time was not, eventually, called upon for the same purpose—to amuse with a relative disregard for probability—as that for which the conventional romantic artist of the day employed it. Rather, the softening that resulted from time's casting its azure tint about events was a softening of surfaces, permitting the author to penetrate through to the psychological realities that came to dominate his greatest works. This method was part of Hawthorne's conscious craft, and, in "The Custom-House," he explains it, in the metaphor of the moonlit, familiar room, as part of his aesthetic and intimately linked with his moral outlook.

Moreover, his choice of seventeenth-century American Puritan settings was not dictated merely by their remoteness. The Puritan outlook, with its acceptance of the active presence of evil in the world, consistently saw a moral drama in the most petty details of daily life. This drama had two stages: one, the soul of the individual concerned, where good and bad held their tug of war; and two, the outward world of nature and the human community, where actions became symbolic of the internal struggle and natural phenomena became ambiguously indicative of the divine intention.

The world of the American Puritans, then, was an appropriate setting for a novelist who was committed to moral drama, investigation of psychological reality, and symbolic use of appearance. Setting his action in such a world, he immediately gained an air of probability for both his subject and its technique. His readers knew that this, indeed, had been a world in which men read actions and natural phenomena symbolically and were thus more receptive to the novelist's intensive manner.

But the setting should not mislead the reader. The Puritan world in which Hawthorne placed his action is not that of history but of art. A superficial indication of the difference lies in the factual changes that Hawthorne unhesitatingly made. As the notes to the following text indicate, he took liberties with the actual dates of historical events, the known characteristics of historical personages, and the particular nature of certain laws and institutions. A more fundamental indication of the difference is that the moral world of Hawthorne's Puritan narratives, including *The Scarlet Letter,* is the product of the author's imagination. The historical facts are that a community of Puritans with certain beliefs about the nature of good and evil did exist in Massachusetts and that these beliefs led them to see all of life as a spiritual struggle. These historical data lend themselves to the sort of drama Nathaniel Hawthorne wished to write. But the specific beliefs explored in *The Scarlet Letter* and the specific actions set forth are not, in any detail, those of the American Puritans. They are, rather, the result of Hawthorne's life, and they stand as an examination of human, not Puritan, experience.

Another habit of style developed to re-enforce the technique of the double alternative is apparent in Hawthorne's color imagery. The outside view is almost always accompanied by bright colors and lights, while the chamber view is conveyed in scenes in which dark colors and shadows dominate. Very frequently, of course, the two color schemes contrast within the same scene in accompaniment to the thematic values of the episode.

III: The Technique of *The Scarlet Letter*

The Scarlet Letter (1850) is the mature embodiment of the art Hawthorne so consciously developed. The very introduction to the work, "The Custom-House," explicitly takes up the conflict of the artist's private habits with the man's public profession. In creating the fiction that he is merely editing a discovered manuscript in the text that will follow, Hawthorne establishes a meeting ground between the remoteness of his tale and the immediacy of his audience. In that essay also, a theory of romance, one that will explain the technique of double alternatives, is offered.

The novel itself almost immediately establishes this technique as central. In the second paragraph of a very brief first chapter, our attention is directed to a wild rosebush growing by the prison door. The next paragraph talks about the bush and closes the chapter with its emphasis on the two possible explanations for its presence. Either the rosebush stood at the prison door because it survived on that spot long after the wilderness gave way to civilization, a realistic explanation; or it sprang up magically as a result of the persecuted Anne Hutchinson's having trod the spot when she was imprisoned, a supernatural explanation. Hawthorne, characteristically, declines to choose an explanation for us, but, also characteristically, having given both, he uses the ambiguity to focus the reader's attention on what results from having both alternatives available. Since the bush is there, he says, he will present the reader with one of its flowers: "It may serve, let us hope, to symbolize some sweet moral blossom, that may be found along the track, or relieve the darkening close of a tale of human frailty and sorrow." We further note that there are two reasons even for presenting the reader with the flower.

If we continue through the novel with rose clutched in hand, as Hawthorne wants us to do, we have accepted a symbolic offering that will perform an implicit function as well as the two mentioned explicitly: it will serve as a constant reminder that, just as its origin may be accounted for in two ways which, taken together, yield a third meaning, so the tale that we are about to read is symbolic and will yield up its fullness symbolically, as does the rose.

iv: The Moral Drama of *The Scarlet Letter*

The act of adultery that sets in motion the plot of *The Scarlet Letter* occurred before the opening of the novel that is concerned with its effects. The first effect to be emphasized is

that the act was a sin against God and a crime against the
sanctity of the community, and the early chapters develop this
view from the point of view of those who hold it, the resi-
dents of the town of Boston.

The novel moves from the community to a consideration of
the effect of the sin on one who was personally wronged by it,
Roger Chillingworth. Unsatisfied with traditional social and
ecclesiastical punishment, he begins a course of private revenge that renders him diabolical. The act, then, not only
begets punishment but also brings about further evil; and, if
we view the further evil as greater than whatever bad attaches
to the act of adultery, then we see that evil is not merely perpetuated by evil, it is multiplied.

When we then turn to the effect on Hester herself, we see
that the complexity of the problem increases. For Hester,
while she outwardly shows a noble acceptance of the consequences of her deed and an heroic perseverance in the face of
them, inwardly does not accept either the interpretation of the
community or that of Roger Chillingworth. While—laws then
and laws today being what they are—she agrees to the fact that
she has committed a social crime, she does not believe she has
committed a sin. Indeed, she maintains that what she did had
a consecration of its own and needed no hallowing from any
source other than that of the natural love from which it sprang.
In her isolation, however, forced to keep this conviction to
herself for want of a sympathetic human community, she is
driven toward psychological imbalance. Not a moment too
soon, she realizes that if she continues in this condition she,
too, will become diabolic—she will have allowed and aided evil
to beget greater evil. Not only will she become a party to the
torturing of Dimmesdale, but she also will have cut off all
human sympathies.

The immediate effect of the act of adultery on Dimmesdale,
who values and, in the last analysis, accepts the community's
frame of reference, is to drive him into hypocrisy, the most
complex sin of the Protestant tradition of which he is an

eminent representative—Spenser's master villain was the master hypocrite, Archimago; Milton's Satan could pass the good angels undetected because only God could tell a hypocrite. This hypocrisy makes Dimmesdale fit prey for Chillingworth, so that the minister too becomes a willing instrument in the multiplication of evil.

These three central characters lead double lives, then, the outward appearance failing to match the inner reality. But relative to Hester's problem, Dimmesdale's is simple, for he accepts the values of the community, and if he can just force himself to confession he will be made whole once more. Hester, however, is the hero of the drama, for she may, if she will, call quits now that she is paying the public price. Nevertheless, she persists in being true to her perceptions even though they bring her further travail. Pearl, the fourth central character, is the only one who appears to be what she is —the act embodied. Fanciful, changeful, and at times supernatural, she openly manifests her spiritual condition in costume and in act.

True to the warning he issued when he handed the reader the symbolic rose, Hawthorne does not clearly stand with any of the characters. The reader, of course, soon sees that he does not side with Chillingworth and also recognizes that Pearl, as a character, represents no point of view at all. But between the community and Hester, Hawthorne will not choose. While he clearly admires Hester, he yet insists on basic virtues in men like Bellingham and Wilson; and while he criticizes the Puritan ethic, he insists as late as Chapter 13 that with regard to Hester "The scarlet letter had not done its office."

Light, color, and shadow re-enforce this ambiguity which, eventually, extends to touch everything in the novel. With regard to setting, for instance, the community of Boston somberly stands for an insistence on the positive presence of evil and views the surrounding sunlit forest as the abode of the natural, the untamed, and, therefore, of evil. That same forest, we see, can be the source of solace for Hester, who has insisted upon the divinity of natural love, and is an area where, correspondingly, Pearl finds her deepest affinities. But, we are shown, the citizens of the town also know how to dress in gay colors and also know how to forgive. And, we are shown, the sun can go out of the forest, and dark acts may very well be performed there.

Although Hawthorne persists in his ambiguity, he never does so to the extent of confusion. We are always aware of the very precise manner in which the symbols come into being and in which one alternative is matched by another; we are always aware, in short, of an artistic purpose in the ambiguity. Hawthorne's meaning is nowhere made explicit, although in Chapter 13, with the examination of the thoughts that visit Hester's consciousness, we come the closest to outright authorial comment. Here we gather the sense that Hester's doctrine may some day be the beautiful guiding theory of life that she wants it to be, but not in her day and not in any day when it must be established as the consequence of human frailty rather than human strength. In the main, however, Hawthorne's meaning is not so to be located. It is, rather, what the reader takes from having experienced the complexity of *The Scarlet Letter*, from having allowed Hawthorne's technique to create experience. Doubtless such a meaning can and perhaps should be articulated by the reader who has finished *The Scarlet Letter*. But, as the rosebush warns at the outset, the major task of the reader and his chief reward is to allow the novel to bring him a meaning that has been tempered in the tension of ambiguity and stands the stronger for it.

LARZER ZIFF

University of California
Berkeley
May 1, 1963

NATHANIEL HAWTHORNE
CHRONOLOGY

1804   Born July 4, in Salem, Massachusetts, son of Nathaniel Hathorne, sea captain, and Elizabeth Clarke Manning Hathorne.

1808   His father died in Surinam (Dutch Guiana) while on a voyage.

1818   Moved with his mother and two sisters to Raymond, Maine, where his mother had family and property.

1819   Returned to school in Salem.

1821   Entered Bowdoin College.

1825   Was graduated from Bowdoin and returned to his mother's house in Salem.

1828   Paid to have *Fanshawe* published.

1837   *Twice-Told Tales* published; continued writing stories for magazines and doing hack work for publishers.

1839   Became engaged to marry Sophia Peabody of Salem; took a post in the Boston Custom House.

1841   Joined Brook Farm.

1842   Married Sophia Peabody and settled at the Old Manse.

1844   A daughter, Una, born.

1846   Moved to Salem and became Surveyor of Customs; published *Mosses from an Old Manse;* a son, Julian, born.

1849   Left Custom House and completed *The Scarlet Letter.*

1850   *The Scarlet Letter* published; good critical reception; moved to "Tanglewood," Lenox, Massachusetts, where he became friendly with Herman Melville, who lived nearby and was working then on *Moby Dick,* which he dedicated to Hawthorne.

1851   *The House of the Seven Gables* and *The Snow-Image and Other Twice-Told Tales* published; moved to West Newton, Massachusetts; a daughter, Rose, born.

1852   *The Blithedale Romance* published; moved to the "Wayside" in Concord.

1853   Went to Liverpool as United States Consul.

1857   Consular appointment ended; traveled on the continent and settled in Italy.

1859   Returned to live for some months in England.
1860   *The Marble Faun* published; returned to the "Wayside."
1863   *Our Old Home,* sketches of England, published.
1864   Died May 19, in Plymouth, New Hampshire, while on a vacation trip with Franklin Pierce; buried May 23, in Concord.

SELECTED BIBLIOGRAPHY

I. Hawthorne's Chief Works

Fanshawe: A Tale, 1828; *Twice-Told Tales*, 1837; *Mosses from an Old Manse*, 1846; *The Scarlet Letter*, 1850; *The House of the Seven Gables*, 1851; *The Snow-Image and Other Twice-Told Tales*, 1851; *The Blithedale Romance*, 1852; *Tanglewood Tales for Girls and Boys*, 1853; *The Marble Faun*, 1860; *Our Old Home*, 1863; *Septimius Felton: or, The Elixir of Life*, 1872; *The Dolliver Romance and Other Pieces*, 1876; *Dr. Grimshawe's Secret*, 1883.

II. Collected Editions

The Complete Works of Nathaniel Hawthorne. 12 vols. "Riverside Edition." Boston, 1883.

The Complete Writings of Nathaniel Hawthorne. 22 vols. "Old Manse Edition." Boston, 1900.

A definitive edition of the complete works of Hawthorne is now in preparation by the Ohio State University Press and began appearing in 1963 as the "Centenary Edition."

III. Letters and Notebooks

Letters of Hawthorne to William D. Ticknor, 1851–1864. 2 vols. Newark, 1910.

Love Letters of Nathaniel Hawthorne, 1833–41 and 1841–63. Chicago, 1907.

Passages from the French and Italian Note-Books, ed. Sophia Hawthorne. Boston, 1872.

The American Notebooks by Nathaniel Hawthorne, ed. Randall Stewart. New Haven, 1932.

The English Notebooks by Nathaniel Hawthorne, ed. Randall Stewart. New York, 1941.

IV. Bibliography

There is no definitive bibliography of Hawthorne's works. A guide to the existing ones is in Robert E. Spiller and others, *Literary History of the United States* (New York, 1948), III, 552–53. For a useful list of works on Hawthorne, see Walter Blair, "Nathaniel Hawthorne," in *Eight American Authors: A Review of Research and Criticism*, ed. Floyd Stovall (New York, 1956).

V. Biography

The standard modern biography is Randall Stewart, *Nathaniel Hawthorne: A Biography* (New Haven, 1948).

The three critical biographies that have been most influential are: Newton Arvin, *Hawthorne* (Boston, 1929); Henry James, *Hawthorne* (London, 1879); and Mark Van Doren, *Nathaniel Hawthorne* (New York, 1949).

In addition, there are several critical biographies that tend to reflect the intellectual climate at the time of their production as much as they do that of Hawthorne's time, and a number of biographies and memoirs of Hawthorne by those who knew him. The most interesting of the latter group are: James T. Fields, *Yesterdays with Authors* (Boston, 1872); Julian Hawthorne, *Nathaniel Hawthorne and His Wife*, 2 vols. (Boston, 1885), and *Hawthorne Reading* (Cleveland, 1902); and George Parsons Lathrop, *A Study of Hawthorne* (Boston, 1876).

VI. Source Studies

Chandler, Elizabeth L. *A Study of the Sources of the Tales and Romances Written by Nathaniel Hawthorne Before 1853.* ("Smith College Studies in Modern Languages," Vol. VI.) Northampton, 1926.

Reid, Alfred S. *The Yellow Ruff & The Scarlet Letter: A Source of Hawthorne's Novel.* Gainesville, 1953.

Ryskamp, Charles. "The New England Sources of *The Scarlet Letter*," *American Literature*, XXXI (November 1959), 257–72.

VII. Special Studies of *The Scarlet Letter*

Feidelson, Charles, Jr. *Symbolism and American Literature.* Chicago, 1953. Contains a consideration of *The Scarlet Letter* as "a kind of exposition of the nature of symbolic perception."

Fogle, Richard H. *Hawthorne's Fiction: The Light and the Dark.* Norman, Okla., 1952. Examines the nature of the "unresolved contradiction" that is the "true conclusion" of *The Scarlet Letter*.

Lawrence, D. H. *Studies in Classic American Literature*. London, 1922. A section on *The Scarlet Letter* tells the reader what he will hear if he listens to the "diabolic undertone" of the novel.

Matthiessen, F. O. *American Renaissance: Art and Expression in the Age of Emerson and Whitman*. New York, 1941. Includes a distinguished consideration of *The Scarlet Letter* as it comes from Hawthorne's talent and as it interrelates with Hawthorne's other works and the great works of the period.

Stewart, Randall, ed. *The American Notebooks by Nathaniel Hawthorne*. New Haven, 1932. See Introduction for an exposition of the characters and themes of *The Scarlet Letter* as they develop from Hawthorne's notes and as they relate to the characters and themes of other Hawthorne works.

Waggoner, Hyatt H. *Hawthorne: A Critical Study*. Cambridge, 1955. A consideration of the types of images in *The Scarlet Letter* and the answers to questions of meaning and value that they suggest.

Winters, Yvor. *Maule's Curse: Seven Studies in the History of American Obscurantism*. Norfolk, 1938. Includes a consideration of the philosophical and theological influences that made Hawthorne an allegorist and *The Scarlet Letter* an allegory.

VIII. Articles on *The Scarlet Letter*

Blair, Walter. "Color, Light and Shadow in Hawthorne's Fiction," *New England Quarterly*, xv (March 1942), 79–94. A study of the way in which Hawthorne uses images of light and color to add to and reveal meaning.

Carpenter, F. I. "Scarlet A Minus," *College English*, v (January 1944), 173–80. Based on the premise that *The Scarlet Letter* is not a major classic because of ambiguous logic and a moralistic conclusion, this essay reconsiders from a modern perspective the problem of evil presented in the work.

Gerber, John. "Form and Content in *The Scarlet Letter*," *New England Quarterly*, xvii (March 1944), 22–55. A discussion of the interdependence of form and content in the novel, revealing the artistic sophistication of the work.

Hart, J. E. "*The Scarlet Letter*: One Hundred Years After," *New England Quarterly*, xxiii (September 1950), 381–95. Hawthorne's characters are related to Hawthorne's life to reveal his views of art and the relation of the individual to the world.

Hawthorne, Julian. "The Making of *The Scarlet Letter*," *Bookman*, LXXIV (December 1931), 401–11. A description of Hawthorne's family life at the time that he was at work on his masterpiece.

Walcutt, Charles Child. "*The Scarlet Letter* and Its Modern Critics," *Nineteenth Century Fiction*, VII (March 1953), 251–64. A classification and estimate of modern interpretations of *The Scarlet Letter*.

Ziff, Larzer. "The Ethical Dimension of 'The Custom-House,' " *Modern Language Notes*, LXXIII (May 1958), 338–44. An attempt to relate Hawthorne's introductory essay to the novel itself.

Preface to the Second Edition

Much to the author's surprise, and (if he may say so without additional offence) considerably to his amusement, he finds that his sketch of official life, introductory to THE SCARLET LETTER, has created an unprecedented excitement in the respectable community immediately around him. It could hardly have been more violent, indeed, had he burned down the Custom-House, and quenched its last smoking ember in the blood of a certain venerable personage, against whom he is supposed to cherish a peculiar malevolence.[1] As the public disapprobation would weigh very heavily on him, were he conscious of deserving it, the author begs leave to say, that he has carefully read over the introductory pages, with a purpose to alter or expunge whatever might be found amiss, and to make the best reparation in his power for the atrocities of which he has been adjudged guilty. But it appears to him, that the only remarkable features of the sketch are its frank and genuine good-humor, and the general accuracy with which he has conveyed his sincere impressions of the characters therein described. As to enmity, or ill-feeling of any kind, personal or political, he utterly disclaims such motives. The sketch might, perhaps, have been wholly omitted, without loss to the public, or detriment to the book; but, having undertaken to write it, he conceives that it could not have been done in a better or a

[1] In "The Custom-House," Hawthorne goes into detail about his political appointment and the controversy that ensued upon the change of federal administration. (See page xviii, Introduction, and Notes 11 and 29, "The Custom-House.") Hawthorne was a Democrat, and this "personage" was the leader of the Salem Whig party, the Reverend Charles Wentworth Upham (1802–1875). He is commonly believed to have been the model for the portrait of Judge Pyncheon in *The House of the Seven Gables*.

kindlier spirit, nor, so far as his abilities availed, with a livelier effect of truth.

The author is constrained, therefore, to republish his introductory sketch without the change of a word.

SALEM, *March 30, 1850.*

CONTENTS

The Scarlet Letter

A Romance

PLAN OF BOSTON
DECEMBER 25, 1645

SHOWING PLACES MENTIONED IN

THE SCARLET LETTER

BASED ON A MAP DRAWN BY GEORGE
LAMB IN 1903: **SERIES OF PLANS OF BOSTON**
(BOSTON. 1905)

WEST HILL

BEACON

THE BURYING GROUND

SCHOOL

WILLIAM HIBBINS' HOUSE

THE SPRINGATE

GOVERNOR WINTHROP'S HOUSE

FORT FIELD

FORT HILL

WINDMILL POINT

The Custom-House

Introductory to "The Scarlet Letter"

It is a little remarkable, that—though disinclined to talk over-much of myself and my affairs at the fireside, and to my personal friends—an autobiographical impulse should twice in my life have taken possession of me, in addressing the public. The first time was three or four years since, when I favored the reader—inexcusably, and for no earthly reason, that either the indulgent reader or the intrusive author could imagine—with a description of my way of life in the deep quietude of an Old Manse.[1] And now—because, beyond my deserts, I was happy enough to find a listener or two on the former occasion—I again seize the public by the button, and talk of my three years' experience in a Custom-House. The example of the famous "P. P., Clerk of this Parish,"[2] was never more faithfully followed. The truth seems to be, however, that, when he casts his leaves forth upon the wind, the author addresses, not the many who will fling aside his volume, or never take it up, but the few who will understand him, better than most of his schoolmates and lifemates. Some authors, indeed, do far more than this, and indulge themselves in such confidential depths of

[1] After his marriage to Sophia Peabody on July 8, 1842, Hawthorne took up his residence at the Old Manse in Concord. This had once been the Emerson family home, and here Ralph Waldo Emerson had written some of his early essays. When Hawthorne published a collection of tales and sketches in 1846, he called them *Mosses from an Old Manse* and, in the introductory chapter, talked of himself and "welcomed" the reader "into the cheery little study," as he notes later on page 6.

[2] The Tory writers in the circle of Alexander Pope found a favorite target in Bishop Burnet. In *The Memoirs of P. P. Clerk of this Parish*, they constructed a satire on the self-important, gossipy manner the Bishop has in his *History of My Own Times*. Now writing another memoir of himself, Hawthorne wryly invites comparison with the egotistical P. P.

revelation as could fittingly be addressed, only and exclusively, to the one heart and mind of perfect sympathy; as if the printed book, thrown at large on the wide world, were certain to find out the divided segment of the writer's own nature, and complete his circle of existence by bringing him into communion with it. It is scarcely decorous, however, to speak all, even where we speak impersonally. But—as thoughts are frozen and utterance benumbed, unless the speaker stand in some true relation with his audience—it may be pardonable to imagine that a friend, a kind and apprehensive, though not the closest friend, is listening to our talk; and then, a native reserve being thawed by this genial consciousness, we may prate of the circumstances that lie around us, and even of ourself, but still keep the inmost Me behind its veil. To this extent and within these limits, an author, methinks, may be autobiographical, without violating either the reader's rights or his own.

It will be seen, likewise, that this Custom-House sketch has a certain propriety, of a kind always recognized in literature, as explaining how a large portion of the following pages came into my possession, and as offering proofs of the authenticity of a narrative therein contained. This, in fact,—a desire to put myself in my true position as editor, or very little more, of the most prolix among the tales that make up my volume,[3]—this, and no other, is my true reason for assuming a personal relation with the public. In accomplishing the main purpose, it has appeared allowable, by a few extra touches, to give a faint representation of a mode of life not heretofore described, together with some of the characters that move in it, among whom the author happened to make one.

In my native town of Salem, at the head of what, half a century ago, in the days of old King Derby,[4] was a bustling

---

[3] See Hawthorne's note, page 44.

[4] Elias Hasket Derby (1739-1799), merchant and shipowner, who pioneered in the Far East trade and whose enterprises were a chief cause of the prosperity of the port of Salem in his day.

wharf,—but which is now burdened with decayed wooden
warehouses, and exhibits few or no symptoms of commercial
life; except, perhaps, a bark or brig, half-way down its melancholy length, discharging hides; or, nearer at hand, a Nova
Scotia schooner, pitching out her cargo of firewood,—at the
head, I say, of this dilapidated wharf, which the tide often
overflows, and along which, at the base and in the rear of the
row of buildings, the track of many languid years is seen in a
border of unthrifty grass,—here, with a view from its front
windows adown this not very enlivening prospect, and thence
across the harbour, stands a spacious edifice of brick. From the
loftiest point of its roof, during precisely three and a half
hours of each forenoon, floats or droops, in breeze or calm,
the banner of the republic; but with the thirteen stripes turned
vertically, instead of horizontally, and thus indicating that a
civil, and not a military post of Uncle Sam's government, is
here established. Its front is ornamented with a portico of half
a dozen wooden pillars, supporting a balcony, beneath which
a flight of wide granite steps descends towards the street. Over
the entrance hovers an enormous specimen of the American
eagle, with outspread wings, a shield before her breast, and, if
I recollect aright, a bunch of intermingled thunderbolts and
barbed arrows in each claw. With the customary infirmity of
temper that characterizes this unhappy fowl, she appears, by
the fierceness of her beak and eye and the general truculency
of her attitude, to threaten mischief to the inoffensive community; and especially to warn all citizens, careful of their
safety, against intruding on the premises which she over-
shadows with her wings. Nevertheless, vixenly as she looks,
many people are seeking, at this very moment, to shelter
themselves under the wing of the federal eagle; imagining, I
presume, that her bosom has all the softness and snugness of an
eider-down pillow. But she has no great tenderness, even in her
best of moods, and, sooner or later,—oftener soon than late,—
is apt to fling off her nestlings with a scratch of her claw, a dab
of her beak, or a rankling wound from her barbed arrows.

The pavement round about the above-described edifice—which we may as well name at once as the Custom-House of the port—has grass enough growing in its chinks to show that it has not, of late days, been worn by any multitudinous resort of business. In some months of the year, however, there often chances a forenoon when affairs move onward with a livelier tread. Such occasions might remind the elderly citizen of that period, before the last war with England, when Salem was a port by itself; not scorned, as she is now, by her own merchants and ship-owners, who permit her wharves to crumble to ruin, while their ventures go to swell, needlessly and imperceptibly, the mighty flood of commerce at New York or Boston. On some such morning, when three or four vessels happen to have arrived at once,—usually from Africa or South America,—or to be on the verge of their departure thitherward, there is a sound of frequent feet, passing briskly up and down the granite steps. Here, before his own wife has greeted him, you may greet the sea-flushed ship-master, just in port, with his vessel's papers under his arm in a tarnished tin box. Here, too, comes his owner, cheerful or sombre, gracious or in the sulks, accordingly as his scheme of the now accomplished voyage has been realized in merchandise that will readily be turned to gold, or has buried him under a bulk of incommodities, such as nobody will care to rid him of. Here, likewise,—the germ of the wrinkle-browed, a grizzly-bearded, careworn merchant,—we have the smart young clerk, who gets the taste of traffic as a wolf-cub does of blood, and already sends adventures in his master's ships, when he had better be sailing mimic boats upon a mill-pond. Another figure in the scene is the outward-bound sailor, in quest of a protection; [5] or the recently arrived one, pale and feeble, seeking a passport to the hospital. Nor must we forget the captains of the rusty little schooners that bring firewood from the British provinces;

[5] A protection is a certificate of American citizenship issued by the customs authorities to seamen.

a rough-looking set of tarpaulins, without the alertness of the Yankee aspect, but contributing an item of no slight importance to our decaying trade.

Cluster all these individuals together, as they sometimes were, with other miscellaneous ones to diversify the group, and, for the time being, it made the Custom-House a stirring scene, More frequently, however, on ascending the steps, you would discern—in the entry, if it were summer time, or in their appropriate rooms, if wintry or inclement weather—a row of venerable figures, sitting in old-fashioned chairs, which were tipped on their hind legs back against the wall. Oftentimes they were asleep, but occasionally might be heard talking together, in voices between speech and a snore, and with that lack of energy that distinguishes the occupants of alms-houses, and all other human beings who depend for subsistence on charity, on monopolized labor, or any thing else but their own independent exertions. These old gentlemen—seated, like Matthew,[6] at the receipt of custom, but not very liable to be summoned thence, like him, for apostolic errands—were Custom-House officers.

Furthermore, on the left hand as you enter the front door, is a certain room or office, about fifteen feet square, and of a lofty height; with two of its arched windows commanding a view of the aforesaid dilapidated wharf, and the third looking across a narrow lane, and along a portion of Derby Street. All three give glimpses of the shops of grocers, block-makers, slop-sellers, and ship-chandlers; around the doors of which are generally to be seen, laughing and gossiping, clusters of old salts, and such other wharf-rats as haunt the Wapping[7] of a seaport. The room itself is cobwebbed, and dingy with old paint; its floor is strewn with gray sand, in a fashion that has

---

[6] Matthew 9:9, "And as Jesus passed forth from thence, he saw a man, named Matthew, sitting at the receipt of custom."

[7] The district of East London on the north bank of the Thames, where vessels docked.

elsewhere fallen into long disuse; and it is easy to conclude, from the general slovenliness of the place, that this is a sanctuary into which womankind, with her tools of magic, the broom and mop, has very infrequent access. In the way of furniture, there is a stove with a voluminous funnel; an old pine desk, with a three-legged stool beside it; two or three wooden-bottom chairs, exceedingly decrepit and infirm; and, —not to forget the library,—on some shelves, a score or two of volumes of the Acts of Congress, and a bulky Digest of the Revenue Laws. A tin pipe ascends through the ceiling, and forms a medium of vocal communication with other parts of the edifice. And here, some six months ago,—pacing from corner to corner, or lounging on the long-legged stool, with his elbow on the desk, and his eyes wandering up and down the columns of the morning newspaper,—you might have recognized, honored reader, the same individual who welcomed you into his cheery little study, where the sunshine glimmered so pleasantly through the willow branches, on the western side of the Old Manse. But now, should you go thither to seek him, you would inquire in vain for the Loco-foco[8] Surveyor. The besom of reform has swept him out of office; and a worthier successor wears his dignity and pockets his emoluments.

This old town of Salem—my native place, though I have dwelt much away from it, both in boyhood and maturer years —possesses, or did possess, a hold on my affections, the force of which I have never realized during my seasons of actual residence here. Indeed, so far as its physical aspect is concerned, with its flat, unvaried surface, covered chiefly with wooden houses, few or none of which pretend to architectural

[8] A familiar name for a member of the Democratic Party, applied especially to the radical or equal-rights section of that party as a result of a meeting in Tammany Hall on October 29, 1835. Because of the great diversity of sentiment, the chairman left his seat and the lights were extinguished in the hope of dissolving the meeting. Those in favor of extreme measures, however, produced locofoco matches—then a comparatively recent (1834) invention— rekindled the lights, continued the meeting, and accomplished their object.

beauty,—its irregularity, which is neither picturesque nor quaint, but only tame,—its long and lazy street, lounging wearisomely through the whole extent of the peninsula, with Gallows Hill and New Guinea at one end, and a view of the alms-house at the other,—such being the features of my native town, it would be quite as reasonable to form a sentimental attachment to a disarranged checkerboard. And yet, though invariably happiest elsewhere, there is within me a feeling for old Salem, which, in lack of a better phrase, I must be content to call affection. The sentiment is probably assignable to the deep and aged roots which my family has struck into the soil. It is now nearly two centuries and a quarter since the original Briton,[9] the earliest emigrant of my name, made his appearance in the wild and forest-bordered settlement, which has since become a city. And here his descendants have been born and died, and have mingled their earthy substance with the soil; until no small portion of it must necessarily be akin to the mortal frame wherewith, for a little while, I walk the streets. In part, therefore, the attachment which I speak of is the mere sensuous sympathy of dust for dust. Few of my countrymen can know what it is; nor, as frequent transplantation is perhaps better for the stock, need they consider it desirable to know.

But the sentiment has likewise its moral quality. The figure

---

[9] William Hathorne (1607–1681) emigrated to America with John Winthrop in 1630 and in 1636 moved to Salem, where, next to John Endicott, he was the most influential figure in the town's early history. He was a merchant but held important political offices, such as speaker of the house of deputies, and he served as a major in King Philip's War. His son John was one of the judges of the Salem witchcraft trials but, unlike the majority of his colleagues, refused to repent his role once the frenzy had passed. The third Hathorne, Joseph, was a farmer; and the fourth, Daniel, was a sea captain and Revolutionary fighter. The fifth, Nathaniel, was also a sea captain. He died in Surinam at the age of thirty-two, four years after the birth of his son Nathaniel, the writer, first of his line to choose a sedentary occupation and to use "w" in the family name.

of that first ancestor, invested by family tradition with a dim and dusky grandeur, was present to my boyish imagination, as far back as I can remember. It still haunts me, and induces a sort of home-feeling with the past, which I scarcely claim in reference to the present phase of the town. I seem to have a stronger claim to a residence here on account of this grave, bearded, sable-cloaked, and steeple-crowned progenitor,—who came so early, with his Bible and his sword, and trode the unworn street with such a stately port, and made so large a figure, as a man of war and peace,—a stronger claim than for myself, whose name is seldom heard and my face hardly known. He was a soldier, legislator, judge; he was a ruler in the Church; he had all the Puritanic traits, both good and evil. He was likewise a bitter persecutor; as witness the Quakers, who have remembered him in their histories, and relate an incident of his hard severity towards a woman of their sect, which will last longer, it is to be feared, than any record of his better deeds, although these were many. His son, too, inherited the persecuting spirit, and made himself so conspicuous in the martyrdom of the witches, that their blood may fairly be said to have left a stain upon him. So deep a stain, indeed, that his old dry bones, in the Charter Street burial-ground, must still retain it, if they have not crumbled utterly to dust! I know not whether these ancestors of mine bethought themselves to repent, and ask pardon of Heaven for their cruelties; or whether they are now groaning under the heavy consequences of them, in another state of being. At all events, I, the present writer, as their representative, hereby take shame upon myself for their sakes, and pray that any curse incurred by them—as I have heard, and as the dreary and unprosperous condition of the race, for many a long year back, would argue to exist—may be now and henceforth removed.

Doubtless, however, either of these stern and black-browed Puritans would have thought it quite a sufficient retribution for his sins, that, after so long a lapse of years, the old trunk of the family tree, with so much venerable moss upon it, should have borne, as its topmost bough, an idler like myself. No aim, that I have ever cherished, would they recognize as laudable; no success of mine—if my life, beyond its domestic scope, had ever been brightened by success—would they deem otherwise than worthless, if not positively disgraceful. "What is he?" murmurs one gray shadow of my forefathers to the other. "A writer of story-books! What kind of a business in life,—what mode of glorifying God, or being serviceable to mankind in his day and generation,—may that be? Why, the degenerate fellow might as well have been a fiddler!" Such are the compliments bandied between my great-grandsires and myself, across the gulf of time! And yet, let them scorn me as they will, strong traits of their nature have intertwined themselves with mine.

Planted deep, in the town's earliest infancy and childhood, by these two earnest and energetic men, the race has ever since subsisted here; always, too, in respectability; never, so far as I have known, disgraced by a single unworthy member; but seldom or never, on the other hand, after the first two generations, performing any memorable deed, or so much as putting forward a claim to public notice. Gradually, they have sunk almost out of sight; as old houses, here and there about the streets, get covered half-way to the eaves by the accumulation of new soil. From father to son, for above a hundred years, they followed the sea; a gray-headed shipmaster, in each generation, retiring from the quarter-deck to the homestead, while a boy of fourteen took the hereditary place before the mast, confronting the salt spray and the gale, which had blustered against his sire and grandsire. The boy, also, in due time, passed from the forecastle to the cabin, spent a tempestuous manhood, and returned from his world-wanderings, to grow old, and die, and mingle his dust with the natal earth. This long connection of a family with one spot, as its place of birth and burial, creates a kindred between the human being and the locality, quite independent of any charm in the scenery or moral circumstances that surround him. It is not love, but

instinct. The new inhabitant—who came himself from a foreign
land, or whose father or grandfather came—has little claim to
be called a Salemite; he has no conception of the oyster-like
tenacity with which an old settler, over whom his third century is creeping, clings to the spot where his successive generations have been imbedded. It is no matter that the place is
joyless for him; that he is weary of the old wooden houses,
the mud and dust, the dead level of site and sentiment, the chill
east wind, and the chillest of social atmospheres;—all these, and
whatever faults besides he may see or imagine, are nothing to
the purpose. The spell survives, and just as powerfully as if
the natal spot were an earthly paradise. So has it been in my
case. I felt it almost as a destiny to make Salem my home; so
that the mould of features and cast of character which had all
along been familiar here—ever, as one representative of the
race lay down in his grave, another assuming, as it were, his
sentry-march along the Main Street—might still in my little
day be seen and recognized in the old town. Nevertheless, this
very sentiment is an evidence that the connection, which has
become an unhealthy one, should at last be severed.[10] Human
nature will not flourish, any more than a potato, if it be planted
and replanted, for too long a series of generations, in the same
worn-out soil. My children have had other birthplaces, and,
so far as their fortunes may be within my control, shall strike
their roots into unaccustomed earth.

On emerging from the Old Manse, it was chiefly this
strange, indolent, unjoyous attachment for my native town,
that brought me to fill a place in Uncle Sam's brick edifice,[11]

[10] The severing of such a connection is a persistent theme in
Hawthorne's works and is the main theme of his next novel, *The
House of the Seven Gables.*

[11] From 1839 to 1841, Hawthorne was employed as a weigher
and gauger in the Boston Custom House, thanks to his friendship
with prominent Democrats, chiefly Franklin Pierce, George Ban-
croft, and Horatio Bridge. In 1845 he again needed to seek a gov-
ernmental office to support himself. With the election of the

when I might as well, or better, have gone somewhere else.
My doom was on me. It was not the first time, nor the second,
that I had gone away,—as it seemed, permanently,—but yet returned, like the bad half-penny; or as if Salem were for me the
inevitable centre of the universe. So, one fine morning, I ascended the flight of granite steps, with the President's commission in my pocket, and was introduced to the corps of
gentlemen who were to aid me in my weighty responsibility,
as chief executive officer of the Custom-House.

I doubt greatly—or rather, I do not doubt at all—whether
any public functionary of the United States, either in the
civil or military line, has ever had such a patriarchal body of
veterans under his orders as myself. The whereabouts of the
Oldest Inhabitant was at once settled, when I looked at them.
For upwards of twenty years before this epoch, the independent position of the Collector had kept the Salem Custom-House
out of the whirlpool of political vicissitude, which makes the
tenure of office generally so fragile. A soldier,—New England's
most distinguished soldier,—he stood firmly on the pedestal of
his gallant services; and, himself secure in the wise liberality
of the successive administrations through which he had held
office, he had been the safety of his subordinates in many an
hour of danger and heart-quake. General Miller [12] was radically

Democrat James K. Polk to the Presidency, the same friends
(Pierce was then U.S. Senator from New Hampshire), together
with Senator Atherton of New Hampshire and Senator Fairfield of
Maine, secured him the position of Surveyor of Customs at Salem.
He entered office in March 1816 and left in June 1849, after the
election of the Whig candidate for President, General Zachary
Taylor.

[12] General James Miller (1776–1851) entered the U.S. Army as
a major in 1808, was brevetted colonel for gallantry at Fort George
in 1813, and distinguished himself at the battle of Lundy's Lane,
where success depended upon the capture of a British battery.
When asked by General Winfield Scott if he could take the battery, Miller replied, "I'll try, Sir!" and executed the task with a
bravery that won him promotion to brigadier general. He served

conservative; a man over whose kindly nature habit had no
slight influence; attaching himself strongly to familiar faces,
and with difficulty moved to change, even when change might
have brought unquestionable improvement. Thus, on taking
charge of my department, I found few but aged men. They
were ancient sea-captains, for the most part, who, after being
tost on every sea, and standing up sturdily against life's tempestuous blast, had finally drifted into this quiet nook; where, with
little to disturb them, except the periodical terrors of a Presi-
dential election, they one and all acquired a new lease of existence. Though by no means less liable than their fellow-men to
age and infirmity, they had evidently some talisman or other
that kept death at bay. Two or three of their number, as I was
assured, being gouty and rheumatic, or perhaps bed-ridden,
never dreamed of making their appearance at the Custom-
House, during a large part of the year; but, after a torpid
winter, would creep out into the warm sunshine of May or
June, go lazily about what they termed duty, and, at their own
leisure and convenience, betake themselves to bed again. I must
plead guilty to the charge of abbreviating the official breath of
more than one of these venerable servants of the republic.
They were allowed, on my representation, to rest from their
arduous labors, and soon afterwards—as if their sole principle
of life had been zeal for their country's service; as I verily believe it was—withdrew to a better world. It is a pious consolation to me, that, through my interference, a sufficient space was
allowed them for repentance of the evil and corrupt practices,
into which, as a matter of course, every Custom-House officer
must be supposed to fall. Neither the front nor the back entrance of the Custom-House opens on the road to Paradise.

The greater part of my officers were Whigs. It was well for
their venerable brotherhood, that the new Surveyor was not
a politician, and, though a faithful Democrat in principle,

---

as governor of Arkansas (1819–1825) and collector of the port of
Salem (1825–1849).

neither received nor held his office with any reference to political services. Had it been otherwise,—had an active politician
been put into this influential post, to assume the easy task of
making head against a Whig Collector, whose infirmities withheld him from the personal administration of his office,—hardly
a man of the old corps would have drawn the breath of official
life, within a month after the exterminating angel had come
up the Custom-House steps. According to the received code
in such matters, it would have been nothing short of duty, in
a politician, to bring every one of those white heads under the
axe of the guillotine. It was plain enough to discern, that the
old fellows dreaded some such discourtesy at my hands. It
pained, and at the same time amused me, to behold the terrors
that attended my advent; to see a furrowed cheek, weather-
beaten by half a century of storm, turn ashy pale at the glance
of so harmless an individual as myself; to detect, as one or another addressed me, the tremor of a voice, which, in long-past
days, had been wont to bellow through a speaking-trumpet,
hoarsely enough to frighten Boreas himself to silence. They
knew, these excellent old persons, that, by all established rule,—
and, as regarded some of them, weighed by their own lack of
efficiency for business,—they ought to have given place to
younger men, more orthodox in politics, and altogether fitter
than themselves to serve our common Uncle. I knew it too, but
could never quite find in my heart to act upon the knowledge.
Much and deservedly to my own discredit, therefore, and considerably to the detriment of my official conscience, they continued, during my incumbency, to creep about the wharves,
and loiter up and down the Custom-House steps. They spent
a good deal of time, also, asleep in their accustomed corners,
with their chairs tilted back against the wall; awaking, however, once or twice in a forenoon, to bore one another with
the several thousandth repetition of old sea-stories, and mouldy
jokes, that had grown to be pass-words and countersigns among
them.

The discovery was soon made, I imagine, that the new Surveyor had no great harm in him. So, with lightsome hearts, and the happy consciousness of being usefully employed,—in their own behalf, at least, if not for our beloved country,— these good old gentlemen went through the various formalities of office. Sagaciously, under their spectacles, did they peep into the holds of vessels! Mighty was their fuss about little matters, and marvellous, sometimes, the obtuseness that allowed greater ones to slip between their fingers! Whenever such a mischance occurred,—when a wagon-load of valuable merchandise had been smuggled ashore, at noonday, perhaps, and directly beneath their unsuspicious noses,—nothing could exceed the vigilance and alacrity with which they proceeded to lock, and double-lock, and secure with tape and sealing-wax, all the avenues of the delinquent vessel. Instead of a reprimand for their previous negligence, the case seemed rather to require an eulogium on their praiseworthy caution, after the mischief had happened; a grateful recognition of the promptitude of their zeal, the moment that there was no longer any remedy!

Unless people are more than commonly disagreeable, it is my foolish habit to contract a kindness for them. The better part of my companion's character, if it have a better part, is that which usually comes uppermost in my regard, and forms the type whereby I recognize the man. As most of these old Custom-House officers had good traits, and as my position in reference to them, being paternal and protective, was favorable to the growth of friendly sentiments, I soon grew to like them all. It was pleasant, in the summer forenoons,—when the fervent heat, that almost liquefied the rest of the human family, merely communicated a genial warmth to their half-torpid systems,—it was pleasant to hear them chatting in the back entry, a row of them all tipped against the wall, as usual; while the frozen witticisms of past generations were thawed out, and came bubbling with laughter from their lips. Externally, the jollity of aged men has much in common with the mirth of children; the intellect, any more than a deep sense of humor, has little to do with the matter; it is, with both, a gleam that plays upon the surface, and imparts a sunny and cheery aspect alike to the green branch, and gray, mouldering trunk. In one case, however, it is real sunshine; in the other, it more resembles the phosphorescent glow of decaying wood.

It would be sad injustice, the reader must understand, to represent all my excellent old friends as in their dotage. In the first place, my coadjutors were not invariably old; there were men among them in their strength and prime, of marked ability and energy, and altogether superior to the sluggish and dependent mode of life on which their evil stars had cast them. Then, moreover, the white locks of age were sometimes found to be the thatch of an intellectual tenement in good repair. But, as respects the majority of my corps of veterans, there will be no wrong done, if I characterize them generally as a set of wearisome old souls, who had gathered nothing worth preservation from their varied experience of life. They seemed to have flung away all the golden grain of practical wisdom, which they had enjoyed so many opportunities of harvesting, and most carefully to have stored their memories with the husks. They spoke with far more interest and unction of their morning's breakfast, or yesterday's, to-day's, or to-morrow's dinner, than of the shipwreck of forty or fifty years ago, and all the world's wonders which they had witnessed with their youthful eyes.

The father of the Custom-House—the patriarch, not only of this little squad of officials, but, I am bold to say, of the respectable body of tide-waiters all over the United States—was a certain permanent Inspector. He might truly be termed a legitimate son of the revenue system, dyed in the wool, or rather, born in the purple; since his sire, a Revolutionary colonel, and formerly collector of the port, had created an office for him, and appointed him to fill it, at a period of the early ages which few living men can now remember. This Inspector, when I first knew him, was a man of fourscore years, or thereabouts, and certainly one of the most wonderful specimens of winter-green that you would be likely to dis-

cover in a·lifetime's search. With his florid cheek, his compact
figure, smartly arrayed in a bright-buttoned blue coat, his brisk
and vigorous step, and his hale and hearty aspect, altogether,
he seemed—not young, indeed—but a kind of new contrivance
of Mother Nature in the shape of man, whom age and infirmity had no business to touch. His voice and laugh, which
perpetually reëchoed through the Custom-House, had nothing
of the tremulous quaver and cackle of an old man's utterance;
they came strutting out of his lungs, like the crow of a cock,
or the blast of a clarion. Looking at him merely as an animal,—
and there was very little else to look at,—he was a most satisfactory object, from the thorough healthfulness and whole-
someness of his system, and his capacity, at that extreme age,
to enjoy all, or nearly all, the delights which he had ever
aimed at, or conceived of. The careless security of his life in
the Custom-House, on a regular income, and with but slight
and infrequent apprehensions of removal, had no doubt contributed to make time pass lightly over him. The original and
more potent causes, however, lay in the rare perfection of his
animal nature, the moderate proportion of intellect, and the
very trifling admixture of moral and spiritual ingredients; these
latter qualities, indeed, being in barely enough measure to keep
the old gentleman from walking on all-fours. He possessed no
power of thought, no depth of feeling, no troublesome sensibilities; nothing, in short, but a few commonplace instincts,
which, aided by the cheerful temper that grew inevitably out
of his physical well-being, did duty very respectably, and to
general acceptance, in lieu of a heart. He had been the husband
of three wives, all long since dead; the father of twenty children, most of whom, at every age of childhood or maturity,
had likewise returned to dust. Here, one would suppose, might
have been sorrow enough to imbue the sunniest disposition,
through and through, with a sable tinge. Not so with our old
Inspector! One brief sigh sufficed to carry off the entire burden of these dismal reminiscences. The next moment, he was as
ready for sport as any unbreeched infant; far readier than the

Collector's junior clerk, who, at nineteen years, was much the elder and graver man of the two.

I used to watch and study this patriarchal personage with, I think, livelier curiosity than any other form of humanity there presented to my notice. He was, in truth, a rare phenomenon; so perfect in one point of view; so shallow, so delusive, so impalpable, such an absolute nonentity, in every other. My conclusion was that he had no soul, no heart, no mind; nothing, as I have already said, but instincts; and yet, withal, so cunningly had the few materials of his character been put together, that there was no painful perception of deficiency, but, on my part, an entire contentment with what I found in him. It might be difficult—and it was so—to conceive how he should exist hereafter, so earthy and sensuous did he seem; but surely his existence here, admitting that it was to terminate with his last breath, had been not unkindly given; with no higher moral responsibilities than the beasts of the field, but with a larger scope of enjoyment than theirs, and with all their blessed immunity from the dreariness and duskiness of age.

One point, in which he had vastly the advantage over his four-footed brethren, was his ability to recollect the good dinners which it had made no small portion of the happiness of his life to eat. His gourmandism was a highly agreeable trait; and to hear him talk of roast-meat was as appetizing as a pickle or an oyster. As he possessed no higher attribute, and neither sacrificed nor vitiated any spiritual endowment by devoting all his energies and ingenuities to subserve the delight and profit of his maw, it always pleased and satisfied me to hear him expatiate on fish, poultry, and butcher's meat, and the most eligible methods of preparing them for the table. His reminiscences of good cheer, however ancient the date of the actual banquet, seemed to bring the savor of pig or turkey under one's very nostrils. There were flavors on his palate, that had lingered there not less than sixty or seventy years, and were still apparently as fresh as that of the mutton-chop which he had just devoured for his breakfast. I have heard him smack his lips over dinners, every guest at which, except himself, had long been food for worms. It was marvellous to observe how the ghosts of bygone meals were continually rising up before him; not in anger or retribution, but as if grateful for his former appreciation, and seeking to reduplicate an endless series of enjoyment, at once shadowy and sensual. A tenderloin of beef, a hind-quarter of veal, a spare-rib of pork, a particular chicken, or a remarkably praiseworthy turkey, which had perhaps adorned his board in the days of the elder Adams, would be remembered; while all the subsequent experience of our race, and all the events that brightened or darkened his individual career, had gone over him with as little permanent effect as the passing breeze. The chief tragic event of the old man's life, so far as I could judge, was his mishap with a certain goose, which lived and died some twenty or forty years ago; a goose of most promising figure, but which, at table, proved so inveterately tough that the carving-knife would make no impression on its carcass; and it could only be divided with an axe and handsaw.

But it is time to quit this sketch; on which, however, I should be glad to dwell at considerably more length, because, of all men whom I have ever known, this individual was fittest to be a Custom-House officer. Most persons, owing to causes which I may not have space to hint at, suffer moral detriment from this peculiar mode of life. The old Inspector was incapable of it, and, were he to continue in office to the end of time, would be just as good as he was then, and sit down to dinner with just as good an appetite.

There is one likeness, without which my gallery of Custom-House portraits would be strangely incomplete; but which my comparatively few opportunities for observation enable me to sketch only in the merest outline. It is that of the Collector, our gallant old General, who, after his brilliant military service, subsequently to which he had ruled over a wild Western territory, had come hither, twenty years before, to spend the decline of his varied and honorable life. The brave soldier had already numbered, nearly or quite, his threescore years and ten, and was pursuing the remainder of his earthly march, burdened with infirmities which even the martial music of his own spirit-stirring recollections could do little towards lightening. The step was palsied now, that had been foremost in the charge. It was only with the assistance of a servant, and by leaning his hand heavily on the iron balustrade, that he could slowly and painfully ascend the Custom-House steps, and, with a toilsome progress across the floor, attain his customary chair beside the fireplace. There he used to sit, gazing with a somewhat dim serenity of aspect at the figures that came and went; amid the rustle of papers, the administering of oaths, the discussion of business, and the casual talk of the office; all which sounds and circumstances seemed but indistinctly to impress his senses, and hardly to make their way into his inner sphere of contemplation. His countenance, in this repose, was mild and kindly. If his notice was sought, an expression of courtesy and interest gleamed out upon his features; proving that there was light within him, and that it was only the outward medium of the intellectual lamp that obstructed the rays in their passage. The closer you penetrated to the substance of his mind, the sounder it appeared. When no longer called upon to speak, or listen, either of which operations cost him an evident effort, his face would briefly subside into its former not uncheerful quietude. It was not painful to behold this look; for, though dim, it had not the imbecility of decaying age. The framework of his nature, originally strong and massive, was not yet crumbled into ruin.

To observe and define his character, however, under such disadvantages, was as difficult a task as to trace out and build up anew, in imagination, an old fortress, like Ticonderoga,[13]

---

[13] In his brief sketch, "Old Ticonderoga: A Picture of the Past," in *The Snow-Image and Other Twice-Told Tales,* Hawthorne did attempt this "difficult" task. Fort Ticonderoga was located at a strategic point near the foot of Lake Champlain and was the site

from a view of its gray and broken ruins. Here and there, perchance, the walls may remain almost complete; but elsewhere may be only a shapeless mound, cumbrous with its very strength, and overgrown, through long years of peace and neglect, with grass and alien weeds.

Nevertheless, looking at the old warrior with affection,—for, slight as was the communication between us, my feeling towards him, like that of all bipeds and quadrupeds who knew him, might not improperly be termed so,—I could discern the main points of his portrait. It was marked with the noble and heroic qualities which showed it to be not by a mere accident, but of good right, that he had won a distinguished name. His spirit could never, I conceive, have been characterized by an uneasy activity; it must, at any period of his life, have required an impulse to set him in motion; but, once stirred up, with obstacles to overcome, and an adequate object to be attained, it was not in the man to give out or fail. The heat that had formerly pervaded his nature, and which was not yet extinct, was never of the kind that flashes and flickers in a blaze, but, rather, a deep, red glow, as of iron in a furnace. Weight, solidity, firmness; this was the expression of his repose, even in such decay as had crept untimely over him, at the period of which I speak. But I could imagine, even then, that, under some excitement which should go deeply into his consciousness,—roused by a trumpet-peal, loud enough to awaken all of his energies that were not dead, but only slumbering,—he was yet capable of flinging off his infirmities like a sick man's gown, dropping the staff of age to seize a battle-sword, and starting up once more a warrior. And, in so intense a moment, his demeanour would have still been calm. Such an exhibition, however, was but to be pictured in fancy; not to be anticipated, nor desired. What I saw in him—as evidently as the in-

---

of battles in the French and Indian Wars and the Revolution. During the latter conflict, it was captured from the British by American forces under the command of Benedict Arnold and Ethan Allen.

destructible ramparts of Old Ticonderoga, already cited as the
most appropriate simile—were the features of stubborn and ponderous endurance, which might well have amounted to obstinacy in his earlier days; of integrity, that, like most of his
other endowments, lay in a somewhat heavy mass, and was just
as unmalleable and unmanageable as a ton of iron ore; and of
benevolence, which, fiercely as he led the bayonets on at Chip-
pewa or Fort Erie, I take to be of quite as genuine a stamp as
what actuates any or all the polemical philanthropists of the
age. He had slain men with his own hand, for aught I know;—
certainly, they had fallen, like blades of grass at the sweep of
the scythe, before the charge to which his spirit imparted its
triumphant energy;—but, be that as it might, there was never in
his heart so much cruelty as would have brushed the down off
a butterfly's wing. I have not known the man, to whose innate
kindliness I would more confidently make an appeal.

Many characteristics—and those, too, which contribute not
the least forcibly to impart resemblance in a sketch—must have
vanished, or been obscured, before I met the General. All
merely graceful attributes are usually the most evanescent; nor
does Nature adorn the human ruin with blossoms of new
beauty, that have their roots and proper nutriment only in the
chinks and crevices of decay, as she sows wall-flowers over the
ruined fortress of Ticonderoga. Still, even in respect of grace
and beauty, there were points well worth noting. A ray of
humor, now and then, would make its way through the veil of
dim obstruction, and glimmer pleasantly upon our faces. A
trait of native elegance, seldom seen in the masculine character
after childhood or early youth, was shown in the General's
fondness for the sight and fragrance of flowers. An old soldier
might be supposed to prize only the bloody laurel on his brow;
but here was one, who seemed to have a young girl's appreciation of the floral tribe.

There, beside the fireplace, the brave old General used to
sit; while the Surveyor—though seldom, when it could be
avoided, taking upon himself the difficult task of engaging him

in conversation—was fond of standing at a distance, and watching his quiet and almost slumberous countenance. He seemed away from us, although we saw him but a few yards off; remote, though we passed close beside his chair; unattainable, though we might have stretched forth our hands and touched his own. It might be, that he lived a more real life within his thoughts, than amid the unappropriate environment of the Collector's office. The evolutions of the parade; the tumult of the battle; the flourish of old, heroic music, heard thirty years before;—such scenes and sounds, perhaps, were all alive before his intellectual sense. Meanwhile, the merchants and shipmasters, the spruce clerks, and uncouth sailors, entered and departed; the bustle of this commercial and Custom-House life kept up its little murmur roundabout him; and neither with the men nor their affairs did the General appear to sustain the most distant relation. He was as much out of place as an old sword—now rusty, but which had flashed once in the battle's front, and showed still a bright gleam along its blade—would have been, among the inkstands, paper-folders, and mahogany rulers, on the Deputy Collector's desk.

There was one thing that much aided me in renewing and re-creating the stalwart soldier of the Niagara frontier,—the man of true and simple energy. It was the recollection of those memorable words of his,—"I'll try, Sir!"—spoken on the very verge of a desperate and heroic enterprise, and breathing the soul and spirit of New England hardihood, comprehending all perils, and encountering all. If, in our country, valor were rewarded by heraldic honor, this phrase—which it seems so easy to speak, but which only he, with such a task of danger and glory before him, has ever spoken—would be the best and fittest of all mottoes for the General's shield of arms.

It contributes greatly towards a man's moral and intellectual health, to be brought into habits of companionship with individuals unlike himself, who care little for his pursuits, and whose sphere and abilities he must go out of himself to ap-

preciate. The accidents of my life have often afforded me this
advantage, but never with more fulness and variety than during my continuance in office. There was one man, especially,
the observation of whose character gave me a new idea of
talent. His gifts were emphatically those of a man of business;
prompt, acute, clear-minded; with an eye that saw through
all perplexities, and a faculty of arrangement that made them
vanish, as by the waving of an enchanter's wand. Bred up from
boyhood in the Custom-House, it was his proper field of activity; and the many intricacies of business, so harassing to the
interloper, presented themselves before him with the regularity
of a perfectly comprehended system. In my contemplation, he
stood as the ideal of his class. He was, indeed, the Custom-
House in himself; or, at all events, the main-spring that kept
its variously revolving wheels in motion; for, in an institution
like this, where its officers are appointed to subserve their own
profit and convenience, and seldom with a leading reference to
their fitness for the duty to be performed, they must perforce
seek elsewhere the dexterity which is not in them. Thus, by
an inevitable necessity, as a magnet attracts steel-filings, so did
our man of business draw to himself the difficulties which
everybody met with. With an easy condescension, and kind
forbearance towards our stupidity,—which, to his order of
mind, must have seemed little short of crime,—would he forthwith, by the merest touch of his finger, make the incomprehensible as clear as daylight. The merchants valued him not less
than we, his esoteric friends. His integrity was perfect; it was a
law of nature with him, rather than a choice or a principle;
nor can it be otherwise than the main condition of an intellect
so remarkably clear and accurate as his, to be honest and regular in the administration of affairs. A stain on his conscience,
as to any thing that came within the range of his vocation,
would trouble such a man very much in the same way, though
to a far greater degree, than an error in the balance of an account, or an ink-blot on the fair page of a book of record.

Here, in a word,—and it is a rare instance in my life,—I had met with a person thoroughly adapted to the situation which he held.

Such were some of the people with whom I now found myself connected. I took it in good part at the hands of Providence, that I was thrown into a position so little akin to my past habits; and set myself seriously to gather from it whatever profit was to be had. After my fellowship of toil and impracticable schemes, with the dreamy brethren of Brook Farm; [14] after living for three years within the subtile influence of an intellect like Emerson's; [15] after those wild, free days on the Assabeth,[16] indulging fantastic speculations beside our fire of

[14] The Brook Farm Institute of Agriculture and Education was an experiment in communal living conducted in the Boston suburb of Roxbury and motivated by the ideals of transcendentalism. In April of 1841, the thirty-seven-year-old Hawthorne joined the group, hoping, in the main, that he could here write free of the usual pressures of earning a living through full-time employment. He left some fourteen months later to be married and to establish his residence at the Old Manse. Of Brook Farm, he said: "The real Me was never an associate of the community; there has been a spectral appearance there, sounding the horn at daybreak, and milking the cows, and hoeing potatoes, and raking hay, toiling in the sun, and doing me the honor to assume my name." He based his third novel, *The Blithedale Romance*, on his Brook Farm experience.

[15] Concord, where Emerson lived, was the center of the Transcendentalist group. Hawthorne's wife was a member of the group, and during his residence in the Old Manse Hawthorne came to know the eminent members of it, although he always remained apart from their philosophy. Of the Concord of his day, he said: "Never was a poor little country village infected with such a variety of queer, strangely dressed, oddly behaved mortals, most of whom took upon themselves to be important agents of the world's destiny, yet were simply bores of the first water." He considered Ralph Waldo Emerson (1803–1882) the town's one "great original thinker," and they visited with one another frequently, although neither seems to have read much of the other's work.

[16] A small stream rising in central Massachusetts and uniting with the Sudbury River at Concord to form the Concord River.

fallen boughs, with Ellery Channing;[17] after talking with Thoreau [18] about pine-trees and Indian relics, in his hermitage at Walden; after growing fastidious by sympathy with the classic refinement of Hillard's [19] culture; after becoming imbued with poetic sentiment at Longfellow's [20] hearth-stone;— it was time, at length, that I should exercise other faculties of my nature, and nourish myself with food for which I had hitherto had little appetite. Even the old Inspector was desir-

[17] Ellery Channing (1818–1901), nephew of the great Unitarian minister, William Ellery Channing; poet, and member of the Concord Transcendentalist group, was on friendly terms with Hawthorne, who described him in his journal as "one of those queer and clever young men whom Mr. Emerson (that everlasting rejector of all that is, and seeker for he knows not what) is continually picking up by way of a genius. . . . I like him well enough, however; but after all, these originals in a small way, after one has seen a few of them, become more dull and commonplace than even those who keep the ordinary pathway of life."

[18] When Hawthorne knew him, Henry David Thoreau (1817–1862) had not yet written his great works and was totally unknown outside the village, near which he had set up his cabin at Walden Pond. Hawthorne was attracted by Thoreau's honesty and profundity, although he at times found the younger man an "intolerable bore." By 1845, he had concluded that Thoreau was both tedious and tiresome, yet gifted with great qualities of intellect and character.

[19] George S. Hillard (1808–1879) was a Boston lawyer and writer who served as Hawthorne's attorney. When Hawthorne worked in Boston in 1839, he lived with the Hillards, and they lent him money from time to time as part of their unceasing encouragement of him. In addition to various legal, political, and historical writings, Hillard produced travel literature and edited a five-volume edition of the works of Edmund Spenser.

[20] Henry Wadsworth Longfellow (1807–1882) was a classmate of Hawthorne's at Bowdoin College, although they were not close friends then. By the time Hawthorne was a struggling writer at the Old Manse, Longfellow was a famous poet and an eminent member of the Harvard faculty. The two became friendly, and Longfellow encouraged Hawthorne's career, although he never seems to have reconciled himself to the fact that Hawthorne's works were not, in the main, cheerful.

able, as a change of diet, to a man who had known Alcott.[21]
I looked upon it as an evidence, in some measure, of a system
naturally well balanced, and lacking no essential part of a
thorough organization, that, with such associates to remember,
I could mingle at once with men of altogether different qualities, and never murmur at the change.

Literature, its exertions and objects, were now of little
moment in my regard. I cared not, at this period, for books;
they were apart from me. Nature,—except it were human nature,—the nature that is developed in earth and sky, was, in
one sense, hidden from me; and all the imaginative delight,
wherewith it had been spiritualized, passed away out of my
mind. A gift, a faculty, if it had not departed, was suspended
and inanimate within me. There would have been something
sad, unutterably dreary, in all this, had I not been conscious
that it lay at my own option to recall whatever was valuable
in the past. It might be true, indeed, that this was a life which
could not, with impunity, be lived too long; else, it might make
me permanently other than I had been, without transforming
me into any shape which it would be worth my while to take.
But I never considered it as other than a transitory life. There
was always a prophetic instinct, a low whisper in my ear, that,
within no long period, and whenever a new change of custom
should be essential to my good, a change would come.

Meanwhile, there I was, a Surveyor of the Revenue, and,
so far as I have been able to understand, as good a Surveyor
as need be. A man of thought, fancy, and sensibility, (had he
ten times the Surveyor's proportion of those qualities,) may, at
any time, be a man of affairs, if he will only choose to give
himself the trouble. My fellow-officers, and the merchants and

[21] Amos Bronson Alcott (1799–1888), educator and philosopher,
was a member of Brook Farm, where Hawthorne knew him, and
later founded his own short-lived cooperative community, Fruit-
lands. When Hawthorne returned to live in Concord in 1852, he
bought his residence, the Wayside, from Alcott. Louisa May was
Alcott's daughter, and *Little Women* is based on Alcott family life.

sea-captains with whom my official duties brought me into any manner of connection, viewed me in no other light, and probably knew me in no other character. None of them, I presume, had ever read a page of my inditing, or would have cared a fig the more for me, if they had read them all; nor would it have mended the matter, in the least, had those same unprofitable pages been written with a pen like that of Burns or of Chaucer, each of whom was a Custom-House officer in his day, as well as I. It is a good lesson—though it may often be a hard one—for a man who has dreamed of literary fame, and of making for himself a rank among the world's dignitaries by such means, to step aside out of the narrow circle in which his claims are recognized, and to find how utterly devoid of significance, beyond that circle, is all that he achieves, and all he aims at. I know not that I especially needed the lesson, either in the way of warning or rebuke; but, at any rate, I learned it thoroughly; nor, it gives me pleasure to reflect, did the truth, as it came home to my perception, ever cost me a pang, or require to be thrown off in a sigh. In the way of literary talk, it is true, the Naval Officer—an excellent fellow, who came into office with me, and went out only a little later—would often engage me in a discussion about one or the other of his favorite topics, Napoleon or Shakspeare. The Collector's junior clerk, too,—a young gentleman who, it was whispered, occasionally covered a sheet of Uncle Sam's letter-paper with what, (at the distance of a few yards,) looked very much like poetry,—used now and then to speak to me of books, as matters with which I might possibly be conversant. This was my all of lettered intercourse; and it was quite sufficient for my necessities.

No longer seeking nor caring that my name should be blazoned abroad on title-pages, I smiled to think that it had now another kind of vogue. The Custom-House marker imprinted it, with a stencil and black paint, on pepper-bags, and baskets of anatto, and cigar-boxes, and bales of all kinds of dutiable merchandise, in testimony that these commodities had paid the impost, and gone regularly through the office. Borne on such queer vehicle of fame, a knowledge of my existence, so far as a name conveys it, was carried where it had never been before, and, I hope, will never go again.

But the past was not dead. Once in a great while, the thoughts, that had seemed so vital and so active, yet had been put to rest so quietly, revived again. One of the most remarkable occasions, when the habit of bygone days awoke in me, was that which brings it within the law of literary propriety to offer the public the sketch which I am now writing.

In the second story of the Custom-House, there is a large room, in which the brick-work and naked rafters have never been covered with panelling and plaster. The edifice—originally projected on a scale adapted to the old commercial enterprise of the port, and with an idea of subsequent prosperity destined never to be realized—contains far more space than its occupants know what to do with. This airy hall, therefore, over the Collector's apartments, remains unfinished to this day, and, in spite of the aged cobwebs that festoon its dusky beams, appears still to await the labor of the carpenter and mason. At one end of the room, in a recess, were a number of barrels, piled one upon another, containing bundles of official documents. Large quantities of similar rubbish lay lumbering the floor. It was sorrowful to think how many days, and weeks, and months, and years of toil, had been wasted on these musty papers, which were now only an encumbrance on earth, and were hidden away in this forgotten corner, never more to be glanced at by human eyes. But, then, what reams of other manuscripts—filled, not with the dulness of official formalities, but with the thought of inventive brains and the rich effusion of deep hearts—had gone equally to oblivion; and that, moreover, without serving a purpose in their day, as these heaped-up papers had, and—saddest of all—without purchasing for their writers the comfortable livelihood which the clerks of the Custom-House had gained by these worthless scratchings of the pen! Yet not altogether worthless, perhaps, as ma-

terials of local history. Here, no doubt, statistics of the former
commerce of Salem might be discovered, and memorials of her
princely merchants,—old King Derby,—old Billy Gray,—old
Simon Forrester,[22]—and many another magnate in his day;
whose powdered head, however, was scarcely in the tomb, before his mountain-pile of wealth began to dwindle. The founders of the greater part of the families which now compose the
aristocracy of Salem might here be traced, from the petty and
obscure beginnings of their traffic, at periods generally much
posterior to the Revolution, upward to what their children
look upon as long-established rank.

Prior to the Revolution, there is a dearth of records; the
earlier documents and archives of the Custom-House having,
probably, been carried off to Halifax, when all the King's officials accompanied the British army in its flight from Boston. It
has often been a matter of regret with me; for, going back,
perhaps, to the days of the Protectorate, those papers must
have contained many references to forgotten or remembered
men, and to antique customs, which would have affected me
with the same pleasure as when I used to pick up Indian arrow-
heads in the field near the Old Manse.

But, one idle and rainy day, it was my fortune to make a
discovery of some little interest. Poking and burrowing into
the heaped-up rubbish in the corner; unfolding one and another document, and reading the names of vessels that had
long ago foundered at sea or rotted at the wharves, and those
of merchants, never heard of now on 'Change, nor very readily
decipherable on their mossy tombstones; glancing at such matters with the saddened, weary, half-reluctant interest which
we bestow on the corpse of dead activity,—and exerting my
fancy, sluggish with little use, to raise up from these dry bones
an image of the old town's brighter aspect, when India was a
new region, and only Salem knew the way thither,—I chanced

[22] William Gray (1780–1825) and Simon Forrester (1776–1851)
were wealthy shipowners in the heyday of the port of Salem.

to lay my hand on a small package, carefully done up in a piece of ancient yellow parchment.[23] This envelope had the air of an official record of some period long past, when clerks engrossed their stiff and formal chirography on more substantial materials than at present. There was something about it that quickened an instinctive curiosity, and made me undo the faded red tape, that tied up the package, with the sense that a treasure would here be brought to light. Unbending the rigid folds of the parchment cover, I found it to be a commission, under the hand and seal of Governor Shirley,[24] in favor of one Jonathan Pue,[25] as Surveyor of his Majesty's Customs for the port of Salem, in the Province of Massachusetts Bay. I remembered to have read (probably in Felt's Annals[26]) a notice of the decease of Mr. Surveyor Pue, about fourscore years ago; and likewise, in a newspaper of recent times, an account of the digging up of his remains in the little grave-yard of St. Peter's Church, during the renewal of that edifice. Nothing, if I rightly

[23] The account of the finding of the documents and the scarlet letter itself is, of course, fictitious.

[24] William Shirley (1694–1771) was appointed governor of Massachusetts in 1741 and served as the royal appointee in that post until 1749, when he went home to England. He returned as governor of Massachusetts in 1753 and in 1756 became commander in chief of all British forces in America. Recalled to England later in 1756, he returned to Massachusetts once again, in 1770, and died there in the following year.

[25] One Jonathan Pue became searcher and surveyor of Salem Custom House in 1752. Felt's Annals records his death under the date March 24, 1760.

[26] Hawthorne had gained a good part of his knowledge of Puritan Massachusetts from Annals of Salem from Its First Settlement (1827) by Joseph B. Felt. Among other items, Felt records the following for May 5, 1694: "Among such laws, passed this session, were two against Adultery and Polygamy. Those guilty of the first crime, were to sit an hour on the gallows, with ropes about their necks,—be severely whipt not above 40 stripes; and forever after wear a capital A, two inches long, cut out of cloth colored differently from their clothes, and sewed on the arms or back parts of their garments so as always to be seen when they were about."

call to mind, was left of my respected predecessor, save an imperfect skeleton, and some fragments of apparel, and a wig of majestic frizzle; which, unlike the head that it once adorned, was in very satisfactory preservation. But, on examining the papers which the parchment commission served to envelop, I found more traces of Mr. Pue's mental part, and the internal operations of his head, than the frizzled wig had contained of the venerable skull itself.

They were documents, in short, not official, but of a private nature, or, at least, written in his private capacity, and apparently with his own hand. I could account for their being included in the heap of Custom-House lumber only by the fact, that Mr. Pue's death had happened suddenly; and that these papers, which he probably kept in his official desk, had never come to the knowledge of his heirs, or were supposed to relate to the business of the revenue. On the transfer of the archives to Halifax, this package, proving to be of no public concern, was left behind, and had remained ever since unopened.

The ancient Surveyor—being little molested, I suppose, at that early day, with business pertaining to his office—seems to have devoted some of his many leisure hours to researches as a local antiquarian, and other inquisitions of a similar nature. These supplied material for petty activity to a mind that would otherwise have been eaten up with rust. A portion of his facts, by the by, did me good service in the preparation of the article entitled "MAIN STREET," [27] included in the present volume. The remainder may perhaps be applied to purposes equally valuable, hereafter; or not impossibly may be worked up, so far as they go, into a regular history of Salem, should my veneration for the natal soil ever impel me to so pious a task. Meanwhile, they shall be at the command of any gentleman, inclined, and competent, to take the unprofitable labor

[27] This historical sketch of Salem is included in Hawthorne's *The Snow-Image and Other Twice-Told Tales.*

off my hands. As a final disposition, I contemplate depositing them with the Essex Historical Society.[28]

But the object that most drew my attention, in the mysterious package, was a certain affair of fine red cloth, much worn and faded. There were traces about it of gold embroidery, which, however, was greatly frayed and defaced; so that none, or very little, of the glitter was left. It had been wrought, as was easy to perceive, with wonderful skill of needlework; and the stitch (as I am assured by ladies conversant with such mysteries) gives evidence of a now forgotten art, not to be recovered even by the process of picking out the threads. This rag of scarlet cloth,—for time, and wear, and a sacrilegious moth, had reduced it to little other than a rag,—on careful examination, assumed the shape of a letter. It was the capital letter A. By an accurate measurement, each limb proved to be precisely three inches and a quarter in length. It had been intended, there could be no doubt, as an ornamental article of dress; but how it was to be worn, or what rank, honor, and dignity, in by-past times, were signified by it, was a riddle which (so evanescent are the fashions of the world in these particulars) I saw little hope of solving. And yet it strangely interested me. My eyes fastened themselves upon the old scarlet letter, and would not be turned aside. Certainly, there was some deep meaning in it, most worthy of interpretation, and which, as it were, streamed forth from the mystic symbol, subtly communicating itself to my sensibilities, but evading the analysis of my mind.

While thus perplexed,—and cogitating, among other hypotheses, whether the letter might not have been one of those decorations which the white men used to contrive, in order to take the eyes of Indians,—I happened to place it on my

[28] Salem is the seat of Essex County, and the Essex Historical Society was instrumental in preserving records of colonial Massachusetts—as it is instrumental today in preserving records about Hawthorne himself. Hawthorne made extensive use of the Society's library.

breast. It seemed to me,—the reader may smile, but must not doubt my word,—it seemed to me, then, that I experienced a sensation not altogether physical, yet almost so, as of burning heat; and as if the letter were not of red cloth, but red-hot iron. I shuddered, and involuntarily let it fall upon the floor.

In the absorbing contemplation of the scarlet letter, I had hitherto neglected to examine a small roll of dingy paper, around which it had been twisted. This I now opened, and had the satisfaction to find, recorded by the old Surveyor's pen, a reasonably complete explanation of the whole affair. There were several foolscap sheets, containing many particulars respecting the life and conversation of one Hester Prynne, who appeared to have been rather a noteworthy personage in the view of our ancestors. She had flourished during a period between the early days of Massachusetts and the close of the seventeenth century. Aged persons, alive in the time of Mr. Surveyor Pue, and from whose oral testimony he had made up his narrative, remembered her, in their youth, as a very old, but not decrepit woman, of a stately and solemn aspect. It had been her habit, from an almost immemorial date, to go about the country as a kind of voluntary nurse, and doing whatever miscellaneous good she might; taking upon herself, likewise, to give advice in all matters, especially those of the heart; by which means, as a person of such propensities inevitably must, she gained from many people the reverence due to an angel, but, I should imagine, was looked upon by others as an intruder and a nuisance. Prying farther into the manuscript, I found the record of other doings and sufferings of this singular woman, for most of which the reader is referred to the story entitled "THE SCARLET LETTER"; and it should be borne carefully in mind, that the main facts of that story are authorized and authenticated by the document of Mr. Surveyor Pue. The original papers, together with the scarlet letter itself,—a most curious relic,—are still in my possession, and shall be freely exhibited to whomsoever, induced by the great interest of the narrative, may desire a sight of them. I must not be understood as affirming, that, in the dressing up of the tale, and imagining the motives and modes of passion that influenced the characters who figure in it, I have invariably confined myself within the limits of the old Surveyor's half a dozen sheets of foolscap. On the contrary, I have allowed myself, as to such points, nearly or altogether as much license as if the facts had been entirely of my own invention. What I contend for is the authenticity of the outline.

This incident recalled my mind, in some degree, to its old track. There seemed to be here the groundwork of a tale. It impressed me as if the ancient Surveyor, in his garb of a hundred years gone by, and wearing his immortal wig,—which was buried with him, but did not perish in the grave,—had met me in the deserted chamber of the Custom-House. In his port was the dignity of one who had borne his Majesty's commission, and who was therefore illuminated by a ray of the splendor that shone so dazzlingly about the throne. How unlike, alas! the hang-dog look of a republican official, who, as the servant of the people, feels himself less than the least, and below the lowest, of his masters. With his own ghostly hand, the obscurely seen, but majestic, figure had imparted to me the scarlet symbol, and the little roll of explanatory manuscript. With his own ghostly voice, he had exhorted me, on the sacred consideration of my filial duty and reverence towards him,—who might reasonably regard himself as my official ancestor,—to bring his mouldy and moth-eaten lucubrations before the public. "Do this," said the ghost of Mr. Surveyor Pue, emphatically nodding the head that looked so imposing within its memorable wig, "do this, and the profit shall be all your own! You will shortly need it; for it is not in your days as it was in mine, when a man's office was a life-lease, and oftentimes an heirloom. But, I charge you, in this matter of old Mistress Prynne, give to your predecessor's memory the credit which will be rightfully its due!" And I said to the ghost of Mr. Surveyor Pue,—"I will!"

On Hester Prynne's story, therefore, I bestowed much

thought. It was the subject of my meditations for many an hour, while pacing to and fro across my room, or traversing, with a hundredfold repetition, the long extent from the front-door of the Custom-House to the side-entrance, and back again. Great were the weariness and annoyance of the old In-spector and the Weighers and Gaugers, whose slumbers were disturbed by the unmercifully lengthened tramp of my passing and returning footsteps. Remembering their own former habits, they used to say that the Surveyor was walking the quarter-deck. They probably fancied that my sole object—and, indeed, the sole object for which a sane man could ever put himself into voluntary motion—was, to get an appetite for dinner. And to say the truth, an appetite, sharpened by the east-wind that generally blew along the passage, was the only valuable result of so much indefatigable exercise. So little adapted is the atmosphere of a Custom-House to the delicate harvest of fancy and sensibility, that, had I remained there through ten Presidencies yet to come, I doubt whether the tale of "The Scarlet Letter" would ever have been brought before the public eye. My imagination was a tarnished mirror. It would not reflect, or only with miserable dimness, the figures with which I did my best to people it. The characters of the narrative would not be warmed and rendered malleable, by any heat that I could kindle at my intellectual forge. They would take neither the glow of passion nor the tenderness of senti-ment, but retained all the rigidity of dead corpses, and stared me in the face with a fixed and ghastly grin of contemptuous defiance. "What have you to do with us?" that expression seemed to say. "The little power you might once have pos-sessed over the tribe of unrealities is gone! You have bartered it for a pittance of the public gold. Go, then, and earn your wages!" In short, the almost torpid creatures of my own fancy twitted me with imbecility, and not without fair occasion.

It was not merely during the three hours and a half which Uncle Sam claimed as his share of my daily life, that this wretched numbness held possession of me. It went with me on

my sea-shore walks and rambles into the country, whenever—
which was seldom and reluctantly—I bestirred myself to seek
that invigorating charm of Nature, which used to give me
such freshness and activity of thought, the moment that I
stepped across the threshold of the Old Manse. The same
torpor, as regarded the capacity for intellectual effort, accompanied me home, and weighed upon me in the chamber which
I most absurdly termed my study. Nor did it quit me, when,
late at night, I sat in the deserted parlour, lighted only by
the glimmering coal-fire and the moon, striving to picture forth
imaginary scenes, which, the next day, might flow out on the
brightening page in many-hued description.

If the imaginative faculty refused to act at such an hour, it
might well be deemed a hopeless case. Moonlight, in a familiar room, falling so white upon the carpet, and showing all
its figures so distinctly,—making every object so minutely
visible, yet so unlike a morning or noontide visibility,—is a
medium the most suitable for a romance-writer to get acquainted with his illusive guests. There is the little domestic
scenery of the well-known apartment; the chairs, with each its
separate individuality; the centre-table, sustaining a work-
basket, a volume or two, and an extinguished lamp; the sofa;
the book-case; the picture on the wall;—all these details, so
completely seen, are so spiritualized by the unusual light, that
they seem to lose their actual substance, and become things
of intellect. Nothing is too small or too trifling to undergo this
change, and acquire dignity thereby. A child's shoe; the doll,
seated in her little wicker carriage; the hobby-horse;—whatever, in a word, has been used or played with, during the day,
is now invested with a quality of strangeness and remoteness,
though still almost as vividly present as by daylight. Thus,
therefore, the floor of our familiar room has become a neutral
territory, somewhere between the real world and fairy-land,
where the Actual and the Imaginary may meet, and each imbue itself with the nature of the other. Ghosts might enter
here, without affrighting us. It would be too much in keeping

with the scene to excite surprise, were we to look about us and discover a form, beloved, but gone hence, now sitting quietly in a streak of this magic moonshine, with an aspect that would make us doubt whether it had returned from afar, or had never once stirred from our fireside.

The somewhat dim coal-fire has an essential influence in producing the effect which I would describe. It throws its unobtrusive tinge throughout the room, with a faint ruddiness upon the walls and ceiling, and a reflected gleam from the polish of the furniture. This warmer light mingles itself with the cold spirituality of the moonbeams, and communicates, as it were, a heart and sensibilities of human tenderness to the forms which fancy summons up. It converts them from snow-images into men and women. Glancing at the looking-glass, we behold—deep within its haunted verge—the smouldering glow of the half-extinguished anthracite, the white moonbeams on the floor, and a repetition of all the gleam and shadow of the picture, with one remove farther from the actual, and nearer to the imaginative. Then, at such an hour, and with this scene before him, if a man, sitting all alone, cannot dream strange things, and make them look like truth, he need never try to write romances.

But, for myself, during the whole of my Custom-House experience, moonlight and sunshine, and the glow of fire-light, were just alike in my regard; and neither of them was of one whit more avail than the twinkle of a tallow-candle. An entire class of susceptibilities, and a gift connected with them,—of no great richness or value, but the best I had,—was gone from me.

It is my belief, however, that, had I attempted a different order of composition, my faculties would not have been found so pointless and inefficacious. I might, for instance, have contented myself with writing out the narratives of a veteran shipmaster, one of the Inspectors, whom I should be most ungrateful not to mention; since scarcely a day passed that he did not stir me to laughter and admiration by his marvellous

gifts as a story-teller. Could I have preserved the picturesque
force of his style, and the humorous coloring which nature
taught him how to throw over his descriptions, the result, I
honestly believe, would have been something new in literature.
Or I might readily have found a more serious task. It was a
folly, with the materiality of this daily life pressing so intru-
sively upon me, to attempt to fling myself back into another
age; or to insist on creating the semblance of a world out of
airy matter, when, at every moment, the impalpable beauty
of my soap-bubble was broken by the rude contact of some
actual circumstance. The wiser effort would have been, to
diffuse thought and imagination through the opaque substance
of to-day, and thus to make it a bright transparency; to spir-
itualize the burden that began to weigh so heavily; to seek,
resolutely, the true and indestructible value that lay hidden
in the petty and wearisome incidents, and ordinary characters,
with which I was now conversant. The fault was mine. The
page of life that was spread out before me seemed dull and
commonplace, only because I had not fathomed its deeper import. A better book than I shall ever write was there; leaf after
leaf presenting itself to me, just as it was written out by the
reality of the flitting hour, and vanishing as fast as written,
only because my brain wanted the insight and my hand the
cunning to transcribe it. At some future day, it may be, I shall
remember a few scattered fragments and broken paragraphs,
and write them down, and find the letters turn to gold upon
the page.

These perceptions have come too late. At the instant, I was
only conscious that what would have been a pleasure once was
now a hopeless toil. There was no occasion to make much
moan about this state of affairs. I had ceased to be a writer of
tolerably poor tales and essays, and had become a tolerably
good Surveyor of the Customs. That was all. But, nevertheless,
it is any thing but agreeable to be haunted by a suspicion that
one's intellect is dwindling away; or exhaling, without your
consciousness, like ether out of a phial; so that, at every glance,

you find a smaller and less volatile residuum. Of the fact, there could be no doubt; and, examining myself and others, I was led to conclusions in reference to the effect of public office on the character, not very favorable to the mode of life in question. In some other form, perhaps, I may hereafter develop these effects. Suffice it here to say, that a Custom-House officer, of long continuance, can hardly be a very praiseworthy or respectable personage, for many reasons; one of them, the tenure by which he holds his situation, and another, the very nature of his business, which—though, I trust, an honest one—is of such a sort that he does not share in the united effort of mankind.

An effect—which I believe to be observable, more or less, in every individual who has occupied the position—is, that, while he leans on the mighty arm of the Republic, his own proper strength departs from him. He loses, in an extent proportioned to the weakness or force of his original nature, the capability of self-support. If he possess an unusual share of native energy, or the enervating magic of place do not operate too long upon him, his forfeited powers may be redeemable. The ejected officer—fortunate in the unkindly shove that sends him forth betimes, to struggle amid a struggling world—may return to himself, and become all that he has ever been. But this seldom happens. He usually keeps his ground just long enough for his own ruin, and is then thrust out, with sinews all unstrung, to totter along the difficult footpath of life as he best may. Conscious of his own infirmity,—that his tempered steel and elasticity are lost,—he for ever afterwards looks wistfully about him in quest of support external to himself. His pervading and continual hope—a hallucination, which, in the face of all discouragement, and making light of impossibilities, haunts him while he lives, and, I fancy, like the convulsive throes of the cholera, torments him for a brief space after death—is, that, finally, and in no long time, by some happy coincidence of circumstances, he shall be restored to office. This faith, more than any thing else, steals the pith and availability out of whatever enterprise he may dream of undertaking. Why should he toil and moil, and be at so much trouble to pick himself up out of the mud, when, in a little while hence, the strong arm of his Uncle will raise and support him? Why should he work for his living here, or go to dig gold in California, when he is so soon to be made happy, at monthly intervals, with a little pile of glittering coin out of his Uncle's pocket? It is sadly curious to observe how slight a taste of office suffices to infect a poor fellow with this singular disease. Uncle Sam's gold—meaning no disrespect to the worthy old gentleman—has, in this respect, a quality of enchantment like that of the Devil's wages. Whoever touches it should look well to himself, or he may find the bargain to go hard against him, involving, if not his soul, yet many of its better attributes; its sturdy force, its courage and constancy, its truth, its self-reliance, and all that gives the emphasis to manly character.

Here was a fine prospect in the distance! Not that the Surveyor brought the lesson home to himself, or admitted that he could be so utterly undone, either by continuance in office, or ejectment. Yet my reflections were not the most comfortable. I began to grow melancholy and restless; continually prying into my mind, to discover which of its poor properties were gone, and what degree of detriment had already accrued to the remainder. I endeavoured to calculate how much longer I could stay in the Custom-House, and yet go forth a man. To confess the truth, it was my greatest apprehension,—as it would never be a measure of policy to turn out so quiet an individual as myself, and it being hardly in the nature of a public officer to resign,—it was my chief trouble, therefore, that I was likely to grow gray and decrepit in the Surveyorship, and become much such another animal as the old Inspector. Might it not, in the tedious lapse of official life that lay before me, finally be with me as it was with this venerable friend,—to make the dinner-hour the nucleus of the day, and to spend the rest of it, as an old dog spends it, asleep in the sunshine or the shade? A dreary look-forward this, for a man who felt it to be the best definition of happiness to live throughout the whole range of his faculties and sensibilities! But, all this while, I was giving myself very unnecessary alarm. Providence had meditated better things for me than I could possibly imagine for myself.

A remarkable event of the third year of my Surveyorship—to adopt the tone of "P.P."—was the election of General Taylor to the Presidency. It is essential, in order to form a complete estimate of the advantages of official life, to view the incumbent at the in-coming of a hostile administration. His position is then one of the most singularly irksome, and, in every contingency, disagreeable, that a wretched mortal can possibly occupy; with seldom an alternative of good, on either hand, although what presents itself to him as the worst event may very probably be the best. But it is a strange experience, to a man of pride and sensibility, to know that his interests are within the control of individuals who neither love nor understand him, and by whom, since one or the other must needs happen, he would rather be injured than obliged. Strange, too, for one who has kept his calmness throughout the contest, to observe the bloodthirstiness that is developed in the hour of triumph, and to be conscious that he is himself among its objects! There are few uglier traits of human nature than this tendency—which I now witnessed in men no worse than their neighbours—to grow cruel, merely because they possessed the power of inflicting harm. If the guillotine, as applied to office-holders, were a literal fact, instead of one of the most apt of metaphors, it is my sincere belief, that the active members of the victorious party were sufficiently excited to have chopped off all our heads, and have thanked Heaven for the opportunity! It appears to me—who have been a calm and curious observer, as well in victory as defeat—that this fierce and bitter spirit of malice and revenge has never distinguished the many triumphs of my own party as it now did that of the Whigs. The Democrats take the offices, as a general rule, because they need them, and because the practice of many years has made it the law of political warfare, which, unless a different system be proclaimed, it were weakness and cowardice to murmur at. But the long habit of victory has made them generous. They know how to spare, when they see occasion; and when they strike, the axe may be sharp, indeed, but its edge is seldom poisoned with ill-will; nor is it their custom ignominiously to kick the head which they have just struck off.

In short, unpleasant as was my predicament, at best, I saw much reason to congratulate myself that I was on the losing side, rather than the triumphant one. If, heretofore, I had been none of the warmest of partisans, I began now, at this season of peril and adversity, to be pretty acutely sensible with which party my predilections lay; nor was it without something like regret and shame, that, according to a reasonable calculation of chances, I saw my own prospect of retaining office to be better than those of my Democratic brethren. But who can see an inch into futurity, beyond his nose? My own head was the first that fell![29]

The moment when a man's head drops off is seldom or never, I am inclined to think, precisely the most agreeable of his life. Nevertheless, like the greater part of our misfortunes, even so serious a contingency brings its remedy and consolation with it, if the sufferer will but make the best, rather than the worst, of the accident which has befallen him. In my particular case, the consolatory topics were close at hand, and, indeed, had suggested themselves to my meditations a considerable time before it was requisite to use them. In view of my previous weariness of office, and vague thoughts of resignation, my fortune somewhat resembled that of a person who should entertain an idea of committing suicide, and, altogether beyond his hopes, meet with the good hap to be murdered. In the Custom-House, as before in the Old Manse, I had spent three years; a term long enough to rest a weary

[29] Although he was a Democrat, Hawthorne believed that he had received his position as a literary man provided for by the government, and he did not expect to be discharged with a change of parties. He protested the action and, for a short time, there was a bitter contest between Hawthorne's friends and those who opposed him, which burst into the public press. The discharge, however, was not reversed.

brain; long enough to break off old intellectual habits, and make room for new ones; long enough, and too long, to have lived in an unnatural state, doing what was really of no advantage nor delight to any human being, and withholding myself from toil that would, at least, have stilled an unquiet impulse in me. Then, moreover, as regarded his unceremonious ejectment, the late Surveyor was not altogether ill-pleased to be recognized by the Whigs as an enemy; since his inactivity in political affairs,—his tendency to roam, at will, in that broad and quiet field where all mankind may meet, rather than confine himself to those narrow paths where brethren of the same household must diverge from one another,—had sometimes made it questionable with his brother Democrats whether he was a friend. Now, after he had won the crown of martyrdom, (though with no longer a head to wear it on,) the point might be looked upon as settled. Finally, little heroic as he was, it seemed more decorous to be overthrown in the downfall of the party with which he had been content to stand, than to remain a forlorn survivor, when so many worthier men were falling; and, at last, after subsisting for four years on the mercy of a hostile administration, to be compelled then to define his position anew, and claim the yet more humiliating mercy of a friendly one.

Meanwhile, the press had taken up my affair, and kept me, for a week or two, careering through the public prints, in my decapitated state, like Irving's Headless Horseman;[30] ghastly and grim, and longing to be buried, as a politically dead man ought. So much for my figurative self. The real human being, all this time, with his head safely on his shoulders, had brought himself to the comfortable conclusion, that every thing was for the best; and, making an investment in ink, paper, and steel-pens, had opened his long-disused writing-desk, and was again a literary man.

Now it was, that the lucubrations of my ancient predeces-

[30] The headless horseman in "The Legend of Sleepy Hollow," by Washington Irving.

sor, Mr. Surveyor Pue, came into play. Rusty through long idleness, some little space was requisite before my intellectual machinery could be brought to work upon the tale, with an effect in any degree satisfactory. Even yet, though my thoughts were ultimately much absorbed in the task, it wears, to my eye, a stern and sombre aspect; too much ungladdened by genial sunshine; too little relieved by the tender and familiar influences which soften almost every scene of nature and real life, and, undoubtedly, should soften every picture of them. This uncaptivating effect is perhaps due to the period of hardly accomplished revolution, and still seething turmoil, in which the story shaped itself. It is no indication, however, of a lack of cheerfulness in the writer's mind; for he was happier, while straying through the gloom of these sunless fantasies, than at any time since he had quitted the Old Manse. Some of the briefer articles, which contribute to make up the volume, have likewise been written since my involuntary withdrawal from the toils and honors of public life, and the remainder are gleaned from annuals and magazines, of such antique date that they have gone round the circle, and come back to novelty again.* Keeping up the metaphor of the political guillotine, the whole may be considered as the POSTHUMOUS PAPERS OF A DECAPITATED SURVEYOR; and the sketch which I am now bringing to a close, if too autobiographical for a modest person to publish in his lifetime, will readily be excused in a gentleman who writes from beyond the grave. Peace be with all the world! My blessing on my friends! My forgiveness to my enemies! For I am in the realm of quiet!

The life of the Custom-House lies like a dream behind me. The old Inspector,—who, by the by, I regret to say, was overthrown and killed by a horse, some time ago; else he would certainly have lived for ever,—he, and all those other vener-

---

* At the time of writing this article, the author intended to publish, along with "The Scarlet Letter," several shorter tales and sketches. These it has been thought advisable to defer. [HAWTHORNE'S NOTE.]

able personages who sat with him at the receipt of custom, are but shadows in my view; white-headed and wrinkled images, which my fancy used to sport with, and has now flung aside for ever. The merchants,—Pingree, Phillips, Shepard, Upton, Kimball, Bertram, Hunt,—these, and many other names, which had such a classic familiarity for my ear six months ago,—these men of traffic, who seemed to occupy so important a position in the world,—how little time has it required to disconnect me from them all, not merely in act, but recollection! It is with an effort that I recall the figures and appellations of these few. Soon, likewise, my old native town will loom upon me through the haze of memory, a mist brooding over and around it; as if it were no portion of the real earth, but an overgrown village in cloud-land, with only imaginary inhabitants to people its wooden houses, and walk its homely lanes, and the unpictur-esque prolixity of its main street. Henceforth, it ceases to be a reality of my life. I am a citizen of somewhere else. My good townspeople will not much regret me; for—though it has been as dear an object as any, in my literary efforts, to be of some importance in their eyes, and to win myself a pleasant memory in this abode and burial-place of so many of my forefathers— there has never been, for me, the genial atmosphere which a literary man requires, in order to ripen the best harvest of his mind. I shall do better amongst other faces; and these familiar ones, it need hardly be said, will do just as well without me.

It may be, however,—O, transporting and triumphant thought!—that the great-grandchildren of the present race may sometimes think kindly of the scribbler of bygone days, when the antiquary of days to come, among the sites memorable in the town's history, shall point out the locality of THE TOWN-PUMP! [31]

---

[31] Hawthorne's sketch, "A Rill from the Town Pump," was in-cluded in *Twice-Told Tales.* It is, among other things, a temperance tract.

1. The Prison-Door

A THRONG of bearded men, in sad-colored garments and gray, steeple-crowned hats, intermixed with women, some wearing hoods, and others bareheaded, was assembled in front of a wooden edifice, the door of which was heavily timbered with oak, and studded with iron spikes.

flat color

The founders of a new colony, whatever Utopia of human virtue and happiness they might originally project, have invariably recognized it among their earliest practical necessities to allot a portion of the virgin soil as a cemetery, and another portion as the site of a prison. In accordance with this rule, it may safely be assumed that the forefathers of Boston had built the first prison-house, somewhere in the vicinity of Cornhill, almost as seasonably as they marked out the first burial-ground, on Isaac Johnson's lot,[1] and round about his grave, which subsequently became the nucleus of all the congregated sepulchres in the old church-yard of King's Chapel. Certain it is, that, some fifteen or twenty years after the settlement of the town, the wooden jail was already marked with weather-stains and other indications of age, which gave a yet darker aspect to its beetle-browed and gloomy front. The rust on the ponderous iron-work of its oaken door looked more antique than any thing else in the new world. Like all that pertains to crime, it seemed never to have known a youthful era. Before this ugly

irony

[1] Isaac Johnson (1601–1630) was the wealthiest of the early immigrants to Massachusetts, to which he came in 1630 with his wife, the Lady Arbella, daughter of the Earl of Lincoln. Boston was settled under Johnson's supervision, but he died within a year of his arrival. He specified not only the lot on which he was to be buried but also the corner of it that he was to occupy.

brings in the imaginary

edifice, and between it and the wheel-track of the street, was a grass-plot, much overgrown with burdock, pig-weed, apple-peru,[2] and such unsightly vegetation, which evidently found something congenial in the soil that had so early borne the black flower of civilized society, a prison. But, on one side of the portal, and rooted almost at the threshold, was a wild rose-bush, covered, in this month of June, with its delicate gems, *metaphor* which might be imagined to offer their fragrance and fragile beauty to the prisoner as he went in, and to the condemned criminal as he came forth to his doom, in token that the deep heart of Nature could pity and be kind to him.

This rose-bush, by a strange chance, has been kept alive in history; but whether it had merely survived out of the stern old wilderness, so long after the fall of the gigantic pines and oaks that originally overshadowed it,—or whether, as there is fair authority for believing, it had sprung up under the foot-steps of the sainted Ann Hutchinson,[3] as she entered the

[2] Sometimes called the Apple of Peru, this is the thorn apple that grows on Jimson weed.

[3] Anne Hutchinson (1590–1643) migrated to Massachusetts with her husband in 1634. She was an extremely personable and vigorous woman, deeply interested in theology, and soon gathered a following among those who strove, within the bounds of the Massachusetts church system, to place an immense premium on the indwelling of the Holy Spirit in a true believer. They stressed the true believer's responsibility to the Spirit within him, even to the point of disobeying the more explicit laws of the Bible or of the Commonwealth. Her doctrine was branded as "antinomianism" by her opponents and condemned as dangerously anarchistic in the emphasis it placed on the personal nature of salvation. After a controversy that came close to wrecking the young colony of Massachusetts, she was banished in 1638, and together with her family and some friends she moved to Rhode Island. In 1642, after the death of her husband, she removed to the present Pelham Bay, New York, then under Dutch control; and there, within a year of her settlement, she and her family were massacred by Indians. She lives on in folklore as an example of an inspired prophet who was *also Hester* persecuted because she was a woman in an age when only men were considered to be the valid revealers of truth.

prison-door,—we shall not take upon us to determine. Finding it so directly on the threshold of our narrative, which is now about to issue from that inauspicious portal, we could hardly do otherwise than pluck one of its flowers and present it to the reader. It may serve, let us hope, to symbolize some sweet moral blossom, that may be found along the track, or relieve the darkening close of a tale of human frailty and sorrow.

Pearl is a kind of relief like the flower

Ch 1-9 : structure

2. The Market-Place

to establish the atmosphere   *people are vengeful (esp. older people)*

THE grass-plot before the jail, in Prison Lane, on a certain summer morning, not less than two centuries ago, was occupied by a pretty large number of the inhabitants of Boston; all with their eyes intently fastened on the iron-clamped oaken door. Amongst any other population, or at a later period in the history of New England, the grim rigidity that petrified the bearded physiognomies of these good people would have augured some awful business in hand. It could have betokened nothing short of the anticipated execution of some noted culprit, on whom the sentence of a legal tribunal had but confirmed the verdict of public sentiment. But, in that early severity of the Puritan character, an inference of this kind could not so indubitably be drawn. It might be that a sluggish bond-servant, or an undutiful child, whom his parents had given over to the civil authority, was to be corrected at the whipping-post. It might be, that an Antinomian,[1] a Quaker, or other heterodox religionist, was to be scourged out of the town, or an idle and vagrant Indian, whom the white man's fire-water had made riotous about the streets, was to be driven with

[1] See Note 3, Chapter 1, page 48.

stripes into the shadow of the forest. It might be, too, that a
witch, like old Mistress Hibbins,[2] the bitter-tempered widow
of the magistrate, was to die upon the gallows. In either case,
there was very much the same solemnity of demeanour on the
part of the spectators; as befitted a people amongst whom
religion and law were almost identical, and in whose character
both were so thoroughly interfused, that the mildest and the
severest acts of public discipline were alike made venerable and
awful. Meagre, indeed, and cold, was the sympathy that a
transgressor might look for, from such bystanders at the scaffold. On the other hand, a penalty which, in our days, would
infer a degree of mocking infamy and ridicule, might then be
invested with almost as stern a dignity as the punishment of
death itself.

It was a circumstance to be noted, on the summer morning
when our story begins its course, that the women, of whom
there were several in the crowd, appeared to take a peculiar
interest in whatever penal infliction might be expected to ensue. The age had not so much refinement, that any sense of
impropriety restrained the wearers of petticoat and farthingale
from stepping forth into the public ways, and wedging their
not unsubstantial persons, if occasion were, into the throng
nearest to the scaffold at an execution. Morally, as well as
materially, there was a coarser fibre in those wives and maidens
of old English birth and breeding, than in their fair descend-

[2] Ann Hibbins, wife of William Hibbins—who had served as the
colony's agent in England and as a magistrate—had a quarrelsome
temper, which brought her under church censure and made her a
most unpopular figure. In 1655, the year after her husband's death,
her disposition rendered her so odious to her neighbors that she
was accused by some of witchcraft. She was tried for this in 1655
and found guilty. When the magistrates tried to reverse the verdict,
the popular clamor against her was so great that she was condemned and put to death (1656). Only one document of the
period mentions that she was Richard Bellingham's sister. While this
is far from conclusive, such a relationship, of course, is very useful
for the economy of the novel, in furtherance of which Hawthorne
also has her in her widowhood some years earlier than was the fact.

ants, separated from them by a series of six or seven generations; for, throughout that chain of ancestry, every successive mother has transmitted to her child a fainter bloom, a more delicate and briefer beauty, and a slighter physical frame, if not a character of less force and solidity, than her own. The women, who were now standing about the prison-door, stood within less than half a century of the period when the manlike Elizabeth[3] had been the not altogether unsuitable representative of the sex. They were her countrywomen; and the beef and ale of their native land, with a moral diet not a whit more refined, entered largely into their composition. The bright morning sun, therefore, shone on broad shoulders and well-developed busts, and on round and ruddy cheeks, that had ripened in the far-off island, and had hardly yet grown paler or thinner in the atmosphere of New England. There was, moreover, a boldness and rotundity of speech among these matrons, as most of them seemed to be, that would startle us at the present day, whether in respect to its purport or its volume of tone.

"Goodwives," said a hard-featured dame of fifty, "I'll tell ye a piece of my mind. It would be greatly for the public behoof, if we women, being of mature age and church-members in good repute, should have the handling of such malefactresses as this Hester Prynne. What think ye, gossips?[4] If the hussy stood up for judgment before us five, that are now here in a knot together, would she come off with such a sentence as the worshipful magistrates have awarded? Marry, I trow not!"

"People say," said another, "that the Reverend Master Dimmesdale, her godly pastor, takes it very grievously to heart that such a scandal should have come upon his congregation "

"The magistrates are God-fearing gentlemen, but merciful

[3] Elizabeth I (1533–1603) reigned as Queen of England and Ireland from 1558 until her death. Although she possessed extraordinary political intelligence and outwitted every statesman in Europe, she was not above justifying her conduct by pleading feminine weakness.

[4] "Good sibs" or "good kin."

overmuch,—that is a truth," added a third autumnal matron. "At the very least, they should have put the brand of a hot iron on Hester Prynne's forehead. Madam Hester would have winced at that, I warrant me. But she,—the naughty baggage,—little will she care what they put upon the bodice of her gown! Why, look you, she may cover it with a brooch, or such like heathenish adornment, and so walk the streets as brave as ever!"

"Ah, but," interposed, more softly, a young wife, holding a child by the hand, "let her cover the mark as she will, the pang of it will be always in her heart."

"What do we talk of marks and brands, whether on the bodice of her gown, or the flesh of her forehead?" cried another female, the ugliest as well as the most pitiless of these self-constituted judges. "This woman has brought shame upon us all, and ought to die. Is there not law for it? Truly there is, both in the Scripture and the statute-book. Then let the magistrates, who have made it of no effect, thank themselves if their own wives and daughters go astray!"

"Mercy on us, goodwife," exclaimed a man in the crowd, "is there no virtue in woman, save what springs from a wholesome fear of the gallows? That is the hardest word yet! Hush, now, gossips; for the lock is turning in the prison-door, and here comes Mistress Prynne herself."

The door of the jail being flung open from within, there appeared, in the first place, like a black shadow emerging into the sunshine, the grim and grisly presence of the town-beadle, with a sword by his side and his staff of office in his hand. This personage prefigured and represented in his aspect the whole dismal severity of the Puritanic code of law, which it was his business to administer in its final and closest application to the offender. Stretching forth the official staff in his left hand, he laid his right upon the shoulder of a young woman, whom he thus drew forward; until, on the threshold of the prison-door, she repelled him, by an action marked with natural dignity and force of character, and stepped into the open air, as if by her own free-will. She bore in her arms a child, a baby of some three months old, who winked and turned aside its little face from the too vivid light of day; because its existence, heretofore, had brought it acquainted only with the gray twilight of a dungeon, or other darksome apartment of the prison.

When the young woman—the mother of this child—stood fully revealed before the crowd, it seemed to be her first impulse to clasp the infant closely to her bosom; not so much by an impulse of motherly affection, as that she might thereby conceal a certain token, which was wrought or fastened into her dress. In a moment, however, wisely judging that one token of her shame would but poorly serve to hide another, she took the baby on her arm, and, with a burning blush, and yet a haughty smile, and a glance that would not be abashed, looked around at her townspeople and neighbours. On the breast of her gown, in fine red cloth, surrounded with an elaborate embroidery and fantastic flourishes of gold thread, appeared the letter A. It was so artistically done, and with so much fertility and gorgeous luxuriance of fancy, that it had all the effect of a last and fitting decoration to the apparel which she wore; and which was of a splendor in accordance with the taste of the age, but greatly beyond what was allowed by the sumptuary regulations of the colony.

The young woman was tall, with a figure of perfect elegance, on a large scale. She had dark and abundant hair, so glossy that it threw off the sunshine with a gleam, and a face which, besides being beautiful from regularity of feature and richness of complexion, had the impressiveness belonging to a marked brow and deep black eyes. She was lady-like, too, after the manner of the feminine gentility of those days; characterized by a certain state and dignity, rather than by the delicate, evanescent, and indescribable grace, which is now recognized as its indication. And never had Hester Prynne appeared more lady-like, in the antique interpretation of the term, than as she issued from the prison. Those who had be-

fore known her, and had expected to behold her dimmed and
obscured by a disastrous cloud, were astonished, and even
startled, to perceive how her beauty shone out, and made a
halo of the misfortune and ignominy in which she was enveloped. It may be true, that, to a sensitive observer, there was
something exquisitely painful in it. Her attire, which, indeed,
she had wrought for the occasion, in prison, and had modelled
much after her own fancy, seemed to express the attitude of
her spirit, the desperate recklessness of her mood, by its wild
and picturesque peculiarity. But the point which drew all eyes,
and, as it were, transfigured the wearer,—so that both men
and women, who had been familiarly acquainted with Hester
Prynne, were now impressed as if they beheld her for the first
time,—was that SCARLET LETTER, so fantastically embroidered
and illuminated upon her bosom. It had the effect of a spell,
taking her out of the ordinary relations with humanity, and
inclosing her in a sphere by herself.

"She hath good skill at her needle, that's certain," remarked
one of the female spectators; "but did ever a woman, before
this brazen hussy, contrive such a way of showing it! Why,
gossips, what is it but to laugh in the faces of our godly magistrates, and make a pride out of what they, worthy gentlemen,
meant for a punishment?"

"It were well," muttered the most iron-visaged of the old
dames, "if we stripped Madam Hester's rich gown off her
dainty shoulders; and as for the red letter, which she hath
stitched so curiously, I'll bestow a rag of mine own rheumatic
flannel, to make a fitter one!"

"O, peace, neighbours, peace!" whispered their youngest
companion. "Do not let her hear you! Not a stitch in that
embroidered letter, but she has felt it in her heart."

The grim beadle now made a gesture with his staff.

"Make way, good people, make way, in the King's name,"
cried he. "Open a passage; and, I promise ye, Mistress Prynne
shall be set where man, woman, and child may have a fair
sight of her brave apparel, from this time till an hour past

meridian. A blessing on the righteous Colony of the Massachusetts, where iniquity is dragged out into the sunshine! Come
along, Madam Hester, and show your scarlet letter in the
market-place!"

A lane was forthwith opened through the crowd of spectators. Preceded by the beadle, and attended by an irregular
procession of stern-browed men and unkindly-visaged women,
Hester Prynne set forth towards the place appointed for her
punishment. A crowd of eager and curious schoolboys, understanding little of the matter in hand, except that it gave them
a half-holiday, ran before her progress, turning their heads
continually to stare into her face, and at the winking baby in
her arms, and at the ignominious letter on her breast. It was
no great distance, in those days, from the prison-door to the
market-place. Measured by the prisoner's experience, however,
it might be reckoned a journey of some length; for, haughty
as her demeanour was, she perchance underwent an agony
from every footstep of those that thronged to see her, as if her
heart had been flung into the street for them all to spurn and
trample upon. In our nature, however, there is a provision,
alike marvellous and merciful, that the sufferer should never
know the intensity of what he endures by its present torture,
but chiefly by the pang that rankles after it. With almost a
serene deportment, therefore, Hester Prynne passed through
this portion of her ordeal, and came to a sort of scaffold, at the
western extremity of the market-place. It stood nearly beneath
the eaves of Boston's earliest church, and appeared to be a fix-
ture there.

In fact, this scaffold constituted a portion of a penal ma-
chine, which now, for two or three generations past, has been
merely historical and traditionary among us, but was held, in
the old time, to be as effectual an agent in the promotion of
good citizenship, as ever was the guillotine among the terror-
ists of France. It was, in short, the platform of the pillory; and
above it rose the framework of that instrument of discipline,
so fashioned as to confine the human head in its tight grasp,

and thus hold it up to the public gaze. The very ideal of ignominy was embodied and made manifest in this contrivance
of wood and iron. There can be no outrage, methinks, against
our common nature,—whatever be the delinquencies of the
individual,—no outrage more flagrant than to forbid the culprit to hide his face for shame; as it was the essence of this
punishment to do. In Hester Prynne's instance, however, as
not unfrequently in other cases, her sentence bore, that she
should stand a certain time upon the platform, but without
undergoing that gripe about the neck and confinement of the
head, the proneness to which was the most devilish characteristic of this ugly engine. Knowing well her part, she ascended
a flight of wooden steps, and was thus displayed to the surrounding multitude, at about the height of a man's shoulders
above the street.

Had there been a Papist among the crowd of Puritans, he
might have seen in this beautiful woman, so picturesque in her
attire and mien, and with the infant at her bosom, an object
to remind him of the image of Divine Maternity, which so
many illustrious painters have vied with one another to represent; something which should remind him, indeed, but only
by contrast, of that sacred image of sinless motherhood, whose
infant was to redeem the world. Here, there was the taint of
deepest sin in the most sacred quality of human life, working
such effect, that the world was only the darker for this
woman's beauty, and the more lost for the infant that she had
borne.

The scene was not without a mixture of awe, such as must
always invest the spectacle of guilt and shame in a fellow-
creature, before society shall have grown corrupt enough to
smile, instead of shuddering, at it. The witnesses of Hester
Prynne's disgrace had not yet passed beyond their simplicity.
They were stern enough to look upon her death, had that been
the sentence, without a murmur at its severity, but had none
of the heartlessness of another social state, which would find
only a theme for jest in an exhibition like the present. Even

had there been a disposition to turn the matter into ridicule, it must have been repressed and overpowered by the solemn presence of men no less dignified than the Governor, and several of his counsellors, a judge, a general, and the ministers of the town; all of whom sat or stood in a balcony of the meeting-house, looking down upon the platform. When such personages could constitute a part of the spectacle, without risking the majesty or reverence of rank and office, it was safely to be inferred that the infliction of a legal sentence would have an earnest and effectual meaning. Accordingly, the crowd was sombre and grave. The unhappy culprit sustained herself as best a woman might, under the heavy weight of a thousand unrelenting eyes, all fastened upon her, and concentred at her bosom. It was almost intolerable to be borne. Of an impulsive and passionate nature, she had fortified herself to encounter the stings and venomous stabs of public contumely, wreaking itself in every variety of insult; but there was a quality so much more terrible in the solemn mood of the popular mind, that she longed rather to behold all those rigid countenances contorted with scornful merriment, and herself the object. Had a roar of laughter burst from the multitude,—each man, each woman, each little shrill-voiced child, contributing their individual parts,—Hester Prynne might have repaid them all with a bitter and disdainful smile. But, under the leaden infliction which it was her doom to endure, she felt, at moments, as if she must needs shriek out with the full power of her lungs, and cast herself from the scaffold down upon the ground, or else go mad at once.

Yet there were intervals when the whole scene, in which she was the most conspicuous object, seemed to vanish from her eyes, or, at least, glimmered indistinctly before them, like a mass of imperfectly shaped and spectral images. Her mind, and especially her memory, was preternaturally active, and kept bringing up other scenes than this roughly hewn street of a little town, on the edge of the Western wilderness; other faces than were lowering upon her from beneath the brims of

those steeple-crowned hats. Reminiscences, the most trifling
and immaterial, passages of infancy and school-days, sports,
childish quarrels, and the little domestic traits of her maiden
years, came swarming back upon her, intermingled with recollections of whatever was gravest in her subsequent life; one
picture precisely as vivid as another; as if all were of similar
importance, or all alike a play. Possibly, it was an instinctive
device of her spirit, to relieve itself, by the exhibition of these
phantasmagoric forms, from the cruel weight and hardness
of the reality.

   Be that as it might, the scaffold of the pillory was a point of
view that revealed to Hester Prynne the entire track along
which she had been treading, since her happy infancy. Standing
on that miserable eminence, she saw again her native village, in
Old England, and her paternal home; a decayed house of gray
stone, with a poverty-stricken aspect, but retaining a half-
obliterated shield of arms over the portal, in token of antique
gentility. She saw her father's face, with its bald brow, and
reverend white beard, that flowed over the old-fashioned Elizabethan ruff; her mother's, too, with the look of heedful and
anxious love which it always wore in her remembrance, and
which, even since her death, had so often laid the impediment
of a gentle remonstrance in her daughter's pathway. She saw
her own face, glowing with girlish beauty, and illuminating
all the interior of the dusky mirror in which she had been
wont to gaze at it. There she beheld another countenance, of
a man well stricken in years, a pale, thin, scholar-like visage,
with eyes dim and bleared by the lamp-light that had served
them to pore over many ponderous books. Yet those same
bleared optics had a strange, penetrating power, when it was
their owner's purpose to read the human soul. This figure of
the study and the cloister, as Hester Prynne's womanly fancy
failed not to recall, was slightly deformed, with the left
shoulder a trifle higher than the right. Next rose before her,
in memory's picture-gallery, the intricate and narrow thor-
oughfares, the tall, gray houses, the huge cathedrals, and the

[marginal note: Roger Chillingworth]

public edifices, ancient in date and quaint in architecture, of a Continental city; where a new life had awaited her, still in connection with the misshapen scholar; a new life, but feeding itself on time-worn materials, like a túft of green moss on a crumbling wall. Lastly, in lieu of these shifting scenes, came back the rude market-place of the Puritan settlement, with all the townspeople assembled and levelling their stern regards at Hester Prynne,—yes, at herself,—who stood on the scaffold of the pillory, an infant on her arm, and the letter A, in scarlet, fantastically embroidered with gold thread, upon her bosom!

Amsterdam

Could it be true? She clutched the child so fiercely to her breast, that it sent forth a cry; she turned her eyes downward at the scarlet letter, and even touched it with her finger, to assure herself that the infant and the shame were real. Yes!— these were the realities,—all else had vanished!

emphasis on the reality of the symbols
she does not recognize her actions to be evil in the eyes of others or of God.

3. The Recognition

emergence of Chillingworth's obsession

FROM this intense consciousness of being the object of severe and universal observation, the wearer of the scarlet letter was at length relieved by discerning, on the outskirts of the crowd, a figure which irresistibly took possession of her thoughts. An Indian, in his native garb, was standing there; but the red men were not so infrequent visitors of the English settlements, that one of them would have attracted any notice from Hester Prynne, at such a time; much less would he have excluded all other objects and ideas from her mind. By the Indian's side, and evidently sustaining a companionship with him, stood a white man, clad in a strange disarray of civilized and savage costume.

He was small in stature, with a furrowed visage, which, as yet, could hardly be termed aged. There was a remarkable intelligence in his features, as of a person who had so cultivated his mental part that it could not fail to mould the physical to itself, and become manifest by unmistakable tokens. Although, by a seemingly careless arrangement of his heterogeneous garb, he had endeavoured to conceal or abate the peculiarity, it was sufficiently evident to Hester Prynne, that one of this man's shoulders rose higher than the other. Again, at the first instant of perceiving that thin visage, and the slight deformity of the figure, she pressed her infant to her bosom, with so convulsive a force that the poor babe uttered another cry of pain. But the mother did not seem to hear it.

At his arrival in the market-place, and some time before she saw him, the stranger had bent his eyes on Hester Prynne. It was carelessly, at first, like a man chiefly accustomed to look inward, and to whom external matters are of little value and import, unless they bear relation to something within his mind. Very soon, however, his look became keen and penetrative. A writhing horror twisted itself across his features, like a snake gliding swiftly over them, and making one little pause, with all its wreathed intervolutions in open sight. His face darkened with some powerful emotion, which, nevertheless, he so instantaneously controlled by an effort of his will, that, save at a single moment, its expression might have passed for calmness. After a brief space, the convulsion grew almost imperceptible, and finally subsided into the depths of his nature. When he found the eyes of Hester Prynne fastened on his own, and saw that she appeared to recognize him, he slowly and calmly raised his finger, make a gesture with it in the air, and laid it on his lips.

Then, touching the shoulder of a townsman, who stood next to him, he addressed him in a formal and courteous manner.

"I pray you, good Sir," said he, "who is this woman?— and wherefore is she here set up to public shame?"

"You must needs be a stranger in this region, friend," answered the townsman, looking curiously at the questioner and

his savage companion; "else you would surely have heard of
Mistress Hester Prynne, and her evil doings. She hath raised
a great scandal, I promise you, in godly Master Dimmesdale's
church."

"You say truly," replied the other. "I am a stranger, and
have been a wanderer, sorely against my will. I have met with
grievous mishaps by sea and land, and have been long held in
bonds among the heathen-folk, to the southward; and am now
brought hither by this Indian, to be redeemed out of my captivity. Will it please you, therefore, to tell me of Hester
Prynne's,—have I her name rightly?—of this woman's offences,
and what has brought her to yonder scaffold?"

"Truly, friend, and methinks it must gladden your heart,
after your troubles and sojourn in the wilderness," said the
townsman, "to find yourself, at length, in a land where iniquity
is searched out, and punished in the sight of rulers and people;
as here in our godly New England. Yonder woman, Sir, you
must know, was the wife of a certain learned man, English by
birth, but who had long dwelt in Amsterdam, whence, some
good time agone, he was minded to cross over and cast in
his lot with us of the Massachusetts. To this purpose, he sent
his wife before him, remaining himself to look after some
necessary affairs. Marry, good Sir, in some two years, or less,
that the woman has been a dweller here in Boston, no tidings
have come of this learned gentleman, Master Prynne; and his
young wife, look you, being left to her own misguidance——"

"Ah!—aha!—I conceive you," said the stranger, with a bitter
smile. "So learned a man as you speak of should have learned
this too in his books. And who, by your favor, Sir, may be
the father of yonder babe—it is some three or four months old,
I should judge—which Mistress Prynne is holding in her arms?"

"Of a truth, friend, that matter remaineth a riddle; and the
Daniel [1] who shall expound it is yet a-wanting," answered the
townsman. "Madam Hester absolutely refuseth to speak, and

---

[1] The Book of Daniel is concerned in great part with that
prophet's skill in interpreting dreams and other signs.

the magistrates have laid their heads together in vain. Peradventure the guilty one stands looking on at this sad spectacle, unknown of man, and forgetting that God sees him."

"The learned man," observed the stranger, with another smile, "should come himself to look into the mystery."

"It behooves him well, if he be still in life," responded the townsman. "Now, good Sir, our Massachusetts magistracy, bethinking themselves that this woman is youthful and fair, and doubtless was strongly tempted to her fall;—and that, moreover, as is most likely, her husband may be at the bottom of the sea;—they have not been bold to put in force the extremity of our righteous law against her. The penalty thereof is death. But, in their great mercy and tenderness of heart, they have doomed Mistress Prynne to stand only a space of three hours on the platform of the pillory, and then and thereafter, for the remainder of her natural life, to wear a mark of shame upon her bosom."

IRONY

"A wise sentence!" remarked the stranger, gravely bowing his head. "Thus she will be a living sermon against sin, until the ignominious letter be engraved upon her tombstone. It irks me, nevertheless, that the partner of her iniquity should not, at least, stand on the scaffold by her side. But he will be known!—he will be known!—he will be known!"

Chillingworth

He bowed courteously to the communicative townsman, and, whispering a few words to his Indian attendant, they both made their way through the crowd.

While this passed, Hester Prynne had been standing on her pedestal, still with a fixed gaze towards the stranger; so fixed a gaze, that, at moments of intense absorption, all other objects in the visible world seemed to vanish, leaving only him and her. Such an interview, perhaps, would have been more terrible than even to meet him as she now did, with the hot, midday sun burning down upon her face, and lighting up its shame; with the scarlet token of infamy on her breast; with the sin-born infant in her arms; with a whole people, drawn forth as to a festival, staring at the features that should have been seen only in the quiet gleam of the fireside, in the happy shadow of a home, or beneath a matronly veil, at church. Dreadful as it was, she was conscious of a shelter in the presence of these thousand witnesses. It was better to stand thus, with so many betwixt him and her, than to greet him, face to face, they two alone. She fled for refuge, as it were, to the public exposure, and dreaded the moment when its protection should be withdrawn from her. Involved in these thoughts, she scarcely heard a voice behind her, until it had repeated her name more than once, in a loud and solemn tone, audible to the whole multitude.

"Hearken unto me, Hester Prynne!" said the voice.

It has already been noticed, that directly over the platform on which Hester Prynne stood was a kind of balcony, or open gallery, appended to the meeting-house. It was the place whence proclamations were wont to be made, amidst an assemblage of the magistracy, with all the ceremonial that attended such public observances in those days. Here, to witness the scene which we are describing, sat Governor Bellingham [2] himself, with four sergeants about his chair, bearing halberds, as a guard of honor. He wore a dark feather in his hat, a border of embroidery on his cloak, and a black velvet tunic beneath; a gentleman advanced in years, and with a hard experience written in his wrinkles. He was not ill fitted to be the head and representative of a community, which owed its origin and progress, and its present state of development, not to the impulses of youth, but to the stern and tempered energies of manhood, and the sombre sagacity of age; accomplishing so much, precisely because it imagined and hoped so little. The other eminent characters, by whom the chief ruler was surrounded, were distinguished by a dignity of mien, belonging to

[2] Richard Bellingham (*c.* 1592–1672) immigrated to Massachusetts in 1634 and was elected governor of that colony in the years 1641, 1654, and 1665–1672. The novel opens in June of 1642; actually Bellingham was not governor at that date, his term having expired the previous month.

a period when the forms of authority were felt to possess the
sacredness of divine institutions. They were, doubtless, good
men, just, and sage. But, out of the whole human family, it
would not have been easy to select the same number of wise
and virtuous persons, who should be less capable of sitting in
judgment on an erring woman's heart, and disentangling its
mesh of good and evil, than the sages of rigid aspect towards
whom Hester Prynne now turned her face. She seemed conscious, indeed, that whatever sympathy she might expect lay
in the larger and warmer heart of the multitude; for, as she
lifted her eyes towards the balcony, the unhappy woman grew
pale and trembled.

The voice which had called her attention was that of the
reverend and famous John Wilson,[3] the eldest clergyman of
Boston, a great scholar, like most of his contemporaries in the
profession, and withal a man of kind and genial spirit. This
last attribute, however, had been less carefully developed than
his intellectual gifts, and was, in truth, rather a matter of shame
than self-congratulation with him. There he stood, with a
border of grizzled locks beneath his skull-cap; while his gray
eyes, accustomed to the shaded light of his study, were winking, like those of Hester's infant, in the unadulterated sunshine.
He looked like the darkly engraved portraits which we see
prefixed to old volumes of sermons; and had no more right than
one of those portraits would have, to step forth, as he now
did, and meddle with a question of human guilt, passion, and
anguish.

"Hester Prynne," said the clergyman, "I have striven with
my young brother here, under whose preaching of the word
you have been privileged to sit,"—here Mr. Wilson laid his
hand on the shoulder of a pale young man beside him,—"I
have sought, I say, to persuade this godly youth, that he
should deal with you, here in the face of Heaven, and before

[3] John Wilson (1588–1667) immigrated to Massachusetts with
John Winthrop in 1630 and was one of the founders, as well as the
minister, of the Boston church. He was the chief clerical opponent
of Anne Hutchinson in the antinomian controversy.

these wise and upright rulers, and in hearing of all the people, as touching the vileness and blackness of your sin. Knowing your natural temper better than I, he could the better judge what arguments to use, whether of tenderness or terror, such as might prevail over your hardness and obstinacy; insomuch that you should no longer hide the name of him who tempted you to this grievous fall. But he opposes to me, (with a young man's oversoftness, albeit wise beyond his years,) that it were wronging the very nature of woman to force her to lay open her heart's secrets in such broad daylight, and in presence of so great a multitude. Truly, as I sought to convince him, the shame lay in the commission of the sin, and not in the showing of it forth. What say you to it, once again, brother Dimmesdale? Must it be thou or I that shall deal with this poor sinner's soul?"

There was a murmur among the dignified and reverend occupants of the balcony; and Governor Bellingham gave expression to its purport, speaking in an authoritative voice, although tempered with respect towards the youthful clergyman whom he addressed.

"Good Master Dimmesdale," said he, "the responsibility of this woman's soul lies greatly with you. It behooves you, therefore, to exhort her to repentance, and to confession, as a proof and consequence thereof."

The directness of this appeal drew the eyes of the whole crowd upon the Reverend Mr. Dimmesdale; a young clergyman, who had come from one of the great English universities, bringing all the learning of the age into our wild forest-land. His eloquence and religious fervor had already given the earnest of high eminence in his profession. He was a person of very striking aspect, with a white, lofty, and impending brow, large, brown, melancholy eyes, and a mouth which, unless when he forcibly compressed it, was apt to be tremulous, expressing both nervous sensibility and a vast power of self-restraint. Notwithstanding his high native gifts and scholar-like attainments, there was an air about this young minister,—an apprehensive, a startled, a half-frightened look,—as of a being who felt himself quite astray and at a loss in the pathway of human existence, and could only be at ease in some seclusion of his own. Therefore, so far as his duties would permit, he trode in the shadowy by-paths, and thus kept himself simple and childlike; coming forth, when occasion was, with a freshness, and fragrance, and dewy purity of thought, which, as many people said, affected them like the speech of an angel.

Such was the young man whom the Reverend Mr. Wilson and the Governor had introduced so openly to the public notice, bidding him speak, in the hearing of all men, to that mystery of a woman's soul, so sacred even in its pollution. The trying nature of his position drove the blood from his cheek, and made his lips tremulous.

"Speak to the woman, my brother," said Mr. Wilson. "It is of moment to her soul, and therefore, as the worshipful Governor says, momentous to thine own, in whose charge hers is. Exhort her to confess the truth!"

The Reverend Mr. Dimmesdale bent his head, in silent prayer, as it seemed, and then came forward.

"Hester Prynne," said he, leaning over the balcony, and looking down stedfastly into her eyes, "thou hearest what this good man says, and seest the accountability under which I labor. If thou feelest it to be for thy soul's peace, and that thy earthly punishment will thereby be made more effectual to salvation, I charge thee to speak out the name of thy fellow-sinner and fellow-sufferer! Be not silent from any mistaken pity and tenderness for him; for, believe me, Hester, though he were to step down from a high place, and stand there beside thee, on thy pedestal of shame, yet better were it so, than to hide a guilty heart through life. What can thy silence do for him, except it tempt him—yea, compel him, as it were—to add hypocrisy to sin? Heaven hath granted thee an open ignominy, that thereby thou mayest work out an open triumph over the evil within thee, and the sorrow without. Take heed how thou deniest to him—who, perchance, hath not the courage to grasp it for himself—the bitter, but wholesome, cup that is now presented to thy lips!"

The young pastor's voice was tremulously sweet, rich, deep, and broken. The feeling that it so evidently manifested, rather than the direct purport of the words, caused it to vibrate within all hearts, and brought the listeners into one accord of sympathy. Even the poor baby, at Hester's bosom, was affected by the same influence; for it directed its hitherto vacant gaze towards Mr. Dimmesdale, and held up its little arms, with a half pleased, half plaintive murmur. So powerful seemed the minister's appeal, that the people could not believe but that Hester Prynne would speak out the guilty name; or else that the guilty one himself, in whatever high or lowly place he stood, would be drawn forth by an inward and inevitable necessity, and compelled to ascend the scaffold.

Hester shook her head.

"Woman, transgress not beyond the limits of Heaven's mercy!" cried the Reverend Mr. Wilson, more harshly than before. "That little babe hath been gifted with a voice, to second and confirm the counsel which thou hast heard. Speak out the name! That, and thy repentance, may avail to take the scarlet letter off thy breast."

"Never!" replied Hester Prynne, looking, not at Mr. Wilson, but into the deep and troubled eyes of the younger clergyman. "It is too deeply branded. Ye cannot take it off. And would that I might endure his agony, as well as mine!"

"Speak, woman!" said another voice, coldly and sternly, proceeding from the crowd about the scaffold. "Speak; and give your child a father!"

"I will not speak!" answered Hester, turning pale as death, but responding to this voice, which she too surely recognized. "And my child must seek a heavenly Father; she shall never know an earthly one!"

"She will not speak!" murmured Mr. Dimmesdale, who, leaning over the balcony, with his hand upon his heart, had awaited the result of his appeal. He now drew back, with a long respiration. "Wondrous strength and generosity of a woman's heart! She will not speak!"

Discerning the impracticable state of the poor culprit's

mind, the elder clergyman, who had carefully prepared himself for the occasion, addressed to the multitude a discourse on sin, in all its branches, but with continual reference to the ignominious letter. So forcibly did he dwell upon this symbol, for the hour or more during which his periods were rolling over the people's heads, that it assumed new terrors in their imagination, and seemed to derive its scarlet hue from the flames of the infernal pit. Hester Prynne, meanwhile, kept her place upon the pedestal of shame, with glazed eyes, and an air of weary indifference. She had borne, that morning, all that nature could endure; and as her temperament was not of the order that escapes from too intense suffering by a swoon, her spirit could only shelter itself beneath a stony crust of insensibility, while the faculties of animal life remained entire. In this state, the voice of the preacher thundered remorselessly, but unavailingly, upon her ears. The infant, during the latter portion of her ordeal, pierced the air with its wailings and screams; she strove to hush it, mechanically, but seemed scarcely to sympathize with its trouble. With the same hard demeanour, she was led back to prison, and vanished from the public gaze within its iron-clamped portal. It was whispered, by those who peered after her, that the scarlet letter threw a lurid gleam along the dark passage-way of the interior.

4. The Interview

Chillingworth head-to-head with Hester

AFTER her return to the prison, Hester Prynne was found to be in a state of nervous excitement that demanded constant watchfulness, lest she should perpetrate violence on herself, or do some half-frenzied mischief to the poor babe. As night approached, it proving impossible to quell her insubordination by rebuke or threats of punishment, Master Brackett, the jailer, thought fit to introduce a physician. He described him as a man of skill in all Christian modes of physical science, and likewise familiar with whatever the savage people could teach, in respect to medicinal herbs and roots that grew in the forest. To say the truth, there was much need of professional assistance, not merely for Hester herself, but still more urgently for the child; who, drawing its sustenance from the maternal bosom, seemed to have drank in with it all the turmoil, the anguish, and despair, which pervaded the mother's system. It now writhed in convulsions of pain, and was a forcible type, in its little frame, of the moral agony which Hester Prynne had borne throughout the day.

Closely following the jailer into the dismal apartment, appeared that individual, of singular aspect, whose presence in the crowd had been of such deep interest to the wearer of the scarlet letter. He was lodged in the prison, not as suspected of any offence, but as the most convenient and suitable mode of disposing of him, until the magistrates should have conferred with the Indian sagamores respecting his ransom. His name was announced as Roger Chillingworth. The jailer, after ushering him into the room, remained a moment, marvelling at the comparative quiet that followed his entrance; for Hester Prynne had immediately become as still as death, although the child continued to moan.

"Prithee, friend, leave me alone with my patient," said the practitioner. "Trust me, good jailer, you shall briefly have peace in your house; and, I promise you, Mistress Prynne shall hereafter be more amenable to just authority than you may have found her heretofore."

"Nay, if your worship can accomplish that," answered Master Brackett, "I shall own you for a man of skill indeed! Verily, the woman hath been like a possessed one; and there lacks little, that I should take in hand to drive Satan out of her with stripes."

The stranger had entered the room with the characteristic quietude of the profession to which he announced himself as belonging. Nor did his demeanour change, when the with-drawal of the prison-keeper left him face to face with the woman, whose absorbed notice of him, in the crowd, had intimated so close a relation between himself and her. His first care was given to the child; whose cries, indeed, as she lay writhing on the trundle-bed, made it of peremptory neces-sity to postpone all other business to the task of soothing her. He examined the infant carefully, and then proceeded to un-clasp a leathern case, which he took from beneath his dress. It appeared to contain certain medical preparations, one of which he mingled with a cup of water.

"My old studies in alchemy," observed he, "and my sojourn, for above a year past, among a people well versed in the kindly properties of simples, have made a better physician of me than many that claim the medical degree. Here, woman! The child is yours,—she is none of mine,—neither will she recognize my voice or aspect as a father's. Administer this draught, there-fore, with thine own hand."

Hester repelled the offered medicine, at the same time gazing with strongly marked apprehension into his face.

"Wouldst thou avenge thyself on the innocent babe?" whispered she.

"Foolish woman!" responded the physician, half coldly, half soothingly. "What should ail me to harm this misbegotten and miserable babe? The medicine is potent for good; and were it my child,—yea, mine own, as well as thine!—I could do no better for it."

As she still hesitated, being, in fact, in no reasonable state of mind, he took the infant in his arms, and himself adminis-tered the draught. It soon proved its efficacy, and redeemed the leech's pledge. The moans of the little patient subsided; its convulsive tossings gradually ceased; and in a few moments, as is the custom of young children after relief from pain, it sank into a profound and dewy slumber. The physician, as he had a fair right to be termed, next bestowed his attention on the mother. With calm and intent scrutiny, he felt her pulse, looked into her eyes,—a gaze that made her heart shrink and shudder, because so familiar, and yet so strange and cold, —and, finally, satisfied with his investigation, proceeded to mingle another draught.

"I know not Lethe nor Nepenthe," remarked he; "but I have learned many new secrets in the wilderness, and here is one of them,—a recipe that an Indian taught me, in requital of some lessons of my own, that were as old as Paracelsus. Drink it! It may be less soothing than a sinless conscience. That I cannot give thee. But it will calm the swell and heaving of thy passion, like oil thrown on the waves of a tempestuous sea."

He presented the cup to Hester, who received it with a slow, earnest look into his face; not precisely a look of fear, yet full of doubt and questioning, as to what his purposes might be. She looked also at her slumbering child.

"I have thought of death," said she,—"have wished for it,— would even have prayed for it, were it fit that such as I should pray for any thing. Yet, if death be in this cup, I bid thee think again, ere thou beholdest me quaff it. See! It is even now at my lips."

"Drink, then," replied he, still with the same cold composure. "Dost thou know me so little, Hester Prynne? Are my purposes wont to be so shallow? Even if I imagine a scheme of vengeance, what could I do better for my object than to let thee live,—than to give thee medicines against all harm and peril of life,—so that this burning shame may still blaze upon thy bosom?"—As he spoke, he laid his long forefinger on the scarlet letter, which forthwith seemed to scorch into Hester's breast, as if it had been red-hot. He noticed her involuntary gesture, and smiled.—"Live, therefore, and bear about thy doom with thee, in the eyes of men and women,—in the eyes of him whom thou didst call thy husband,—in the eyes of yonder child! And, that thou mayest live, take off this draught."

Without further expostulation or delay, Hester Prynne

drained the cup, and, at the motion of the man of skill, seated
herself on the bed where the child was sleeping; while he
drew the only chair which the room afforded, and took his
own seat beside her. She could not but tremble at these preparations; for she felt that—having now done all that humanity,
or principle, or, if so it were, a refined cruelty, impelled him
to do, for the relief of physical suffering—he was next to treat
with her as the man whom she had most deeply and irreparably
injured.

"Hester," said he, "I ask not wherefore, nor how, thou hast
fallen into the pit, or say rather, thou hast ascended to the
pedestal of infamy, on which I found thee. The reason is not
far to seek. It was my folly, and thy weakness. I,—a man of
thought,—the book-worm of great libraries,—a man already
in decay, having given my best years to feed the hungry dream
of knowledge,—what had I to do with youth and beauty like
thine own! Misshapen from my birth-hour, how could I de-
lude myself with the idea that intellectual gifts might veil
physical deformity in a young girl's fantasy! Men call me wise.
If sages were ever wise in their own behoof, I might have fore-
seen all this. I might have known that, as I came out of the
vast and dismal forest, and entered this settlement of Christian
men, the very first object to meet my eyes would be thyself,
Hester Prynne, standing up, a statue of ignominy, before the
people. Nay, from the moment when we came down the old
church-steps together, a married pair, I might have beheld
the bale-fire of that scarlet letter blazing at the end of our
path!"

"Thou knowest," said Hester,—for, depressed as she was,
she could not endure this last quiet stab at the token of her
shame,—"thou knowest that I was frank with thee. I felt no
love, nor feigned any."

"True!" replied he. "It was my folly! I have said it. But, up
to that epoch of my life, I had lived in vain. The world had
been so cheerless! My heart was a habitation large enough for
many guests, but lonely and chill, and without a household

fire. I longed to kindle one! It seemed not so wild a dream,—old as I was, and sombre as I was, and misshapen as I was,—that the simple bliss, which is scattered far and wide, for all mankind to gather up, might yet be mine. And so, Hester, I drew thee into my heart, into its innermost chamber, and sought to warm thee by the warmth which thy presence made there!"

"I have greatly wronged thee," murmured Hester.

"We have wronged each other," answered he. "Mine was the first wrong, when I betrayed thy budding youth into a false and unnatural relation with my decay. Therefore, as a man who has not thought and philosophized in vain, I seek no vengeance, plot no evil against thee. Between thee and me, the scale hangs fairly balanced. But, Hester, the man lives who has wronged us both! Who is he?"

"Ask me not!" replied Hester Prynne, looking firmly into his face. "That thou shalt never know!"

"Never, sayest thou?" rejoined he, with a smile of dark and self-relying intelligence. "Never know him! Believe me, Hester, there are few things,—whether in the outward world, or, to a certain depth, in the invisible sphere of thought,—few things hidden from the man, who devotes himself earnestly and un-reservedly to the solution of a mystery. Thou mayest cover up thy secret from the prying multitude. Thou mayest con-ceal it, too, from the ministers and magistrates, even as thou didst this day, when they sought to wrench the name out of thy heart, and give thee a partner on thy pedestal. But, as for me, I come to the inquest with other senses than they possess. I shall seek this man, as I have sought truth in books; as I have sought gold in alchemy. There is a sympathy that will make me conscious of him. I shall see him tremble. I shall feel my-self shudder, suddenly and unawares. Sooner or later, he must needs be mine!"

The eyes of the wrinkled scholar glowed so intensely upon her, that Hester Prynne clasped her hands over her heart, dreading lest he should read the secret there at once.

"Thou wilt not reveal his name? Not the less he is mine," resumed he, with a look of confidence, as if destiny were at one with him. "He bears no letter of infamy wrought into his garment, as thou dost; but I shall read it on his heart. Yet fear not for him! Think not that I shall interfere with Heaven's own method of retribution, or, to my own loss, betray him to the gripe of human law. Neither do thou imagine that I shall contrive aught against his life; no, nor against his fame, if, as I judge, he be a man of fair repute. Let him live! Let him hide himself in outward honor, if he may! Not the less he shall be mine!"

"Thy acts are like mercy," said Hester, bewildered and appalled. "But thy words interpret thee as a terror!"

"One thing, thou that wast my wife, I would enjoin upon thee," continued the scholar. "Thou hast kept the secret of thy paramour. Keep, likewise, mine! There are none in this land that know me. Breathe not, to any human soul, that thou didst ever call me husband! Here, on this wild outskirt of the earth, I shall pitch my tent; for, elsewhere a wanderer, and isolated from human interests, I find here a woman, a man, a child, amongst whom and myself there exist the closest ligaments. No matter whether of love or hate; no matter whether of right or wrong! Thou and thine, Hester Prynne, belong to me. My home is where thou art, and where he is. But betray me not!"

"Wherefore dost thou desire it?" inquired Hester, shrinking, she hardly knew why, from this secret bond. "Why not announce thyself openly, and cast me off at once?"

"It may be," he replied, "because I will not encounter the dishonor that besmirches the husband of a faithless woman. It may be for other reasons. Enough, it is my purpose to live and die unknown. Let, therefore, thy husband be to the world as one already dead, and of whom no tidings shall ever come. Recognize me not, by word, by sign, by look! Breathe not the secret, above all, to the man thou wottest of. Shouldst thou fail me in this, beware! His fame, his position, his life, will be in my hands. Beware!"

"I will keep thy secret, as I have his," said Hester.

"Swear it!" rejoined he.

And she took the oath.

"And now, Mistress Prynne," said old Roger Chillingworth, as he was hereafter to be named, "I leave thee alone; alone with thy infant, and the scarlet letter! How is it, Hester? Doth thy sentence bind thee to wear the token in thy sleep? Art thou not afraid of nightmares and hideous dreams?"

"Why does thou smile so at me?" inquired Hester, troubled at the expression of his eyes. "Art thou like the Black Man that haunts the forest round about us? Hast thou enticed me into a bond that will prove the ruin of my soul?"

"Not thy soul," he answered, with another smile. "No, not thine!"

5. Hester at Her Needle

HESTER PRYNNE's term of confinement was now at an end. Her prison-door was thrown open, and she came forth into the sunshine, which, falling on all alike, seemed, to her sick and morbid heart, as if meant for no other purpose than to reveal the scarlet letter on her breast. Perhaps there was a more real torture in her first unattended footsteps from the threshold of the prison, than even in the procession and spectacle that have been described, where she was made the common infamy, at which all mankind was summoned to point its finger. Then, she was supported by an unnatural tension of the nerves, and by all the combative energy of her character, which enabled her to convert the scene into a kind of lurid triumph. It was, moreover, a separate and insulated event, to occur but once in her lifetime, and to meet which, therefore, reckless of economy, she might call up the vital strength that would have sufficed for many quiet years. The very law that condemned her—a giant of stern features, but with vigor to support, as well as to annihilate, in his iron arm—had held her up, through the terrible ordeal of her ignominy. But now, with this un-attended walk from her prison-door, began the daily custom, and she must either sustain and carry it forward by the ordi-nary resources of her nature, or sink beneath it. She could no longer borrow from the future, to help her through the pres-ent grief. To-morrow would bring its own trial with it; so would the next day, and so would the next; each its own trial, and yet the very same that was now so unutterably grievous to be borne. The days of the far-off future would toil onward, still with the same burden for her to take up, and bear along with her, but never to fling down; for the accumulating days, and added years, would pile up their misery upon the heap of shame. Throughout them all, giving up her individuality, she would become the general symbol at which the preacher and moralist might point, and in which they might vivify and em-body their images of woman's frailty and sinful passion. Thus the young and pure would be taught to look at her, with the scarlet letter flaming on her breast,—at her, the child of hon-orable parents,—at her, the mother of a babe, that would here-after be a woman,—at her, who had once been innocent,—as the figure, the body, the reality of sin. And over her grave, the infamy that she must carry thither would be her only monument.

It may seem marvellous, that, with the world before her,—kept by no restrictive clause of her condemnation within the limits of the Puritan settlement, so remote and so obscure,—free to return to her birthplace, or to any other European land, and there hide her character and identity under a new exterior, as completely as if emerging into another state of being,—and having also the passes of the dark, inscrutable forest open to her, where the wildness of her nature might assimilate itself with a people whose customs and life were alien from the law that had condemned her,—it may seem marvellous, that this woman should still call that place her home, where, and where only, she must needs be the type of shame. But there is a fatality, a feeling so irresistible and inevitable that it has the force of doom, which almost invariably compels human beings to linger around and haunt, ghost-like, the spot where some great and marked event has given the color to their lifetime; and still the more irresistibly, the darker the tinge that saddens it. Her sin, her ignominy, were the roots which she had struck into the soil. It was as if a new birth, with stronger assimilations than the first, had converted the forest-land, still so uncongenial to every other pilgrim and wanderer, into Hester Prynne's wild and dreary, but life-long home. All other scenes of earth—even that village of rural England, where happy infancy and stainless maidenhood seemed yet to be in her mother's keeping, like garments put off long ago—were foreign to her, in comparison. The chain that bound her here was of iron links, and galling to her inmost soul, but never could be broken.

It might be, too,—doubtless it was so, although she hid the secret from herself, and grew pale whenever it struggled out of her heart, like a serpent from its hole,—it might be that another feeling kept her within the scene and pathway that had been so fatal. There dwelt, there trode the feet of one with whom she deemed herself connected in a union, that, unrecognized on earth, would bring them together before the bar of final judgment, and make that their marriage-altar, for a joint futurity of endless retribution. Over and over again, the tempter of souls had thrust this idea upon Hester's contemplation, and laughed at the passionate and desperate joy with which she seized, and then strove to cast it from her. She barely looked the idea in the face, and hastened to bar it in its dungeon. What she compelled herself to believe,—what, finally, she reasoned upon, as her motive for continuing a resident of New England,—was half a truth, and half a self-delusion. Here, she said to herself, had been the scene of her guilt, and here should be the scene of her earthly punishment; and so, perchance, the torture of her daily shame would at length purge her soul, and work out another purity than that which she had lost; more saint-like, because the result of martyrdom.

Hester Prynne, therefore, did not flee. On the outskirts of the town, within the verge of the peninsula, but not in close vicinity to any other habitation, there was a small thatched cottage. It had been built by an earlier settler, and abandoned, because the soil about it was too sterile for cultivation, while its comparative remoteness put it out of the sphere of that social activity which already marked the habits of the emigrants. It stood on the shore, looking across a basin of the sea at the forest-covered hills, towards the west. A clump of scrubby trees, such as alone grew on the peninsula, did not so much conceal the cottage from view, as seem to denote that here was some object which would fain have been, or at least ought to be, concealed. In this little, lonesome dwelling, with some slender means that she possessed, and by the license of the magistrates, who still kept an inquisitorial watch over her, Hester established herself, with her infant child. A mystic shadow of suspicion immediately attached itself to the spot. Children, too young to comprehend wherefore this woman should be shut out from the sphere of human charities, would creep nigh enough to behold her plying her needle at the cottage-window, or standing in the door-way, or laboring in her little garden, or coming forth along the pathway that led townward; and, discerning the scarlet letter on her breast, would scamper off, with a strange, contagious fear.

Lonely as was Hester's situation, and without a friend on earth who dared to show himself, she, however, incurred no risk of want. She possessed an art that sufficed, even in a land that afforded comparatively little scope for its exercise, to supply food for her thriving infant and herself. It was the art—then, as now, almost the only one within a woman's grasp —of needle-work. She bore on her breast, in the curiously embroidered letter, a specimen of her delicate and imaginative skill, of which the dames of a court might gladly have availed themselves, to add the richer and more spiritual adornment of human ingenuity to their fabrics of silk and gold. Here, indeed, in the sable simplicity that generally characterized the Puritanic modes of dress, there might be an infrequent call for the finer productions of her handiwork. Yet the taste of the age, demanding whatever was elaborate in compositions of this kind, did not fail to extend its influence over our stern progenitors, who had cast behind them so many fashions which it might seem harder to dispense with. Public ceremonies, such as ordinations, the installation of magistrates, and all that could give majesty to the forms in which a new government manifested itself to the people, were, as a matter of policy, marked by a stately and well-conducted ceremonial, and a sombre, but yet a studied magnificence. Deep ruffs, painfully wrought bands, and gorgeously embroidered gloves, were all deemed necessary to the official state of men assuming the reins of power; and were readily allowed to individuals dignified by rank or wealth, even while sumptuary laws forbade these and similar extravagances to the plebeian order. In the array of funerals, too,—whether for the apparel of the dead body, or to typify, by manifold emblematic devices of sable cloth and snowy lawn, the sorrow of the survivors,—there was a frequent and characteristic demand for such labor as Hester Prynne could supply. Baby-linen—for babies then wore robes of state—afforded still another possibility of toil and emolument.

By degrees, nor very slowly, her handiwork became what would now be termed the fashion. Whether from commiseration for a woman of so miserable a destiny; or from the morbid curiosity that gives a fictitious value even to common or worthless things; or by whatever other intangible circumstance was then, as now, sufficient to bestow, on some persons, what others might seek in vain; or because Hester really filled a gap which must otherwise have remained vacant; it is certain that she had ready and fairly requited employment for as many hours as she saw fit to occupy with her needle. Vanity, it may be, chose to mortify itself, by putting on, for ceremonials of pomp and state, the garments that had been wrought by her sinful hands. Her needle-work was seen on the ruff of the Governor; military men wore it on their scarfs, and the minister on his band; it decked the baby's little cap; it was shut up, to be mildewed and moulder away, in the coffins of the dead. But it is not recorded that, in a single instance, her skill was called in aid to embroider the white veil which was to cover the pure blushes of a bride. The exception indicated the ever relentless vigor with which society frowned upon her sin.

Hester sought not to acquire any thing beyond a subsistence, of the plainest and most ascetic description, for herself, and a simple abundance for her child. Her own dress was of the coarsest materials and the most sombre hue; with only that one ornament,—the scarlet letter,—which it was her doom to wear. The child's attire, on the other hand, was distinguished by a fanciful, or, we might rather say, a fantastic ingenuity, which served, indeed, to heighten the airy charm that early began to develop itself in the little girl, but which appeared to have also a deeper meaning. We may speak further of it hereafter. Except for that small expenditure in the decoration of her infant, Hester bestowed all her superfluous means in charity, on wretches less miserable than herself, and who not unfrequently insulted the hand that fed them. Much of the time, which she might readily have applied to the better efforts of her art, she employed in making coarse garments for the poor. It is probable that there was an idea of penance in this mode of occupation, and that she offered up a real sacrifice of enjoyment, in devoting so many hours to such rude handi-work. She had in her nature a rich, voluptuous, Oriental char-acteristic,—a taste for the gorgeously beautiful, which, save in the exquisite productions of her needle, found nothing else, in all the possibilities of her life, to exercise itself upon. Women derive a pleasure, incomprehensible to the other sex, from the delicate toil of the needle. To Hester Prynne it might have been a mode of expressing, and therefore soothing, the passion of her life. Like all other joys, she rejected it as sin. This morbid meddling of conscience with an immaterial matter betokened, it is to be feared, no genuine and stedfast penitence, but something doubtful, something that might be deeply wrong, beneath.

In this manner, Hester Prynne came to have a part to perform in the world. With her native energy of character, and rare capacity, it could not entirely cast her off, although it had set a mark upon her, more intolerable to a woman's heart than that which branded the brow of Cain. In all her intercourse with society, however, there was nothing that made her feel as if she belonged to it. Every gesture, every word, and even the silence of those with whom she came in contact, implied, and often expressed, that she was banished, and as much alone as if she inhabited another sphere, or communicated with the common nature by other organs and senses than the rest of human kind. She stood apart from mortal interests, yet close beside them, like a ghost that revisits the familiar fireside, and can no longer make itself seen or felt; no more smile with the household joy, nor mourn with the kindred sorrow; or, should it succeed in manifesting its forbidden sympathy, awakening only terror and horrible repugnance. These emotions, in fact, and its bitterest scorn besides, seemed to be the sole portion that she retained in the universal heart. It was not an age of delicacy; and her position, although she understood it well, and was in little danger of forgetting it, was often brought before her vivid self-perception, like a new anguish, by the rudest touch upon the tenderest spot. The poor, as we have already said, whom she sought out to be the objects of her bounty, often reviled the hand that was stretched forth to succor them. Dames of elevated rank, likewise, whose doors she entered in the way of her occupation, were accustomed to distil drops of bitterness into her heart; sometimes through that alchemy of quiet malice, by which women can concoct a subtile poison from ordinary trifles; and sometimes, also, by a coarser expression, that fell upon the sufferer's defenceless breast like a rough blow upon an ulcerated wound. Hester had schooled herself long and well; she never responded to these attacks, save by a flush of crimson that rose irrepressibly over her pale cheek, and again subsided into the depths of her bosom. She was patient,—a martyr, indeed,—but she forbore to pray for her enemies; lest, in spite of her forgiving aspirations, the words of the blessing should stubbornly twist themselves into a curse.

Continually, and in a thousand other ways, did she feel the innumerable throbs of anguish that had been so cunningly contrived for her by the undying, the ever-active sentence of the Puritan tribunal. Clergymen paused in the street to address words of exhortation, that brought a crowd, with its mingled grin and frown, around the poor, sinful woman. If she entered a church, trusting to share the Sabbath smile of the Universal Father, it was often her mishap to find herself the text of the discourse. She grew to have a dread of children; for they had imbibed from their parents a vague idea of something horrible in this dreary woman, gliding silently through the town, with never any companion but one only child. Therefore, first allowing her to pass, they pursued her at a distance with shrill cries, and the utterance of a word that had no distinct purport to their own minds, but was none the less terrible to her, as proceeding from lips that babbled it unconsciously. It seemed to argue so wide a diffusion of her shame, that all nature knew of it; it could have caused her no deeper pang, had the leaves of the trees whispered the dark story among themselves,—had the summer breeze murmured about it,—had the wintry blast shrieked it aloud! Another peculiar torture was felt in the gaze of a new eye. When strangers looked curiously at the scarlet letter,—and none ever failed to do so,—they branded it afresh into Hester's soul; so that, oftentimes, she could scarcely refrain, yet always did refrain, from covering the symbol with her hand. But then, again, an accustomed eye had likewise its own anguish to inflict. Its cool stare of familiarity was intolerable. From first to last, in short, Hester Prynne had always this dreadful agony in feeling a human eye upon the token; the spot never grew callous; it seemed, on the contrary, to grow more sensitive with daily torture.

But sometimes, once in many days, or perchance in many months, she felt an eye—a human eye—upon the ignominious brand, that seemed to give a momentary relief, as if half of her agony were shared. The next instant, back it all rushed again, with still a deeper throb of pain; for, in that brief interval, she had sinned anew. Had Hester sinned alone?

Her imagination was somewhat affected, and, had she been of a softer moral and intellectual fibre, would have been still more so, by the strange and solitary anguish of her life. Walking to and fro, with those lonely footsteps, in the little world with which she was outwardly connected, it now and then appeared to Hester,—if altogether fancy, it was nevertheless too potent to be resisted,—she felt or fancied, then, that the scarlet letter had endowed her with a new sense. She shuddered to believe, yet could not help believing, that it gave her a sympathetic knowledge of the hidden sin in other hearts. She was terror-stricken by the revelations that were thus made. What were they? Could they be other than the insidious whispers of the bad angel, who would fain have persuaded the struggling woman, as yet only half his victim, that the outward guise of purity was but a lie, and that, if truth were everywhere to be shown, a scarlet letter would blaze forth on many a bosom besides Hester Prynne's? Or, must she receive those intimations—so obscure, yet so distinct—as truth? In all her miserable experience, there was nothing else so awful and so loathsome as this sense. It perplexed, as well as shocked her, by the irreverent inopportuneness of the occasions that brought it into vivid action. Sometimes, the red infamy upon her breast would give a sympathetic throb, as she passed near a venerable minister or magistrate, the model of piety and justice, to whom that age of antique reverence looked up, as to a mortal man in fellowship with angels. "What evil thing is at hand?" would Hester say to herself. Lifting her reluctant eyes, there would be nothing human within the scope of view,

save the form of this earthly saint! Again, a mystic sisterhood would contumaciously assert itself, as she met the sanctified frown of some matron, who, according to the rumor of all
tongues, had kept cold snow within her bosom throughout
life. That unsunned snow in the matron's bosom, and the
burning shame on Hester Prynne's,—what had the two in
common? Or, once more, the electric thrill would give her
warning,—"Behold, Hester, here is a companion!"—and, looking up, she would detect the eyes of a young maiden glancing
at the scarlet letter, shyly and aside, and quickly averted, with
a faint, chill crimson in her cheeks; as if her purity were somewhat sullied by that momentary glance. O Fiend, whose talisman was that fatal symbol, wouldst thou leave nothing,
whether in youth or age, for this poor sinner to revere?—Such
loss of faith is ever one of the saddest results of sin. Be it accepted as a proof that all was not corrupt in this poor victim
of her own frailty, and man's hard law, that Hester Prynne yet
struggled to believe that no fellow-mortal was guilty like herself.

The vulgar, who, in those dreary old times, were always
contributing a grotesque horror to what interested their imagi-
nations, had a story about the scarlet letter which we might
readily work up into a terrific legend. They averred, that the
symbol was not mere scarlet cloth, tinged in an earthly dye-
pot, but was red-hot with infernal fire, and could be seen
glowing all alight, whenever Hester Prynne walked abroad in
the night-time. And we must needs say, it seared Hester's
bosom so deeply, that perhaps there was more truth in the
rumor than our modern incredulity may be inclined to admit.

6. Pearl

WE HAVE as yet hardly spoken of the infant; that little creature, whose innocent life had sprung, by the inscrutable decree
of Providence, a lovely and immortal flower, out of the rank
luxuriance of a guilty passion. How strange it seemed to the
sad woman, as she watched the growth, and the beauty that
became every day more brilliant, and the intelligence that
threw its quivering sunshine over the tiny features of this
child! Her Pearl!—For so had Hester called her; not as a name
expressive of her aspect, which had nothing of the calm, white,
unimpassioned lustre that would be indicated by the comparison. But she named the infant "Pearl," as being of great price,[1]
—purchased with all she had,—her mother's only treasure! How
strange, indeed! Man had marked this woman's sin by a scarlet
letter, which had such potent and disastrous efficacy that no
human sympathy could reach her, save it were sinful like herself. God, as a direct consequence of the sin which man thus
punished, had given her a lovely child, whose place was on
that same dishonored bosom, to connect her parent for ever
with the race and descent of mortals, and to be finally a blessed
soul in heaven! Yet these thoughts affected Hester Prynne less
with hope than apprehension. She knew that her deed had
been evil; she could have no faith, therefore, that its result
would be for good. Day after day, she looked fearfully into
the child's expanding nature; ever dreading to detect some
dark and wild peculiarity, that should correspond with the
guiltiness to which she owed her being.

Certainly, there was no physical defect. By its perfect shape,
its vigor, and its natural dexterity in the use of all its untried

---

[1] Matthew 13:45–46, "Again, the kingdom of heaven is like unto
a merchant man, seeking goodly pearls: Who, when he had found
one pearl of great price, went and sold all that he had, and bought
it."

limbs, the infant was worthy to have been brought forth in Eden; worthy to have been left there, to be the plaything of the angels, after the world's first parents were driven out. The child had a native grace which does not invariably coexist with faultless beauty; its attire, however simple, always impressed the beholder as if it were the very garb that precisely became it best. But little Pearl was not clad in rustic weeds. Her mother, with a morbid purpose that may be better understood hereafter, had bought the richest tissues that could be procured, and allowed her imaginative faculty its full play in the arrangement and decoration of the dresses which the child wore, before the public eye. So magnificent was the small figure, when thus arrayed, and such was the splendor of Pearl's own proper beauty, shining through the gorgeous robes which might have extinguished a paler loveliness, that there was an absolute circle of radiance around her, on the darksome cottage-floor. And yet a russet gown, torn and soiled with the child's rude play, made a picture of her just as perfect. Pearl's aspect was imbued with a spell of infinite variety; in this one child there were many children, comprehending the full scope between the wild-flower prettiness of a peasant-baby, and the pomp, in little, of an infant princess. Throughout all, however, there was a trait of passion, a certain depth of hue, which she never lost; and if, in any of her changes, she had grown fainter or paler, she would have ceased to be herself;—it would have been no longer Pearl!

This outward mutability indicated, and did not more than fairly express, the various properties of her inner life. Her nature appeared to possess depth, too, as well as variety; but— or else Hester's fears deceived her—it lacked reference and adaptation to the world into which she was born. The child could not be made amenable to rules. In giving her existence, a great law had been broken; and the result was a being, whose elements were perhaps beautiful and brilliant, but all in disorder; or with an order peculiar to themselves, amidst which the point of variety and arrangement was difficult or impossible to be discovered. Hester could only account for the child's character—and even then, most vaguely and imperfectly—by recalling what she herself had been, during that momentous period while Pearl was imbibing her soul from the spiritual world, and her bodily frame from its material of earth. The mother's impassioned state had been the medium through which were transmitted to the unborn infant the rays of its moral life; and, however white and clear originally, they had taken the deep stains of crimson and gold, the fiery lustre, the black shadow, and the untempered light, of the intervening substance. Above all, the warfare of Hester's spirit, at that epoch, was perpetuated in Pearl. She could recognize her wild, desperate, defiant mood, the flightiness of her temper, and even some of the very cloud-shapes of gloom and despondency that had brooded in her heart. They were now illuminated by the morning radiance of a young child's disposition, but, later in the day of earthly existence, might be prolific of the storm and whirlwind.

The discipline of the family, in those days, was of a far more rigid kind than now. The frown, the harsh rebuke, the frequent application of the rod, enjoined by Scriptural authority, were used, not merely in the way of punishment for actual offences, but as a wholesome regimen for the growth and promotion of all childish virtues. Hester Prynne, nevertheless, the lonely mother of this one child, ran little risk of erring on the side of undue severity. Mindful, however, of her own errors and misfortunes, she early sought to impose a tender, but strict, control over the infant immortality that was committed to her charge. But the task was beyond her skill. After testing both smiles and frowns, and proving that neither mode of treatment possessed any calculable influence, Hester was ultimately compelled to stand aside, and permit the child to be swayed by her own impulses. Physical compulsion or restraint was effectual, of course, while it lasted. As to any other kind of discipline, whether addressed to her mind or heart, little Pearl might or might not be within its reach, in accordance

with the caprice that ruled the moment. Her mother, while
Pearl was yet an infant, grew acquainted with a certain peculiar look, that warned her when it would be labor thrown
away to insist, persuade, or plead. It was a look so intelligent,
yet inexplicable, so perverse, sometimes so malicious, but generally accompanied by a wild flow of spirits, that Hester could
not help questioning, at such moments, whether Pearl was a
human child. She seemed rather an airy sprite, which, after
playing its fantastic sports for a little while upon the cottage-
floor, would flit away with a mocking smile. Whenever that
look appeared in her wild, bright, deeply black eyes, it invested her with a strange remoteness and intangibility; it was
as if she were hovering in the air and might vanish, like a glimmering light that comes we know not whence, and goes we
know not whither. Beholding it, Hester was constrained to
rush towards the child,—to pursue the little elf in the flight
which she invariably began,—to snatch her to her bosom, with
a close pressure and earnest kisses,—not so much from overflowing love, as to assure herself that Pearl was flesh and blood,
and not utterly delusive. But Pearl's laugh, when she was
caught, though full of merriment and music, made her mother
more doubtful than before.

Heart-smitten at this bewildering and baffling spell, that so
often came between herself and her sole treasure, whom she
had bought so dear, and who was all her world, Hester sometimes burst into passionate tears. Then, perhaps,—for there
was no foreseeing how it might affect her,—Pearl would frown,
and clench her little fist, and harden her small features into
a stern, unsympathizing look of discontent. Not seldom, she
would laugh anew, and louder than before, like a thing incapable and unintelligent of human sorrow. Or—but this more
rarely happened—she would be convulsed with a rage of grief,
and sob out her love for her mother, in broken words, and
seem intent on proving that she had a heart, by breaking it.
Yet Hester was hardly safe in confiding herself to that gusty
tenderness; it passed, as suddenly as it came. Brooding over

all these matters, the mother felt like one who has evoked a spirit, but, by some irregularity in the process of conjuration, has failed to win the master-word that should control this new and incomprehensible intelligence. Her only real comfort was when the child lay in the placidity of sleep. Then she was sure of her, and tasted hours of quiet, sad, delicious happiness; until—perhaps with that perverse expression glimmering from beneath her opening lids—little Pearl awoke!

How soon—with what strange rapidity, indeed!—did Pearl arrive at an age that was capable of social intercourse, beyond the mother's ever-ready smile and nonsense-words! And then what a happiness would it have been, could Hester Prynne have heard her clear, bird-like voice mingling with the uproar of other childish voices, and have distinguished and unravelled her own darling's tones, amid all the entangled outcry of a group of sportive children! But this could never be. Pearl was a born outcast of the infantile world. An imp of evil, emblem and product of sin, she had no right among christened infants. Nothing was more remarkable than the instinct, as it seemed, with which the child comprehended her loneliness; the destiny that had drawn an inviolable circle round about her; the whole peculiarity, in short, of her position in respect to other children. Never, since her release from prison, had Hester met the public gaze without her. In all her walks about the town, Pearl, too, was there; first as the babe in arms, and afterwards as the little girl, small companion of her mother, holding a forefinger with her whole grasp, and tripping along at the rate of three or four footsteps to one of Hester's. She saw the children of the settlement, on the grassy margin of the street, or at the domestic thresholds, disporting themselves in such grim fashion as the Puritanic nurture would permit; playing at going to church, perchance; or at scourging Quakers; or taking scalps in a sham-fight with the Indians; or scaring one another with freaks of imitative witchcraft. Pearl saw, and gazed intently, but never sought to make acquaintance. If spoken to, she would not speak again. If the children gathered about her, as they sometimes did, Pearl would grow positively terrible in her puny wrath, snatching up stones to fling at them, with shrill, incoherent exclamations that made her mother tremble, because they had so much the sound of a witch's anathemas in some unknown tongue.

The truth was, that the little Puritans, being of the most intolerant brood that ever lived, had got a vague idea of something outlandish, unearthly, or at variance with ordinary fashions, in the mother and child; and therefore scorned them in their hearts, and not unfequently reviled them with their tongues. Pearl felt the sentiment, and requited it with the bitterest hatred that can be supposed to rankle in a childish bosom. These outbreaks of a fierce temper had a kind of value, and even comfort, for her mother; because there was at least an intelligible earnestness in the mood, instead of the fitful caprice that so often thwarted her in the child's manifestations. It appalled her, nevertheless, to discern here, again, a shadowy reflection of the evil that had existed in herself. All this enmity and passion had Pearl inherited, by inalienable right, out of Hester's heart. Mother and daughter stood together in the same circle of seclusion from human society; and in the nature of the child seemed to be perpetuated those unquiet elements that had distracted Hester Prynne before Pearl's birth, but had since begun to be soothed away by the softening influences of maternity.

At home, within and around her mother's cottage, Pearl wanted not a wide and various circle of acquaintance. The spell of life went forth from her ever creative spirit, and communicated itself to a thousand objects, as a torch kindles a flame wherever it may be applied. The unlikeliest materials, a stick, a bunch of rags, a flower, were the puppets of Pearl's witchcraft, and, without undergoing any outward change, became spiritually adapted to whatever drama occupied the stage of her inner world. Her one baby-voice served a multitude of imaginary personages, old and young, to talk withal.

The pine-trees, aged, black, and solemn, and flinging groans and other melancholy utterances on the breeze, needed little transformation to figure as Puritan elders; the ugliest weeds of the garden were their children, whom Pearl smote down and uprooted, most unmercifully. It was wonderful, the vast variety of forms into which she threw her intellect, with no continuity, indeed, but darting up and dancing, always in a state of preternatural activity,—soon sinking down, as if exhausted by so rapid and feverish a tide of life,—and succeeded by other shapes of a similar wild energy. It was like nothing so much as the phantasmagoric play of the northern lights. In the mere exercise of the fancy, however, and the sportiveness of a growing mind, there might be little more than was observable in other children of bright faculties; except as Pearl, in the dearth of human playmates, was thrown more upon the visionary throng which she created. The singularity lay in the hostile feelings with which the child regarded all these offspring of her own heart and mind. She never created a friend, but seemed always to be sowing broadcast the dragon's teeth,[2] whence sprung a harvest of armed enemies, against whom she rushed to battle. It was inexpressibly sad—then what depth of sorrow to a mother, who felt in her own heart the cause!— to observe, in one so young, this constant recognition of an adverse world, and so fierce a training of the energies that were to make good her cause, in the contest that must ensue.

Gazing at Pearl, Hester Prynne often dropped her work upon her knees, and cried out, with an agony which she would fain have hidden, but which made utterance for itself, betwixt speech and a groan,—"O Father in Heaven,—if Thou art still my Father,—what is this being which I have brought into the world!" And Pearl, overhearing the ejaculation, or aware, through some more subtle channel, of those throbs of an-

---

[2] In the myth, Cadmus sowed dragon's teeth, which produced a harvest of fierce armed warriors. Hawthorne retold the story for children as "The Dragon's Teeth" in *Tanglewood Tales.*

guish, would turn her vivid and beautiful little face upon her mother, smile with sprite-like intelligence, and resume her play.

One peculiarity of the child's deportment remains yet to be told. The very first thing which she had noticed, in her life, was—what?—not the mother's smile, responding to it, as other babies do, by that faint, embryo smile of the little mouth, remembered so doubtfully afterwards, and with such fond discussion whether it were indeed a smile. By no means! But that first object of which Pearl seemed to become aware was —shall we say it?—the scarlet letter on Hester's bosom! One day, as her mother stooped over the cradle, the infant's eyes had been caught by the glimmering of the gold embroidery about the letter; and, putting up her little hand, she grasped at it, smiling, not doubtfully, but with a decided gleam that gave her face the look of a much older child. Then, gasping for breath, did Hester Prynne clutch the fatal token, instinctively endeavouring to tear it away; so infinite was the torture inflicted by the intelligent touch of Pearl's baby-hand. Again, as if her mother's agonized gesture were meant only to make sport for her, did little Pearl look into her eyes, and smile! From that epoch, except when the child was asleep, Hester had never felt a moment's safety; not a moment's calm enjoyment of her. Weeks, it is true, would sometimes elapse, during which Pearl's gaze might never once be fixed upon the scarlet letter; but then, again, it would come at unawares, like the stroke of sudden death, and always with that peculiar smile, and odd expression of the eyes.

Once, this freakish, elfish cast came into the child's eyes, while Hester was looking at her own image in them, as mothers are fond of doing; and, suddenly,—for women in solitude, and with troubled hearts, are pestered with unaccountable delusions,—she fancied that she beheld, not her own miniature portrait, but another face in the small black mirror of Pearl's eye. It was a face, fiend-like, full of smiling malice, yet bearing the semblance of features that she had known full well, though seldom with a smile, and never with malice, in them. It was as if an evil spirit possessed the child, and had just then peeped forth in mockery. Many a time afterwards had Hester been tortured, though less vividly, by the same illusion.

In the afternoon of a certain summer's day, after Pearl grew big enough to run about, she amused herself with gathering handfuls of wild-flowers, and flinging them, one by one, at her mother's bosom; dancing up and down, like a little elf, whenever she hit the scarlet letter. Hester's first motion had been to cover her bosom with her clasped hands. But, whether from pride or resignation, or a feeling that her penance might best be wrought out by this unutterable pain, she resisted the impulse, and sat erect, pale as death, looking sadly into little Pearl's wild eyes. Still came the battery of flowers, almost invariably hitting the mark, and covering the mother's breast with hurts for which she could find no balm in this world, nor knew how to seek it in another. At last, her shot being all expended, the child stood still and gazed at Hester, with that little, laughing image of a fiend peeping out —or, whether it peeped or no, her mother so imagined it— from the unsearchable abyss of her black eyes.

"Child, what art thou?" cried the mother.

"O, I am your little Pearl!" answered the child.

But, while she said it, Pearl laughed and began to dance up and down, with the humorsome gesticulation of a little imp, whose next freak might be to fly up the chimney.

"Art thou my child, in very truth?" asked Hester.

Nor did she put the question altogether idly, but, for the moment, with a portion of genuine earnestness; for, such was Pearl's wonderful intelligence, that her mother half doubted whether she were not acquainted with the secret spell of her existence, and might not now reveal herself.

"Yes; I am little Pearl!" repeated the child, continuing her antics.

"Thou art not my child! Thou art no Pearl of mine!" said the mother, half playfully; for it was often the case that a sportive impulse came over her, in the midst of her deepest suffering. "Tell me, then, what thou art, and who sent thee hither?"

"Tell me, mother!" said the child, seriously, coming up to Hester, and pressing herself close to her knees. "Do thou tell me!"

"Thy Heavenly Father sent thee!" answered Hester Prynne.

But she said it with a hesitation that did not escape the acuteness of the child. Whether moved only by her ordinary freakishness, or because an evil spirit prompted her, she put up her small forefinger, and touched the scarlet letter.

"He did not send me!" cried she, positively. "I have no Heavenly Father!"

"Hush, Pearl, hush! Thou must not talk so!" answered the mother, suppressing a groan. "He sent us all into this world. He sent even me, thy mother. Then, much more, thee! Or, if not, thou strange and elfish child, whence didst thou come?"

"Tell me! Tell me!" repeated Pearl, no longer seriously, but laughing, and capering about the floor. "It is thou that must tell me!"

But Hester could not resolve the query, being herself in a dismal labyrinth of doubt. She remembered—betwixt a smile and a shudder—the talk of the neighbouring townspeople; who, seeking vainly elsewhere for the child's paternity, and observing some of her odd attributes, had given out that poor little Pearl was a demon offspring; such as, ever since old Catholic times, had occasionally been seen on earth, through the agency of their mothers' sin, and to promote some foul and wicked purpose. Luther, according to the scandal of his monkish enemies, was a brat of that hellish breed; nor was Pearl the only child to whom this inauspicious origin was assigned, among the New England Puritans.

7. The Governor's Hall

HESTER PRYNNE went, one day, to the mansion of Governor Bellingham, with a pair of gloves, which she had fringed and embroidered to his order, and which were to be worn on some great occasion of state; for, though the chances of a popular election had caused this former ruler to descend a step or two from the highest rank, he still held an honorable and influential place among the colonial magistracy.

Another and far more important reason than the delivery of a pair of embroidered gloves impelled Hester, at this time, to seek an interview with a personage of so much power and activity in the affairs of the settlement. It had reached her ears, that there was a design on the part of some of the leading inhabitants, cherishing the more rigid order of principles in religion and government, to deprive her of her child. On the supposition that Pearl, as already hinted, was of demon origin, these good people not unreasonably argued that a Christian interest in the mother's soul required them to remove such a stumbling-block from her path. If the child, on the other hand, were really capable of moral and religious growth, and possessed the elements of ultimate salvation, then, surely, it would enjoy all the fairer prospect of these advantages by being transferred to wiser and better guardianship than Hester Prynne's. Among those who promoted the design, Governor Bellingham was said to be one of the most busy. It may appear singular, and, indeed, not a little ludicrous, that an affair of this kind, which, in later days, would have been referred to no higher jurisdiction than that of the selectmen of the town, should then have been a question publicly discussed, and on which statesmen of eminence took sides. At that epoch of pristine simplicity, however, matters of even slighter public interest, and of far less intrinsic weight than the welfare of Hester and her child, were strangely mixed up with the deliberations of legislators and acts of state. The period was hardly, if at all, earlier than that of our story, when a dispute concerning the right of property in a pig, not only caused a fierce and bitter contest in the legislative body of the colony, but resulted in an important modification of the framework itself of the legislature.[1]

Full of concern, therefore,—but so conscious of her own right, that it seemed scarcely an unequal match between the public, on the one side, and a lonely woman, backed by the sympathies of nature, on the other,—Hester Prynne set forth from her solitary cottage. Little Pearl, of course, was her companion. She was now of an age to run lightly along by her mother's side, and, constantly in motion from morn till sunset, could have accomplished a much longer journey than that before her. Often, nevertheless, more from caprice than necessity, she demanded to be taken up in arms, but was soon as imperious to be set down again, and frisked onward before Hester on the grassy pathway, with many a harmless trip and tumble. We have spoken of Pearl's rich and luxuriant beauty; a beauty that shone with deep and vivid tints; a bright complexion, eyes possessing intensity both of depth and glow, and hair already of a deep, glossy brown, and which, in after years, would be nearly akin to black. There was fire in her and throughout her; she seemed the unpremeditated offshoot of a passionate moment. Her mother, in contriving the child's garb, had allowed the gorgeous tendencies of her imagination their full play; arraying her in a crimson velvet tunic, of a peculiar cut, abundantly embroidered with fantasies and flourishes of gold thread. So much strength of coloring, which must have

---

[1] Until 1644, the deputies, elected from each town, and the magistrates, elected at large, sat together in one governing body, the general court. They split into two houses as the result of a dispute over ownership of a white sow, the majority of magistrates favoring one party and the majority of deputies another. The underlying issue that was brought to a head in this trivial case was one that had been troubling the government of the colony for a decade.

given a wan and pallid aspect to cheeks of a fainter bloom, was admirably adapted to Pearl's beauty, and made her the very brightest little jet of flame that ever danced upon the earth.

But it was a remarkable attribute of this garb, and, indeed, of the child's whole appearance, that it irresistibly and inevitably reminded the beholder of the token which Hester Prynne was doomed to wear upon her bosom. It was the scarlet letter in another form; the scarlet letter endowed with life! The mother herself—as if the red ignominy were so deeply scorched into her brain, that all her conceptions assumed its form—had carefully wrought out the similitude; lavishing many hours of morbid ingenuity, to create an analogy between the object of her affection, and the emblem of her guilt and torture. But, in truth, Pearl was the one, as well as the other; and only in consequence of that identity had Hester contrived so perfectly to represent the scarlet letter in her appearance.

As the two wayfarers came within the precincts of the town, the children of the Puritans looked up from their play,—or what passed for play with those sombre little urchins,—and spake gravely one to another:—

"Behold, verily, there is the woman of the scarlet letter; and, of a truth, moreover, there is the likeness of the scarlet letter running along by her side! Come, therefore, and let us fling mud at them!"

But Pearl, who was a dauntless child, after frowning, stamping her foot, and shaking her little hand with a variety of threatening gestures, suddenly made a rush at the knot of her enemies, and put them all to flight. She resembled, in her fierce pursuit of them, an infant pestilence,—the scarlet fever, or some such half-fledged angel of judgment,—whose mission was to punish the sins of the rising generation. She screamed and shouted, too, with a terrific volume of sound, which doubtless caused the hearts of the fugitives to quake within them. The victory accomplished, Pearl returned quietly to her mother, and looked up smiling into her face.

Without further adventure, they reached the dwelling of Governor Bellingham. This was a large wooden house, built in a fashion of which there are specimens still extant in the streets of our elder towns; now moss-grown, crumbling to decay, and melancholy at heart with the many sorrowful or joyful occurrences, remembered or forgotten, that have happened, and passed away, within their dusky chambers. Then, however, there was the freshness of the passing year on its exterior, and the cheerfulness, gleaming forth from the sunny windows, of a human habitation into which death had never entered. It had indeed a very cheery aspect; the walls being overspread with a kind of stucco, in which fragments of broken glass were plentifully intermixed; so that, when the sunshine fell aslantwise over the front of the edifice, it glittered and sparkled as if diamonds had been flung against it by the double handful. The brilliancy might have befitted Aladdin's palace, rather than the mansion of a grave old Puritan ruler. It was further decorated with strange and seemingly cabalistic figures and diagrams, suitable to the quaint taste of the age, which had been drawn in the stucco when newly laid on, and had now grown hard and durable, for the admiration of after times.

Pearl, looking at this bright wonder of a house, began to caper and dance, and imperatively required that the whole breadth of sunshine should be stripped off its front, and given her to play with.

"No, my little Pearl!" said her mother. "Thou must gather thine own sunshine. I have none to give thee!"

They approached the door; which was of an arched form, and flanked on each side by a narrow tower or projection of the edifice, in both of which were lattice-windows, with wooden shutters to close over them at need. Lifting the iron hammer that hung at the portal, Hester Prynne gave a summons, which was answered by one of the Governor's bond-servants; a free-born Englishman, but now a seven years' slave. During that term he was to be the property of his master, and as much a commodity of bargain and sale as an ox, or a joint-stool. The serf wore the blue coat, which was the customary garb of serving-men at that period, and long before, in the old hereditary halls of England.

"Is the worshipful Governor Bellingham within?" inquired Hester.

"Yea, forsooth," replied the bond-servant, staring with wide-open eyes at the scarlet letter, which, being a new-comer in the country, he had never before seen. "Yea, his honorable worship is within. But he hath a godly minister or two with him, and likewise a leech. Ye may not see his worship now."

"Nevertheless, I will enter," answered Hester Prynne; and the bond-servant, perhaps judging from the decision of her air and the glittering symbol in her bosom, that she was a great lady in the land, offered no opposition.

So the mother and little Pearl were admitted into the hall of entrance. With many variations, suggested by the nature of his building-materials, diversity of climate, and a different mode of social life, Governor Bellingham had planned his new habitation after the residences of gentlemen of fair estate in his native land. Here, then, was a wide and reasonably lofty hall, extending through the whole depth of the house, and forming a medium of general communication, more or less directly, with all the other apartments. At one extremity, this spacious room was lighted by the windows of the two towers, which formed a small recess on either side of the portal. At the other end, though partly muffled by a curtain, it was more powerfully illuminated by one of those embowed hall-windows which we read of in old books, and which was provided with a deep and cushioned seat. Here, on the cushion, lay a folio tome, probably of the Chronicles of England, or other such substantial literature; even as, in our own days, we scatter gilded volumes on the centre-table, to be turned over by the casual guest. The furniture of the hall consisted of some ponderous chairs, the backs of which were elaborately carved with wreaths of oaken flowers; and likewise a table in the same taste; the whole being of the Elizabethan age, or perhaps earlier, and heirlooms, transferred hither from the Governor's paternal home. On the table—in token that the sentiment of old English hospitality had not been left behind—stood a large pewter tankard, at the bottom of which, had Hester or Pearl peeped into it, they might have seen the frothy remnant of a recent draught of ale.

On the wall hung a row of portraits, representing the fore-fathers of the Bellingham lineage, some with armour on their breasts, and others with stately ruffs and robes of peace. All were characterized by the sternness and severity which old portraits so invariably put on; as if they were the ghosts, rather than the pictures, of departed worthies, and were gazing with harsh and intolerant criticism at the pursuits and enjoyments of living men.

At about the centre of the oaken panels, that lined the hall, was suspended a suit of mail, not, like the pictures, an ancestral relic, but of the most modern date; for it had been manufactured by a skilful armorer in London, the same year in which Governor Bellingham came over to New England. There was a steel head-piece, a cuirass, a gorget, and greaves, with a pair of gauntlets and a sword hanging beneath; all, and especially the helmet and breastplate, so highly burnished as to glow with white radiance, and scatter an illumination everywhere about upon the floor. This bright panoply was not meant for mere idle show, but had been worn by the Governor on many a solemn muster and training field, and had glittered, moreover, at the head of a regiment in the Pequod war.[2] For, though bred a lawyer, and accustomed to speak of Bacon, Coke, Noye, and Finch,[3] as his professional associates, the

[2] The Pequod War (1633–1637) began with the killing of several English traders by the Pequods, a Connecticut River tribe, and ended with the slaughter of nearly eight hundred Indian men, women, and children at the hands of troops from Massachusetts Bay, Plymouth, and Connecticut.

[3] Sir Francis Bacon (1561–1626), statesman, philosopher, and essayist, was admitted to the bar in 1582, was active in the great

exigencies of this new country had transformed Governor Bellingham into a soldier, as well as a statesman and ruler.

Little Pearl—who was as greatly pleased with the gleaming armour as she had been with the glittering frontispiece of the house—spent some time looking into the polished mirror of the breastplate.

"Mother," cried she, "I see you here. Look! Look!"

Hester looked, by way of humoring the child; and she saw that, owing to the peculiar effect of this convex mirror, the scarlet letter was represented in exaggerated and gigantic proportions, so as to be greatly the most prominent feature of her appearance. In truth, she seemed absolutely hidden behind it. Pearl pointed upward, also, at a similar picture in the headpiece; smiling at her mother, with the elfish intelligence that was so familiar an expression on her small physiognomy. That look of naughty merriment was likewise reflected in the mirror, with so much breadth and intensity of effect, that it made Hester Prynne feel as if it could not be the image of her own child, but of an imp who was seeking to mould itself into Pearl's shape.

---

legal events of his day, and, in 1613, was promoted to the attorney generalship, in which capacity he had Sir Edward Coke, his persistent enemy, removed from the King's Bench.

Sir Edward Coke (1552–1634), English jurist, was appointed Chief Justice of the King's Bench in 1613. His *Institutes of the Laws of England* (1628–1644) is his best-known legal work; the first part, containing a translation from Norman French and a commentary on Sir Thomas Littleton's work, is known as *Coke on Littleton.*

Sir John Finch (1584–1660) became speaker of the House of Commons in 1628 and Chief Justice of the Court of Common Pleas in 1634. He was a rigorous supporter of Charles I against the Puritans.

William Noye (1577–1634) was attorney general to Charles I and a highly inventive legal counselor. He was responsible for some of the more tyrannical measures of that reign: e.g., the revival of the forest laws, the soap monopoly, and the writ of ship money.

"Come along, Pearl!" said she, drawing her away. "Come and look into this fair garden. It may be, we shall see flowers there; more beautiful ones than we find in the woods."

Pearl, accordingly, ran to the bow-window, at the farther end of the hall, and looked along the vista of a garden-walk, carpeted with closely shaven grass, and bordered with some rude and immature attempt at shrubbery. But the proprietor appeared already to have relinquished, as hopeless, the effort to perpetuate on this side of the Atlantic, in a hard soil and amid the close struggle for subsistence, the native English taste for ornamental gardening. Cabbages grew in plain sight; and a pumpkin vine, rooted at some distance, had run across the intervening space, and deposited one of its gigantic products directly beneath the hall-window; as if to warn the Governor that this great lump of vegetable gold was as rich an ornament as New England earth would offer him. There were a few rose-bushes, however, and a number of apple-trees, probably the descendants of those planted by the Reverend Mr. Blackstone,[4] the first settler of the peninsula; that half mythological personage who rides through our early annals, seated on the back of a bull.

Pearl, seeing the rose-bushes, began to cry for a red rose, and would not be pacified.

"Hush, child, hush!" said her mother earnestly. "Do not cry, dear little Pearl! I hear voices in the garden. The Governor is coming, and gentlemen along with him!"

In fact, adown the vista of the garden-avenue, a number of persons were seen approaching towards the house. Pearl, in utter scorn of her mother's attempt to quiet her, gave an

[4] William Blackstone (1595–1675), a minister in the Church of England, left Britain in 1623 because of a difference with the authorities and became the first white settler on the site of Boston, seven years in advance of the Puritans. When the latter did arrive, Blackstone, disliking them and preferring the company of Indians, moved to Rhode Island, where he devoted himself to agriculture and to his library.

eldritch scream, and then became silent; not from any notion
of obedience, but because the quick and mobile curiosity of
her disposition was excited by the appearance of these new
personages.

8. The Elf-Child
and the Minister

GOVERNOR BELLINGHAM, in a loose gown and easy cap,—such
as elderly gentlemen loved to indue themselves with, in their
domestic privacy,—walked foremost, and appeared to be showing off his estate, and expatiating on his projected improve-
ments. The wide circumference of an elaborate ruff, beneath
his gray beard, in the antiquated fashion of King James's reign,[1]
caused his head to look not a little like that of John the Baptist
in a charger. The impression made by his aspect, so rigid and
severe, and frostbitten with more than autumnal age, was
hardly in keeping with the appliances of worldly enjoyment
wherewith he had evidently done his utmost to surround himself. But it is an error to suppose that our grave forefathers—
though accustomed to speak and think of human existence as a
state merely of trial and warfare, and though unfeignedly prepared to sacrifice goods and life at the behest of duty—made it
a matter of conscience to reject such means of comfort, or
even luxury, as lay fairly within their grasp. This creed was
never taught, for instance, by the venerable pastor, John Wilson, whose beard, white as a snow-drift, was seen over Governor Bellingham's shoulder; while its wearer suggested that

---

[1] James (1566–1625) reigned as James VI of Scotland from 1567
and as James I of England from 1603 until his death.

pears and peaches might yet be naturalized in the New England climate, and that purple grapes might possibly be compelled to flourish, against the sunny garden-wall. The old clergyman, nurtured at the rich bosom of the English Church, had a long established and legitimate taste for all good and comfortable things; and however stern he might show himself in the pulpit, or in his public reproof of such transgressions as that of Hester Prynne, still, the genial benevolence of his private life had won him warmer affection than was accorded to any of his professional contemporaries.

Behind the Governor and Mr. Wilson came two other guests; one, the Reverend Arthur Dimmesdale, whom the reader may remember, as having taken a brief and reluctant part in the scene of Hester Prynne's disgrace; and, in close companionship with him, old Roger Chillingworth, a person of great skill in physic, who, for two or three years past, had been settled in the town. It was understood that this learned man was the physician as well as friend of the young minister, whose health had severely suffered, of late, by his too unreserved self-sacrifice to the labors and duties of the pastoral relation.

The Governor, in advance of his visitors, ascended one or two steps, and, throwing open the leaves of the great hall window, found himself close to little Pearl. The shadow of the curtain fell on Hester Prynne, and partially concealed her.

"What have we here?" said Governor Bellingham, looking with surprise at the scarlet little figure before him. "I profess, I have never seen the like, since my days of vanity, in old King James's time, when I was wont to esteem it a high favor to be admitted to a court mask! There used to be a swarm of these small apparitions, in holiday-time; and we called them children of the Lord of Misrule.[2] But how gat such a guest into my hall?"

"Ay, indeed!" cried good old Mr. Wilson. "What little bird

[2] The one chosen to preside over the Christmas games and revels at a great man's house.

of scarlet plumage may this be? Methinks I have seen just such figures, when the sun has been shining through a richly painted window, and tracing out the golden and crimson images across the floor. But that was in the old land. Prithee, young one, who art thou, and what has ailed thy mother to bedizen thee in this strange fashion? Art thou a Christian child,—ha? Dost know thy catechism? Or art thou one of those naughty elfs or fairies, whom we thought to have left behind us, with other relics of Papistry, in merry old England?"

"I am mother's child," answered the scarlet vision, "and my name is Pearl!"

"Pearl?—Ruby, rather!—or Coral!—or Red Rose, at the very least, judging from thy hue!" responded the old minister, putting forth his hand in a vain attempt to pat little Pearl on the cheek. "But where is this mother of thine? Ah! I see," he added; and, turning to Governor Bellingham, whispered,— "This is the selfsame child of whom we have held speech together; and behold here the unhappy woman, Hester Prynne, her mother!"

"Sayest thou so?" cried the Governor. "Nay, we might have judged that such a child's mother must needs be a scarlet woman, and a worthy type of her of Babylon![3] But she comes at a good time; and we will look into this matter forthwith."

Governor Bellingham stepped through the window into the hall, followed by his three guests.

"Hester Prynne," said he, fixing his naturally stern regard on the wearer of the scarlet letter, "there hath been much question concerning thee, of late. The point hath been weight-

---

[3] Revelation 17:3–5, "So he carried me away in the spirit into the wilderness: and I saw a woman sit upon a scarlet coloured beast, full of names of blasphemy, having seven heads and ten horns. And the woman was arrayed in purple and scarlet colour, and decked with gold and precious stones and pearls, having a golden cup in her hand full of abominations and filthiness of her fornication: And upon her forehead was a name written, MYSTERY, BABYLON THE GREAT, THE MOTHER OF HARLOTS AND ABOMINATIONS OF THE EARTH."

ily discussed, whether we, that are of authority and influence, do well discharge our consciences by trusting an immortal soul, such as there is in yonder child, to the guidance of one who hath stumbled and fallen, amid the pitfalls of this world. Speak thou, the child's own mother! Were it not, thinkest thou, for thy little one's temporal and eternal welfare, that she be taken out of thy charge, and clad soberly, and disciplined strictly, and instructed in the truths of heaven and earth? What canst thou do for the child, in this kind?"

"I can teach my little Pearl what I have learned from this!" answered Hester Prynne, laying her finger on the red token.

"Woman, it is thy badge of shame!" replied the stern magistrate. "It is because of the stain which that letter indicates, that we would transfer thy child to other hands."

"Nevertheless," said the mother calmly, though growing more pale, "this badge hath taught me,—it daily teaches me, —it is teaching me at this moment,—lessons whereof my child may be the wiser and better, albeit they can profit nothing to myself."

"We will judge warily," said Bellingham, "and look well what we are about to do. Good Master Wilson, I pray you, examine this Pearl,—since that is her name,—and see whether she hath had such Christian nurture as befits a child of her age."

The old minister seated himself in an arm-chair, and made an effort to draw Pearl betwixt his knees. But the child, unaccustomed to the touch or familiarity of any but her mother, escaped through the open window and stood on the upper step, looking like a wild, tropical bird, of rich plumage, ready to take flight into the upper air. Mr. Wilson, not a little astonished at this outbreak,—for he was a grandfatherly sort of personage, and usually a vast favorite with children,—essayed, however, to proceed with the examination.

"Pearl," said he, with great solemnity, "thou must take heed to instruction, that so, in due season, thou mayest wear in thy bosom the pearl of great price. Canst thou tell me, my child, who made thee?"

Now Pearl knew well enough who made her; for Hester Prynne, the daughter of a pious home, very soon after her talk with the child about her Heavenly Father, had begun to inform her of those truths which the human spirit, at whatever stage of immaturity, imbibes with such eager interest. Pearl, therefore, so large were the attainments of her three years' lifetime, could have borne a fair examination in the New England Primer,[4] or the first column of the Westminster Catechism,[5] although unacquainted with the outward form of either of those celebrated works. But that perversity, which all children have more or less of, and of which little Pearl had a tenfold portion, now, at the most inopportune moment, took thorough possession of her, and closed her lips, or impelled her to speak words amiss. After putting her finger in her mouth, with many ungracious refusals to answer good Mr. Wilson's question, the child finally announced that she had not been made at all, but had been plucked by her mother off the bush of wild roses, that grew by the prison-door.

This fantasy was probably suggested by the near proximity of the Governor's red roses, as Pearl stood outside of the window; together with her recollection of the prison rose-bush, which she had passed in coming hither.

---

[4] A famous children's schoolbook of late seventeenth-century Massachusetts, the most famous feature of which is the series of woodcuts that illustrate the alphabet. These are followed by moral and religious couplets: e.g., for the letter A, "By *Adam's* fall/We sinned all."

[5] The standard Presbyterian catechism was that compiled by the Westminster Assembly of ministers in 1647. The shorter catechism is divided into two parts: the doctrine we are to believe, and the duties we are to perform. It has 107 questions and answers. While the Boston Puritans were Congregationalists, their differences from Presbyterianism were chiefly in the area of church government, and they catechized their children in the same doctrine.

Old Roger Chillingworth, with a smile on his face, whispered something in the young clergyman's ear. Hester Prynne looked at the man of skill, and even then, with her fate hanging in the balance, was startled to perceive what a change had come over his features,—how much uglier they were,—how his dark complexion seemed to have grown duskier, and his figure more misshapen,—since the days when she had familiarly known him. She met his eyes for an instant, but was immediately constrained to give all her attention to the scene now going forward.

"This is awful!" cried the Governor, slowly recovering from the astonishment into which Pearl's response had thrown him. "Here is a child of three years old, and she cannot tell who made her! Without question, she is equally in the dark as to her soul, its present depravity, and future destiny! Methinks, gentlemen, we need inquire no further."

Hester caught hold of Pearl, and drew her forcibly into her arms, confronting the old Puritan magistrate with almost a fierce expression. Alone in the world, cast off by it, and with this sole treasure to keep her heart alive, she felt that she possessed indefeasible rights against the world, and was ready to defend them to the death.

"God gave me the child!" cried she. "He gave her, in requital of all things else, which ye had taken from me. She is my happiness!—she is my torture, none the less! Pearl keeps me here in life! Pearl punishes me too! See ye not, she is the scarlet letter, only capable of being loved, and so endowed with a million-fold the power of retribution for my sin? Ye shall not take her! I will die first!"

"My poor woman," said the not unkind old minister, "the child shall be well cared for!—far better than thou canst do it."

"God gave her into my keeping," repeated Hester Prynne, raising her voice almost to a shriek. "I will not give her up!"— And here, by a sudden impulse, she turned to the young clergyman, Mr. Dimmesdale, at whom, up to this moment, she had seemed hardly so much as once to direct her eyes.—"Speak thou for me!" cried she. "Thou wast my pastor, and hadst charge of my soul, and knowest me better than these men can. I will not lose the child! Speak for me! Thou knowest,—for thou hast sympathies which these men lack!—thou knowest what is in my heart, and what are a mother's rights, and how much the stronger they are, when that mother has but her child and the scarlet letter! Look thou to it! I will not lose the child! Look to it!"

At this wild and singular appeal, which indicated that Hester Prynne's situation had provoked her to little less than madness, the young minister at once came forward, pale, and holding his hand over his heart, as was his custom whenever his peculiarly nervous temperament was thrown into agitation. He looked now more careworn and emaciated than as we described him at the scene of Hester's public ignominy; and whether it were his failing health, or whatever the cause might be, his large dark eyes had a world of pain in their troubled and melancholy depth.

"There is truth in what she says," began the minister, with a voice sweet, tremulous, but powerful, insomuch that the hall reëchoed, and the hollow armour rang with it,—"truth in what Hester says, and in the feeling which inspires her! God gave her the child, and gave her, too, an instinctive knowledge of its nature and requirements,—both seemingly so peculiar,—which no other mortal being can possess. And, moreover, is there not a quality of awful sacredness in the relation between this mother and this child?"

"Ay!—how is that, good Master Dimmesdale?" interrupted the Governor. "Make that plain, I pray you!"

"It must be even so," resumed the minister. "For, if we deem it otherwise, do we not thereby say that the Heavenly Father, the Creator of all flesh, hath lightly recognized a deed of sin, and made of no account the distinction between unhallowed lust and holy love? This child of its father's guilt and its mother's shame hath come from the hand of God, to work in many ways upon her heart, who pleads so earnestly, and with such bitterness of spirit, the right to keep her. It was meant for a blessing; for the one blessing of her life! It was meant, doubtless, as the mother herself hath told us, for a retribution too; a torture, to be felt at many an unthought of moment; a pang, a sting, an ever-recurring agony, in the midst of a troubled joy! Hath she not expressed this thought in the garb of the poor child, so forcibly reminding us of that red symbol which sears her bosom?"

"Well said, again!" cried good Mr. Wilson. "I feared the woman had no better thought than to make a mountebank of her child!"

"O, not so!—not so!" continued Mr. Dimmesdale. "She recognizes, believe me, the solemn miracle which God hath wrought, in the existence of that child. And may she feel, too, —what, methinks, is the very truth,—that this boon·was meant, above all things else, to keep the mother's soul alive, and to preserve her from blacker depths of sin into which Satan might else have sought to plunge her! Therefore it is good for this poor, sinful woman that she hath an infant immortality, a being capable of eternal joy or sorrow, confided to her care, —to be trained up by her to righteousness,—to remind her, at every moment, of her fall,—but yet to teach her, as it were by the Creator's sacred pledge, that, if she bring the child to heaven, the child also will bring its parent thither! Herein is the sinful mother happier than the sinful father. For Hester Prynne's sake, then, and no less for the poor child's sake, let us leave them as Providence hath seen fit to place them!"

"You speak, my friend, with a strange earnestness," said old Roger Chillingworth, smiling at him.

"And there is weighty import in what my young brother hath spoken," added the Reverend Mr. Wilson. "What say you, worshipful Master Bellingham? Hath he not pleaded well for the poor woman?"

"Indeed hath he," answered the magistrate, "and hath adduced such arguments, that we will even leave the matter as it now stands; so long, at least, as there shall be no further scan-

dal in the woman. Care must be had, nevertheless, to put the
child to due and stated examination in the catechism at thy
hands or Master Dimmesdale's. Moreover, at a proper season,
the tithing-men[6] must take heed that she go both to school and
to meeting."

The young minister, on ceasing to speak, had withdrawn a
few steps from the group, and stood with his face partially concealed in the heavy folds of the window-curtain; while the
shadow of his figure, which the sunlight cast upon the floor,
was tremulous with the vehemence of his appeal. Pearl, that
wild and flighty little elf, stole softly towards him, and, taking
his hand in the grasp of both her own, laid her cheek against it;
a caress so tender, and withal so unobtrusive, that her mother,
who was looking on, asked herself,—"Is that my Pearl?" Yet
she knew that there was love in the child's heart, although it
mostly revealed itself in passion, and hardly twice in her lifetime had been softened by such gentleness as now. The minister,—for, save the long-sought regards of woman, nothing is
sweeter than these marks of childish preference, accorded spon-
taneously by a spiritual instinct, and therefore seeming to im-
ply in us something truly worthy to be loved,—the minister
looked round, laid his hand on the child's head, hesitated an
instant, and then kissed her brow. Little Pearl's unwonted
mood of sentiment lasted no longer; she laughed, and went
capering down the hall, so airily, that old Mr. Wilson raised a
question whether even her tiptoes touched the floor.

"The little baggage hath witchcraft in her, I profess," said
he to Mr. Dimmesdale. "She needs no old woman's broomstick
to fly withal!"

"A strange child!" remarked old Roger Chillingworth. "It is

[6] The "tithing" was an old English subdivision of the population
that consisted of a company of about ten households. The tithing-
man was at its head, directly responsible to the magistrates for the
peaceable behavior of his constituency. In seventeenth-century
Massachusetts, the tithingmen resembled modern police officers
more closely than they did their old English models.

easy to see the mother's part in her. Would it be beyond a philosopher's research, think ye, gentlemen, to analyze that child's nature, and, from its make and mould, to give a shrewd guess at the father?"

"Nay; it would be sinful, in such a question, to follow the clew of profane philosophy," said Mr. Wilson. "Better to fast and pray upon it; and still better, it may be, to leave the mystery as we find it, unless Providence reveal it of its own accord. Thereby, every good Christian man hath a title to show a father's kindness towards the poor, deserted babe."

The affair being so satisfactorily concluded, Hester Prynne, with Pearl, departed from the house. As they descended the steps, it is averred that the lattice of a chamber-window was thrown open, and forth into the sunny day was thrust the face of Mistress Hibbins, Governor Bellingham's bitter-tempered sister, and the same who, a few years later, was·executed as a witch.

"Hist, hist!" said she, while her ill-omened physiognomy seemed to cast a shadow over the cheerful newness of the house. "Wilt thou go with us to-night? There will be a merry company in the forest; and I wellnigh promised the Black Man that comely Hester Prynne should make one."

"Make my excuse to him, so please you!" answered Hester, with a triumphant smile. "I must tarry at home, and keep watch over my little Pearl. Had they taken her from me, I would willingly have gone with thee into the forest, and signed my name in the Black Man's book too, and that with mine own blood!"

"We shall have thee there anon!" said the witch-lady, frowning, as she drew back her head.

But here—if we suppose this interview betwixt Mistress Hibbins and Hester Prynne to be authentic, and not a parable—was already an illustration of the young minister's argument against sundering the relation of a fallen mother to the offspring of her frailty. Even thus early had the child saved her from Satan's snare.

9. The Leech

UNDER the appellation of Roger Chillingworth, the reader will remember, was hidden another name, which its former wearer had resolved should never more be spoken. It has been related, how, in the crowd that witnessed Hester Prynne's ignominious exposure, stood a man, elderly, travel-worn, who, just emerging from the perilous wilderness, beheld the woman, in whom he hoped to find embodied the warmth and cheerfulness of home, set up as a type of sin before the people. Her matronly fame was trodden under all men's feet. Infamy was babbling around her in the public market-place. For her kindred, should the tidings ever reach them, and for the companions of her unspotted life, there remained nothing but the contagion of her dishonor; which would not fail to be distributed in strict accordance and proportion with the intimacy and sacredness of their previous relationship. Then why—since the choice was with himself—should the individual, whose connection with the fallen woman had been the most intimate and sacred of them all, come forward to vindicate his claim to an inheritance so little desirable? He resolved not to be pilloried beside her on her pedestal of shame. Unknown to all but Hester Prynne, and possessing the lock and key of her silence, he chose to withdraw his name from the roll of mankind, and, as regarded his former ties and interests, to vanish out of life as completely as if he indeed lay at the bottom of the ocean, whither rumor had long ago consigned him. This purpose once effected, new interests would immediately spring up, and likewise a new purpose; dark, it is true, if not guilty, but of force enough to engage the full strength of his faculties.

In pursuance of this resolve, he took up his residence in the Puritan town, as Roger Chillingworth, without other introduction than the learning and intelligence of which he possessed more than a common measure. As his studies, at a pre-

vious period of his life, had made him extensively acquainted
with the medical science of the day, it was as a physician that
he presented himself, and as such was cordially received.
Skilful men, of the medical and chirurgical profession, were
of rare occurrence in the colony. They seldom, it would appear, partook of the religious zeal that brought other emigrants
across the Atlantic. In their researches into the human frame,
it may be that the higher and more subtile faculties of such
men were materialized, and that they lost the spiritual view of
existence amid the intricacies of that wondrous mechanism,
which seemed to involve art enough to comprise all of life
within itself. At all events, the health of the good town of Boston, so far as medicine had aught to do with it, had hitherto
lain in the guardianship of an aged deacon and apothecary,
whose piety and godly deportment were stronger testimonials
in his favor, than any that he could have produced in the
shape of a diploma. The only surgeon was one who combined
the occasional exercise of that noble art with the daily and
habitual flourish of a razor. To such a professional body Roger
Chillingworth was a brilliant acquisition. He soon manifested
his familiarity with the ponderous and imposing machinery of
antique physic; in which every remedy contained a multitude
of far-fetched and heterogeneous ingredients, as elaborately
compounded as if the proposed result had been the Elixir of
Life. In his Indian captivity, moreover, he had gained much
knowledge of the properties of native herbs and roots; nor did
he conceal from his patients, that these simple medicines, Nature's boon to the untutored savage, had quite as large a share
of his own confidence as the European pharmacopœia, which
so many learned doctors had spent centuries in elaborating.

This learned stranger was exemplary, as regarded at least the
outward forms of a religious life, and, early after his arrival,
had chosen for his spiritual guide the Reverend Mr. Dimmesdale. The young divine, whose scholar-like renown still lived
in Oxford, was considered by his more fervent admirers as

was heard to speak of Sir Kenelm Digby,[1] and other famous men,—whose scientific attainments were esteemed hardly less than supernatural,—as having been his correspondents or associates. Why, with such rank in the learned world, had he come hither? What could he, whose sphere was in great cities, be seeking in the wilderness? In answer to this query, a rumor gained ground,—and, however absurd, was entertained by some very sensible people,—that Heaven had wrought an absolute miracle, by transporting an eminent Doctor of Physic, from a German university, bodily through the air, and setting him down at the door of Mr. Dimmesdale's study! Individuals of wiser faith, indeed, who knew that Heaven promotes its purposes without aiming at the stage-effect of what is called miraculous interposition, were inclined to see a providential hand in Roger Chillingworth's so opportune arrival.

This idea was countenanced by the strong interest which the physician ever manifested in the young clergyman; he attached himself to him as a parishioner, and sought to win a friendly regard and confidence from his naturally reserved sensibility. He expressed great alarm at his pastor's state of health, but was anxious to attempt the cure, and, if early undertaken, seemed not despondent of a favorable result. The elders, the deacons, the motherly dames, and the young and fair maidens, of Mr. Dimmesdale's flock, were alike importunate that he should make trial of the physician's frankly offered skill. Mr. Dimmesdale gently repelled their entreaties.

"I need no medicine," said he.

But how could the young minister say so, when, with every successive Sabbath, his cheek was paler and thinner, and his voice more tremulous than before,—when it had now become

---

[1] Sir Kenelm Digby (1603–1665), diplomat, naval commander, philosopher, and author, is frequently cited as an exemplification of the Renaissance ideal of the "complete man." He opposed the Puritans in England and was imprisoned by Commons, 1642–1643, after which, until the Restoration, he lived mainly on the Continent and busied himself on behalf of the royal house.

a constant habit, rather than a casual gesture, to press his hand
over his heart? Was he weary of his labors? Did he wish to
die? These questions were solemnly propounded to Mr. Dimmesdale by the elder ministers of Boston and the deacons of
his church, who, to use their own phrase, "dealt with him," on
the sin of rejecting the aid which Providence so manifestly
held out. He listened in silence, and finally promised to confer
with the physician.

"Were it God's will," said the Reverend Mr. Dimmesdale,
when, in fulfillment of this pledge, he requested old Roger
Chillingworth's professional advice, "I could be well content,
that my labors, and my sorrows, and my sins, and my pains,
should shortly end with me, and what is earthly of them be
buried in my grave, and the spiritual go with me to my eternal
state, rather than that you should put your skill to the proof in
my behalf."

"Ah," replied Roger Chillingworth, with that quietness
which, whether imposed or natural, marked all his deportment, "it is thus that a young clergyman is apt to speak. Youthful men, not having taken a deep root, give up their hold
of life so easily! And saintly men, who walk with God on
earth, would fain be away, to walk with him on the golden
pavements of the New Jerusalem."

"Nay," rejoined the young minister, putting his hand to his
heart, with a flush of pain flitting over his brow, "were I
worthier to walk there, I could be better content to toil here."

"Good men ever interpret themselves too meanly," said the
physician.

In this manner, the mysterious old Roger Chillingworth became the medical adviser of the Reverend Mr. Dimmesdale. As
not only the disease interested the physician, but he was
strongly moved to look into the character and qualities of the
patient, these two men, so different in age, came gradually to
spend much time together. For the sake of the minister's health,
and to enable the leech to gather plants with healing balm
in them, they took long walks on the sea-shore, or in the forest;

mingling various talk with the plash and murmur of the waves, and the solemn wind-anthem among the tree-tops. Often, likewise, one was the guest of the other, in his place of study and retirement. There was a fascination for the minister in the company of the man of science, in whom he recognized an intellectual cultivation of no moderate depth or scope; together with a range and freedom of ideas, that he would have vainly looked for among the members of his own profession. In truth, he was startled, if not shocked, to find this attribute in the physician. Mr. Dimmesdale was a true priest, a true religionist, with the reverential sentiment largely developed, and an order of mind that impelled itself powerfully along the track of a creed, and wore its passage continually deeper with the lapse of time. In no state of society would he have been what is called a man of liberal views; it would always be essential to his peace to feel the pressure of a faith about him, supporting, while it confined him within its iron framework. Not the less, however, though with a tremulous enjoyment, did he feel the occasional relief of looking at the universe through the medium of another kind of intellect than those with which he habitually held converse. It was as if a window were thrown open, admitting a freer atmosphere into the close and stifled study, where his life was wasting itself away, amid lamp-light, or obstructed day-beams, and the musty fragrance, be it sensual or moral, that exhales from books. But the air was too fresh and chill to be long breathed, with comfort. So the minister, and the physician with him, withdrew again within the limits of what their church defined as orthodox.

Thus Roger Chillingworth scrutinized his patient carefully, both as he saw him in his ordinary life, keeping an accustomed pathway in the range of thoughts familiar to him, and as he appeared when thrown amidst other moral scenery, the novelty of which might call out something new to the surface of his character. He deemed it essential, it would seem, to know the man, before attempting to do him good. Wherever there is a heart and an intellect, the diseases of the physical frame are tinged with the peculiarities of these. In Arthur Dimmesdale, thought and imagination were so active, and sensibility so intense, that the bodily infirmity would be likely to have its groundwork there. So Roger Chillingworth—the man of skill, the kind and friendly physician—strove to go deep into his patient's bosom, delving among his principles, prying into his recollections, and probing every thing with a cautious touch, like a treasure-seeker in a dark cavern. Few secrets can escape an investigator, who has opportunity and license to undertake such a quest, and skill to follow it up. A man burdened with a secret should especially avoid the intimacy of his physician. If the latter possess native sagacity, and a nameless something more,—let us call it intuition; if he show no intrusive egotism, nor disagreeably prominent characteristics of his own; if he have the power, which must be born with him, to bring his mind into such affinity with his patient's, that this last shall unawares have spoken what he imagines himself only to have thought; if such revelations be received without tumult, and acknowledged not so often by an uttered sympathy, as by silence, an inarticulate breath, and here and there a word, to indicate that all is understood; if, to these qualifications of a confidant be joined the advantages afforded by his recognized character as a physician;—then, at some inevitable moment, will the soul of the sufferer be dissolved, and flow forth in a dark, but transparent stream, bringing all its mysteries into the daylight.

Roger Chillingworth possessed all, or most, of the attributes above enumerated. Nevertheless, time went on; a kind of intimacy, as we have said, grew up between these two cultivated minds, which had as wide a field as the whole sphere of human thought and study, to meet upon; they discussed every topic of ethics and religion, of public affairs, and private character; they talked much, on both sides, of matters that seemed personal to themselves; and yet no secret, such as the physician fancied must exist there, ever stole out of the minister's consciousness into his companion's ear. The latter had his suspicions, indeed, that even the nature of Mr. Dimmesdale's bodily disease had never fairly been revealed to him. It was a strange reserve!

After a time, at a hint from Roger Chillingworth, the friends of Mr. Dimmesdale effected an arrangement by which the two were lodged in the same house; so that every ebb and flow of the minister's life-tide might pass under the eye of his anxious and attached physician. There was much joy throughout the town, when this greatly desirable object was attained. It was held to be the best possible measure for the young clergyman's welfare; unless, indeed, as often urged by such as felt authorized to do so, he had selected some one of the many blooming damsels, spiritually devoted to him, to become his devoted wife. This latter step, however, there was no present prospect that Arthur Dimmesdale would be prevailed upon to take; he rejected all suggestions of the kind, as if priestly celibacy were one of his articles of church-discipline. Doomed by his own choice, therefore, as Mr. Dimmesdale so evidently was, to eat his unsavory morsel always at another's board, and endure the life-long chill which must be his lot who seeks to warm himself only at another's fireside, it truly seemed that this sagacious, experienced, benevolent, old physician, with his concord of paternal and reverential love for the young pastor, was the very man, of all mankind, to be constantly within reach of his voice.

The new abode of the two friends was with a pious widow, of good social rank, who dwelt in a house covering pretty nearly the site on which the venerable structure of King's Chapel has since been built. It had the grave-yard, originally Isaac Johnson's home-field, on one side, and so was well adapted to call up serious reflections, suited to their respective employments, in both minister and man of physic. The motherly care of the good widow assigned to Mr. Dimmesdale a front apartment, with a sunny exposure, and heavy window-curtains to create a noontide shadow, when desirable. The walls were hung round with tapestry, said to be from the

Gobelin[2] looms, and, at all events, representing the Scriptural
story of David and Bathsheba, and Nathan the Prophet,[3] in
colors still unfaded, but which made the fair woman of the
scene almost as grimly picturesque as the woe-denouncing seer.
Here, the pale clergyman piled up his library, rich with parch-
ment-bound folios of the Fathers, and the lore of Rabbis, and
monkish erudition, of which the Protestant divines, even while
they vilified and decried that class of writers, were yet constrained often to avail themselves. On the other side of the
house, old Roger Chillingworth arranged his study and laboratory; not such as a modern man of science would reckon even
tolerably complete, but provided with a distilling apparatus,
and the means of compounding drugs and chemicals, which
the practised alchemist knew well how to turn to purpose.
With such commodiousness of situation, these two learned persons sat themselves down, each in his own domain, yet
familiarly passing from one apartment to the other, and
bestowing a mutual and not incurious inspection into one
another's business.

And the Reverend Arthur Dimmesdale's best discerning
friends, as we have intimated, very reasonably imagined that
the hand of Providence had done all this, for the purpose—
besought in so many public, and domestic, and secret prayers
—of restoring the young minister to health. But—it must now
be said—another portion of the community had latterly begun
to take its own view of the relation betwixt Mr. Dimmesdale
and the mysterious old physician. When an uninstructed multitude attempts to see with its eyes, it is exceedingly apt to be
deceived. When, however, it forms its judgment, as it usually
does, on the intuitions of its great and warm heart, the con-

[2] The Gobelin family, beginning in the mid-fifteenth century,
were dyers and clothmakers in Paris. In 1601, Henry IV set up two
hundred workmen from Flanders at the Gobelin works to make
tapestries, and since that time the name Gobelin has become synonymous with the highest achievements in tapestry weaving.
[3] The story is told in II Samuel: 12–13.

clusions thus attained are often so profound and so unerring, as to possess the character of truths supernaturally revealed. The people, in the case of which we speak, could justify its prejudice against Roger Chillingworth by no fact or argument worthy of serious refutation. There was an aged handicrafts-man, it is true, who had been a citizen of London at the period of Sir Thomas Overbury's murder,[4] now some thirty years agone; he testified to having seen the physician, under some other name, which the narrator of the story had now for-gotten, in company with Doctor Forman,[5] the famous old conjurer, who was implicated in the affair of Overbury. Two or three individuals hinted, that the man of skill, during his Indian captivity, had enlarged his medical attainments by join-ing in the incantations of the savage priests; who were univer-sally acknowledged to be powerful enchanters, often perform-ing seemingly miraculous cures by their skill in the black art. A large number—and many of these were persons of such sober sense and practical observation, that their opinions would have been valuable, in other matters—affirmed that Roger Chillingworth's aspect had undergone a remarkable change while he had dwelt in town, and especially since his abode with Mr. Dimmesdale. At first, his expression had been calm, medi-

[4] Sir Thomas Overbury (1581–1613) opposed the marriage of his employer and confidant, the King's favorite, Robert Carr, Earl of Rochester, to Frances Howard, Countess of Essex. As a conse-quence, Lady Essex plotted against him, managed to have him imprisoned in the Tower for disrespect to the King, and then em-ployed the jailer, a physician's widow named Ann Turner, and an apothecary to poison Overbury. A year after his death, the plot was discovered and the accomplices were hanged. Lady Essex, now married to Carr, was spared, but she and her husband lived the rest of their lives in ignominy.

[5] Simon Forman (1552–1611), astrologer and quack doctor, was in and out of trouble with the law throughout his career for fraudulently practicing medicine. Nevertheless, his great personal charm, especially with the ladies, brought him powerful clients. Ann Turner constantly consulted with him in her own intrigues and in those of Lady Essex, for whom Forman was asked to pro-duce magical love philters.

tative, scholar-like. Now, there was something ugly and evil in his face, which they had not previously noticed, and which grew still the more obvious to sight, the oftener they looked upon him. According to the vulgar idea, the fire in his laboratory has been brought from the lower regions, and was fed with infernal fuel; and so, as might be expected, his visage was getting sooty with the smoke.

To sum up the matter, it grew to be a widely diffused opinion, that the Reverend Arthur Dimmesdale, like many other personages of especial sanctity, in all ages of the Christian world, was haunted either by Satan himself, or Satan's emissary, in the guise of old Roger Chillingworth. This diabolical agent had the Divine permission, for a season, to burrow into the clergyman's intimacy, and plot against his soul. No sensible man, it was confessed, could doubt on which side the victory would turn. The people looked, with an unshaken hope, to see the minister come forth out of the conflict, transfigured with the glory which he would unquestionably win. Meanwhile, nevertheless, it was sad to think of the perchance mortal agony through which he must struggle towards his triumph.

Alas, to judge from the gloom and terror in the depths of the poor minister's eyes, the battle was a sore one, and the victory any thing but secure!

10. The Leech and His Patient

OLD Roger Chillingworth, throughout life, had been calm in temperament, kindly, though not of warm affections, but ever, and in all his relations with the world, a pure and upright man.

He had begun an investigation, as he imagined, with the severe
and equal integrity of a judge, desirous only of truth, even as
if the question involved no more than the air-drawn lines and
figures of a geometrical problem, instead of human passions,
and wrongs inflicted on himself. But, as he proceeded, a terrible fascination, a kind of fierce, though still calm, necessity
seized the old man within its gripe, and never set him free
again, until he had done all its bidding. He now dug into the
poor clergyman's heart, like a miner searching for gold; or,
rather, like a sexton delving into a grave, possibly in quest of a
jewel that had been buried on the dead man's bosom, but likely
to find nothing save mortality and corruption. Alas for his own
soul, if these were what he sought!

Sometimes, a light glimmered out of the physician's eyes,
burning blue and ominous, like the reflection of a furnace, or,
let us say, like one of those gleams of ghastly fire that darted
from Bunyan's awful door-way in the hill-side,[1] and quivered
on the pilgrim's face. The soil where this dark miner was
working had perchance shown indications that encouraged
him.

"This man," said he, at one such moment, to himself, "pure
as they deem him,—all spiritual as he seems,—hath inherited a
strong animal nature from his father or his mother. Let us dig
a little farther in the direction of this vein!"

Then, after long search into the minister's dim interior, and
turning over many precious materials, in the shape of high
aspirations for the welfare of his race, warm love of souls, pure
sentiments, natural piety, strengthened by thought and study,
and illuminated by revelation,—all of which invaluable gold
was perhaps no better than rubbish to the seeker,—he would
turn back, discouraged, and begin his quest towards another
point. He groped along as stealthily, with as cautious a tread,
and as wary an outlook, as a thief entering a chamber where

---

[1] In *The Pilgrim's Progress*, by John Bunyan, a door that opens
directly into Hell is located on the hill that leads to the gate of
Heaven.

a man lies only half asleep,—or, it may be, broad awake,—with purpose to steal the very treasure which this man guards as the apple of his eye. In spite of his premeditated carefulness, the floor would now and then creak; his garments would rustle; the shadow of his presence, in a forbidden proximity, would be thrown across his victim. In other words, Mr. Dimmesdale, whose sensibility of nerve often produced the effect of spiritual intuition, would become vaguely aware that something inimical to his peace had thrust itself into relation with him. But old Roger Chillingworth, too, had perceptions that were almost intuitive; and when the minister threw his startled eyes towards him, there the physician sat; his kind, watchful, sympathizing, but never intrusive friend.

Yet Mr. Dimmesdale would perhaps have seen this individual's character more perfectly, if a certain morbidness, to which sick hearts are liable, had not rendered him suspicious of all mankind. Trusting no man as his friend, he could not recognize his enemy when the latter actually appeared. He therefore still kept up a familiar intercourse with him, daily receiving the old physician in his study; or visiting the laboratory, and, for recreation's sake, watching the processes by which weeds were converted into drugs of potency.

One day, leaning his forehead on his hand, and his elbow on the sill of the open window, that looked towards the graveyard, he talked with Roger Chillingworth, while the old man was examining a bundle of unsightly plants.

"Where," asked he, with a look askance at them,—for it was the clergyman's peculiarity that he seldom, now-a-days, looked straightforth at any object, whether human or inanimate,— "where, my kind doctor, did you gather those herbs, with such a dark, flabby leaf?"

"Even in the grave-yard, here at hand," answered the physician, continuing his employment. "They are new to me. I found them growing on a grave, which bore no tombstone, nor other memorial of the dead man, save these ugly weeds that have taken upon themselves to keep him in remembrance.

They grew out of his heart, and typify, it may be, some hideous secret that was buried with him, and which he had done better to confess during his lifetime."

"Perchance," said Mr. Dimmesdale, "he earnestly desired it, but could not."

"And wherefore?" rejoined the physician. "Wherefore not; since all the powers of nature call so earnestly for the confession of sin, that these black weeds have sprung up out of a buried heart, to make manifest an unspoken crime?"

"That, good Sir, is but a fantasy of yours," replied the minister. "There can be, if I forebode aright, no power, short of the Divine mercy, to disclose, whether by uttered words, or by type or emblem, the secrets that may be buried with a human heart. The heart, making itself guilty of such secrets, must perforce hold them, until the day when all hidden things shall be revealed. Nor have I so read or interpreted Holy Writ, as to understand that the disclosure of human thoughts and deeds, then to be made, is intended as a part of the retribution. That, surely, were a shallow view of it. No; these revelations, unless I greatly err, are meant merely to promote the intellectual satisfaction of all intelligent beings, who will stand waiting, on that day, to see the dark problem of this life made plain. A knowledge of men's hearts will be needful to the completest solution of that problem. And I conceive, moreover, that the hearts holding such miserable secrets as you speak of will yield them up, at that last day, not with reluctance, but with a joy unutterable."

"Then why not reveal them here?" asked Roger Chillingworth, glancing quietly aside at the minister. "Why should not the guilty ones sooner avail themselves of this unutterable solace?"

"They mostly do," said the clergyman, griping hard at his breast, as if afflicted with an importunate throb of pain. "Many, many a poor soul hath given its confidence to me, not only on the death-bed, but while strong in life, and fair in reputation. And ever, after such an outpouring, O, what a relief have

I witnessed in those sinful brethren! even as in one who at last draws free air, after long stifling with his own polluted breath. How can it be otherwise? Why should a wretched man, guilty, we will say, of murder, prefer to keep the dead corpse buried in his own heart, rather than fling it forth at once, and let the universe take care of it!"

"Yet some men bury their secrets thus," observed the calm physician.

"True; there are such men," answered Mr. Dimmesdale. "But, not to suggest more obvious reasons, it may be that they are kept silent by the very constitution of their nature. Or,—can we not suppose it?—guilty as they may be, retaining, nevertheless, a zeal for God's glory and man's welfare, they shrink from displaying themselves black and filthy in the view of men; because, thenceforward, no good can be achieved by them; no evil of the past be redeemed by better service. So, to their own unutterable torment, they go about among their fellow-creatures, looking pure as new-fallen snow; while their hearts are all speckled and spotted with iniquity of which they cannot rid themselves."

"These men deceive themselves," said Roger Chillingworth, with somewhat more emphasis than usual, and making a slight gesture with his forefinger. "They fear to take up the shame that rightfully belongs to them. Their love for man, their zeal for God's service,—these holy impulses may or may not coexist in their hearts with the evil inmates to which their guilt has unbarred the door, and which must needs propagate a hellish breed within them. But, if they seek to glorify God, let them not lift heavenward their unclean hands! If they would serve their fellow-men, let them do it by making manifest the power and reality of conscience, in constraining them to penitential self-abasement! Wouldst thou have me to believe, O wise and pious friend, that a false show can be better—can be more for God's glory, or man's welfare—than God's own truth? Trust me, such men deceive themselves!"

"It may be so," said the young clergyman indifferently, as

waiving a discussion that he considered irrelevant or unseasonable. He had a ready faculty, indeed, of escaping from any topic that agitated his too sensitive and nervous temperament. —"But, now, I would ask of my well-skilled physician, whether, in good sooth, he deems me to have profited by his kindly care of this weak frame of mine?"

Before Roger Chillingworth could answer, they heard the clear, wild laughter of a young child's voice, proceeding from the adjacent burial-ground. Looking instinctively from the open window,—for it was summer-time,—the minister beheld Hester Prynne and little Pearl passing along the footpath that traversed the inclosure. Pearl looked as beautiful as the day, but was in one of those moods of perverse merriment which, whenever they occurred, seemed to remove her entirely out of the sphere of sympathy or human contact. She now skipped irreverently from one grave to another; until, coming to the broad, flat, armorial tombstone of a departed worthy,—perhaps of Isaac Johnson himself,—she began to dance upon it. In reply to her mother's command and entreaty that she would behave more decorously, little Pearl paused to gather the prickly burrs from a tall burdock, which grew beside the tomb. Taking a handful of these, she arranged them along the lines of the scarlet letter that decorated the maternal bosom, to which the burrs, as their nature was, tenaciously adhered. Hester did not pluck them off.

Roger Chillingworth had by this time approached the window, and smiled grimly down.

"There is no law, nor reverence for authority, no regard for human ordinances or opinions, right or wrong, mixed up with that child's composition," remarked he, as much to himself as to his companion. "I saw her, the other day, bespatter the Governor himself with water, at the cattle-trough in Spring Lane. What, in Heaven's name, is she? Is the imp altogether evil? Hath she affections? Hath she any discoverable principle of being?"

"None,—save the freedom of a broken law," answered Mr.

Dimmesdale, in a quiet way, as if he had been discussing the point within himself. "Whether capable of good, I know not."

The child probably overheard their voices; for, looking up to the window, with a bright, but naughty smile of mirth and intelligence, she threw one of the prickly burrs at the Reverend Mr. Dimmesdale. The sensitive clergyman shrunk, with nervous dread, from the light missile. Detecting his emotion, Pearl clapped her little hands in the most extravagant ecstasy. Hester Prynne, likewise, had involuntarily looked up; and all these four persons, old and young, regarded one another in silence, till the child laughed aloud, and shouted,—"Come away, mother! Come away, or yonder old Black Man will catch you! He hath got hold of the minister already. Come away, mother, or he will catch you! But he cannot catch little Pearl!"

So she drew her mother away, skipping, dancing, and frisking fantastically among the hillocks of the dead people, like a creature that had nothing in common with a bygone and buried generation, nor owned herself akin to it. It was as if she had been made afresh, out of new elements, and must perforce be permitted to live her own life, and be a law unto herself, without her eccentricities being reckoned to her for a crime.

"There goes a woman," resumed Roger Chillingworth, after a pause, "who, be her demerits what they may, hath none of that mystery of hidden sinfulness which you deem so grievous to be borne. Is Hester Prynne the less miserable, think you, for that scarlet letter on her breast?"

"I do verily believe it," answered the clergyman. "Nevertheless, I cannot answer for her. There was a look of pain in her face, which I would gladly have been spared the sight of. But still, methinks, it must needs be better for the sufferer to be free to show his pain, as this poor woman Hester is, than to cover it all up in his heart."

There was another pause; and the physician began anew to examine and arrange the plants which he had gathered.

"You inquired of me, a little time agone," said he, at length, "my judgment as touching your health."

"I did," answered the clergyman, "and would gladly learn it. Speak frankly, I pray you, be it for life or death."

"Freely, then, and plainly," said the physician, still busy with his plants, but keeping a wary eye on Mr. Dimmesdale, "the disorder is a strange one; not so much in itself, nor as out-wardly manifested,—in so far, at least, as the symptoms have been laid open to my observation. Looking daily at you, my good Sir, and watching the tokens of your aspect, now for months gone by, I should deem you a man sore sick, it may be, yet not so sick but that an instructed and watchful physi-cian might well hope to cure you. But—I know not what to say—the disease is what I seem to know, yet know it not."

"You speak in riddles, learned Sir," said the pale minister, glancing aside out of the window.

"Then, to speak more plainly," continued the physician, "and I crave pardon, Sir,—should it seem to require pardon, —for this needful plainness of my speech. Let me ask,—as your friend,—as one having charge, under Providence, of your life and physical well-being,—hath all the operation of this disorder been fairly laid open and recounted to me?"

"How can you question it?" asked the minister. "Surely, it were child's play to call in a physician, and then hide the sore!"

"You would tell me, then, that I know all?" said Roger Chillingworth, deliberately, and fixing an eye, bright with in-tense and concentrated intelligence, on the minister's face. "Be it so! But, again! He to whom only the outward and physical evil is laid open knoweth, oftentimes, but half the evil which he is called upon to cure. A bodily disease, which we look upon as whole and entire within itself, may, after all, be but a symptom of some ailment in the spiritual part. Your pardon, once again, good Sir, if my speech give the shadow of offence. You, Sir, of all men whom I have known, are he whose body is the closest conjoined, and imbued, and identified, so to speak, with the spirit whereof it is the instrument."

"Then I need ask no further," said the clergyman, somewhat

hastily rising from his chair. "You deal not, I take it, in medicine for the soul!"

"Thus, a sickness," continued Roger Chillingworth, going on, in an unaltered tone, without heeding the interruption,—but standing up, and confronting the emaciated and white-cheeked minister with his low, dark, and misshapen figure,—"a sickness, a sore place, if we may so call it, in your spirit, hath immediately its appropriate manifestation in your bodily frame. Would you, therefore, that your physician heal the bodily evil? How may this be, unless you first lay open to him the wound or trouble in your soul?"

"No!—not to thee!—not to an earthly physician!" cried Mr. Dimmesdale, passionately, and turning his eyes, full and bright, and with a kind of fierceness, on old Roger Chillingworth. "Not to thee! But, if it be the soul's disease, then do I commit myself to the one Physician of the soul! He, if it stand with his good pleasure, can cure; or he can kill! Let him do with me as, in his justice and wisdom, he shall see good. But who art thou, that meddlest in this matter?—that dares thrust himself between the sufferer and his God?"

With a frantic gesture, he rushed out of the room.

"It is as well to have made this step," said Roger Chillingworth to himself, looking after the minister with a grave smile. "There is nothing lost. We shall be friends again anon. But see, now, how passion takes hold upon this man, and hurrieth him out of himself! As with one passion, so with another! He hath done a wild thing ere now, this pious Master Dimmesdale, in the hot passion of his heart!"

It proved not difficult to reëstablish the intimacy of the two companions, on the same footing and in the same degree as heretofore. The young clergyman, after a few hours of privacy, was sensible that the disorder of his nerves had hurried him into an unseemly outbreak of temper, which there had been nothing in the physician's words to excuse or palliate. He marvelled, indeed, at the violence with which he had thrust back the kind old man, when merely proffering the advice which it was his duty to bestow, and which the minister himself had expressly sought. With these remorseful feelings, he lost no time in making the amplest apologies, and besought his friend still to continue the care, which, if not successful in restoring him to health, had, in all probability, been the means of prolonging his feeble existence to that hour. Roger Chillingworth readily assented, and went on with his medical supervision of the minister; doing his best for him, in all good faith, but always quitting the patient's apartment, at the close of a professional interview, with a mysterious and puzzled smile upon his lips. This expression was invisible in Mr. Dimmesdale's presence, but grew strongly evident as the physician crossed the threshold.

"A rare case!" he muttered. "I must needs look deeper into it. A strange sympathy betwixt soul and body! Were it only for the art's sake, I must search this matter to the bottom!"

It came to pass, not long after the scene above recorded, that the Reverend Mr. Dimmesdale, at noonday, and entirely unawares, fell into a deep, deep slumber, sitting in his chair, with a large black-letter volume open before him on the table. It must have been a work of vast ability in the somniferous school of literature. The profound depth of the minister's repose was the more remarkable; inasmuch as he was one of those persons whose sleep, ordinarily, is as light, as fitful, and as easily scared away, as a small bird hopping on a twig. To such an unwonted remoteness, however, had his spirit now withdrawn into itself, that he stirred not in his chair, when old Roger Chillingworth, without any extraordinary precaution, came into the room. The physician advanced directly in front of his patient, laid his hand upon his bosom, and thrust aside the vestment, that, hitherto, had always covered it even from the professional eye.

Then, indeed, Mr. Dimmesdale shuddered, and slightly stirred.

After a brief pause, the physician turned away.

But with what a wild look of wonder, joy, and horror! With

what a ghastly rapture, as it were, too mighty to be expressed only by the eye and features, and therefore bursting forth through the whole ugliness of his figure, and making itself even riotously manifest by the extravagant gestures with which he threw up his arms towards the ceiling, and stamped his foot upon the floor! Had a man seen old Roger Chillingworth, at that moment of his ecstasy, he would have had no need to ask how Satan comports himself, when a precious human soul is lost to heaven, and won into his kingdom.

But what distinguished the physician's ecstasy from Satan's was the trait of wonder in it!

11. The Interior of a Heart

AFTER the incident last described, the intercourse between the clergyman and the physician, though externally the same, was really of another character than it had previously been. The intellect of Roger Chillingworth had now a sufficiently plain path before it. It was not, indeed, precisely that which he had laid out for himself to tread. Calm, gentle, passionless, as he appeared, there was yet, we fear, a quiet depth of malice, hitherto latent, but active now, in this unfortunate old man, which led him to imagine a more intimate revenge than any mortal had ever wreaked upon an enemy. To make himself the one trusted friend, to whom should be confided all the fear, the remorse, the agony, the ineffectual repentance, the backward rush of sinful thoughts, expelled in vain! All that guilty sorrow, hidden from the world, whose great heart would have pitied and forgiven, to be revealed to him, the Pitiless, to him, the Unforgiving! All that dark treasure to be lavished on the very man, to whom nothing else could so adequately pay the debt of vengeance!

The clergyman's shy and sensitive reserve had balked this scheme. Roger Chillingworth, however, was inclined to be hardly, if at all, less satisfied with the aspect of affairs, which Providence—using the avenger and his victim for its own purposes, and, perchance, pardoning, where it seemed most to punish—had substituted for his black devices. A revelation, he could almost say, had been granted to him. It mattered little, for his object, whether celestial, or from what other region. By its aid, in all the subsequent relations betwixt him and Mr. Dimmesdale, not merely the external presence, but the very inmost soul of the latter seemed to be brought out before his eyes, so that he could see and comprehend its every movement. He became, thenceforth, not a spectator only, but a chief actor, in the poor minister's interior world. He could play upon him as he chose. Would he arouse him with a throb of agony? The victim was for ever on the rack; it needed only to know the spring that controlled the engine;—and the physician knew it well! Would he startle him with sudden fear? As at the waving of a magician's wand, uprose a grisly phantom, —uprose a thousand phantoms,—in many shapes, of death, or more awful shame, all flocking roundabout the clergyman, and pointing with their fingers at his breast!

All this was accomplished with a subtlety so perfect, that the minister, though he had constantly a dim perception of some evil influence watching over him, could never gain a knowledge of its actual nature. True, he looked doubtfully, fearfully,—even, at times, with horror and the bitterness of hatred,—at the deformed figure of the old physician. His gestures, his gait, his grizzled beard, his slightest and most indifferent acts, the very fashion of his garments, were odious in the clergyman's sight; a token, implicitly to be relied on, of a deeper antipathy in the breast of the latter than he was will-

ing to acknowledge to himself. For, as it was impossible to
assign a reason for such distrust and abhorrence, so Mr. Dimmesdale, conscious that the poison of one morbid spot was
infecting his heart's entire substance, attributed all his presenti-
ments to no other cause. He took himself to task for his bad
sympathies in reference to Roger Chillingworth, disregarded
the lesson that he should have drawn from them, and did his
best to root them out. Unable to accomplish this, he nevertheless, as a matter of principle, continued his habits of social
familiarity with the old man, and thus gave him constant opportunities for perfecting the purpose to which—poor, forlorn
creature that he was, and more wretched than his victim—the
avenger had devoted himself.

While thus suffering under bodily disease, and gnawed and
tortured by some black trouble of the soul, and given over to
the machinations of his deadliest enemy, the Reverend Mr.
Dimmesdale had achieved a brilliant popularity in his sacred
office. He won it, indeed, in great part, by his sorrows. His
intellectual gifts, his moral perceptions, his power of experi-
encing and communicating emotion, were kept in a state of
preternatural activity by the prick and anguish of his daily life.
His fame, though still on its upward slope, already overshadowed the soberer reputations of his fellow-clergymen, eminent
as several of them were. There were scholars among them,
who had spent more years in acquiring abstruse lore, connected with the divine profession, than Mr. Dimmesdale had
lived; and who might well, therefore, be more profoundly
versed in such solid and valuable attainments than their youthful brother. There were men, too, of a sturdier texture of mind
than his, and endowed with a far greater share of shrewd, hard,
iron or granite understanding; which, duly mingled with a fair
proportion of doctrinal ingredient, constitutes a highly respectable, efficacious, and unamiable variety of the clerical
species. There were others, again, true saintly fathers, whose
faculties had been elaborated by weary toil among their books,
and by patient thought, and etherealized, moreover, by spir-

itual communications with the better world, into which their purity of life had almost introduced these holy personages, with their garments of mortality still clinging to them. All that they lacked was the gift that descended upon the chosen disciples, at Pentecost, in tongues of flame;[1] symbolizing, it would seem, not the power of speech in foreign and unknown languages, but that of addressing the whole human brotherhood in the heart's native language. These fathers, otherwise so apostolic, lacked Heaven's last and rarest attestation of their office, the Tongue of Flame. They would have vainly sought—had they ever dreamed of seeking—to express the highest truths through the humblest medium of familiar words and images. Their voices came down, afar and indistinctly, from the upper heights where they habitually dwelt.

Not improbably, it was to this latter class of men that Mr. Dimmesdale, by many of his traits of character, naturally belonged. To their high mountain-peaks of faith and sanctity he would have climbed, had not the tendency been thwarted by the burden, whatever it might be, of crime or anguish, beneath which it was his doom to totter. It kept him down, on a level with the lowest; him, the man of ethereal attributes, whose voice the angels might else have listened to and answered! But this very burden it was, that gave him sympathies so intimate with the sinful brotherhood of mankind; so that his heart vibrated in unison with theirs, and received their pain into itself, and sent its own throb of pain through a thousand other hearts, in gushes of sad, persuasive eloquence. Oftenest persuasive, but sometimes terrible! The people knew not the power that moved them thus. They deemed the young clergy-

---

[1] Acts 2:1–4, "And when the day of Pentecost was fully come, they were all with one accord in one place. And suddenly there came a sound from heaven as of a rushing mighty wind, and it filled all the house where they were sitting. And there appeared unto them cloven tongues like as of fire, and it sat upon each of them. And they were all filled with the Holy Ghost, and began to speak with other tongues, as the Spirit gave them utterance."

man a miracle of holiness. They fancied him the mouth-piece of Heaven's messages of wisdom, and rebuke, and love. In their eyes, the very ground on which he trod was sanctified. The virgins of his church grew pale around him, victims of a passion so imbued with religious sentiment that they imagined it to be all religion, and brought it openly, in their white bosoms, as their most acceptable sacrifice before the altar. The aged members of his flock, beholding Mr. Dimmesdale's frame so feeble, while they were themselves so rugged in their infirmity, believed that he would go heavenward before them, and enjoined it upon their children, that their old bones should be buried close to their young pastor's holy grave. And, all this time, perchance, when poor Mr. Dimmesdale was thinking of his grave, he questioned with himself whether the grass would ever grow on it, because an accursed thing must there be buried!

It is inconceivable, the agony with which this public veneration tortured him! It was his genuine impulse to adore the truth, and to reckon all things shadow-like, and utterly devoid of weight or value, that had not its divine essence as the life within their life. Then, what was he?—a substance?—or the dimmest of all shadows? He longed to speak out, from his own pulpit, at the full height of his voice, and tell the people what he was. "I, whom you behold in these black garments of the priesthood,—I, who ascend the sacred desk, and turn my pale face heavenward, taking upon myself to hold communion, in your behalf, with the Most High Omniscience,—I, in whose daily life you discern the sanctity of Enoch,[2]—I, whose footsteps, as you suppose, leave a gleam along my earthly track, whereby the pilgrims that shall come after me may be guided to the regions of the blest,—I, who have laid the hand of baptism upon your children,—I, who have breathed the parting prayer over your dying friends, to whom the Amen sounded faintly from a world which they had quitted,—I, your pastor,

[2] "And Enoch walked with God": Genesis 5:22, 24.

whom you so reverence and trust, am utterly a pollution and a lie!"

More than once, Mr. Dimmesdale had gone into the pulpit, with a purpose never to come down its steps, until he should have spoken words like the above. More than once, he had cleared his throat, and drawn in the long, deep, and tremulous breath, which, when sent forth again, would come burdened with the black secret of his soul. More than once—nay, more than a hundred times—he had actually spoken! Spoken! But how? He had told his hearers that he was altogether vile, a viler companion of the vilest, the worst of sinners, an abomination, a thing of unimaginable iniquity; and that the only wonder was, that they did not see his wretched body shrivelled up before their eyes, by the burning wrath of the Almighty! Could there be plainer speech than this? Would not the people start up in their seats, by a simultaneous impulse, and tear him down out of the pulpit which he defiled? Not so, indeed! They heard it all, and did but reverence him the more. They little guessed what deadly purport lurked in those self-condemning words. "The godly youth!" said they among themselves. "The saint on earth! Alas, if he discern such sinfulness in his own white soul, what horrid spectacle would he behold in thine or mine!" The minister well knew—subtle, but remorseful hypocrite that he was!—the light in which his vague confession would be viewed. He had striven to put a cheat upon himself by making the avowal of a guilty conscience, but had gained only one other sin, and a self-acknowledged shame, without the momentary relief of being self-deceived. He had spoken the very truth, and transformed it into the veriest falsehood. And yet, by the constitution of his nature, he loved the truth, and loathed the lie, as few men ever did. Therefore, above all things else, he loathed his miserable self!

His inward trouble drove him to practices, more in accordance with the old, corrupted faith of Rome, than with the better light of the church in which he had been born and bred. In Mr. Dimmesdale's secret closet, under lock and key, there

was a bloody scourge. Oftentimes, this Protestant and Puritan
divine had plied it on his own shoulders; laughing bitterly at
himself the while, and smiting so much the more pitilessly, because of that bitter laugh. It was his custom, too, as it has been
that of many other pious Puritans, to fast,—not, however, like
them, in order to purify the body and render it the fitter
medium of celestial illumination,—but rigorously, and until his
knees trembled beneath him, as an act of penance. He kept
vigils, likewise, night after night, sometimes in utter darkness;
sometimes with a glimmering lamp; and sometimes, viewing his
own face in a looking-glass, by the most powerful light which
he could throw upon it. He thus typified the constant introspection wherewith he tortured, but could not purify, himself.
In these lengthened vigils, his brain often reeled, and visions
seemed to flit before him; perhaps seen doubtfully, and by a
faint light of their own, in the remote dimness of the chamber,
or more vividly, and close beside him, within the looking-glass.
Now it was a herd of diabolic shapes, that grinned and mocked
at the pale minister, and beckoned him away with them; now
a group of shining angels, who flew upward heavily, as
sorrow-laden, but grew more ethereal as they rose. Now came
the dead friends of his youth, and his white-bearded father,
with a saint-like frown, and his mother, turning her face away
as she passed by. Ghost of a mother,—thinnest fantasy of a
mother,—methinks she might yet have thrown a pitying glance
towards her son! And now, through the chamber which these
spectral thoughts had made so ghastly, glided Hester Prynne,
leading along little Pearl, in her scarlet garb, and pointing her
forefinger, first, at the scarlet letter on her bosom, and then at
the clergyman's own breast.

None of these visions ever quite deluded him. At any moment, by an effort of his will, he could discern substances
through their misty lack of substance, and convince himself
that they were not solid in their nature, like yonder table of
carved oak, or that big, square, leathern-bound and brazen-
clasped volume of divinity. But, for all that, they were, in one

sense, the truest and most substantial things which the poor minister now dealt with. It is the unspeakable misery of a life so false as his, that it steals the pith and substance out of whatever realities there are around us, and which were meant by Heaven to be the spirit's joy and nutriment. To the untrue man, the whole universe is false,—it is impalpable,—it shrinks to nothing within his grasp. And he himself, in so far as he shows himself in a false light, becomes a shadow, or, indeed, ceases to exist. The only truth, that continued to give Mr. Dimmesdale a real existence on this earth, was the anguish in his inmost soul, and the undissembled expression of it in his aspect. Had he once found power to smile, and wear a face of gayety, there would have been no such man!

On one of those ugly nights, which we have faintly hinted at, but forborne to picture forth, the minister started from his chair. A new thought had struck him. There might be a moment's peace in it. Attiring himself with as much care as if it had been for public worship, and precisely in the same manner, he stole softly down the staircase, undid the door, and issued forth.

12. The Minister's Vigil

WALKING in the shadow of a dream, as it were, and perhaps actually under the influence of a species of somnambulism, Mr. Dimmesdale reached the spot, where, now so long since, Hester Prynne had lived through her first hour of public ignominy. The same platform or scaffold, black and weather-stained with the storm or sunshine of seven long years, and foot-worn, too, with the tread of many culprits who had since ascended it, re-

mained standing beneath the balcony of the meeting-house.
The minister went up the steps.

It was an obscure night of early May. An unvaried pall of
cloud muffled the whole expanse of sky from zenith to hori-
zon. If the same multitude which had stood as eyewitnesses
while Hester Prynne sustained her punishment could now have
been summoned forth, they would have discerned no face
above the platform, nor hardly the outline of a human shape,
in the dark gray of the midnight. But the town was all asleep.
There was no peril of discovery. The minister might stand
there, if it so pleased him, until morning should redden in the
east, without other risk than that the dank and chill night-air
would creep into his frame, and stiffen his joints with rheu-
matism, and clog his throat with catarrh and cough; thereby
defrauding the expectant audience of to-morrow's prayer and
sermon. No eye could see him, save that ever-wakeful one
which had seen him in his closet, wielding the bloody scourge.
Why, then, had he come hither? Was it but the mockery of
penitence? A mockery, indeed, but in which his soul trifled
with itself! A mockery at which angels blushed and wept,
while fiends rejoiced, with jeering laughter! He had been
driven hither by the impulse of that Remorse which dogged
him everywhere, and whose own sister and closely linked companion was that Cowardice which invariably drew him back,
with her tremulous gripe, just when the other impulse had
hurried him to the verge of a disclosure. Poor, miserable man!
what right had infirmity like his to burden itself with crime?
Crime is for the iron-nerved, who have their choice either to
endure it, or, if it press too hard, to exert their fierce and savage
strength for a good purpose, and fling it off at once! This
feeble and most sensitive of spirits could do neither, yet continually did one thing or another, which intertwined, in the
same inextricable knot, the agony of heaven-defying guilt and
vain repentance.

And thus, while standing on the scaffold, in this vain show
of expiation, Mr. Dimmesdale was overcome with a great hor-

ror of mind, as if the universe were gazing at a scarlet token on his naked breast, right over his heart. On that spot, in very truth, there was, and there had long been, the gnawing and poisonous tooth of bodily pain. Without any effort of his will, or power to restrain himself, he shrieked aloud; an outcry that went pealing through the night, and was beaten back from one house to another, and reverberated from the hills in the background; as if a company of devils, detecting so much misery and terror in it, had made a plaything of the sound, and were bandying it to and fro.

"It is done!" muttered the minister, covering his face with his hands. "The whole town will awake, and hurry forth, and find me here!"

But it was not so. The shriek had perhaps sounded with a far greater power, to his own startled ears, than it actually possessed. The town did not awake; or, if it did, the drowsy slumberers mistook the cry either for something frightful in a dream, or for the noise of witches; whose voices, at that period, were often heard to pass over the settlements or lonely cottages, as they rode with Satan through the air. The clergyman, therefore, hearing no symptoms of disturbance, uncovered his eyes and looked about him. At one of the chamber-windows of Governor Bellingham's mansion, which stood at some distance, on the line of another street, he beheld the appearance of the old magistrate himself, with a lamp in his hand, a white night-cap on his head, and a long white gown enveloping his figure. He looked like a ghost, evoked unseasonably from the grave. The cry had evidently startled him. At another window of the same house, moreover, appeared old Mistress Hibbins, the Governor's sister, also with a lamp, which, even thus far off, revealed the expression of her sour and discontented face. She thrust forth her head from the lattice, and looked anxiously upward. Beyond the shadow of a doubt, this venerable witch-lady had heard Mr. Dimmesdale's outcry, and interpreted it, with its multitudinous echoes and reverberations, as the clamor of the fiends and night-hags, with whom she was well known to make excursions into the forest.

Detecting the gleam of Governor Bellingham's lamp, the old lady quickly extinguished her own, and vanished. Possibly, she went up among the clouds. The minister saw nothing further of her motions. The magistrate, after a wary observation of the darkness—into which, nevertheless, he could see but little farther than he might into a mill-stone—retired from the window.

The minister grew comparatively calm. His eyes, however, were soon greeted by a little, glimmering light, which, at first a long way off, was approaching up the street. It threw a gleam of recognition on here a post, and there a garden-fence, and here a latticed window-pane, and there a pump, with its full trough of water, and here, again, an arched door of oak, with an iron knocker, and a rough log for the door-step. The Reverend Mr. Dimmesdale noted all these minute particulars, even while firmly convinced that the doom of his existence was stealing onward, in the footsteps which he now heard; and that the gleam of the lantern would fall upon him, in a few moments more, and reveal his long-hidden secret. As the light drew nearer, he beheld, within its illuminated circle, his brother clergyman,—or, to speak more accurately, his professional father, as well as highly valued friend,—the Reverend Mr. Wilson; who, as Mr. Dimmesdale now conjectured, had been praying at the bedside of some dying man. And so he had. The good old minister came freshly from the death-chamber of Governor Winthrop,[1] who had passed from earth to heaven within that very hour. And now, surrounded, like the saint-like personages of olden times, with a radiant halo, that glorified him amid this gloomy night of sin,—as if the departed

[1] John Winthrop (1588–1649) arrived in Massachusetts as the chosen governor in 1630 and was among the founders of Boston. He governed until 1634 and again in the years 1637–1640, 1642–1644, and 1646–1649. He was certainly the most influential figure in early Massachusetts and, more than any other man, left the imprint of his character on the colony. His journal, *History of New England 1630–1649*, is perhaps the best single document of American Puritan character and history. Winthrop died in March, but Hawthorne sets this scene in early May of the same year.

Governor had left him an inheritance of his glory, or as if he
had caught upon himself the distant shine of the celestial city,
while looking thitherward to see the triumphant pilgrim pass
within its gates,—now, in short, good Father Wilson was moving homeward, aiding his footsteps with a lighted lantern! The
glimmer of this luminary suggested the above conceits to Mr.
Dimmesdale, who smiled,—nay, almost laughed at them,—and
then wondered if he were going mad.

As the Reverend Mr. Wilson passed beside the scaffold,
closely muffling his Geneva cloak about him with one arm,
and holding the lantern before his breast with the other, the
minister could hardly restrain himself from speaking.

"A good evening to you, venerable Father Wilson! Come
up hither, I pray you, and pass a pleasant hour with me!"

Good heavens! Had Mr. Dimmesdale actually spoken? For
one instant, he believed that these words had passed his lips.
But they were uttered only within his imagination. The venerable Father Wilson continued to step slowly onward, looking carefully at the muddy pathway before his feet, and never
once turning his head towards the guilty platform. When the
light of the glimmering lantern had faded quite away, the minister discovered, by the faintness which came over him, that
the last few moments had been a crisis of terrible anxiety; although his mind had made an involuntary effort to relieve itself
by a kind of lurid playfulness.

Shortly afterwards, the like grisly sense of the humorous
again stole in among the solemn phantoms of his thought. He
felt his limbs growing stiff with the unaccustomed chilliness
of the night, and doubted whether he should be able to descend the steps of the scaffold. Morning would break, and find
him there. The neighbourhood would begin to rouse itself. The
earliest riser, coming forth in the dim twilight, would perceive
a vaguely defined figure aloft on the place of shame; and, half
crazed betwixt alarm and curiosity, would go, knocking from
door to door, summoning all the people to behold the ghost—
as he needs must think it—of some defunct transgressor. A

dusky tumult would flap its wings from one house to another. Then—the morning light still waxing stronger—old patriarchs would rise up in great haste, each in his flannel gown, and matronly dames, without pausing to put off their night-gear. The whole tribe of decorous personages, who had never heretofore been seen with a single hair of their heads awry, would start into public view, with the disorder of a nightmare in their aspects. Old Governor Bellingham would come grimly forth, with his King James's ruff fastened askew; and Mistress Hibbins, with some twigs of the forest clinging to her skirts, and looking sourer than ever, as having hardly got a wink of sleep after her night ride; and good Father Wilson, too, after spending half the night at a death-bed, and liking ill to be disturbed, thus early, out of his dreams about the glorified saints. Hither, likewise, would come the elders and deacons of Mr. Dimmesdale's church, and the young virgins who so idolized their minister, and had made a shrine for him in their white bosoms; which, now, by the by, in their hurry and confusion, they would scantly have given themselves time to cover with their kerchiefs. All people, in a word, would come stumbling over their thresholds, and turning up their amazed and horror-stricken visages around the scaffold. Whom would they discern there, with the red eastern light upon his brow? Whom, but the Reverend Arthur Dimmesdale, half frozen to death, overwhelmed with shame, and standing where Hester Prynne had stood!

Carried away by the grotesque horror of this picture, the minister, unawares, and to his own infinite alarm, burst into a great peal of laughter. It was immediately responded to by a light, airy, childish laugh, in which, with a thrill of the heart,—but he knew not whether of exquisite pain, or pleasure as acute,—he recognized the tones of little Pearl.

"Pearl! Little Pearl!" cried he, after a moment's pause; then, suppressing his voice,—"Hester! Hester Prynne! Are you there?"

"Yes; it is Hester Prynne!" she replied, in a tone of surprise;

and the minister heard her footsteps approaching from the sidewalk, along which she had been passing.—"It is I, and my little Pearl."

"Whence come you, Hester?" asked the minister. "What sent you hither?"

"I have been watching at a death-bed," answered Hester Prynne;—"at Governor Winthrop's death-bed, and have taken his measure for a robe, and am now going homeward to my dwelling."

"Come up hither, Hester, thou and little Pearl," said the Reverend Mr. Dimmesdale. "Ye have both been here before, but I was not with you. Come up hither once again, and we will stand all three together!"

She silently ascended the steps, and stood on the platform, holding little Pearl by the hand. The minister felt for the child's other hand, and took it. The moment that he did so, there came what seemed a tumultuous rush of new life, other life than his own, pouring like a torrent into his heart, and hurrying through all his veins, as if the mother and the child were communicating their vital warmth to his half-torpid system. The three formed an electric chain.

"Minister!" whispered little Pearl.

"What wouldst thou say, child?" asked Mr. Dimmesdale.

"Wilt thou stand here with mother and me, to-morrow noontide?" inquired Pearl.

"Nay; not so, my little Pearl!" answered the minister; for, with the new energy of the moment, all the dread of public exposure, that had so long been the anguish of his life, had returned upon him; and he was already trembling at the conjunction in which—with a strange joy, nevertheless—he now found himself. "Not so, my child. I shall, indeed, stand with thy mother and thee one other day, but not to-morrow!"

Pearl laughed, and attempted to pull away her hand. But the minister held it fast.

"A moment longer, my child!" said he.

"But wilt thou promise," asked Pearl, "to take my hand, and mother's hand, to-morrow noontide?"

"Not then, Pearl!" said the minister, "but another time!"

"And what other time?" persisted the child.

"At the great judgment day!" whispered the minister,—and, strangely enough, the sense that he was a professional teacher of the truth impelled him to answer the child so. "Then, and there, before the judgment-seat, thy mother, and thou, and I, must stand together! But the daylight of this world shall not see our meeting!"

Pearl laughed again.

But, before Mr. Dimmesdale had done speaking, a light gleamed far and wide over all the muffled sky. It was doubtless caused by one of those meteors, which the night-watcher may so often observe burning out to waste, in the vacant regions of the atmosphere. So powerful was its radiance, that it thoroughly illuminated the dense medium of cloud betwixt the sky and earth. The great vault brightened, like the dome of an immense lamp. It showed the familiar scene of the street, with the distinctness of mid-day, but also with the awfulness that is always imparted to familiar objects by an unaccustomed light. The wooden houses, with their jutting stories and quaint gable-peaks; the doorsteps and thresholds, with the early grass springing up about them; the garden-plots, black with freshly turned earth; the wheel-track, little worn, and, even in the market-place, margined with green on either side;—all were visible, but with a singularity of aspect that seemed to give another moral interpretation to the things of this world than they had ever borne before. And there stood the minister, with his hand over his heart; and Hester Prynne, with the embroidered letter glimmering on her bosom; and little Pearl, herself a symbol, and the connecting link between those two. They stood in the noon of that strange and solemn splendor, as if it were the light that is to reveal all secrets, and the daybreak that shall unite all who belong to one another.

There was witchcraft in little Pearl's eyes; and her face, as she glanced upward at the minister, wore that naughty smile which made its expression frequently so elfish. She withdrew her hand from Mr. Dimmesdale's, and pointed across the street.

But he clasped both his hands over his breast, and cast his eyes towards the zenith.

Nothing was more common, in those days, than to interpret all meteoric appearances, and other natural phenomena, that occurred with less regularity than the rise and set of sun and moon, as so many revelations from a supernatural source. Thus, a blazing spear, a sword of flame, a bow, or a sheaf of arrows, seen in the midnight sky, prefigured Indian warfare. Pestilence was known to have been foreboded by a shower of crimson light. We doubt whether any marked event, for good or evil, ever befell New England, from its settlement down to Revolutionary times, of which the inhabitants had not been previously warned by some spectacle of this nature. Not seldom, it had been seen by multitudes. Oftener, however, its credibility rested on the faith of some lonely eyewitness, who beheld the wonder through the colored, magnifying, and distorting medium of his imagination, and shaped it more distinctly in his after-thought. It was, indeed, a majestic idea, that the destiny of nations should be revealed, in these awful hieroglyphics, on the cope of heaven. A scroll so wide might not be deemed too expansive for Providence to write a people's doom upon. The belief was a favorite one with our forefathers, as betokening that their infant commonwealth was under a celestial guardianship of peculiar intimacy and strictness. But what shall we say, when an individual discovers a revelation, addressed to himself alone, on the same vast sheet of record! In such a case, it could only be the symptom of a highly disordered mental state, when a man, rendered morbidly self-contemplative by long, intense, and secret pain, had extended his egotism over the whole expanse of nature, until the firmament itself should appear no more than a fitting page for his soul's history and fate.

We impute it, therefore, solely to the disease in his own eye and heart, that the minister, looking upward to the zenith, beheld there the appearance of an immense letter,—the letter A,—marked out in lines of dull red light. Not but the meteor may have shown itself at that point, burning duskily through a veil of cloud; but with no such shape as his guilty imagination gave it; or, at least, with so little definiteness, that another's guilt might have seen another symbol in it.

There was a singular circumstance that characterized Mr. Dimmesdale's psychological state, at this moment. All the time that he gazed upward to the zenith, he was, nevertheless, perfectly aware that little Pearl was pointing her finger towards old Roger Chillingworth, who stood at no great distance from the scaffold. The minister appeared to see him, with the same glance that discerned the miraculous letter. To his features, as to all other objects, the meteoric light imparted a new expression; or it might well be that the physician was not careful then, as at all other times, to hide the malevolence with which he looked upon his victim. Certainly, if the meteor kindled up the sky, and disclosed the earth, with an awfulness that admonished Hester Prynne and the clergyman of the day of judgment, then might Roger Chillingworth have passed with them for the arch-fiend, standing there, with a smile and scowl, to claim his own. So vivid was the expression, or so intense the minister's perception of it, that it seemed still to remain painted on the darkness, after the meteor had vanished, with an effect as if the street and all things else were at once annihilated.

"Who is that man, Hester?" gasped Mr. Dimmesdale, overcome with terror. "I shiver at him! Dost thou know the man? I hate him, Hester!"

She remembered her oath, and was silent.

"I tell thee, my soul shivers at him," muttered the minister again. "Who is he? Who is he? Canst thou do nothing for me? I have a nameless horror of the man."

"Minister," said little Pearl, "I can tell thee who he is!"

"Quickly, then, child!" said the minister, bending his ear close to her lips. "Quickly!—and as low as thou canst whisper."

Pearl mumbled something into his ear, that sounded, indeed, like human language, but was only such gibberish as children may be heard amusing themselves with, by the hour together. At all events, if it involved any secret information in regard to old Roger Chillingworth, it was in a tongue unknown to the erudite clergyman, and did but increase the bewilderment of his mind. The elfish child then laughed aloud.

"Dost thou mock me now?" said the minister.

"Thou wast not bold!—thou wast not true!" answered the child. "Thou wouldst not promise to take my hand, and mother's hand, to-morrow noontide!"

"Worthy Sir," said the physician, who had now advanced to the foot of the platform. "Pious Master Dimmesdale! can this be you? Well, well, indeed! We men of study, whose heads are in our books, have need to be straitly looked after! We dream in our waking moments, and walk in our sleep. Come, good Sir, and my dear friend, I pray you, let me lead you home!"

"How knewest thou that I was here?" asked the minister, fearfully.

"Verily, and in good faith," answered Roger Chillingworth, "I knew nothing of the matter. I had spent the better part of the night at the bedside of the worshipful Governor Winthrop, doing what my poor skill might to give him ease. He going home to a better world, I, likewise, was on my way homeward, when this strange light shone out. Come with me, I beseech you, Reverend Sir; else you will be poorly able to do Sabbath duty to-morrow. Aha! see now, how they trouble the brain,—these books!—these books! You should study less, good Sir, and take a little pastime; or these night-whimseys will grow upon you!"

"I will go home with you," said Mr. Dimmesdale.

With a chill despondency, like one awaking, all nerveless, from an ugly dream, he yielded himself to the physician, and was led away.

The next day, however, being the Sabbath, he preached a discourse which was held to be the richest and most powerful, and the most replete with heavenly influences, that had ever proceeded from his lips. Souls, it is said, more souls than one, were brought to the truth by the efficacy of that sermon, and vowed within themselves to cherish a holy gratitude towards Mr. Dimmesdale throughout the long hereafter. But, as he came down the pulpit-steps, the gray-bearded sexton met him, holding up a black glove, which the minister recognized as his own.

"It was found," said the sexton, "this morning, on the scaffold, where evil-doers are set up to public shame. Satan dropped it there, I take it, intending a scurrilous jest against your reverence. But, indeed, he was blind and foolish, as he ever and always is. A pure hand needs no glove to cover it!"

"Thank you, my good friend," said the minister gravely, but startled at heart; for, so confused was his remembrance, that he had almost brought himself to look at the events of the past night as visionary. "Yes, it seems to be my glove indeed!"

"And, since Satan saw fit to steal it, your reverence must needs handle him without gloves, henceforward," remarked the old sexton, grimly smiling. "But did your reverence hear of the portent that was seen last night? A great red letter in the sky,—the letter A,—which we interpret to stand for Angel. For, as our good Governor Winthrop was made an angel this past night, it was doubtless held fit that there should be some notice thereof!"

"No," answered the minister. "I had not heard of it."

13. Another View of Hester

In her late singular interview with Mr. Dimmesdale, Hester Prynne was shocked at the condition to which she found the clergyman reduced. His nerve seemed absolutely destroyed. His moral force was abased into more than childish weakness.

It grovelled helpless on the ground, even while his intellectual faculties retained their pristine strength, or had perhaps acquired a morbid energy, which disease only could have given them. With her knowledge of a train of circumstances hidden from all others, she could readily infer, that, besides the legitimate action of his own conscience, a terrible machinery had been brought to bear, and was still operating, on Mr. Dimmesdale's well-being and repose. Knowing what this poor, fallen man had once been, her whole soul was moved by the shuddering terror with which he had appealed to her,—the outcast woman,—for support against his instinctively discovered enemy. She decided, moreover, that he had a right to her utmost aid. Little accustomed, in her long seclusion from society, to measure her ideas of right and wrong by any standard external to herself, Hester saw—or seemed to see—that there lay a responsibility upon her, in reference to the clergyman, which she owed to no other, nor to the whole world besides. The links that united her to the rest of human kind—links of flowers, or silk, or gold, or whatever the material—had all been broken. Here was the iron link of mutual crime, which neither he nor she could break. Like all other ties, it brought along with it its obligations.

Hester Prynne did not now occupy precisely the same position in which we beheld her during the earlier periods of her ignominy. Years had come, and gone. Pearl was now seven years old. Her mother, with the scarlet letter on her breast, glittering in its fantastic embroidery, had long been a familiar object to the townspeople. As is apt to be the case when a person stands out in any prominence before the community, and, at the same time, interferes neither with public nor individual interests and convenience, a species of general regard had ultimately grown up in reference to Hester Prynne. It is to the credit of human nature, that, except where its selfishness is brought into play, it loves more readily than it hates. Hatred, by a gradual and quiet process, will even be transformed to love, unless the change be impeded by a continually new irritation of the original feeling of hostility. In this matter of Hester Prynne, there was neither irritation nor irksomeness. She never battled with the public, but submitted uncomplainingly to its worst usage; she made no claim upon it, in requital for what she suffered; she did not weigh upon its sympathies. Then, also, the blameless purity of her life, during all these years in which she had been set apart to infamy, was reckoned largely in her favor. With nothing now to lose, in the sight of mankind, and with no hope, and seemingly no wish, of gaining any thing, it could only be a genuine regard for virtue that had brought back the poor wanderer to its paths.

It was perceived, too, that, while Hester never put forward even the humblest title to share in the world's privileges,— farther than to breathe the common air, and earn daily bread for little Pearl and herself by the faithful labor of her hands, —she was quick to acknowledge her sisterhood with the race of man, whenever benefits were to be conferred. None so ready as she to give of her little substance to every demand of poverty; even though the bitter-hearted pauper threw back a gibe in requital of the food brought regularly to his door, or the garments wrought for him by the fingers that could have embroidered a monarch's robe. None so self-devoted as Hester, when pestilence stalked through the town. In all seasons of calamity, indeed, whether general or of individuals, the outcast of society at once found her place. She came, not as a guest, but as a rightful inmate, into the household that was darkened by trouble; as if its gloomy twilight were a medium in which she was entitled to hold intercourse with her fellow-creatures. There glimmered the embroidered letter, with comfort in its unearthly ray. Elsewhere the token of sin, it was the taper of the sick-chamber. It had even thrown its gleam, in the sufferer's hard extremity, across the verge of time. It had shown him where to set his foot, while the light of earth was fast becoming dim, and ere the light of futurity could reach him. In such emergencies, Hester's nature showed itself warm and rich; a well-spring of human tenderness, unfailing to every

real demand, and inexhaustible by the largest. Her breast, with
its badge of shame, was but the softer pillow for the head that
needed one. She was self-ordained a Sister of Mercy; or, we
may rather say, the world's heavy hand had so ordained her,
when neither the world nor she looked forward to this result.
The letter was the symbol of her calling. Such helpfulness was
found in her,—so much power to do, and power to sympathize,
—that many people refused to interpret the scarlet A by its
original signification. They said that it meant Able; so strong
was Hester Prynne, with a woman's strength.

It was only the darkened house that could contain her.
When sunshine came again, she was not there. Her shadow
had faded across the threshold. The helpful inmate had departed, without one backward glance to gather up the meed
of gratitude, if any were in the hearts of those whom she had
served so zealously. Meeting them in the street, she never
raised her head to receive their greeting. If they were resolute
to accost her, she laid her finger on the scarlet letter, and
passed on. This might be pride, but was so like humility, that
it produced all the softening influence of the latter quality on
the public mind. The public is despotic in its temper; it is
capable of denying common justice, when too strenuously demanded as a right; but quite as frequently it awards more than
justice, when the appeal is made, as despots love to have it
made, entirely to its generosity. Interpreting Hester Prynne's
deportment as an appeal of this nature, society was inclined to
show its former victim a more benign countenance than she
cared to be favored with, or, perchance, than she deserved.

The rulers, and the wise and learned men of the community, were longer in acknowledging the influence of Hester's
good qualities than the people. The prejudices which they
shared in common with the latter were fortified in themselves
by an iron framework of reasoning, that made it a far tougher
labor to expel them. Day by day, nevertheless, their sour and
rigid wrinkles were relaxing into something which, in the due
course of years, might grow to be an expression of almost

benevolence. Thus it was with the men of rank, on whom their eminent position imposed the guardianship of the public morals. Individuals in private life, meanwhile, had quite forgiven Hester Prynne for her frailty; nay, more, they had begun to look upon the scarlet letter as the token, not of that one sin, for which she had borne so long and dreary a penance, but of her many good deeds since. "Do you see that woman with the embroidered badge?" they would say to strangers. "It is our Hester,—the town's own Hester,—who is so kind to the poor, so helpful to the sick, so comfortable to the afflicted!" Then, it is true, the propensity of human nature to tell the very worst of itself, when embodied in the person of another, would constrain them to whisper the black scandal of bygone years. It was none the less a fact, however, that, in the eyes of the very men who spoke thus, the scarlet letter had the effect of the cross on a nun's bosom. It imparted to the wearer a kind of sacredness, which enabled her to walk securely amid all peril. Had she fallen among thieves, it would have kept her safe. It was reported, and believed by many, that an Indian had drawn his arrow against the badge, and that the missile struck it, but fell harmless to the ground.

The effect of the symbol—or rather, of the position in respect to society that was indicated by it—on the mind of Hester Prynne herself, was powerful and peculiar. All the light and graceful foliage of her character had been withered up by this red-hot brand, and had long ago fallen away, leaving a bare and harsh outline, which might have been repulsive, had she possessed friends or companions to be repelled by it. Even the attractiveness of her person had undergone a similar change. It might be partly owing to the studied austerity of her dress, and partly to the lack of demonstration in her manners. It was a sad transformation, too, that her rich and luxuriant hair had either been cut off, or was so completely hidden by a cap, that not a shining lock of it ever once gushed into the sunshine. It was due in part to all these causes, but still more to something else, that there seemed to be no longer

any thing in Hester's face for Love to dwell upon; nothing
in Hester's form, though majestic and statue-like, that Passion would ever dream of clasping in its embrace; nothing in
Hester's bosom, to make it ever again the pillow of Affection.
Some attribute had departed from her, the permanence of
which had been essential to keep her a woman. Such is frequently the fate, and such the stern development, of the feminine character and person, when the woman has encountered,
and lived through, an experience of peculiar severity. If she
be all tenderness, she will die. If she survive, the tenderness
will either be crushed out of her, or—and the outward semblance is the same—crushed so deeply into her heart that it
can never show itself more. The latter is perhaps the truest
theory. She who has once been woman, and ceased to be so,
might at any moment become a woman again, if there were
only the magic touch to effect the transfiguration. We shall see
whether Hester Prynne were ever afterwards so touched, and
so transfigured.

Much of the marble coldness of Hester's impression was to
be attributed to the circumstance that her life had turned, in
a great measure, from passion and feeling, to thought. Standing alone in the world,—alone, as to any dependence on society, and with little Pearl to be guided and protected,—alone,
and hopeless of retrieving her position, even had she not
scorned to consider it desirable,—she cast away the fragments
of a broken chain. The world's law was no law for her mind.
It was an age in which the human intellect, newly emanci-
pated, had taken a more active and a wider range than for
many centuries before. Men of the sword had overthrown
nobles and kings. Men bolder than these had overthrown and
rearranged—not actually, but within the sphere of theory,
which was their most real abode—the whole system of ancient prejudice, wherewith was linked much of ancient principle. Hester Prynne imbibed this spirit. She assumed a freedom of speculation, then common enough on the other side
of the Atlantic, but which our forefathers, had they known

of it, would have held to be a deadlier crime than that stig-
matized by the scarlet letter. In her lonesome cottage, by the
sea-shore, thoughts visited her, such as dared to enter no other
dwelling in New England; shadowy guests, that would have
been as perilous as demons to their entertainer, could they
have been seen so much as knocking at her door.

It is remarkable, that persons who speculate the most boldly
often conform with the most perfect quietude to the external regulations of society. The thought suffices them, without
investing itself in the flesh and blood of action. So it seemed
to be with Hester. Yet, had little Pearl never come to her
from the spiritual world, it might have been far otherwise.
Then, she might have come down to us in history, hand in
hand with Ann Hutchinson, as the foundress of a religious
sect. She might, in one of her phases, have been a prophetess.
She might, and not improbably would, have suffered death
from the stern tribunals of the period, for attempting to un-
dermine the foundations of the Puritan establishment. But,
in the education of her child, the mother's enthusiasm of
thought had something to wreak itself upon. Providence, in
the person of this little girl, had assigned to Hester's charge
the germ and blossom of womanhood, to be cherished and developed amid a host of difficulties. Every thing was against
her. The world was hostile. The child's own nature had something wrong in it, which continually betokened that she had
been born amiss,—the effluence of her mother's lawless passion,—and often impelled Hester to ask, in bitterness of heart,
whether it were for ill or good that the poor little creature
had been born at all.

Indeed, the same dark question often rose into her mind,
with reference to the whole race of womanhood. Was existence worth accepting, even to the happiest among them? As
concerned her own individual existence, she had long ago decided in the negative, and dismissed the point as settled. A
tendency to speculation, though it may keep woman quiet,
as it does man, yet makes her sad. She discerns, it may be,

such a hopeless task before her. As a first step, the whole system of society is to be torn down, and built up anew. Then, the very nature of the opposite sex, or its long hereditary habit, which has become like nature, is to be essentially modified, before woman can be allowed to assume what seems a fair and suitable position. Finally, all other difficulties being obviated, woman cannot take advantage of these preliminary reforms, until she herself shall have undergone a still mightier change; in which, perhaps, the ethereal essence, wherein she has her truest life, will be found to have evaporated. A woman never overcomes these problems by any exercise of thought. They are not to be solved, or only in one way. If her heart chance to come uppermost, they vanish. Thus, Hester Prynne, whose heart had lost its regular and healthy throb, wandered without a clew in the dark labyrinth of mind; now turned aside by an insurmountable precipice; now starting back from a deep chasm. There was wild and ghastly scenery all around her, and a home and comfort nowhere. At times, a fearful doubt strove to possess her soul, whether it were not better to send Pearl at once to heaven, and go herself to such futurity as Eternal Justice should provide.

The scarlet letter had not done its office.

Now, however, her interview with the Reverend Mr. Dimmesdale, on the night of his vigil, had given her a new theme of reflection, and held up to her an object that appeared worthy of any exertion and sacrifice for its attainment. She had witnessed the intense misery beneath which the minister struggled, or, to speak more accurately, had ceased to struggle. She saw that he stood on the verge of lunacy, if he had not already stepped across it. It was impossible to doubt, that, whatever painful efficacy there might be in the secret sting of remorse, a deadlier venom had been infused into it by the hand that proffered relief. A secret enemy had been continually by his side, under the semblance of a friend and helper, and had availed himself of the opportunities thus afforded for tampering with the delicate springs of Mr. Dimmes-

dale's nature. Hester could not but ask herself, whether there
had not originally been a defect of truth, courage, and loyalty,
on her own part, in allowing the minister to be thrown into
a position where so much evil was to be foreboded, and nothing auspicious to be hoped. Her only justification lay in the
fact, that she had been able to discern no method of rescuing
him from a blacker ruin than had overwhelmed herself, except
by acquiescing in Roger Chillingworth's scheme of disguise.
Under that impulse, she had made her choice, and had chosen,
as it now appeared, the more wretched alternative of the two.
She determined to redeem her error, so far as it might yet be
possible. Strengthened by years of hard and solemn trial, she
felt herself no longer so inadequate to cope with Roger Chillingworth as on that night, abased by sin, and half maddened
by the ignominy that was still new, when they had talked
together in the prison-chamber. She had climbed her way,
since then, to a higher point. The old man, on the other hand,
had brought himself nearer to her level, or perhaps below it,
by the revenge which he had stooped for.

In fine, Hester Prynne resolved to meet her former husband,
and do what might be in her power for the rescue of the victim on whom he had so evidently set his gripe. The occasion
was not long to seek. One afternoon, walking with Pearl in a
retired part of the peninsula, she beheld the old physician, with
a basket on one arm, and a staff in the other hand, stooping
along the ground, in quest of roots and herbs to concoct his
medicines withal.

14. Hester and the Physician

HESTER bade little Pearl run down to the margin of the water, and play with the shells and tangled sea-weed, until she should have talked awhile with yonder gatherer of herbs. So the child flew away like a bird, and, making bare her small white feet, went pattering along the moist margin of the sea. Here and there, she came to a full stop, and peeped curiously into a pool, left by the retiring tide as a mirror for Pearl to see her face in. Forth peeped at her, out of the pool, with dark, glistening curls around her head, and an elf-smile in her eyes, the image of a little maid, whom Pearl, having no other playmate, invited to take her hand and run a race with her. But the visionary little maid, on her part, beckoned likewise, as if to say,—"This is a better place! Come thou into the pool!" And Pearl, stepping in, mid-leg deep, beheld her own white feet at the bottom; while, out of a still lower depth, came the gleam of a kind of fragmentary smile, floating to and fro in the agitated water.

Meanwhile, her mother had accosted the physician.

"I would speak a word with you," said she,—"a word that concerns us much."

"Aha! And is it Mistress Hester that has a word for old Roger Chillingworth?" answered he, raising himself from his stooping posture. "With all my heart! Why, Mistress, I hear good tidings of you on all hands! No longer ago than yester-eve, a magistrate, a wise and godly man, was discoursing of your affairs, Mistress Hester, and whispered me that there had been question concerning you in the council. It was debated whether or no, with safety to the common weal, yonder scarlet letter might be taken off your bosom. On my life, Hester, I made my entreaty to the worshipful magistrate that it might be done forthwith!"

"It lies not in the pleasure of the magistrates to take off this badge," calmly replied Hester. "Were I worthy to be quit of it, it would fall away of its own nature, or be transformed into something that should speak a different purport."

"Nay, then, wear it, if it suit you better," rejoined he. "A woman must needs follow her own fancy, touching the adornment of her person. The letter is gayly embroidered, and shows right bravely on your bosom!"

All this while, Hester had been looking steadily at the old man, and was shocked, as well as wonder-smitten, to discern what a change had been wrought upon him within the past seven years. It was not so much that he had grown older; for though the traces of advancing life were visible, he bore his age well, and seemed to retain a wiry vigor and alertness. But the former aspect of an intellectual and studious man, calm and quiet, which was what she best remembered in him, had altogether vanished, and been succeeded by an eager, searching, almost fierce, yet carefully guarded look. It seemed to be his wish and purpose to mask this expression with a smile; but the latter played him false, and flickered over his visage so derisively, that the spectator could see his blackness all the better for it. Ever and anon, too, there came a glare of red light out of his eyes; as if the old man's soul were on fire, and kept on smouldering duskily within his breast, until, by some casual puff of passion, it was blown into a momentary flame. This he repressed as speedily as possible, and strove to look as if nothing of the kind had happened.

In a word, old Roger Chillingworth was a striking evidence of man's faculty of transforming himself into a devil, if he will only, for a reasonable space of time, undertake a devil's office. This unhappy person had effected such a transformation by devoting himself, for seven years, to the constant analysis of a heart full of torture, and deriving his enjoyment thence, and adding fuel to those fiery tortures which he analyzed and gloated over.

The scarlet letter burned on Hester Prynne's bosom. Here was another ruin, the responsibility of which came partly home to her.

"What see you in my face," asked the physician, "that you look at it so earnestly?"

"Something that would make me weep, if there were any tears bitter enough for it," answered she. "But let it pass! It is of yonder miserable man that I would speak."

"And what of him?" cried Roger Chillingworth eagerly, as if he loved the topic, and were glad of an opportunity to discuss it with the only person of whom he could make a confidant. "Not to hide the truth, Mistress ·Hester, my thoughts happen just now to be busy with the gentleman. So speak freely; and I will make answer."

"When we last spake together," said Hester, "now seven years ago, it was your pleasure to extort a promise of secrecy, as touching the former relation betwixt yourself and me. As the life and good fame of yonder man were in your hands, there seemed no choice to me, save to be silent, in accordance with your behest. Yet it was not without heavy misgivings that I thus bound myself; for, having cast off all duty towards other human beings, there remained a duty towards him; and something whispered me that I was betraying it, in pledging myself to keep your counsel. Since that day, no man is so near to him as you. You tread behind his every footstep. You are beside him, sleeping and waking. You search his thoughts. You burrow and rankle in his heart! Your clutch is on his life, and you cause him to die daily a living death; and still he knows you not. In permitting this, I have surely acted a false part by the only man to whom the power was left me to be true!"

"What choice had you?" asked Roger Chillingworth. "My finger, pointed at this man, would have hurled him from his pulpit into a dungeon,—thence, peradventure, to the gallows!"

"It had been better so!" said Hester Prynne.

"What evil have I done the man?" asked Roger Chilling-worth again. "I tell thee, Hester Prynne, the richest fee that ever physician earned from monarch could not have bought such care as I have wasted on this miserable priest! But for my aid, his life would have burned away in torments, within the first two years after the perpetration of his crime and thine. For, Hester, his spirit lacked the strength that could have borne up, as thine has, beneath a burden like thy scarlet letter. O, I could reveal a goodly secret! But enough! What art can do, I have exhausted on him. That he now breathes, and creeps about on earth, is owing all to me!"

"Better he had died at once!" said Hester Prynne.

"Yea, woman, thou sayest truly!" cried old Roger Chilling-worth, letting the lurid fire of his heart blaze out before her eyes. "Better had he died at once! Never did mortal suffer what this man has suffered. And all, all, in the sight of his worst enemy! He had been conscious of me. He has felt an influence dwelling always upon him like a curse. He knew, by some spiritual sense,—for the Creator never made another being so sensitive as this,—he knew that no friendly hand was pulling at his heart-strings, and that an eye was looking curi-ously into him, which sought only evil, and found it. But he knew not that the eye and hand were mine! With the super-stition common to his brotherhood, he fancied himself given over to a fiend, to be tortured with frightful dreams, and desperate thoughts, the sting of remorse, and despair of par-don; as a foretaste of what awaits him beyond the grave. But it was the constant shadow of my presence!—the closest pro-pinquity of the man whom he had most vilely wronged!—and who had grown to exist only by this perpetual poison of the direst revenge! Yea, indeed!—he did not err!—there was a fiend at his elbow! A mortal man, with once a human heart, has become a fiend for his especial torment!"

The unfortunate physician, while uttering these words, lifted his hands with a look of horror, as if he had beheld some frightful shape, which he could not recognize, usurping the place of his own image in a glass. It was one of those moments —which sometimes occur only at the interval of years—when a man's moral aspect is faithfully revealed to his mind's eye. Not improbably, he had never before viewed himself as he did now.

"Hast thou not tortured him enough?" said Hester, noticing the old man's look. "Has he not paid thee all?"

"No!—no!—He has but increased the debt!" answered the physician; and, as he proceeded, his manner lost its fiercer characteristics, and subsided into gloom. "Dost thou remember me, Hester, as I was nine years agone? Even then, I was in the autumn of my days, nor was it the early autumn. But all my life had been made up of earnest, studious, thoughtful, quiet years, bestowed faithfully for the increase of mine own knowledge, and faithfully, too, though this latter object was but casual to the other,—faithfully for the advancement of human welfare. No life had been more peaceful and innocent than mine; few lives so rich with benefits conferred. Dost thou remember me? Was I not, though you might deem me cold, nevertheless a man thoughtful for others, craving little for himself,—kind, true, just, and of constant, if not warm affections? Was I not all this?"

"All this, and more," said Hester.

"And what am I now?" demanded he, looking into her face, and permitting the whole evil within him to be written on his features. "I have already told thee what I am! A fiend! Who made me so?"

"It was myself!" cried Hester, shuddering. "It was I, not less than he. Why hast thou not avenged thyself on me?"

"I have left thee to the scarlet letter," replied Roger Chillingworth. "If that have not avenged me, I can do no more!"

He laid his finger on it, with a smile.

"It has avenged thee!" answered Hester Prynne.

"I judged no less," said the physician. "And now, what wouldst thou with me touching this man?"

"I must reveal the secret," answered Hester, firmly. "He must discern thee in thy true character. What may be the result, I know not. But this long debt of confidence, due from me to him, whose bane and ruin I have been, shall at length be paid. So far as concerns the overthrow or preservation of his fair fame and his earthly state, and perchance his life, he is in thy hands. Nor do I,—whom the scarlet letter has disciplined to truth, though it be the truth of red-hot iron, entering into the soul,—nor do I perceive such advantage in his living any longer a life of ghastly emptiness, that I shall stoop to implore thy mercy. Do with him as thou wilt! There is no good for him,—no good for me,—no good for thee! There is no good for little Pearl! There is no path to guide us out of this dismal maze!"

"Woman, I could wellnigh pity thee!" said Roger Chillingworth, unable to restrain a thrill of admiration too; for there was a quality almost majestic in the despair which she expressed. "Thou hadst great elements. Peradventure, hadst thou met earlier with a better love than mine, this evil had not been. I pity thee, for the good that has been wasted in thy nature!"

"And I thee," answered Hester Prynne, "for the hatred that has transformed a wise and just man to a fiend! Wilt thou yet purge it out of thee, and be once more human? If not for his sake, then doubly for thine own! Forgive, and leave his further retribution to the Power that claims it! I said, but now, that there could be no good event for him, or thee, or me, who are here wandering together in this gloomy maze of evil, and stumbling, at every step, over the guilt wherewith we have strewn our path. It is not so! There might be good for thee, and thee alone, since thou hast been deeply wronged, and hast it at thy will to pardon. Wilt thou give up that only privilege? Wilt thou reject that priceless benefit?"

"Peace, Hester, peace!" replied the old man, with gloomy sternness. "It is not granted me to pardon. I have no such power as thou tellest me of. My old faith, long forgotten, comes back to me, and explains all that we do, and all we suffer. By thy first step awry, thou didst plant the germ of evil; but, since that moment, it has all been a dark necessity. Ye that have wronged me are not sinful, save in a kind of typical illusion; neither am I fiend-like, who have snatched a fiend's office from his hands. It is our fate. Let the black flower blossom as it may! Now go thy ways, and deal as thou wilt with yonder man."

He waved his hand, and betook himself again to his employment of gathering herbs.

15. Hester and Pearl

So ROGER CHILLINGWORTH—a deformed old figure, with a face that haunted men's memories longer than they liked—took leave of Hester Prynne, and went stooping away along the earth. He gathered here and there an herb, or grubbed up a root, and put it into the basket on his arm. His gray beard almost touched the ground, as he crept onward. Hester gazed after him a little while, looking with a half-fantastic curiosity to see whether the tender grass of early spring would not be blighted beneath him, and show the wavering track of his footsteps, sere and brown, across its cheerful verdure. She wondered what sort of herbs they were, which the old man was so sedulous to gather. Would not the earth, quickened to an evil purpose by the sympathy of his eye, greet him with poisonous shrubs, of species hitherto unknown, that would start up under his fingers? Or might it suffice him, that every wholesome growth should be converted into something deleterious and malignant at his touch? Did the sun, which shone so brightly everywhere else, really fall upon him? Or was there, as it rather seemed, a circle of ominous shadow moving along with his deformity, whichever way he turned himself? And whither was he now going? Would he not suddenly sink into the earth, leaving a barren and blasted spot, where, in due course of time, would be seen deadly nightshade, dogwood, henbane, and whatever else of vegetable wickedness the climate could produce, all flourishing with hideous luxuriance? Or would he spread bat's wings and flee away, looking so much the uglier, the higher he rose towards heaven?

"Be it sin or no," said Hester Prynne bitterly, as she still gazed after him, "I hate the man!"

She upbraided herself for the sentiment, but could not overcome or lessen it. Attempting to do so, she thought of those long-past days, in a distant land, when he used to emerge at eventide from the seclusion of his study, and sit down in the fire-light of their home, and in the light of her nuptial smile. He needed to bask himself in that smile, he said, in order that the chill of so many lonely hours among his books might be taken off the scholar's heart. Such scenes had once appeared not otherwise than happy, but now, as viewed through the dismal medium of her subsequent life, they classed themselves among her ugliest remembrances. She marvelled how such scenes could have been! She marvelled how she could ever have been wrought upon to marry him! She deemed it her crime most to be repented of, that she had ever endured, and reciprocated, the lukewarm grasp of his hand, and had suffered the smile of her lips and eyes to mingle and melt into his own. And it seemed a fouler offence committed by Roger Chillingworth, than any which had since been done him, that, in the time when her heart knew no better, he had persuaded her to fancy herself happy by his side.

"Yes, I hate him!" repeated Hester, more bitterly than before. "He betrayed me! He has done me worse wrong than I did him!"

Let men tremble to win the hand of woman, unless they

win along with it the utmost passion of her heart! Else it may
be their miserable fortune, as it was Roger Chillingworth's,
when some mightier touch than their own may have awakened
all her sensibilities, to be reproached even for the calm content, the marble image of happiness, which they will have imposed upon her as the warm reality. But Hester ought long
ago to have done with this injustice. What did it betoken?
Had seven long years, under the torture of the scarlet letter,
inflicted so much of misery, and wrought out no repentance?

The emotions of that brief space, while she stood gazing
after the crooked figure of old Roger Chillingworth, threw
a dark light on Hester's state of mind, revealing much that
she might not otherwise have acknowledged to herself.

He being gone, she summoned back her child.

"Pearl! Little Pearl! Where are you?"

Pearl, whose activity of spirit never flagged, had been at
no loss for amusement while her mother talked with the old
gatherer of herbs. At first, as already told, she had flirted fanci-
fully with her own image in a pool of water, beckoning the
phantom forth, and—as it declined to venture—seeking a passage for herself into its sphere of impalpable earth and unattainable sky. Soon finding, however, that either she or the
image was unreal, she turned elsewhere for better pastime.
She made little boats out of birch-bark, and freighted them
with snail-shells, and sent out more ventures on the mighty
deep than any merchant in New England; but the larger part
of them foundered near the shore. She seized a live horseshoe
by the tail, and made prize of several five-fingers, and laid out
a jelly-fish to melt in the warm sun. Then she took up the
white foam, that streaked the line of the advancing tide, and
threw it upon the breeze, scampering after it with winged
footsteps, to catch the great snow-flakes ere they fell. Perceiving a flock of beach-birds, that fed and fluttered along the
shore, the naughty child picked up her apron full of pebbles,
and, creeping from rock to rock after these small sea-fowl,
displayed remarkable dexterity in pelting them. One little gray

bird, with a white breast, Pearl was almost sure, had been hit by a pebble, and fluttered away with a broken wing. But then the elf-child sighed, and gave up her sport; because it grieved her to have done harm to a little being that was as wild as the sea-breeze, or as wild as Pearl herself.

Her final employment was to gather sea-weed, of various kinds, and make herself a scarf, or mantle, and a head-dress, and thus assume the aspect of a little mermaid. She inherited her mother's gift for devising drapery and costume. As the last touch to her mermaid's garb, Pearl took some eel-grass, and imitated, as best she could, on her own bosom, the decoration with which she was so familiar on her mother's. A letter, —the letter A,—but freshly green, instead of scarlet! The child bent her chin upon her breast, and contemplated this device with strange interest; even as if the one only thing for which she had been sent into the world was to make out its hidden import.

"I wonder if mother will ask me what it means!" thought Pearl.

Just then, she heard her mother's voice, and, flitting along as lightly as one of the little sea-birds, appeared before Hester Prynne, dancing, laughing, and pointing her finger to the ornament upon her bosom.

"My little Pearl," said Hester, after a moment's silence, "the green letter, and on thy childish bosom, has no purport. But dost thou know, my child, what this letter means which thy mother is doomed to wear?"

"Yes, mother," said the child. "It is the great letter A. Thou hast taught it me in the horn-book."

Hester looked steadily into her little face; but, though there was that singular expression which she had so often remarked in her black eyes, she could not satisfy herself whether Pearl really attached any meaning to the symbol. She felt a morbid desire to ascertain the point.

"Dost thou know, child, wherefore thy mother wears this letter?"

"Truly do I!" answered Pearl, looking brightly into her mother's face. "It is for the same reason that the minister keeps his hand over his heart!"

"And what reason is that?" asked Hester, half smiling at the absurd incongruity of the child's observation; but, on second thoughts, turning pale. "What has the letter to do with any heart, save mine?"

"Nay, mother, I have told all I know," said Pearl, more seriously than she was wont to speak. "Ask yonder old man whom thou hast been talking with! It may be he can tell. But in good earnest now, mother dear, what does this scarlet letter mean?—and why dost thou wear it on thy bosom?—and why does the minister keep his hand over his heart?"

She took her mother's hand in both her own, and gazed into her eyes with an earnestness that was seldom seen in her wild and capricious character. The thought occurred to Hester, that the child might really be seeking to approach her with childlike confidence, and doing what she could, and as intelligently as she knew how, to establish a meeting-point of sympathy. It showed Pearl in an unwonted aspect. Heretofore, the mother, while loving her child with the intensity of a sole affection, had schooled herself to hope for little other return than the waywardness of an April breeze; which spends its time in airy sport, and has its gusts of inexplicable passion, and is petulant in its best of moods, and chills oftener than caresses you, when you take it to your bosom; in requital of which misdemeanours, it will sometimes, of its own vague purpose, kiss your cheek with a kind of doubtful tenderness, and play gently with your hair, and then begone about its other idle business, leaving a dreamy pleasure at your heart. And this, moreover, was a mother's estimate of the child's disposition. Any other observer might have seen few but unamiable traits, and have given them a far darker coloring. But now the idea came strongly into Hester's mind, that Pearl, with her remarkable precocity and acuteness, might already have approached the age when she could be made a friend, and intrusted with as much of her mother's sorrows as could be imparted, without irreverence either to the parent or the child. In the little chaos of Pearl's character, there might be seen emerging—and could have been, from the very first— the stedfast principles of an unflinching courage,—an uncontrollable will,—a sturdy pride, which might be disciplined into self-respect,—and a bitter scorn of many things, which, when examined, might be found to have the taint of falsehood in them. She possessed affections, too, though hitherto acrid and disagreeable, as are the richest flavors of unripe fruit. With all these sterling attributes, thought Hester, the evil which she inherited from her mother must be great indeed, if a noble woman do not grow out of this elfish child.

Pearl's inevitable tendency to hover about the enigma of the scarlet letter seemed an innate quality of her being. From the earliest epoch of her conscious life, she had entered upon this as her appointed mission. Hester had often fancied that Providence had a design of justice and retribution, in endowing the child with this marked propensity; but never, until now, had she bethought herself to ask, whether, linked with that design, there might not likewise be a purpose of mercy and beneficence. If little Pearl were entertained with faith and trust, as a spirit-messenger no less than an earthly child, might it not be her errand to soothe away the sorrow that lay cold in her mother's heart, and converted it into a tomb?— and to help her to overcome the passion, once so wild, and even yet neither dead nor asleep, but only imprisoned within the same tomb-like heart?

Such were some of the thoughts that now stirred in Hester's mind, with as much vivacity of impression as if they had actually been whispered into her ear. And there was little Pearl, all this while, holding her mother's hand in both her own, and turning her face upward, while she put these searching questions, once, and again, and still a third time.

"What does the letter mean, mother?—and why dost thou wear it?—and why does the minister keep his hand over his heart?"

"What shall I say?" thought Hester to herself.—"No! If this be the price of the child's sympathy, I cannot pay it!"

Then she spoke aloud.

"Silly Pearl," said she, "what questions are these? There are many things in this world that a child must not ask about. What know I of the minister's heart? And as for the scarlet letter, I wear it for the sake of its gold thread!"

In all the seven bygone years, Hester Prynne had never before been false to the symbol on her bosom. It may be that it was the talisman of a stern and severe, but yet a guardian spirit, who now forsook her; as recognizing that, in spite of his strict watch over her heart, some new evil had crept into it, or some old one had never been expelled. As for little Pearl, the earnestness soon passed out of her face.

But the child did not see fit to let the matter drop. Two or three times, as her mother and she went homeward, and as often at supper-time, and while Hester was putting her to bed, and once after she seemed to be fairly asleep, Pearl looked up, with mischief gleaming in her black eyes.

"Mother," said she, "what does the scarlet letter mean?"

And the next morning, the first indication the child gave of being awake was by popping up her head from the pillow, and making that other inquiry, which she had so unaccountably connected with her investigations about the scarlet letter:—

"Mother!—Mother!—Why does the minister keep his hand over his heart?"

"Hold thy tongue, naughty child!" answered her mother, with an asperity that she had never permitted to herself before. "Do not tease me; else I shall shut thee into the dark closet!"

16. A Forest Walk

HESTER PRYNNE remained constant in her resolve to make known to Mr. Dimmesdale, at whatever risk of present pain or ulterior consequences, the true character of the man who had crept into his intimacy. For several days, however, she vainly sought an opportunity of addressing him in some of the meditative walks which she knew him to be in the habit of taking, along the shores of the peninsula, or on the wooded hills of the neighbouring country. There would have been no scandal, indeed, nor peril to the holy whiteness of the clergyman's good fame, had she visited him in his own study; where many a penitent, ere now, had confessed sins of perhaps as deep a dye as the one betokened by the scarlet letter. But, partly that she dreaded the secret or undisguised interference of old Roger Chillingworth, and partly that her conscious heart imputed suspicion where none could have been felt, and partly that both the minister and she would need the whole wide world to breathe in, while they talked together,—for all these reasons, Hester never thought of meeting him in any narrower privacy than beneath the open sky.

At last, while attending in a sick-chamber, whither the Reverend Mr. Dimmesdale had been summoned to make a prayer, she learnt that he had gone, the day before, to visit the Apostle Eliot,[1] among his Indian converts. He would probably return, by a certain hour, in the afternoon of the morrow. Betimes, therefore, the next day, Hester took little Pearl, —who was necessarily the companion of all her mother's expeditions, however inconvenient her presence,—and set forth.

The road, after the two wayfarers had crossed from the

[1] John Eliot (1604–1690), "Apostle of the Indians," was minister of the church of Roxbury and one of the Puritans' few missionaries to the Indians. He translated the Bible into the Indian language and wrote an Indian grammar and catechism.

peninsula to the mainland, was no other than a footpath. It straggled onward into the mystery of the primeval forest. This hemmed it in so narrowly, and stood so black and dense on either side, and disclosed such imperfect glimpses of the sky above, that, to Hester's mind, it imaged not amiss the moral wilderness in which she had so long been wandering. The day was chill and sombre. Overhead was a gray expanse of cloud, slightly stirred, however, by a breeze; so that a gleam of flickering sunshine might now and then be seen at its solitary play upon the path. This flitting cheerfulness was always at the farther extremity of some long vista through the forest. The sportive sunlight—feebly sportive, at best, in the predominant pensiveness of the day and scene—withdrew itself as they came nigh, and left the spots where it had danced the drearier, because they had hoped to find them bright.

"Mother," said little Pearl, "the sunshine does not love you. It runs away and hides itself, because it is afraid of something on your bosom. Now, see! There it is, playing, a good way off. Stand you here, and let me run and catch it. I am but a child. It will not flee from me; for I wear nothing on my bosom yet!"

"Nor ever will, my child, I hope," said Hester.

"And why not, mother?" asked Pearl, stopping short, just at the beginning of her race. "Will not it come of its own accord, when I am a woman grown?"

"Run away, child," answered her mother, "and catch the sunshine! It will soon be gone."

Pearl set forth, at a great pace, and, as Hester smiled to perceive, did actually catch the sunshine, and stood laughing in the midst of it, all brightened by its splendor, and scintillating with the vivacity excited by rapid motion. The light lingered about the lonely child, as if glad of such a playmate, until her mother had drawn almost nigh enough to step into the magic circle too.

"It will go now!" said Pearl, shaking her head.

"See!" answered Hester, smiling. "Now I can stretch out my hand, and grasp some of it."

As she attempted to do so, the sunshine vanished; or, to judge from the bright expression that was dancing on Pearl's features, her mother could have fancied that the child had absorbed it into herself, and would give it forth again, with a gleam about her path, as they should plunge into some gloomier shade. There was no other attribute that so much impressed her with a sense of new and untransmitted vigor in Pearl's nature, as this never-failing vivacity of spirits; she had not the disease of sadness, which almost all children, in these latter days, inherit, with the scrofula, from the troubles of their ancestors. Perhaps this too was a disease, and but the reflex of the wild energy with which Hester had fought against her sorrows, before Pearl's birth. It was certainly a doubtful charm, imparting a hard, metallic lustre to the child's character. She wanted—what some people want throughout life— a grief that should deeply touch her, and thus humanize and make her capable of sympathy. But there was time enough yet for little Pearl!

"Come, my child!" said Hester, looking about her, from the spot where Pearl had stood still in the sunshine. "We will sit down a little way within the wood, and rest ourselves."

"I am not aweary, mother," replied the little girl. "But you may sit down, if you will tell me a story meanwhile."

"A story, child!" said Hester. "And about what?"

"O, a story about the Black Man!" answered Pearl, taking hold of her mother's gown, and looking up, half earnestly, half mischievously, into her face. "How he haunts this forest, and carries a book with him,—a big, heavy book, with iron clasps; and how this ugly Black Man offers his book and an iron pen to every body that meets him here among the trees; and they are to write their names with their own blood. And then he sets his mark on their bosoms! Didst thou ever meet the Black Man, mother?"

"And who told you this story, Pearl?" asked her mother, recognizing a common superstition of the period.

"It was the old dame in the chimney-corner, at the house where you watched last night," said the child. "But she fancied me asleep while she was talking of it. She said that a thousand and a thousand people had met him here, and had written in his book, and have his mark on them. And that ugly-tempered lady, old Mistress Hibbins, was one. And, mother, the old dame said that this scarlet letter was the Black Man's mark on thee, and that it glows like a red flame when thou meetest him at midnight, here in the dark wood. Is it true, mother? And dost thou go to meet him in the night-time?"

"Didst thou ever awake, and find thy mother gone?" asked Hester.

"Not that I remember," said the child. "If thou fearest to leave me in our cottage, thou mightest take me along with thee. I would very gladly go! But, mother, tell me now! Is there such a Black Man? And didst thou ever meet him? And is this his mark?"

"Wilt thou let me be at peace, if I once tell thee?" asked her mother.

"Yes, if thou tellest me all," answered Pearl.

"Once in my life I met the Black Man!" said her mother. "This scarlet letter is his mark!"

Thus conversing, they entered sufficiently deep into the wood to secure themselves from the observation of any casual passenger along the forest-track. Here they sat down on a luxuriant heap of moss; which, at some epoch of the preceding century, had been a gigantic pine, with its roots and trunk in the darksome shade, and its head aloft in the upper atmosphere. It was a little dell where they had seated themselves, with a leaf-strewn bank rising gently on either side, and a brook flowing through the midst, over a bed of fallen and drowned leaves. The trees impending over it had flung down great branches, from time to time, which choked up the current, and compelled it to form eddies and black depths at some points; while, in its swifter and livelier passages, there appeared a channel-way of pebbles, and brown, sparkling sand. Letting the eyes follow along the course of the stream, they could catch the reflected light from its water, at some short distance within the forest, but soon lost all traces of it amid the bewilderment of tree-trunks and underbrush, and here and there a huge rock, covered over with gray lichens. All these giant trees and boulders of granite seemed intent on making a mystery of the course of this small brook; fearing, perhaps, that, with its never-ceasing loquacity, it should whisper tales out of the heart of the old forest whence it flowed, or mirror its revelations on the smooth surface of a pool. Continually, indeed, as it stole onward, the streamlet kept up a babble, kind, quiet, soothing, but melancholy, like the voice of a young child that was spending its infancy without playfulness, and knew not how to be merry among sad acquaintance and events of sombre hue.

"O brook! O foolish and tiresome little brook!" cried Pearl, after listening awhile to its talk. "Why art thou so sad? Pluck up a spirit, and do not be all the time sighing and murmuring!"

But the brook, in the course of its little lifetime among the forest-trees, had gone through so solemn an experience that it could not help talking about it, and seemed to have nothing else to say. Pearl resembled the brook, inasmuch as the current of her life gushed from a well-spring as mysterious, and had flowed through scenes shadowed as heavily with gloom. But, unlike the little stream, she danced and sparkled, and prattled airily along her course.

"What does this sad little brook say, mother?" inquired she.

"If thou hadst a sorrow of thine own, the brook might tell thee of it," answered her mother, "even as it is telling me of mine! But now, Pearl, I hear a footstep along the path, and the noise of one putting aside the branches. I would have thee betake thyself to play, and leave me to speak with him that comes yonder."

"Is it the Black Man?" asked Pearl.

"Wilt thou go and play, child?" repeated her mother. "But do not stray far into the wood. And take heed that thou come at my first call."

"Yes, mother," answered Pearl. "But, if it be the Black Man, wilt thou not let me stay a moment, and look at him, with his big book under his arm?"

"Go, silly child!" said her mother, impatiently. "It is no Black Man! Thou canst see him now through the trees. It is the minister!"

"And so it is!" said the child. "And, mother, he has his hand over his heart! Is it because, when the minister wrote his name in the book, the Black Man set his mark in that place? But why does he not wear it outside his bosom, as thou dost, mother?"

"Go now, child, and thou shalt tease me as thou wilt another time!" cried Hester Prynne. "But do not stray far. Keep where thou canst hear the babble of the brook."

The child went singing away, following up the current of the brook, and striving to mingle a more lightsome cadence with its melancholy voice. But the little stream would not be comforted, and still kept telling its unintelligible secret of some very mournful mystery that had happened—or making a prophetic lamentation about something that was yet to happen—within the verge of the dismal forest. So Pearl, who had enough of shadow in her own little life, chose to break off all acquaintance with this repining brook. She set herself, therefore, to gathering violets and wood-anemones, and some scarlet columbines that she found growing in the crevices of a high rock.

When her elf-child had departed, Hester Prynne made a step or two towards the track that led through the forest, but still remained under the deep shadow of the trees. She beheld the minister advancing along the path, entirely alone, and leaning on a staff which he had cut by the way-side. He looked haggard and feeble, and betrayed a nerveless despondency in his air, which had never so remarkably characterized him in his walks about the settlement, nor in any other situation where he deemed himself liable to notice. Here it was wofully visible, in this intense seclusion of the forest, which of itself would have been a heavy trial to the spirits. There was a listlessness in his gait; as if he saw no reason for taking one step farther, nor felt any desire to do so, but would have been glad, could he be glad of any thing, to fling himself down at the root of the nearest tree, and lie there passive for evermore. The leaves might bestrew him, and the soil gradually accumulate and form a little hillock over his frame, no matter whether there were life in it or no. Death was too definite an object to be wished for, or avoided.

To Hester's eye, the Reverend Mr. Dimmesdale exhibited no symptom of positive and vivacious suffering, except that, as little Pearl had remarked, he kept his hand over his heart.

17. The Pastor and His Parishioner

SLOWLY as the minister walked, he had almost gone by, before Hester Prynne could gather voice enough to attract his observation. At length, she succeeded.

"Arthur Dimmesdale!" she said, faintly at first; then louder, but hoarsely. "Arthur Dimmesdale!"

"Who speaks?" answered the minister.

Gathering himself quickly up, he stood more erect, like a man taken by surprise in a mood to which he was reluctant to have witnesses. Throwing his eyes anxiously in the direction of the voice, he indistinctly beheld a form under the trees, clad in garments so sombre, and so little relieved from the gray twilight into which the clouded sky and the heavy foliage had darkened the noontide, that he knew not whether it were a woman or a shadow. It may be, that his pathway through life was haunted thus, by a spectre that had stolen out from among his thoughts.

He made a step nigher, and discovered the scarlet letter.

"Hester! Hester Prynne!" said he. "Is it thou? Art thou in life?"

"Even so!" she answered. "In such life as has been mine these seven years past! And thou, Arthur Dimmesdale, dost thou yet live?"

It was no wonder that they thus questioned one another's actual and bodily existence, and even doubted of their own. So strangely did they meet, in the dim wood, that it was like the first encounter, in the world beyond the grave, of two spirits who had been intimately connected in their former life, but now stood coldly shuddering, in mutual dread; as not yet familiar with their state, nor wonted to the companionship of disembodied beings. Each a ghost, and awe-stricken at the other ghost! They were awe-stricken likewise at themselves; because the crisis flung back to them their consciousness, and revealed to each heart its history and experience, as life never does, except at such breathless epochs. The soul beheld its features in the mirror of the passing moment. It was with fear, and tremulously, and, as it were, by a slow, reluctant necessity, that Arthur Dimmesdale put forth his hand, chill as death, and touched the chill hand of Hester Prynne. The grasp, cold as it was, took away what was dreariest in the interview. They now felt themselves, at least, inhabitants of the same sphere.

Without a word more spoken,—neither he nor she assuming the guidance, but with an unexpressed consent,—they glided back into the shadow of the woods, whence Hester had emerged, and sat down on the heap of moss where she and Pearl had before been sitting. When they found voice to speak, it was, at first, only to utter remarks and inquiries such as any two acquaintance might have made, about the gloomy sky,

the threatening storm, and, next, the health of each. Thus they
went onward, not boldly, but step by step, into the themes that
were brooding deepest in their hearts. So long estranged by
fate and circumstances, they needed something slight and
casual to run before, and throw open the doors of intercourse,
so that their real thoughts might be led across the threshold.

After a while, the minister fixed his eyes on Hester Prynne's.

"Hester," said he, "hast thou found peace?"

She smiled drearily, looking down upon her bosom.

"Hast thou?" she asked.

"None!—nothing but despair!" he answered. "What else
could I look for, being what I am, and leading such a life as
mine? Were I an atheist,—a man devoid of conscience,—a
wretch with coarse and brutal instincts,—I might have found
peace, long ere now. Nay, I never should have lost it! But, as
matters stand with my soul, whatever of good capacity there
originally was in me, all of God's gifts that were the choicest
have become the ministers of spiritual torment. Hester, I am
most miserable!"

"The people reverence thee," said Hester. "And surely thou
workest good among them! Doth this bring thee no comfort?"

"More misery, Hester!—only the more misery!" answered
the clergyman, with a bitter smile. "As concerns the good
which I may appear to do, I have no faith in it. It must needs
be a delusion. What can a ruined soul, like mine, effect towards the redemption of other souls?—or a polluted soul,
towards their purification? And as for the people's reverence,
would that it were turned to scorn and hatred! Canst thou
deem it, Hester, a consolation, that I must stand up in my
pulpit, and meet so many eyes turned upward to my face, as
if the light of heaven were beaming from it!—must see my
flock hungry for the truth, and listening to my words as if a
tongue of Pentecost were speaking!—and then look inward,
and discern the black reality of what they idolize? I have
laughed, in bitterness and agony of heart, at the contrast between what I seem and what I am! And Satan laughs at it!"

"You wrong yourself in this," said Hester, gently. "You

have deeply and sorely repented. Your sin is left behind you, in the days long past. Your present life is not less holy, in very truth, than it seems in people's eyes. Is there no reality in the penitence thus sealed and witnessed by good works? And wherefore should it not bring you peace?"

"No, Hester, no!" replied the clergyman. "There is no substance in it! It is cold and dead, and can do nothing for me! Of penance I have had enough! Of penitence there has been none! Else, I should long ago have thrown off these garments of mock holiness, and have shown myself to mankind as they will see me at the judgment-seat. Happy are you, Hester, that wear the scarlet letter openly upon your bosom! Mine burns in secret! Thou little knowest what a relief it is, after the torment of a seven years' cheat, to look into an eye that recognizes me for what I am! Had I one friend,—or were it my worst enemy!—to whom, when sickened with the praises of all other men, I could daily betake myself, and be known as the vilest of all sinners, methinks my soul might keep itself alive thereby. Even thus much of truth would save me! But, now, it is all falsehood!—all emptiness!—all death!"

Hester Prynne looked into his face, but hesitated to speak. Yet, uttering his long-restrained emotions so vehemently as he did, his words here offered her the very point of circumstances in which to interpose what she came to say. She conquered her fears, and spoke.

"Such a friend as thou hast even now wished for," said she, "with whom to weep over thy sin, thou hast in me, the partner of it!"—Again she hesitated, but brought out the words with an effort.—"Thou hast long had such an enemy, and dwellest with him under the same roof!"

The minister started to his feet, gasping for breath, and clutching at his heart as if he would have torn it out of his bosom.

"Ha! What sayest thou?" cried he. "An enemy! And under mine own roof! What mean you?"

Hester Prynne was now fully sensible of the deep injury

for which she was responsible to this unhappy man, in permitting him to lie for so many years, or, indeed, for a single moment, at the mercy of one, whose purposes could not be other than malevolent. The very contiguity of his enemy, beneath whatever mask the latter might conceal himself, was enough to disturb the magnetic sphere of a being so sensitive as Arthur Dimmesdale. There had been a period when Hester was less alive to this consideration; or, perhaps, in the misanthropy of her own trouble, she left the minister to bear what she might picture to herself as a more tolerable doom. But of late, since the night of his vigil, all her sympathies towards him had been both softened and invigorated. She now read his heart more accurately. She doubted not, that the continual presence of Roger Chillingworth,—the secret poison of his malignity, infecting all the air about him,—and his authorized interference, as a physician, with the minister's physical and spiritual infirmities,—that these bad opportunities had been turned to a cruel purpose. By means of them, the sufferer's conscience had been kept in an irritated state, the tendency of which was, not to cure by wholesome pain, but to disorganize and corrupt his spiritual being. Its result, on earth, could hardly fail to be insanity, and hereafter, that eternal alienation from the Good and True, of which madness is perhaps the earthly type.

Such was the ruin to which she had brought the man, once, —nay, why should we not speak it?—still so passionately loved! Hester felt that the sacrifice of the clergyman's good name, and death itself, as she had already told Roger Chillingworth, would have been infinitely preferable to the alternative which she had taken upon herself to choose. And now, rather than have had this grievous wrong to confess, she would gladly have lain down on the forest-leaves, and died there, at Arthur Dimmesdale's feet.

"O Arthur," cried she, "forgive me! In all things else, I have striven to be true! Truth was the one virtue which I might have held fast, and did hold fast through all extremity;

save when thy good,—thy life,—thy fame,—were put in question! Then I consented to a deception. But a lie is never good, even though death threaten on the other side! Dost thou not see what I would say? That old man!—the physician!—he whom they call Roger Chillingworth!—he was my husband!"

The minister looked at her, for an instant, with all that violence of passion, which—intermixed, in more shapes than one, with his higher, purer, softer qualities—was, in fact, the portion of him which the Devil claimed, and through which he sought to win the rest. Never was there a blacker or a fiercer frown, than Hester now encountered. For the brief space that it lasted, it was a dark transfiguration. But his character had been so much enfeebled by suffering, that even its lower energies were incapable of more than a temporary struggle. He sank down on the ground, and buried his face in his hands.

"I might have known it!" murmured he. "I did know it! Was not the secret told me in the natural recoil of my heart, at the first sight of him, and as often as I have seen him since? Why did I not understand? O Hester Prynne, thou little, little knowest all the horror of this thing! And the shame!—the indelicacy!—the horrible ugliness of this exposure of a sick and guilty heart to the very eye that would gloat over it! Woman, woman, thou art accountable for this! I cannot forgive thee!"

"Thou shalt forgive me!" cried Hester, flinging herself on the fallen leaves beside him. "Let God punish! Thou shalt forgive!"

With sudden and desperate tenderness, she threw her arms around him, and pressed his head against her bosom; little caring though his cheek rested on the scarlet letter. He would have released himself, but strove in vain to do so. Hester would not set him free, lest he should look her sternly in the face. All the world had frowned on her,—for seven long years had it frowned upon this lonely woman,—and still she bore it all, nor ever once turned away her firm, sad eyes. Heaven, likewise, had frowned upon her, and she had not died. But the frown of this pale, weak, sinful, and sorrow-stricken man was what Hester could not bear, and live!

"Wilt thou yet forgive me?" she repeated, over and over again. "Wilt thou not frown? Wilt thou forgive?"

"I do forgive you, Hester," replied the minister, at length, with a deep utterance out of an abyss of sadness, but no anger. "I freely forgive you now. May God forgive us both! We are not, Hester, the worst sinners in the world. There is one worse than even the polluted priest! That old man's revenge has been blacker than my sin. He has violated, in cold blood, the sanctity of a human heart. Thou and I, Hester, never did so!"

"Never, never!" whispered she. "What we did had a consecration of its own. We felt it so! We said so to each other! Hast thou forgotten it?"

"Hush, Hester!" said Arthur Dimmesdale, rising from the ground. "No; I have not forgotten!"

They sat down again, side by side, and hand clasped in hand, on the mossy trunk of the fallen tree. Life had never brought them a gloomier hour; it was the point whither their pathway had so long been tending, and darkening ever, as it stole along;—and yet it inclosed a charm that made them linger upon it, and claim another, and another, and, after all, another moment. The forest was obscure around them, and creaked with a blast that was passing through it. The boughs were tossing heavily above their heads; while one solemn old tree groaned dolefully to another, as if telling the sad story of the pair that sat beneath, or constrained to forebode evil to come.

And yet they lingered. How dreary looked the forest-track that led backward to the settlement, where Hester Prynne must take up again the burden of her ignominy, and the minister the hollow mockery of his good name! So they lingered an instant longer. No golden light had ever been so precious as the gloom of this dark forest. Here, seen only by his eyes, the scarlet letter need not burn into the bosom of the fallen woman! Here, seen only by her eyes, Arthur Dimmesdale, false to God and man, might be, for one moment, true!

He started at a thought that suddenly occurred to him.

"Hester," cried he, "here is a new horror! Roger Chillingworth knows your purpose to reveal his true character. Will he continue, then, to keep our secret? What will now be the course of his revenge?"

"There is a strange secrecy in his nature," replied Hester, thoughtfully; "and it has grown upon him by the hidden practices of his revenge. I deem it not likely that he will betray the secret. He will doubtless seek other means of satiating his dark passion."

"And I!—how am I to live longer, breathing the same air with this deadly enemy?" exclaimed Arthur Dimmesdale, shrinking within himself, and pressing his hand nervously against his heart,—a gesture that had grown involuntary with him. "Think for me, Hester! Thou art strong. Resolve for me!"

"Thou must dwell no longer with this man," said Hester, slowly and firmly. "Thy heart must be no longer under his evil eye!"

"It were far worse than death!" replied the minister. "But how to avoid it? What choice remains to me? Shall I lie down again on these withered leaves, where I cast myself when thou didst tell me what he was? Must I sink down there, and die at once?"

"Alas, what a ruin has befallen thee!" said Hester, with the tears gushing into her eyes. "Wilt thou die for very weakness? There is no other cause!"

"The judgment of God is on me," answered the conscience-stricken priest. "It is too mighty for me to struggle with!"

"Heaven would show mercy," rejoined Hester, "hadst thou but the strength to take advantage of it."

"Be thou strong for me!" answered he. "Advise me what to do."

"Is the world then so narrow?" exclaimed Hester Prynne, fixing her deep eyes on the minister's, and instinctively exercising a magnetic power over a spirit so shattered and subdued, that it could hardly hold itself erect. "Doth the universe lie within the compass of yonder town, which only a little time ago was but a leaf-strewn desert, as lonely as this around us? Whither leads yonder forest-track? Backward to the settlement, thou sayest! Yes; but onward, too! Deeper it goes, and deeper, into the wilderness, less plainly to be seen at every step; until, some few miles hence, the yellow leaves will show no vestige of the white man's tread. There thou art free! So brief a journey would bring thee from a world where thou hast been most wretched, to one where thou mayest still be happy! Is there not shade enough in all this boundless forest to hide thy heart from the gaze of Roger Chillingworth?"

"Yes, Hester; but only under the fallen leaves!" replied the minister, with a sad smile.

"Then there is the broad pathway of the sea!" continued Hester. "It brought thee hither. If thou so choose, it will bear thee back again. In our native land, whether in some remote rural village or in vast London,—or, surely, in Germany, in France, in pleasant Italy,—thou wouldst be beyond his power and knowledge! And what hast thou to do with all these iron men, and their opinions? They have kept thy better part in bondage too long already!"

"It cannot be!" answered the minister, listening as if he were called upon to realize a dream. "I am powerless to go. Wretched and sinful as I am, I have had no other thought than to drag on my earthly existence in the sphere where Providence hath placed me. Lost as my own soul is, I would still do what I may for other human souls! I dare not quit my post, though an unfaithful sentinel, whose sure reward is death and dishonor, when his dreary watch shall come to an end!"

"Thou art crushed under this seven years' weight of misery," replied Hester, fervently resolved to buoy him up with her own energy. "But thou shalt leave it all behind thee! It shall not cumber thy steps, as thou treadest along the forest-path; neither shalt thou freight the ship with it, if thou prefer to cross the sea. Leave this wreck and ruin here where it hath happened! Meddle no more with it! Begin all anew! Hast thou exhausted possibility in the failure of this one trial? Not so! The future is yet full of trial and success. There is happiness to be enjoyed! There is good to be done! Exchange this false life of thine for a true one. Be, if thy spirit summon thee to such a mission, the teacher and apostle of the red men. Or, —as is more thy nature,—be a scholar and a sage among the wisest and the most renowned of the cultivated world. Preach! Write! Act! Do any thing, save to lie down and die! Give up this name of Arthur Dimmesdale, and make thyself another, and a high one, such as thou canst wear without fear or shame. Why shouldst thou tarry so much as one other day in the torments that have so gnawed into thy life!—that have made thee feeble to will and to do!—that will leave thee powerless even to repent! Up, and away!"

"O Hester!" cried Arthur Dimmesdale, in whose eyes a fitful light, kindled by her enthusiasm, flashed up and died away, "thou tellest of running a race to a man whose knees are tottering beneath him! I must die here. There is not the strength or courage left me to venture into the wide, strange, difficult world, alone!"

It was the last expression of the despondency of a broken spirit. He lacked energy to grasp the better fortune that seemed within his reach.

He repeated the word.

"Alone, Hester!"

"Thou shalt not go alone!" answered she, in a deep whisper. Then, all was spoken!

18. A Flood of Sunshine

ARTHUR DIMMESDALE gazed into Hester's face with a look in which hope and joy shone out, indeed, but with fear betwixt them, and a kind of horror at her boldness, who had spoken what he vaguely hinted at, but dared not speak.

But Hester Prynne, with a mind of native courage and activity, and for so long a period not merely estranged, but outlawed, from society, had habituated herself to such latitude of speculation as was altogether foreign to the clergyman. She had wandered, without rule or guidance, in a moral wilderness; as vast, as intricate and shadowy, as the untamed forest, amid the gloom of which they were now holding a colloquy that was to decide their fate. Her intellect and heart had their home, as it were, in desert places, where she roamed as freely as the wild Indian in his woods. For years past she had looked from this estranged point of view at human institutions, and whatever priests or legislators had established; criticizing all with hardly more reverence than the Indian would feel for the clerical band, the judicial robe, the pillory, the gallows, the fireside, or the church. The tendency of her fate and fortunes had been to set her free. The scarlet letter was her passport into regions where other women dared not tread. Shame, Despair, Solitude! These had been her teachers,—stern and wild ones,—and they had made her strong, but taught her much amiss.

The minister, on the other hand, had never gone through an experience calculated to lead him beyond the scope of generally received laws; although, in a single instance, he had so fearfully transgressed one of the most sacred of them. But this had been a sin of passion, not of principle, nor even purpose. Since that wretched epoch, he had watched, with morbid zeal and minuteness, not his acts,—for those it was easy to arrange,—but each breath of emotion, and his every thought. At the head of the social system, as the clergymen of that day stood, he was only the more trammelled by its regulations, its principles, and even its prejudices. As a priest, the framework of his order inevitably hemmed him in. As a man who had once sinned, but who kept his conscience all alive and painfully sensitive by the fretting of an unhealed wound, he might have been supposed safer within the line of virtue, than if he had never sinned at all.

Thus, we seem to see that, as regarded Hester Prynne, the whole seven years of outlaw and ignominy had been little other than a preparation for this very hour. But Arthur Dimmesdale! Were such a man once more to fall, what plea could be urged in extenuation of his crime? None; unless it avail him somewhat, that he was broken down by long and exquisite suffering; that his mind was darkened and confused by the very remorse which harrowed it; that, between fleeing as an avowed criminal, and remaining as a hypocrite, conscience might find it hard to strike the balance; that it was human to avoid the peril of death and infamy, and the inscrutable machinations of an enemy; that, finally, to this poor pilgrim, on his dreary and desert path, faint, sick, miserable, there appeared a glimpse of human affection and sympathy, a new life, and a true one, in exchange for the heavy doom which he was now expiating. And be the stern and sad truth spoken, that the breach which guilt has once made into the human soul is never, in this mortal state, repaired. It may be watched and guarded; so that the enemy shall not force his way again into the citadel, and might even, in his subsequent assaults, select some other avenue, in preference to that where he had formerly succeeded. But there is still the ruined wall, and, near it, the stealthy tread of the foe that would win over again his unforgotten triumph.

The struggle, if there were one, need not be described. Let it suffice, that the clergyman resolved to flee, and not alone. "If, in all these past seven years," thought he, "I could recall one instant of peace or hope, I would yet endure, for the sake of that earnest of Heaven's mercy. But now,—since I am irrevocably doomed,—wherefore should I not snatch the solace allowed to the condemned culprit before his execution? Or, if this be the path to a better life, as Hester would persuade me, I surely give up no fairer prospect by pursuing it! Neither can I any longer live without her companionship; so powerful is she to sustain,—so tender to soothe! O Thou to whom I dare not lift mine eyes, wilt Thou yet pardon me!"

"Thou wilt go!" said Hester calmly, as he met her glance.

The decision once made, a glow of strange enjoyment threw its flickering brightness over the trouble of his breast. It was the exhilarating effect—upon a prisoner just escaped from the dungeon of his own heart—of breathing the wild, free atmosphere of an unredeemed, unchristianized, lawless region. His spirit rose, as it were, with a bound, and attained a nearer prospect of the sky, than throughout all the misery which had kept him grovelling on the earth. Of a deeply religious temperament, there was inevitably a tinge of the devotional in his mood.

"Do I feel joy again?" cried he, wondering at himself. "Methought the germ of it was dead in me! O Hester, thou art my better angel! I seem to have flung myself—sick, sin-stained, and sorrow-blackened—down upon these forest-leaves, and to have risen up all made anew, and with new powers to glorify Him that hath been merciful! This is already the better life! Why did we not find it sooner?"

"Let us not look back," answered Hester Prynne. "The past is gone! Wherefore should we linger upon it now? See! With this symbol, I undo it all, and make it as it had never been!"

So speaking, she undid the clasp that fastened the scarlet letter, and, taking it from her bosom, threw it to a distance among the withered leaves. The mystic token alighted on the hither verge of the stream. With a hand's breadth farther flight it would have fallen into the water, and have given the little brook another woe to carry onward, besides the unintelligible tale which it still kept murmuring about. But there lay the embroidered letter, glittering like a lost jewel, which some ill-fated wanderer might pick up, and thenceforth be haunted by strange phantoms of guilt, sinkings of the heart, and unaccountable misfortune.

The stigma gone, Hester heaved a long, deep sigh, in which the burden of shame and anguish departed from her spirit. O exquisite relief! She had not known the weight, until she felt the freedom! By another impulse, she took off the formal cap that confined her hair; and down it fell upon her shoulders, dark and rich, with at once a shadow and a light in its abundance, and imparting the charm of softness to her features. There played around her mouth, and beamed out of her eyes, a radiant and tender smile, that seemed gushing from the very heart of womanhood. A crimson flush was glowing on her cheek, that had been long so pale. Her sex, her youth, and the whole richness of her beauty, came back from what men call the irrevocable past, and clustered themselves, with her maiden hope, and a happiness before unknown, within the magic circle of this hour. And, as if the gloom of the earth and sky had been but the effluence of these two mortal hearts, it vanished with their sorrow. All at once, as with a sudden smile of heaven, forth burst the sunshine, pouring a very flood into the obscure forest, gladdening each green leaf, transmuting the yellow fallen ones to gold, and gleaming adown the gray trunks of the solemn trees. The objects that had made a shadow hitherto, embodied the brightness now. The course of the little brook might be traced by its merry gleam afar into the wood's heart of mystery, which had become a mystery of joy.

Such was the sympathy of Nature—that wild, heathen Nature of the forest, never subjugated by human law, nor illumined by higher truth—with the bliss of these two spirits! Love, whether newly born, or aroused from a deathlike slumber, must always create a sunshine, filling the heart so full of radiance, that it overflows upon the outward world. Had the forest still kept its gloom, it would have been bright in Hester's eyes, and bright in Arthur Dimmesdale's!

Hester looked at him with the thrill of another joy.

"Thou must know Pearl!" said she. "Our little Pearl! Thou hast seen her,—yes, I know it!—but thou wilt see her now with other eyes. She is a strange child! I hardly comprehend her! But thou wilt love her dearly, as I do, and wilt advise me how to deal with her."

"Dost thou think the child will be glad to know me?" asked the minister, somewhat uneasily. "I have long shrunk from

children, because they often show a distrust,—a backwardness
to be familiar with me. I have even been afraid of little Pearl!"

"Ah, that was sad!" answered the mother. "But she will
love thee dearly, and thou her. She is not far off. I will call
her! Pearl! Pearl!"

"I see the child," observed the minister. "Yonder she is,
standing in a streak of sunshine, a good way off, on the other
side of the brook. So thou thinkest the child will love me?"

Hester smiled, and again called to Pearl, who was visible,
at some distance, as the minister had described her, like a
bright-apparelled vision, in a sunbeam, which fell down upon
her through an arch of boughs. The ray quivered to and fro,
making her figure dim or distinct,—now like a real child, now
like a child's spirit,—as the splendor went and came again. She
heard her mother's voice, and approached slowly through the
forest.

Pearl had not found the hour pass wearisomely, while her
mother sat talking with the clergyman. The great black forest
—stern as it showed itself to those who brought the guilt and
troubles of the world into its bosom—became the playmate
of the lonely infant, as well as it knew how. Sombre as it was,
it put on the kindest of its moods to welcome her. It offered
her the partridge-berries, the growth of the preceding autumn,
but ripening only in the spring, and now red as drops of blood
upon the withered leaves. These Pearl gathered, and was
pleased with their wild flavor. The small denizens of the wilderness hardly took pains to move out of her path. A partridge,
indeed, with a brood of ten behind her, ran forward threat-
eningly, but soon repented of her fierceness and clucked to
her young ones not to be afraid. A pigeon, alone on a low
branch, allowed Pearl to come beneath, and uttered a sound
as much of greeting as alarm. A squirrel, from the lofty depths
of his domestic tree, chattered either in anger or merriment,—
for a squirrel is such a choleric and humorous little personage
that it is hard to distinguish between his moods,—so he chattered at the child, and flung down a nut upon her head. It was
a last year's nut, and already gnawed by his sharp tooth. A fox,

startled from his sleep by her light footsteps on the leaves, looked inquisitively at Pearl, as doubting whether it were better to steal off, or renew his nap on the same spot. A wolf, it is said,—but here the tale has surely lapsed into the improbable,—came up, and smelt of Pearl's robe, and offered his savage head to be patted by her hand. The truth seems to be, however, that the mother-forest, and these wild things which it nourished, all recognized a kindred wildness in the human child.

And she was gentler here than in the grassy-margined streets of the settlement, or in her mother's cottage. The flowers appeared to know it; and one and another whispered, as she passed, "Adorn thyself with me, thou beautiful child, adorn thyself with me!"—and, to please them, Pearl gathered the violets, and anemones, and columbines, and some twigs of the freshest green, which the old trees held down before her eyes. With these she decorated her hair, and her young waist, and became a nymph-child, or an infant dryad, or whatever else was in closest sympathy with the antique wood. In such guise had Pearl adorned herself, when she heard her mother's voice, and came slowly back.

Slowly; for she saw the clergyman!

19. The Child at the Brook-Side

THOU wilt love her dearly," repeated Hester Prynne, as she and the minister sat watching little Pearl. "Dost thou not think her beautiful? And see with what natural skill she has made those simple flowers adorn her! Had she gathered pearls, and diamonds, and rubies, in the wood, they could not have become her better. She is a splendid child! But I know whose brow she has!"

"Dost thou know, Hester," said Arthur Dimmesdale, with an unquiet smile, "that this dear child, tripping about always at thy side, hath caused me many an alarm? Methought—O Hester, what a thought is that, and how terrible to dread it!— that my own features were partly repeated in her face, and so strikingly that the world might see them! But she is mostly thine!"

"No, no! Not mostly!" answered the mother with a tender smile. "A little longer, and thou needst not to be afraid to trace whose child she is. But how strangely beautiful she looks, with those wild flowers in her hair! It is as if one of the fairies, whom we left in our dear old England, had decked her out to meet us."

It was with a feeling which neither of them had ever before experienced, that they sat and watched Pearl's slow advance. In her was visible the tie that united them. She had been offered to the world, these seven years past, as the living hieroglyphic, in which was revealed the secret they so darkly sought to hide,—all written in this symbol,—all plainly manifest,—had there been a prophet or magician skilled to read the character of flame! And Pearl was the oneness of their being. Be the foregone evil what it might, how could they doubt that their earthly lives and future destinies were conjoined, when they beheld at once the material union, and the spiritual idea, in whom they met, and were to dwell immortally together? Thoughts like these—and perhaps other thoughts, which they did not acknowledge or define—threw an awe about the child, as she came onward.

"Let her see nothing strange—no passion nor eagerness—in thy way of accosting her," whispered Hester. "Our Pearl is a fitful and fantastic little elf, sometimes. Especially, she is seldom tolerant of emotion, when she does not fully comprehend the why and wherefore. But the child hath strong affections! She loves me, and will love thee!"

"Thou canst not think," said the minister, glancing aside at Hester Prynne, "how my heart dreads this interview, and yearns for it! But, in truth, as I already told thee, children are not readily won to be familiar with me. They will not climb my knee, nor prattle in my ear, nor answer to my smile; but stand apart, and eye me strangely. Even little babes, when I take them in my arms, weep bitterly. Yet Pearl, twice in her little lifetime, hath been kind to me! The first time,—thou knowest it well! The last was when thou ledst her with thee to the house of yonder stern old Governor."

"And thou didst plead so bravely in her behalf and mine!" answered the mother. "I remember it; and so shall little Pearl. Fear nothing! She may be strange and shy at first, but will soon learn to love thee!"

By this time Pearl had reached the margin of the brook, and stood on the farther side, gazing silently at Hester and the clergyman, who still sat together on the mossy tree-trunk, waiting to receive her. Just where she had paused the brook chanced to form a pool, so smooth and quiet that it reflected a perfect image of her little figure, with all the brilliant picturesqueness of her beauty, in its adornment of flowers and wreathed foliage, but more refined and spiritualized than the reality. This image, so nearly identical with the living Pearl, seemed to communicate somewhat of its own shadowy and intangible quality to the child herself. It was strange, the way in which Pearl stood, looking so stedfastly at them through the dim medium of the forest-gloom; herself, meanwhile, all glorified with a ray of sunshine, that was attracted thitherward as by a certain sympathy. In the brook beneath stood another child,—another and the same,—with likewise its ray of golden light. Hester felt herself, in some indistinct and tantalizing manner, estranged from Pearl; as if the child, in her lonely ramble through the forest, had strayed out of the sphere in which she and her mother dwelt together, and was now vainly seeking to return to it.

There was both truth and error in the impression; the child and mother were estranged, but through Hester's fault, not Pearl's. Since the latter rambled from her side, another inmate had been admitted within the circle of the mother's feelings, and so modified the aspect of them all, that Pearl, the returning wanderer, could not find her wonted place, and hardly knew where she was.

"I have a strange fancy," observed the sensitive minister, "that this brook is the boundary between two worlds, and that thou canst never meet thy Pearl again. Or is she an elfish spirit, who, as the legends of our childhood taught us, is forbidden to cross a running stream? Pray hasten her; for this delay has already imparted a tremor to my nerves."

"Come, dearest child!" said Hester encouragingly, and stretching out both her arms. "How slow thou art! When hast thou been so sluggish before now? Here is a friend of mine, who must be thy friend also. Thou wilt have twice as much love, henceforward, as thy mother alone could give thee! Leap across the brook and come to us. Thou canst leap like a young deer!"

Pearl, without responding in any manner to these honey-sweet expressions, remained on the other side of the brook. Now she fixed her bright, wild eyes on her mother, now on the minister, and now included them both in the same glance; as if to detect and explain to herself the relation which they bore to one another. For some unaccountable reason, as Arthur Dimmesdale felt the child's eyes upon himself, his hand—with that gesture so habitual as to have become in-voluntary—stole over his heart. At length, assuming a singular air of authority, Pearl stretched out her hand, with the small forefinger extended, and pointing evidently towards her mother's breast. And beneath, in the mirror of the brook, there was the flower-girdled and sunny image of little Pearl, point-ing her small forefinger too.

"Thou strange child, why dost thou not come to me?" exclaimed Hester.

Pearl still pointed with her forefinger; and a frown gathered on her brow; the more impressive from the childish, the almost baby-like aspect of the features that conveyed it. As her mother still kept beckoning to her, and arraying her face in a holiday suit of unaccustomed smiles, the child stamped her foot with a yet more imperious look and gesture. In the brook, again, was the fantastic beauty of the image, with its reflected frown, its pointed finger, and imperious gesture, giving emphasis to the aspect of little Pearl.

"Hasten, Pearl; or I shall be angry with thee!" cried Hester Prynne, who, however inured to such behaviour on the elf-child's part at other seasons, was naturally anxious for a more seemly deportment now. "Leap across the brook, naughty child, and run hither! Else I must come to thee!"

But Pearl, not a whit startled at her mother's threats, any more than mollified by her entreaties, now suddenly burst into a fit of passion, gesticulating violently, and throwing her small figure into the most extravagant contortions. She accompanied this wild outbreak with piercing shrieks, which the woods reverberated on all sides; so that, alone as she was in her childish and unreasonable wrath, it seemed as if a hidden multitude were lending her their sympathy and encouragement. Seen in the brook, once more, was the shadowy wrath of Pearl's image, crowned and girdled with flowers, but stamping its foot, wildly gesticulating, and, in the midst of all, still pointing its small forefinger at Hester's bosom!

"I see what ails the child," whispered Hester to the clergyman, and turning pale in spite of a strong effort to conceal her trouble and annoyance. "Children will not abide any, the slightest, change in the accustomed aspect of things that are daily before their eyes. Pearl misses something which she has always seen me wear!"

"I pray you," answered the minister, "if thou hast any means of pacifying the child, do it forthwith! Save it were the

cankered wrath of an old witch, like Mistress Hibbins," added
he, attempting to smile, "I know nothing that I would not
sooner encounter than this passion in a child. In Pearl's young
beauty, as in the wrinkled witch, it has a preternatural effect.
Pacify her, if thou lovest me!"

Hester turned again towards Pearl, with a crimson blush
upon her cheek, a conscious glance aside at the clergyman, and
then a heavy sigh; while, even before she had time to speak,
the blush yielded to a deadly pallor.

"Pearl," said she, sadly, "look down at thy feet! There!—
before thee!—on the hither side of the brook!"

The child turned her eyes to the point indicated; and there
lay the scarlet letter, so close upon the margin of the stream,
that the gold embroidery was reflected in it.

"Bring it hither!" said Hester.

"Come thou and take it up!" answered Pearl.

"Was ever such a child!" observed Hester aside to the minister. "Oh, I have much to tell thee about her. But, in very
truth, she is right as regards this hateful token. I must bear its
torture yet a little longer,—only a few days longer,— until we
shall have left this region, and look back hither as to a land
which we have dreamed of. The forest cannot hide it! The
mid-ocean shall take it from my hand, and swallow it up for
ever!"

With these words, she advanced to the margin of the brook,
took up the scarlet letter, and fastened it again into her bosom.
Hopefully, but a moment ago, as Hester had spoken of drown-
ing it in the deep sea, there was a sense of inevitable doom
upon her, as she thus received back this deadly symbol from
the hand of fate. She had flung it into infinite space!—she had
drawn an hour's free breath!—and here again was the scarlet
misery, glittering on the old spot! So it ever is, whether thus
typified or no, that an evil deed invests itself with the character of doom. Hester next gathered up the heavy tresses of
her hair, and confined them beneath her cap. As if there were
a withering spell in the sad letter, her beauty, the warmth and

richness of her womanhood, departed, like fading sunshine; and a gray shadow seemed to fall across her.

When the dreary change was wrought, she extended her hand to Pearl.

"Dost thou know thy mother now, child?" asked she, reproachfully, but with a subdued tone. "Wilt thou come across the brook, and own thy mother, now that she has her shame upon her,—now that she is sad?"

"Yes; now I will!" answered the child, bounding across the brook, and clasping Hester in her arms. "Now thou art my mother indeed! And I am thy little Pearl!"

In a mood of tenderness that was not usual with her, she drew down her mother's head, and kissed her brow and both her cheeks. But then—by a kind of necessity that always impelled this child to alloy whatever comfort she might chance to give with a throb of anguish—Pearl put up her mouth, and kissed the scarlet letter too!

"That was not kind!" said Hester. "When thou hast shown me a little love, thou mockest me!"

"Why doth the minister sit yonder?" asked Pearl.

"He waits to welcome thee," replied her mother. "Come thou, and entreat his blessing! He loves thee, my little Pearl, and loves thy mother too. Wilt thou not love him? Come! he longs to greet thee!"

"Doth he love us?" said Pearl, looking up with acute intelligence into her mother's face. "Will he go back with us, hand in hand, we three together, into the town?"

"Not now, dear child," answered Hester. "But in days to come he will walk hand in hand with us. We will have a home and fireside of our own; and thou shalt sit upon his knee; and he will teach thee many things, and love thee dearly. Thou wilt love him; wilt thou not?"

"And will he always keep his hand over his heart?" inquired Pearl.

"Foolish child, what a question is that!" exclaimed her mother. "Come and ask his blessing!"

But, whether influenced by the jealousy that seems instinctive with every petted child towards a dangerous rival, or from whatever caprice of her freakish nature, Pearl would show no favor to the clergyman. It was only by an exertion of force that her mother brought her up to him, hanging back, and manifesting her reluctance by odd grimaces; of which, ever since her babyhood, she had possessed a singular variety, and could transform her mobile physiognomy into a series of different aspects, with a new mischief in them, each and all. The minister—painfully embarrassed, but hoping that a kiss might prove a talisman to admit him into the child's kindlier regards—bent forward, and impressed one on her brow. Hereupon, Pearl broke away from her mother, and, running to the brook, stooped over it, and bathed her forehead, until the unwelcome kiss was quite washed off, and diffused through a long lapse of the gliding water. She then remained apart, silently watching Hester and the clergyman; while they talked together, and made such arrangements as were suggested by their new position, and the purposes soon to be fulfilled.

And now this fateful interview had come to a close. The dell was to be left a solitude among its dark, old trees, which, with their multitudinous tongues, would whisper long of what had passed there, and no mortal be the wiser. And the melancholy brook would add this other tale to the mystery with which its little heart was already overburdened, and whereof it still kept up a murmuring babble, with not a whit more cheerfulness of tone than for ages heretofore.

20. The Minister in a Maze

As THE minister departed, in advance of Hester Prynne and little Pearl, he threw a backward glance; half expecting that he should discover only some faintly traced features or outline of the mother and the child, slowly fading into the twilight of the woods. So great a vicissitude in his life could not at once be received as real. But there was Hester, clad in her gray robe, still standing beside the tree-trunk, which some blast had overthrown a long antiquity ago, and which time had ever since been covering with moss, so that these two fated ones, with earth's heaviest burden on them, might there sit down together, and find a single hour's rest and solace. And there was Pearl, too, lightly dancing from the margin of the brook, —now that the intrusive third person was gone,—and taking her old place by her mother's side. So the minister had not fallen asleep, and dreamed!

In order to free his mind from this indistinctness and duplicity of impression, which vexed it with a strange disquietude, he recalled and more thoroughly defined the plans which Hester and himself had sketched for their departure. It had been determined between them, that the Old World, with its crowds and cities, offered them a more eligible shelter and concealment than the wilds of New England, or all America, with its alternatives of an Indian wigwam, or the few settlements of Europeans, scattered thinly along the seaboard. Not to speak of the clergyman's health, so inadequate to sustain the hardships of a forest life, his native gifts, his culture, and his entire development would secure him a home only in the midst of civilization and refinement; the higher the state, the more delicately adapted to it the man. In furtherance of this choice, it so happened that a ship lay in the harbour; one of those questionable cruisers, frequent at that day, which, with-

out being absolutely outlaws of the deep, yet roamed over its
surface with a remarkable irresponsibility of character. This
vessel had recently arrived from the Spanish Main, and, within
three days' time, would sail for Bristol. Hester Prynne—whose
vocation, as a self-enlisted Sister of Charity, had brought her
acquainted with the captain and crew—could take upon herself
to secure the passage of two individuals and a child, with all
the secrecy which circumstances rendered more than desirable.

The minister had inquired of Hester, with no little interest,
the precise time at which the vessel might be expected to depart. It would probably be on the fourth day from the present. "That is most fortunate!" he had then said to himself.
Now, why the Reverend Mr. Dimmesdale considered it so
very fortunate, we hesitate to reveal. Nevertheless,—to hold
nothing back from the reader,—it was because, on the third
day from the present, he was to preach the Election Sermon; [1]
and, as such an occasion formed an honorable epoch in the
life of a New England clergyman, he could not have chanced
upon a more suitable mode and time of terminating his professional career. "At least, they shall say of me," thought this
exemplary man, "that I leave no public duty unperformed, nor
ill performed!" Sad, indeed, that an introspection so profound
and acute as this poor minister's should be so miserably deceived! We have had, and may still have, worse things to tell
of him; but none, we apprehend, so pitiably weak; no evidence,
at once so slight and irrefragable, of a subtle disease, that had
long since begun to eat into the real substance of his character.
No man, for any considerable period, can wear one face to
himself, and another to the multitude, without finally getting
bewildered as to which may be the true.

The excitement of Mr. Dimmesdale's feelings, as he returned

---

[1] Until the dissolution of their charter in 1684, the freemen of
Massachusetts elected a new governor annually, in May or June;
and the apex of the political year was his installation, at which an
election sermon was preached. Selecting him to preach the election
sermon was regarded as the greatest honor the civil body could
bestow on a clergyman.

from his interview with Hester, lent him unaccustomed physical energy, and hurried him townward at a rapid pace. The pathway among the woods seemed wilder, more uncouth with its rude natural obstacles, and less trodden by the foot of man, than he remembered it on his outward journey. But he leaped across the plashy places, thrust himself through the clinging underbrush, climbed the ascent, plunged into the hollow, and overcame, in short, all the difficulties of the track, with an unweariable activity that astonished him. He could not but recall how feebly, and with what frequent pauses for breath, he had toiled over the same ground only two days before. As he drew near the town, he took an impression of change from the series of familiar objects that presented themselves. It seemed not yesterday, not one, nor two, but many days, or even years ago, since he had quitted them. There, indeed, was each former trace of the street, as he remembered it, and all the peculiarities of the houses, with the due multitude of gable-peaks, and a weathercock at every point where his memory suggested one. Not the less, however, came this importunately obtrusive sense of change. The same was true as regarded the acquaintances whom he met, and all the well-known shapes of human life, about the little town. They looked neither older nor younger, now; the beards of the aged were no whiter, nor could the creeping babe of yesterday walk on his feet to-day; it was impossible to describe in what respect they differed from the individuals on whom he had so recently bestowed a parting glance; and yet the minister's deepest sense seemed to inform him of their mutability. A similar impression struck him most remarkably, as he passed under the walls of his own church. The edifice had so very strange, and yet so familiar, an aspect, that Mr. Dimmesdale's mind vibrated between two ideas; either that he had seen it only in a dream hitherto, or that he was merely dreaming about it now.

This phenomenon, in the various shapes which it assumed, indicated no external change, but so sudden and important a change in the spectator of the familiar scene, that the intervening space of a single day had operated on his consciousness like the lapse of years. The minister's own will, and Hester's will, and the fate that grew between them, had wrought this transformation. It was the same town as heretofore; but the same minister returned not from the forest. He might have said to the friends who greeted him,—"I am not the man for whom you take me! I left him yonder in the forest, withdrawn into a secret dell, by a mossy tree-trunk, and near a melancholy brook! Go, seek your minister, and see if his emaciated figure, his thin cheek, his white, heavy, pain-wrinkled brow, be not flung down there like a cast-off garment!" His friends, no doubt, would still have insisted with him,—"Thou art thyself the man!"—but the error would have been their own, not his.

Before Mr. Dimmesdale reached home, his inner man gave him other evidences of a revolution in the sphere of thought and feeling. In truth, nothing short of a total change of dynasty and moral code, in that interior kingdom, was adequate to account for the impulses now communicated to the unfortunate and startled minister. At every step he was incited to do some strange, wild, wicked thing or other, with a sense that it would be at once involuntary and intentional; in spite of himself, yet growing out of a profounder self than that which opposed the impulse. For instance, he met one of his own deacons. The good old man addressed him with the paternal affection and patriarchal privilege, which his venerable age, his upright and holy character, and his station in the Church, entitled him to use; and, conjoined with this, the deep, almost worshipping respect, which the minister's professional and private claims alike demanded. Never was there a more beautiful example of how the majesty of age and wisdom may comport with the obeisance and respect enjoined upon it, as from a lower social rank and inferior order of endowment, towards a higher. Now, during a conversation of some two or three moments between the Reverend Mr. Dimmesdale and this excellent and hoary-bearded deacon, it was only by the most careful self-control that the former could refrain from uttering certain blasphemous suggestions that rose into his mind, respecting the communion-supper. He absolutely trembled and turned pale as ashes, lest his tongue should wag itself, in utterance of these horrible matters, and plead his own consent for so doing, without his having fairly given it. And, even with this terror in his heart, he could hardly avoid laughing to imagine how the sanctified old patriarchal deacon would have been petrified by his minister's impiety!

Again, another incident of the same nature. Hurrying along the street, the Reverend Mr. Dimmesdale encountered the eldest female member of his church; a most pious and exemplary old dame; poor, widowed, lonely, and with a heart as full of reminiscences about her dead husband and children, and her dead friends of long ago, as a burial-ground is full of storied grave-stones. Yet all this, which would else have been such heavy sorrow, was made almost a solemn joy to her devout old soul by religious consolations and the truths of Scripture, wherewith she had fed herself continually for more than thirty years. And, since Mr. Dimmesdale had taken her in charge, the good grandam's chief earthly comfort—which, unless it had been likewise a heavenly comfort, could have been none at all—was to meet her pastor, whether casually, or of set purpose, and be refreshed with a word of warm, fragrant, heaven-breathing Gospel truth from his beloved lips into her dulled, but rapturously attentive ear. But, on this occasion, up to the moment of putting his lips to the old woman's ear, Mr. Dimmesdale, as the great enemy of souls would have it, could recall no text of Scripture, nor aught else, except a brief, pithy, and, as it then appeared to him, unanswerable argument against the immortality of the human soul. The instilment thereof into her mind would probably have caused this aged sister to drop down dead, at once, as by the effect of an intensely poisonous infusion. What he really did whisper, the minister could never afterwards recollect. There was, perhaps, a fortunate disorder in his utterance, which failed to impart any distinct idea to the good widow's comprehension, or which Providence interpreted after a method of its own. Assuredly, as the minister looked back, he beheld an expression of divine gratitude and ecstasy that seemed like the shine of the celestial city on her face, so wrinkled and ashy pale.

Again, a third instance. After parting from the old church-member, he met the youngest sister of them all. It was a maiden newly won—and won by the Reverend Mr. Dimmes-dale's own sermon, on the Sabbath after his vigil—to barter the transitory pleasures of the world for the heavenly hope, that was to assume brighter substance as life grew dark around her, and which would gild the utter gloom with final glory. She was fair and pure as a lily that had bloomed in Paradise. The minister knew well that he was himself enshrined within the stainless sanctity of her heart, which hung its snowy cur-tains about his image, imparting to religion the warmth of love, and to love a religious purity. Satan, that afternoon, had surely led the poor young girl away from her mother's side, and thrown her into the pathway of this sorely tempted, or—shall we not rather say?—this lost and desperate man. As she drew nigh, the arch-fiend whispered him to condense into small compass and drop into her tender bosom a germ of evil that would be sure to blossom darkly soon, and bear black fruit betimes. Such was his sense of power over this virgin soul, trusting him as she did, that the minister felt potent to blight all the field of innocence with but one wicked look, and develop all its opposite with but a word. So—with a mightier struggle than he had yet sustained—he held his Geneva cloak before his face, and hurried onward, making no sign of recog-nition, and leaving the young sister to digest his rudeness as she might. She ransacked her conscience,—which was full of harmless little matters, like her pocket or her work-bag,—and took herself to task, poor thing, for a thousand imaginary faults; and went about her household duties with swollen eye-lids the next morning.

Before the minister had time to celebrate his victory over this last temptation, he was conscious of another impulse, more

ludicrous, and almost as horrible. It was,—we blush to tell it,—
it was to stop short in the road, and teach some very wicked
words to a knot of little Puritan children who were playing
there, and had but just begun to talk. Denying himself this
freak, as unworthy of his cloth, he met a drunken seaman, one
of the ship's crew from the Spanish Main. And, here, since he
had so valiantly forborne all other wickedness, poor Mr.
Dimmesdale longed, at least, to shake hands with the tarry
blackguard, and recreate himself with a few improper jests,
such as dissolute sailors so abound with, and a volley of good,
round, solid, satisfactory, and heaven-defying oaths! It was
not so much a better principle, as partly his natural good taste,
and still more his buckramed habit of clerical decorum, that
carried him safely through the latter crisis.

"What is it that haunts and tempts me thus?" cried the
minister to himself, at length, pausing in the street, and striking his hand against his forehead. "Am I mad? or am I given
over utterly to the fiend? Did I make a contract with him in
the forest, and sign it with my blood? And does he now summon me to its fulfilment, by suggesting the performance of
every wickedness which his most foul imagination can conceive?"

At the moment when the Reverend Mr. Dimmesdale thus
communed with himself, and struck his forehead with his
hand, old Mistress Hibbins, the reputed witch-lady, is said to
have been passing by. She made a very grand appearance;
having on a high head-dress, a rich gown of velvet, and a ruff
done up with the famous yellow starch, of which Ann Turner,
her especial friend, had taught her the secret,[2] before this last
good lady had been hanged for Sir Thomas Overbury's mur-

[2] Ann Turner's notoriety (see Note 4, Chapter 9, p. 122) was
heightened by her habit of wearing a ruff and cuffs starched in
yellow, a costume which she is said to have invented. By order of
the court, she wore these when she was hanged, and popular ac-
counts of the trial made the yellow starch synonymous with Ann
Turner and her evil doings.

der. Whether the witch had read the minister's thoughts, or
no, she came to a full stop, looked shrewdly into his face,
smiled craftily, and—though little given to converse with
clergymen—began a conversation.

"So, reverend Sir, you have made a visit into the forest,"
observed the witch-lady, nodding her high head-dress at him.
"The next time, I pray you to allow me only a fair warning,
and I shall be proud to bear you company. Without taking
overmuch upon myself, my good word will go far towards
gaining any strange gentleman a fair reception from yonder
potentate you wot of!"

"I profess, madam," answered the clergyman, with a grave
obeisance, such as the lady's rank demanded, and his own good-
breeding made imperative,—"I profess, on my conscience and
character, that I am utterly bewildered as touching the purport of your words! I went not into the forest to seek a potentate; neither do I, at any future time, design a visit thither, with
a view to gaining the favour of such personage. My one sufficient object was to greet that pious friend of mine, the Apostle
Eliot, and rejoice with him over the many precious souls he
hath won from heathendom!"

"Ha, ha, ha!" cackled the old witch-lady, still nodding her
high head-dress at the minister. "Well, well, we must needs
talk thus in the daytime! You carry it off like an old hand!
But at midnight, and in the forest, we shall have other talk
together!"

She passed on with her aged stateliness, but often turning
back her head and smiling at him, like one willing to recognize a secret intimacy of connection.

"Have I then sold myself," thought the minister, "to the
fiend whom, if men say true, this yellow-starched and velveted
old hag has chosen for her prince and master!"

The wretched minister! He had made a bargain very like
it! Tempted by a dream of happiness, he had yielded himself
with deliberate choice, as he had never done before, to what
he knew was deadly sin. And the infectious poison of that

sin had been thus rapidly diffused throughout his moral system. It had stupefied all blessed impulses, and awakened into
vivid life the whole brotherhood of bad ones. Scorn, bitterness,
unprovoked malignity, gratuitous desire of ill, ridicule of
whatever was good and holy, all awoke, to tempt, even while
they frightened him. And his encounter with old Mistress
Hibbins, if it were a real incident, did but show his sympathy
and fellowship with wicked mortals and the world of per-
verted spirits.

He had by this time reached his dwelling, on the edge of
the burial-ground, and, hastening up the stairs, took refuge
in his study. The minister was glad to have reached this shelter,
without first betraying himself to the world by any of those
strange and wicked eccentricities to which he had been continually impelled while passing through the streets. He entered
the accustomed room, and looked around him on its books,
its windows, its fireplace, and the tapestried comfort of the
walls, with the same perception of strangeness that had haunted
him throughout his walk from the forest-dell into the town,
and thitherward. Here he had studied and written; here, gone
through fast and vigil, and come forth half alive; here, striven
to pray; here, borne a hundred thousand agonies! There was
the Bible, in its rich old Hebrew, with Moses and the Prophets
speaking to him, and God's voice through all! There, on the
table, with the inky pen beside it, was an unfinished sermon,
with a sentence broken in the midst, where his thoughts had
ceased to gush out upon the page two days before. He knew
that it was himself, the thin and white-cheeked minister, who
had done and suffered these things, and written thus far into
the Election Sermon! But he seemed to stand apart, and eye
this former self with scornful, pitying, but half-envious curiosity. That self was gone! Another man had returned out of
the forest; a wiser one; with a knowledge of hidden mysteries
which the simplicity of the former never could have reached.
A bitter kind of knowledge that!

While occupied with these reflections, a knock came at

the door of the study, and the minister said, "Come in!"—
not wholly devoid of an idea that he might behold an evil
spirit. And so he did! It was old Roger Chillingworth that
entered. The minister stood, white and speechless, with one
hand on the Hebrew Scriptures, and the other spread upon
his breast.

"Welcome home, reverend Sir!" said the physician. "And
how found you that godly man, the Apostle Eliot? But methinks, dear Sir, you look pale; as if the travel through the
wilderness had been too sore for you. Will not my aid be
requisite to put you in heart and strength to preach your
Election Sermon?"

"Nay, I think not so," rejoined the Reverend Mr. Dimmesdale. "My journey, and the sight of the holy Apostle yonder,
and the free air which I have breathed, have done me good,
after so long confinement in my study. I think to need no
more of your drugs, my kind physician, good though they be,
and administered by a friendly hand."

All this time, Roger Chillingworth was looking at the minister with the grave and intent regard of a physician towards
his patient. But, in spite of this outward show, the latter was
almost convinced of the old man's knowledge, or, at least,
his confident suspicion, with respect to his own interview with
Hester Prynne. The physician knew, then, that, in the minister's regard, he was no longer a trusted friend, but his bitterest enemy. So much being known, it would appear natural
that a part of it should be expressed. It is singular, however,
how long a time often passes before words embody things;
and with what security two persons, who choose to avoid a
certain subject, may approach its very verge, and retire without disturbing it. Thus, the minister felt no apprehension that
Roger Chillingworth would touch, in express words, upon
the real position which they sustained towards one another.
Yet did the physician, in his dark way, creep frightfully near
the secret.

"Were it not better," said he, "that you use my poor skill

to-night? Verily, dear Sir, we must take pains to make you strong and vigorous for this occasion of the Election discourse. The people look for great things from you; apprehending that another year may come about, and find their pastor gone."

"Yea, to another world," replied the minister, with pious resignation. "Heaven grant it be a better one; for, in good sooth, I hardly think to tarry with my flock through the flitting seasons of another year! But, touching your medicine, kind Sir, in my present frame of body I need it not."

"I joy to hear it," answered the physician. "It may be that my remedies, so long administered in vain, begin now to take due effect. Happy man were I, and well deserving of New England's gratitude, could I achieve this cure!"

"I thank you from my heart, most watchful friend," said the Reverend Mr. Dimmesdale, with a solemn smile. "I thank you, and can but requite your good deeds with my prayers."

"A good man's prayers are golden recompense!" rejoined old Roger Chillingworth, as he took his leave. "Yea, they are the current gold coin of the New Jerusalem, with the King's own mint-mark on them!"

Left alone, the minister summoned a servant of the house, and requested food, which, being set before him, he ate with ravenous appetite. Then, flinging the already written pages of the Election Sermon into the fire, he forthwith began another, which he wrote with such an impulsive flow of thought and emotion, that he fancied himself inspired; and only wondered that Heaven should see fit to transmit the grand and solemn music of its oracles through so foul an organ-pipe as he. However, leaving that mystery to solve itself, or go unsolved for ever, he drove his task onward, with earnest haste and ecstasy. Thus the night fled away, as if it were a winged steed, and he careering on it; morning came, and peeped blushing through the curtains; and at last sunrise threw a golden beam into the study, and laid it right across the minister's bedazzled eyes. There he was, with the pen still between his fingers, and a vast, immeasurable tract of written space behind him!

21. The New England Holiday

BETIMES in the morning of the day on which the new Governor was to receive his office at the hands of the people, Hester Prynne and little Pearl came into the market-place. It was already thronged with the craftsmen and other plebeian inhabitants of the town, in considerable numbers; among whom, likewise, were many rough figures, whose attire of deer-skins marked them as belonging to some of the forest settlements, which surrounded the little metropolis of the colony.

On this public holiday, as on all other occasions, for seven years past, Hester was clad in a garment of coarse gray cloth. Not more by its hue than by some indescribable peculiarity in its fashion, it had the effect of making her fade personally out of sight and outline; while, again, the scarlet letter brought her back from this twilight indistinctness, and revealed her under the moral aspect of its own illumination. Her face, so long familiar to the townspeople, showed the marble quietude which they were accustomed to behold there. It was like a mask; or rather, like the frozen calmness of a dead woman's features; owing this dreary resemblance to the fact that Hester was actually dead, in respect to any claim of sympathy, and had departed out of the world with which she still seemed to mingle.

It might be, on this one day, that there was an expression unseen before, nor, indeed, vivid enough to be detected now; unless some preternaturally gifted observer should have first read the heart, and have afterwards sought a corresponding development in the countenance and mien. Such a spiritual seer might have conceived, that, after sustaining the gaze of the multitude through seven miserable years as a necessity, a penance, and something which it was a stern religion to endure, she now, for one last time more, encountered it freely and voluntarily, in order to convert what had so long been agony into a kind of triumph. "Look your last on the scarlet letter and its wearer!"—the people's victim and life-long bond-slave, as they fancied her, might say to them. "Yet a little while, and she will be beyond your reach! A few hours longer, and the deep, mysterious ocean will quench and hide for ever the symbol which ye have caused to burn upon her bosom!" Nor were it an inconsistency too improbable to be assigned to human nature, should we suppose a feeling of regret in Hester's mind, at the moment when she was about to win her freedom from the pain which had been thus deeply incorporated with her being. Might there not be an irresistible desire to quaff a last, long, breathless draught of the cup of wormwood and aloes, with which nearly all her years of womanhood had been perpetually flavored? The wine of life, henceforth to be presented to her lips, must be indeed rich, delicious, and exhilarating, in its chased and golden beaker; or else leave an inevitable and weary languor, after the lees of bitterness wherewith she had been drugged, as with a cordial of intensest potency.

Pearl was decked out with airy gayety. It would have been impossible to guess that this bright and sunny apparition owed its existence to the shape of gloomy gray; or that a fancy, at once so gorgeous and so delicate as must have been requisite to contrive the child's apparel, was the same that had achieved a task perhaps more difficult, in imparting so distinct a peculiarity to Hester's simple robe. The dress, so proper was it to little Pearl, seemed an effluence, or inevitable development and outward manifestation of her character, no more to be separated from her than the many-hued brilliancy from a butterfly's wing, or the painted glory from the leaf of a bright flower. As with these, so with the child; her garb was all of one idea with her nature. On this eventful day, moreover, there was a certain singular inquietude and excitement in her mood, resembling nothing so much as the shimmer of a diamond, that sparkles and flashes with the varied throbbings of the breast on which it is displayed. Children have always a sympathy in the agitations of those connected with them; always, especially, a sense of any trouble or impending revolution, of whatever kind, in domestic circumstances; and therefore Pearl, who was the gem on her mother's unquiet bosom, betrayed, by the very dance of her spirits, the emotions which none could detect in the marble passiveness of Hester's brow.

This effervescence made her flit with a bird-like movement, rather than walk by her mother's side. She broke continually into shouts of a wild, inarticulate, and sometimes piercing music. When they reached the market-place, she became still more restless, on perceiving the stir and bustle that enlivened the spot; for it was usually more like the broad and lonesome green before a village meeting-house, than the centre of a town's business.

"Why, what is this, mother?" cried she. "Wherefore have all the people left their work to-day? Is it a play-day for the whole world? See, there is the blacksmith! He has washed his sooty face, and put on his Sabbath-day clothes, and looks as if he would gladly be merry, if any kind body would only teach him how! And there is Master Brackett, the old jailer, nodding and smiling at me. Why does he do so, mother?"

"He remembers thee a little babe, my child," answered Hester.

"He should not nod and smile at me, for all that,—the black, grim, ugly-eyed old man!" said Pearl. "He may nod at thee if he will; for thou art clad in gray, and wearest the scarlet letter. But, see, mother, how many faces of strange people, and Indians among them, and sailors! What have they all come to do here in the market-place?"

"They wait to see the procession pass," said Hester. "For the Governor and the magistrates are to go by, and the ministers, and all the great people and good people, with the music, and the soldiers marching before them."

"And will the minister be there?" asked Pearl. "And will he hold out both his hands to me, as when thou ledst me to him from the brook-side?"

"He will be there, child," answered her mother. "But he will not greet thee to-day; nor must thou greet him."

"What a strange, sad man is he!" said the child, as if speaking partly to herself. "In the dark night-time, he calls us to him, and holds thy hand and mine, as when we stood with him on the scaffold yonder! And in the deep forest, where only the old trees can hear, and the strip of sky see it, he talks with thee, sitting on a heap of moss! And he kisses my forehead, too, so that the little brook would hardly wash it off! But here in the sunny day, and among all the people, he knows us not; nor must we know him! A strange, sad man is he, with his hand always over his heart!"

"Be quiet, Pearl! Thou understandest not these things," said her mother. "Think not now of the minister, but look about thee, and see how cheery is every body's face to-day. The children have come from their schools, and the grown people from their workshops and their fields, on purpose to be happy. For, to-day, a new man is beginning to rule over them; and so —as has been the custom of mankind ever since a nation was first gathered—they make merry and rejoice; as if a good and golden year were at length to pass over the poor old world!"

It was as Hester said, in regard to the unwonted jollity that brightened the faces of the people. Into this festal season of the year—as it already was, and continued to be during the greater part of two centuries—the Puritans compressed whatever mirth and public joy they deemed allowable to human infirmity; thereby so far dispelling the customary cloud, that, for the space of a single holiday, they appeared scarcely more grave than most other communities at a period of general affliction.

But we perhaps exaggerate the gray or sable tinge, which undoubtedly characterized the mood and manners of the age. The persons now in the market-place of Boston had not been

born to an inheritance of Puritanic gloom. They were native
Englishmen, whose fathers had lived in the sunny richness
of the Elizabethan epoch; a time when the life of England,
viewed as one great mass, would appear to have been as stately,
magnificent, and joyous, as the world has ever witnessed. Had
they followed their hereditary taste, the New England settlers
would have illustrated all events of public importance by bon-
fires, banquets, pageantries, and processions. Nor would it have
been impracticable, in the observance of majestic ceremonies,
to combine mirthful recreation with solemnity, and give, as it
were, a grotesque and brilliant embroidery to the great robe
of state, which a nation, at such festivals, puts on. There was
some shadow of an attempt of this kind in the mode of cele-
brating the day on which the political year of the colony com-
menced. The dim reflection of a remembered splendor, a color-
less and manifold diluted repetition of what they had beheld
in proud old London,—we will not say at a royal coronation,
but at a Lord Mayor's show,—might be traced in the customs
which our forefathers instituted, with reference to the annual
installation of magistrates. The fathers and founders of the
commonwealth—the statesman, the priest, and the soldier—
deemed it a duty then to assume the outward state and majesty,
which, in accordance with antique style, was looked upon as
the proper garb of public or social eminence. All came forth,
to move in procession before the people's eye, and thus impart
a needed dignity to the simple framework of a government so
newly constructed.

Then, too, the people were countenanced, if not encouraged,
in relaxing the severe and close application to their various
modes of rugged industry, which, at all other times, seemed of
the same piece and material with their religion. Here, it is true,
were none of the appliances which popular merriment would
so readily have found in the England of Elizabeth's time, or
that of James;—no rude shows of a theatrical kind; no minstrel
with his harp and legendary ballad, nor gleeman, with an ape
dancing to his music; no juggler, with his tricks of mimic

witchcraft; no Merry Andrew, to stir up the multitude with jests, perhaps hundreds of years old, but still effective, by their appeals to the very broadest sources of mirthful sympathy. All such professors of the several branches of jocularity would have been sternly repressed, not only by the rigid discipline of law, but by the general sentiment which gives law its vitality. Not the less, however, the great, honest face of the people smiled, grimly, perhaps, but widely too. Nor were sports wanting, such as the colonists had witnessed, and shared in, long ago, at the country fairs and on the village-greens of England; and which it was thought well to keep alive on this new soil, for the sake of the courage and manliness that were essential in them. Wrestling-matches, in the differing fashions of Cornwall and Devonshire, were seen here and there about the market-place; in one corner, there was a friendly bout at quarterstaff; and—what attracted most interest of all—on the platform of the pillory, already so noted in our pages, two masters of defence were commencing an exhibition with the buckler and broadsword. But, much to the disappointment of the crowd, this latter business was broken off by the interposition of the town beadle, who had no idea of permitting the majesty of the law to be violated by such an abuse of one of its consecrated places.

It may not be too much to affirm, on the whole, (the people being then in the first stages of joyless deportment, and the offspring of sires who had known how to be merry, in their day,) that they would compare favorably, in point of holiday keeping, with their descendants, even at so long an interval as ourselves. Their immediate posterity, the generation next to the early emigrants, wore the blackest shade of Puritanism, and so darkened the national visage with it, that all the subsequent years have not sufficed to clear it up. We have yet to learn again the forgotten art of gayety.

The picture of human life in the market-place, though its general tint was the sad gray, brown, or black of the English emigrants, was yet enlivened by some diversity of hue. A

party of Indians—in their savage finery of curiously embroidered deer-skin robes, wampum-belts, red and yellow ochre,
and feathers, and armed with the bow and arrow and stone-
headed spear—stood apart, with countenances of inflexible
gravity, beyond what even the Puritan aspect could attain.
Nor, wild as were these painted barbarians, were they the
wildest feature of the scene. This distinction could more justly
be claimed by some mariners,—a part of the crew of the vessel
from the Spanish Main,—who had come ashore to see the
humors of Election Day. They were rough-looking despera-
does, with sun-blackened faces, and an immensity of beard;
their wide, short trousers were confined about the waist by
belts, often clasped with a rough plate of gold, and sustaining
always a long knife, and, in some instances, a sword. From
beneath their broad-brimmed hats of palm-leaf, gleamed eyes
which, even in good nature and merriment, had a kind of animal ferocity. They transgressed, without fear or scruple, the
rules of behaviour that were binding on all others; smoking
tobacco under the beadle's very nose, although each whiff
would have cost a townsman a shilling; and quaffing, at their
pleasure, draughts of wine or aqua-vitæ from pocket-flasks,
which they freely tendered to the gaping crowd around them.
It remarkably characterized the incomplete morality of the
age, rigid as we call it, that a license was allowed the seafaring class, not merely for their freaks on shore, but for far more
desperate deeds on their proper element. The sailor of that
day would go near to be arraigned as a pirate in our own.
There could be little doubt, for instance, that this very ship's
crew, though no unfavorable specimens of the nautical brotherhood, had been guilty, as we should phrase it, of depreda-
tions on the Spanish commerce, such as would have perilled
all their necks in a modern court of justice.

But the sea, in those old times, heaved, swelled, and foamed
very much at its own will, or subject only to the tempestuous
wind, with hardly any attempts at regulation by human law.
The buccaneer on the wave might relinquish his calling, and

become at once, if he chose, a man of probity and piety on land; nor, even in the full career of his reckless life, was he regarded as a personage with whom it was disreputable to traffic, or casually associate. Thus, the Puritan elders, in their black cloaks, starched bands, and steeple-crowned hats, smiled not unbenignantly at the clamor and rude deportment of these jolly seafaring men; and it excited neither surprise nor animadversion when so reputable a citizen as old Roger Chillingworth, the physician, was seen to enter the market-place, in close and familiar talk with the commander of the questionable vessel.

The latter was by far the most showy and gallant figure, so far as apparel went, anywhere to be seen among the multitude. He wore a profusion of ribbons on his garment, and gold lace on his hat, which was also encircled by a gold chain, and surmounted with a feather. There was a sword at his side, and a sword-cut on his forehead, which, by the arrangement of his hair, he seemed anxious rather to display than hide. A landsman could hardly have worn this garb and shown this face, and worn and shown them both with such a galliard air, without undergoing stern question before a magistrate, and probably incurring fine or imprisonment, or perhaps an exhibition in the stocks. As regarded the shipmaster, however, all was looked upon as pertaining to the character, as to a fish his glistening scales.

After parting from the physician, the commander of the Bristol ship strolled idly through the market-place; until, happening to approach the spot where Hester Prynne was standing, he appeared to recognize, and did not hesistate to address her. As was usually the case wherever Hester stood, a small, vacant area—a sort of magic circle—had formed itself about her, into which, though the people were elbowing one another at a little distance, none ventured, or felt disposed to intrude. It was a forcible type of the moral solitude in which the scarlet letter enveloped its fated wearer; partly by her own reserve, and partly by the instinctive, though no longer so unkindly, withdrawal of her fellow-creatures. Now, if never before, it answered a good purpose, by enabling Hester and the seaman to speak together without risk of being overheard; and so changed was Hester Prynne's repute before the public, that the matron in town most eminent for rigid morality could not have held such intercourse with less result of scandal than herself.

"So, mistress," said the mariner, "I must bid the steward make ready one more berth than you bargained for! No fear of scurvy or ship-fever, this voyage! What with the ship's surgeon and this other doctor, our only danger will be from drug or pill; more by token, as there is a lot of apothecary's stuff aboard, which I traded for with a Spanish vessel."

"What mean you?" inquired Hester, startled more than she permitted to appear. "Have you another passenger?"

"Why, know you not," cried the shipmaster, "that this physician here—Chillingworth, he calls himself—is minded to try my cabin-fare with you? Ay, ay, you must have known it; for he tells me he is of your party, and a close friend to the gentleman you spoke of,—he that is in peril from these sour old Puritan rulers!"

"They know each other well, indeed," replied Hester, with a mien of calmness, though in the utmost consternation. "They have long dwelt together."

Nothing further passed between the mariner and Hester Prynne. But, at that instant, she beheld old Roger Chillingworth himself, standing in the remotest corner of the market-place, and smiling on her; a smile which—across the wide and bustling square, and through all the talk and laughter, and various thoughts, moods, and interests of the crowd—conveyed secret and fearful meaning.

22. The Procession

BEFORE Hester Prynne could call together her thoughts, and consider what was practicable to be done in this new and startling aspect of affairs, the sound of military music was heard approaching along a contiguous street. It denoted the advance of the procession of magistrates and citizens, on its way towards the meeting-house; where, in compliance with a custom thus early established, and ever since observed, the Reverend Mr. Dimmesdale was to deliver an Election Sermon.

Soon the head of the procession showed itself, with a slow and stately march, turning a corner, and making its way across the market-place. First came the music. It comprised a variety of instruments, perhaps imperfectly adapted to one another, and played with no great skill, but yet attaining the great object for which the harmony of drum and clarion addresses itself to the multitude,—that of imparting a higher and more heroic air to the scene of life that passes before the eye. Little Pearl at first clapped her hands, but then lost, for an instant, the restless agitation that had kept her in a continual effervescence throughout the morning; she gazed silently, and seemed to be borne upward, like a floating sea-bird, on the long heaves and swells of sound. But she was brought back to her former mood by the shimmer of the sunshine on the weapons and bright armour of the military company, which followed after the music, and formed the honorary escort of the procession. This body of soldiery—which still sustains a corporate existence, and marches down from past ages with an ancient and honorable fame—was composed of no mercenary materials. Its ranks were filled with gentlemen, who felt the stirrings of martial impulse, and sought to establish a kind of College of Arms, where, as in an association of Knights Templars, they might learn the science, and, so far as peaceful exercise would teach them, the practices of war.

The high estimation then placed upon the military character might be seen in the lofty port of each individual member of the company. Some of them, indeed, by their services in the Low Countries and on other fields of European warfare, had fairly won their title to assume the name and pomp of soldiership. The entire array, moreover, clad in burnished steel, and with plumage nodding over their bright morions, had a brilliancy of effect which no modern display can aspire to equal.

And yet the men of civil eminence, who came immediately behind the military escort, were better worth a thoughtful observer's eye. Even in outward demeanour they showed a stamp of majesty that made the warrior's haughty stride look vulgar, if not absurd. It was an age when what we call talent had far less consideration than now, but the massive materials which produce stability and dignity of character a great deal more. The people possessed, by hereditary right, the quality of reverence; which, in their descendants, if it survive at all, exists in smaller proportion, and with a vastly diminished force in the selection and estimate of public men. The change may be for good or ill, and is partly, perhaps, for both. In that old day, the English settler on these rude shores,—having left king, nobles, and all degrees of awful rank behind, while still the faculty and necessity of reverence were strong in him,—bestowed it on the white hair and venerable brow of age; on long-tried integrity; on solid wisdom and sad-colored experience; on endowments of that grave and weighty order, which gives the idea of permanence, and comes under the general definition of respectability. These primitive statesmen, therefore,—Bradstreet, Endicott, Dudley,[1] Bellingham, and their

---

[1] John Endicott (*c.* 1589–1665) was one of the incorporators to whom the royal charter for the Massachusetts settlement was granted, and from 1628 to Winthrop's arrival in 1630 he served as governor. He was the principal founder of Salem and served again as governor in 1644, 1649, 1651–1653, and 1655–1664. Endicott possessed a militant and colorful character, and Hawthorne based two

compeers,—who were elevated to power by the early choice of the people, seem to have been not often brilliant, but distinguished by a ponderous sobriety, rather than activity of intellect. They had a fortitude and self-reliance, and, in time of difficulty or peril, stood up for the welfare of the state like a line of cliffs against a tempestuous tide. The traits of character here indicated were well represented in the square cast of countenance and large physical development of the new colonial magistrates. So far as a demeanour of natural authority was concerned, the mother country need not have been ashamed to see these foremost men of an actual democracy adopted into the House of Peers, or made the Privy Council of the sovereign.

Next in order to the magistrates came the young and eminently distinguished divine, from whose lips the religious discourse of the anniversary was expected. His was the profession, at that era, in which intellectual ability displayed itself far more than in political life; for—leaving a higher motive out of the question—it offered inducements powerful enough, in the almost worshipping respect of the community, to win the most aspiring ambition into its service. Even political power—as in the case of Increase Mather [2]—was within the grasp of a successful priest.

---

stories in *Twice-Told Tales* on his exploits: "Endicott and the Red Cross," and "The May-Pole of Merry Mount."

Simon Bradstreet (1603–1697), husband of the poet Anne Bradstreet, was governor of Massachusetts in 1679–1686 and 1689–1692. When the New England Confederation was formed, Bradstreet and William Hathorne, Hawthorne's ancestor, served as commissioners for Massachusetts. Unlike the two men with whom he is joined in Hawthorne's text, Bradstreet was a moderate.

Thomas Dudley (1576–1653) was elected governor of Massachusetts in 1634, 1640, 1645, and 1650. He was noted for his strictness and clashed even with Winthrop, whom he believed to be too lax.

[2] Increase Mather (1639–1723) was one of the most distinguished members of the first American-born Puritan generation. He was minister of the North Church in Boston, served (1685–1701) as

It was the observation of those who beheld him now, that never, since Mr. Dimmesdale first set his foot on the New England shore, had he exhibited such energy as was seen in the gait and air with which he kept his pace in the procession. There was no feebleness of step, as at other times; his frame was not bent; nor did his hand rest ominously upon his heart. Yet, if the clergyman were rightly viewed, his strength seemed not of the body. It might be spiritual, and imparted to him by angelic ministrations. It might be the exhilaration of that potent cordial, which is distilled only in the furnace-glow of earnest and long-continued thought. Or, perchance, his sensitive temperament was invigorated by the loud and piercing music, that swelled heavenward, and uplifted him on its ascending wave. Nevertheless, so abstracted was his look, it might be questioned whether Mr. Dimmesdale even heard the music. There was his body, moving onward, and with an unaccustomed force. But where was his mind? Far and deep in its own region, busying itself, with preternatural activity, to marshal a procession of stately thoughts that were soon to issue thence; and so he saw nothing, heard nothing, knew nothing, of what was around him; but the spiritual element took up the feeble frame, and carried it along, unconscious of the burden, and converting it to spirit like itself. Men of uncommon intellect, who have grown morbid, possess this occasional power of mighty effort, into which they throw the life of many days, and then are lifeless for as many more.

Hester Prynne, gazing stedfastly at the clergyman, felt a dreary influence come over her, but wherefore or whence she knew not; unless that he seemed so remote from her own sphere, and utterly beyond her reach. One glance of recogni-

---

president of Harvard, and undertook the very important post of Massachusetts ambassador to the royal court, where, in 1689, he negotiated a new charter for the colony. His father's generation had rigorously separated civil and religious offices, but Increase Mather served in both because of his extraordinary abilities. He was the father of Cotton Mather.

tion, she had imagined, must needs pass between them. She thought of the dim forest, with its little dell of solitude, and love, and anguish, and the mossy tree-trunk, where, sitting hand in hand, they had mingled their sad and passionate talk with the melancholy murmur of the brook. How deeply had they known each other then! And was this the man? She hardly knew him now! He, moving proudly past, enveloped, as it were, in the rich music, with the procession of majestic and venerable fathers; he, so unattainable in his wordly position, and still more so in that far vista of his unsympathizing thoughts, through which she now beheld him! Her spirit sank with the idea that all must have been a delusion, and that, vividly as she had dreamed it, there could be no real bond betwixt the clergyman and herself. And thus much of woman was there in Hester, that she could scarcely forgive him,— least of all now, when the heavy foostep of their approaching Fate might be heard, nearer, nearer, nearer!—for being able so completely to withdraw himself from their mutual world; while she groped darkly, and stretched forth her cold hands, and found him not.

Pearl either saw and responded to her mother's feelings, or herself felt the remoteness and intangibility that had fallen around the minister. While the procession passed, the child was uneasy, fluttering up and down, like a bird on the point of taking flight. When the whole had gone by, she looked up into Hester's face.

"Mother," said she, "was that the same minister that kissed me by the brook?"

"Hold thy peace, dear little Pearl!" whispered her mother. "We must not always talk in the market-place of what happens to us in the forest."

"I could not be sure that it was he; so strange he looked," continued the child. "Else I would have run to him, and bid him kiss me now, before all the people; even as he did yonder among the dark old trees. What would the minister have said, mother? Would he have clapped his hand over his heart, and scowled on me, and bid me begone?"

"What should he say, Pearl," answered Hester, "save that it was no time to kiss, and that kisses are not to be given in the market-place? Well for thee, foolish child, that thou didst not speak to him!"

Another shade of the same sentiment, in reference to Mr. Dimmesdale, was expressed by a person whose eccentricities —or insanity, as we should term it—led her to do what few of the townspeople would have ventured on; to begin a conversation with the wearer of the scarlet letter, in public. It was Mistress Hibbins, who, arrayed in great magnificence, with a triple ruff, a broidered stomacher, a gown of rich velvet, and a gold-headed cane, had come forth to see the procession. As this ancient lady had the renown (which subsequently cost her no less a price than her life) of being a principal actor in all the works of necromancy that were continually going forward, the crowd gave way before her, and seemed to fear the touch of her garment, as if it carried the plague among its gorgeous folds. Seen in conjunction with Hester Prynne,— kindly as so many now felt towards the latter,—the dread inspired by Mistress Hibbins was doubled, and caused a general movement from that part of the market-place in which the two women stood.

"Now, what mortal imagination could conceive it!" whispered the old lady confidentially to Hester. "Yonder divine man! That saint on earth, as the people uphold him to be, and as—I must needs say—he really looks! Who, now, that saw him pass in the procession, would think how little while it is since he went forth out of his study,—chewing a Hebrew text of Scripture in his mouth, I warrant,—to take an airing in the forest! Aha! we know what that means, Hester Prynne! But, truly, forsooth, I find it hard to believe him the same man. Many a church-member saw I, walking behind the music, that has danced in the same measure with me, when Somebody was fiddler, and, it might be, an Indian powwow[3] or a Lapland wizard changing hands with us! That is but a trifle, when

[3] A priest or medicine man.

a woman knows the world. But this minister! Couldst thou surely tell, Hester, whether he was the same man that encountered thee on the forest-path!"

"Madam, I know not of what you speak," answered Hester Prynne, feeling Mistress Hibbins to be of infirm mind; yet strangely startled and awe-stricken by the confidence with which she affirmed a personal connection between so many persons (herself among them) and the Evil One. "It is not for me to talk lightly of a learned and pious minister of the Word, like the Reverend Mr. Dimmesdale!"

"Fie, woman, fie!" cried the old lady, shaking her finger at Hester. "Dost thou think I have been to the forest so many times, and have yet no skill to judge who else has been there? Yea; though no leaf of the wild garlands, which they wore while they danced, be left in their hair! I know thee, Hester; for I behold the token. We may all see it in the sunshine; and it glows like a red flame in the dark. Thou wearest it openly; so there need be no question about that. But this minister! Let me tell thee in thine ear! When the Black Man sees one of his own servants, signed and sealed, so shy of owning to the bond as is the Reverend Mr. Dimmesdale, he hath a way of ordering matters so that the mark shall be disclosed in open daylight to the eyes of all the world! What is it that the minister seeks to hide, with his hand always over his heart? Ha, Hester Prynne!"

"What is it, good Mistress Hibbins?" eagerly asked little Pearl. "Hast thou seen it?"

"No matter, darling!" responded Mistress Hibbins, making Pearl a profound reverence. "Thou thyself wilt see it, one time or another. They say, child, thou art of the lineage of the Prince of the Air! Wilt thou ride with me, some fine night, to see thy father? Then thou shalt know wherefore the minister keeps his hand over his heart!"

Laughing so shrilly that all the market-place could hear her, the weird old gentlewoman took her departure.

By this time the preliminary prayer had been offered in the

meeting-house, and the accents of the Reverend Mr. Dimmesdale were heard commencing his discourse. An irresistible feeling kept Hester near the spot. As the sacred edifice was too much thronged to admit another auditor, she took up her position close beside the scaffold of the pillory. It was in sufficient proximity to bring the whole sermon to her ears, in the shape of an indistinct, but varied, murmur and flow of the minister's very peculiar voice.

This vocal organ was in itself a rich endowment; insomuch that a listener, comprehending nothing of the language in which the preacher spoke, might still have been swayed to and fro by the mere tone and cadence. Like all other music, it breathed passion and pathos, and emotions high or tender, in a tongue native to the human heart, wherever educated. Muffled as the sound was by its passage through the church-walls, Hester Prynne listened with such intentness, and sympathized so intimately, that the sermon had throughout a meaning for her, entirely apart from its indistinguishable words. These, perhaps, if more distinctly heard, might have been only a grosser medium, and have clogged the spiritual sense. Now she caught the low undertone, as of the wind sinking down to repose itself; then ascended with it, as it rose through progressive gradations of sweetness and power, until its volume seemed to envelop her with an atmosphere of awe and solemn grandeur. And yet, majestic as the voice sometimes became, there was for ever in it an essential character of plaintiveness. A loud or low expression of anguish,—the whisper, or the shriek, as it might be conceived, of suffering humanity, that touched a sensibility in every bosom! At times this deep strain of pathos was all that could be heard, and scarcely heard, sighing amid a desolate silence. But even when the minister's voice grew high and commanding,—when it gushed irrepressibly upward,—when it assumed its utmost breadth and power, so overfilling the church as to burst its way through the solid walls, and diffuse itself in the open air,—still, if the auditor listened intently, and for the purpose, he could detect the same

cry of pain. What was it? The complaint of a human heart,
sorrow-laden, perchance guilty, telling its secret, whether of
guilt or sorrow, to the great heart of mankind; beseeching its
sympathy or forgiveness,—at every moment,—in each accent,—
and never in vain! It was this profound and continual undertone that gave the clergyman his most appropriate power.

During all this time Hester stood, statue-like, at the foot of
the scaffold. If the minister's voice had not kept her there,
there would nevertheless have been an inevitable magnetism
in that spot, whence she dated the first hour of her life of
ignominy. There was a sense within her,—too ill-defined to be
made a thought, but weighing heavily on her mind,—that her
whole orb of life, both before and after, was connected with
this spot, as with the one point that gave it unity.

Little Pearl, meanwhile, had quitted her mother's side, and
was playing at her own will about the market-place. She made
the sombre crowd cheerful by her erratic and glistening ray;
even as a bird of bright plumage illuminates a whole tree of
dusky foliage by darting to and fro, half seen and half concealed, amid the twilight of the clustering leaves. She had an
undulating, but, oftentimes, a sharp and irregular movement.
It indicated the restless vivacity of her spirit, which to-day was
doubly indefatigable in its tiptoe dance, because it was played
upon and vibrated with her mother's disquietude. Whenever
Pearl saw any thing to excite her ever active and wandering
curiosity, she flew thitherward, and, as we might say, seized
upon that man or thing as her own property, so far as she
desired it; but without yielding the minutest degree of control over her motions in requital. The Puritans looked on, and,
if they smiled, were none the less inclined to pronounce the
child a demon offspring, from the indescribable charm of
beauty and eccentricity that shone through her little figure,
and sparkled with its activity. She ran and looked the wild Indian in the face; and he grew conscious of a nature wilder than
his own. Thence, with native audacity, but still with a reserve
as characteristic, she flew into the midst of a group of mariners,

the swarthy-cheeked wild men of the ocean, as the Indians were of the land; and they gazed wonderingly and admiringly at Pearl, as if a flake of the sea-foam had taken the shape of a little maid, and were gifted with a soul of the sea-fire, that flashes beneath the prow in the night-time.

One of these seafaring men—the shipmaster, indeed, who had spoken to Hester Prynne—was ,so smitten with Pearl's aspect, that he attempted to lay hands upon her, with purpose to snatch a kiss. Finding it as impossible to touch her as to catch a humming-bird in the air, he took from his hat the gold chain that was twisted about it, and threw it to the child. Pearl immediately twined it around her neck and waist, with such happy skill, that, once seen there, it became a part of her, and it was difficult to imagine her without it.

"Thy mother is yonder woman with the scarlet letter," said the seaman. "Wilt thou carry her a message from me?"

"If the message pleases me I will," answered Pearl.

"Then tell her," rejoined he, "that I spake again with the black-a-visaged, hump-shouldered old doctor, and he engages to bring his friend, the gentleman she wots of, aboard with him. So let thy mother take no thought, save for herself and thee. Wilt thou tell her this, thou witch-baby?'

"Mistress Hibbins says my father is the Prince of the Air!" cried Pearl, with her naughty smile. "If thou callest me that ill name, I shall tell him of thee; and he will chase thy ship with a tempest!"

Pursuing a zigzag course across the market-place, the child returned to her mother, and communicated what the mariner had said. Hester's strong, calm, stedfastly enduring spirit almost sank, at last, on beholding this dark and grim countenance of an inevitable doom, which—at the moment when a passage seemed to open for the minister and herself out of their labyrinth of misery—showed itself, with an unrelenting smile, right in the midst of their path.

With her mind harassed by the terrible perplexity in which the shipmaster's intelligence involved her, she was also sub-

jected to another trial. There were many people present, from
the country roundabout, who had often heard of the scarlet
letter, and to whom it had been made terrific by a hundred
false or exaggerated rumors, but who had never beheld it with
their own bodily eyes. These, after exhausting other modes of
amusement, now thronged about Hester Prynne with rude and
boorish intrusiveness. Unscrupulous as it was, however, it
could not bring them nearer than a circuit of several yards. At
that distance they accordingly stood, fixed there by the cen-
trifugal force of the repugnance which the mystic symbol
inspired. The whole gang of sailors, likewise, observing the
press of spectators, and learning the purport of the scarlet
letter, came and thrust their sunburnt and desperado-looking
faces into the ring. Even the Indians were affected by a sort
of cold shadow of the white man's curiosity, and, gliding
through the crowd, fastened their snake-like black eyes on
Hester's bosom; conceiving, perhaps, that the wearer of this
brilliantly embroidered badge must needs be a personage of
high dignity among her people. Lastly, the inhabitants of the
town (their own interest in this worn-out subject languidly
reviving itself, by sympathy with what they saw others feel)
lounged idly to the same quarter, and tormented Hester
Prynne, perhaps more than all the rest, with their cool, well-
acquainted gaze at her familiar shame. Hester saw and recognized the self-same faces of that group of matrons, who had
awaited her forthcoming from the prison-door, seven years
ago; all save one, the youngest and only compassionate among
them, whose burial-robe she had since made. At the final hour,
when she was so soon to fling aside the burning letter, it had
strangely become the centre of more remark and excitement,
and was thus made to sear her breast more painfully, than at
any time since the first day she put it on.

While Hester stood in that magic circle of ignominy, where
the cunning cruelty of her sentence seemed to have fixed her
for ever, the admirable preacher was looking down from the
sacred pulpit upon an audience, whose very inmost spirits had

yielded to his control. The sainted minister in the church! The woman of the scarlet letter in the market-place! What imagination would have been irreverent enough to surmise that the same scorching stigma was on them both?

23. The Revelation of the Scarlet Letter

THE eloquent voice, on which the souls of the listening audience had been borne aloft, as on the swelling waves of the sea, at length came to a pause. There was a momentary silence, profound as what should follow the utterance of oracles. Then ensued a murmur and half-hushed tumult; as if the auditors, released from the high spell that had transported them into the region of another's mind, were returning into themselves, with all their awe and wonder still heavy on them. In a moment more, the crowd began to gush forth from the doors of the church. Now that there was an end, they needed other breath, more fit to support the gross and earthly life into which they relapsed, than that atmosphere which the preacher had converted into words of flame, and had burdened with the rich fragrance of his thought.

In the open air their rapture broke into speech. The street and the market-place absolutely babbled, from side to side, with applauses of the minister. His hearers could not rest until they had told one another of what each knew better than he could tell or hear. According to their united testimony, never had man spoken in so wise, so high, and so holy a spirit, as he that spake this day; nor had inspiration ever breathed

through mortal lips more evidently than it did through his.
Its influence could be seen, as it were, descending upon him,
and possessing him, and continually lifting him out of the
written discourse that lay before him, and filling him with
ideas that must have been as marvellous to himself as to his
audience. His subject, it appeared, had been the relation
between the Deity and the communities of mankind, with a
special reference to the New England which they were here
planting in the wilderness. And, as he drew towards the close,
a spirit as of prophecy had come upon him, constraining him
to its purpose as mightily as the old prophets of Israel were
constrained; only with this difference, that, whereas the
Jewish seers had denounced judgments and ruin on their country, it was his mission to foretell a high and glorious destiny
for the newly gathered people of the Lord. But, throughout
it all, and through the whole discourse, there had been a
certain deep, sad undertone of pathos, which could not be interpreted otherwise than as the natural regret of one soon to
pass away. Yes; their minister whom they so loved—and who
so loved them all, that he could not depart heavenward without a sigh—had the foreboding of untimely death upon him,
and would soon leave them in their tears! This idea of his
transitory stay on earth gave the last emphasis to the effect
which the preacher had produced; it was as if an angel, in his
passage to the skies, had shaken his bright wings over the people for an instant,—at once a shadow and a splendor,—and had
shed down a shower of golden truths upon them.

Thus, there had come to the Reverend Mr. Dimmesdale—
as to most men, in their various spheres, though seldom
recognized until they see it far behind them—an epoch of life
more brilliant and full of triumph than any previous one, or
than any which could hereafter be. He stood, at this moment,
on the very proudest eminence of superiority, to which the gifts
of intellect, rich lore, prevailing eloquence, and a reputation
of whitest sanctity, could exalt a clergyman in New England's
earliest days, when the professional character was of it-

self a lofty pedestal. Such was the position which the minister occupied, as he bowed his head forward on the cushions of the pulpit, at the close of his Election Sermon. Meanwhile, Hester Prynne was standing beside the scaffold of the pillory, with the scarlet letter still burning on her breast!

Now was heard again the clangor of the music, and the measured tramp of the military escort, issuing from the church-door. The procession was to be marshalled thence to the town-hall, where a solemn banquet would complete the ceremonies of the day.

Once more, therefore, the train of venerable and majestic fathers was seen moving through a broad pathway of the people, who drew back reverently, on either side, as the Governor and magistrates, the old and wise men, the holy ministers, and all that were eminent and renowned, advanced into the midst of them. When they were fairly in the market-place, their presence was greeted by a shout. This—though doubtless it might acquire additional force and volume from the childlike loyalty which the age awarded to its rulers—was felt to be an irrepressible outburst of the enthusiasm kindled in the auditors by that high strain of eloquence which was yet reverberating in their ears. Each felt the impulse in himself, and, in the same breath, caught it from his neighbour. Within the church, it had hardly been kept down; beneath the sky, it pealed upward to the zenith. There were human beings enough, and enough of highly wrought and symphonious feeling, to produce that more impressive sound than the organ-tones of the blast, or the thunder, or the roar of the sea; even that mighty swell of many voices, blended into one great voice by the universal impulse which makes likewise one vast heart out of the many. Never, from the soil of New England, had gone up such a shout! Never, on New England soil, had stood the man so honored by his mortal brethren as the preacher!

How fared it with him then? Were there not the brilliant particles of a halo in the air about his head? So etherealized by spirit as he was, and so apotheosized by worshipping admirers, did his footsteps in the procession really tread upon the dust of earth?

As the ranks of military men and civil fathers moved onward, all eyes were turned towards the point where the minister was seen to approach among them. The shout died into a murmur, as one portion of the crowd after another obtained a glimpse of him. How feeble and pale he looked amid all his triumph! The energy—or say, rather, the inspiration which had held him up, until he should have delivered the sacred message that brought its own strength along with it from heaven—was withdrawn, now that it had so faithfully performed its office. The glow, which they had just before beheld burning on his cheek, was extinguished, like a flame that sinks down hopelessly among the late-decaying embers. It seemed hardly the face of a man alive, with such a deathlike hue; it was hardly a man with life in him, that tottered on his path so nervelessly, yet tottered, and did not fall!

One of his clerical brethren,—it was the venerable John Wilson,—observing the state in which Mr. Dimmesdale was left by the retiring wave of intellect and sensibility, stepped forward hastily to offer his support. The minister tremulously, but decidedly, repelled the old man's arm. He still walked onward, if that movement could be so described, which rather resembled the wavering effort of an infant, with its mother's arms in view, outstretched to tempt him forward. And now, almost imperceptible as were the latter steps of his progress, he had come opposite the well-remembered and weather-darkened scaffold, where, long since, with all that dreary lapse of time between, Hester Prynne had encountered the world's ignominious stare. There stood Hester, holding little Pearl by the hand! And there was the scarlet letter on her breast! The minister here made a pause; although the music still played the stately and rejoicing march to which the procession moved. It summoned him onward,—onward to the festival! —but here he made a pause.

Bellingham, for the last few moments, had kept an anxious eye upon him. He now left his own place in the procession, and advanced to give assistance; judging from Mr. Dimmesdale's aspect that he must otherwise inevitably fall. But there was something in the latter's expression that warned back the magistrate, although a man not readily obeying the vague intimations that pass from one spirit to another. The crowd, meanwhile, looked on with awe and wonder. This earthly faintness was, in their view, only another phase of the minister's celestial strength; nor would it have seemed a miracle too high to be wrought for one so holy, had he ascended before their eyes, waxing dimmer and brighter, and fading at last into the light of heaven!

He turned towards the scaffold, and stretched forth his arms.

"Hester," said he, "come hither! Come, my little Pearl!"

It was a ghastly look with which he regarded them; but there was something at once tender and strangely triumphant in it. The child, with the bird-like motion which was one of her characteristics, flew to him, and clasped her arms about his knees. Hester Prynne—slowly, as if impelled by inevitable fate, and against her strongest will—likewise drew near, but paused before she reached him. At this instant old Roger Chillingworth thrust himself through the crowd,—or, perhaps, so dark, disturbed, and evil was his look, he rose up out of some nether region,—to snatch back his victim from what he sought to do! Be that as it might, the old man rushed forward and caught the minister by the arm.

"Madman, hold! What is your purpose?" whispered he. "Wave back that woman! Cast off this child! All shall be well! Do not blacken your fame, and perish in dishonor! I can yet save you! Would you bring infamy on your sacred profession?"

"Ha, tempter! Methinks thou art too late!" answered the minister, encountering his eye, fearfully, but firmly. "Thy power is not what it was! With God's help, I shall escape thee now!"

He again extended his hand to the woman of the scarlet letter.

"Hester Prynne," cried he, with a piercing earnestness, "in

the name of Him, so terrible and so merciful, who gives me grace, at this last moment, to do what—for my own heavy sin and miserable agony—I withheld myself from doing seven years ago, come hither now, and twine thy strength about me! Thy strength, Hester; but let it be guided by the will which God hath granted me! This wretched and wronged old man is opposing it with all his might!—with all his own might and the fiend's! Come, Hester, come! Support me up yonder scaffold!"

The crowd was in a tumult. The men of rank and dignity, who stood more immediately around the clergyman, were so taken by surprise, and so perplexed as to the purport of what they saw,—unable to receive the explanation which most readily presented itself, or to imagine any other,—that they remained silent and inactive spectators of the judgment which Providence seemed about to work. They beheld the minister, leaning on Hester's shoulder and supported by her arm around him, approach the scaffold, and ascend its steps; while still the little hand of the sin-born child was clasped in his. Old Roger Chillingworth followed, as one intimately connected with the drama of guilt and sorrow in which they had all been actors, and well entitled, therefore, to be present at its closing scene.

"Hadst thou sought the whole earth over," said he, looking darkly at the clergyman, "there was no one place so secret,—no high place nor lowly place, where thou couldst have escaped me,—save on this very scaffold!"

"Thanks be to Him who hath led me hither!" answered the minister.

Yet he trembled, and turned to Hester with an expression of doubt and anxiety in his eyes, not the less evidently betrayed, that there was a feeble smile upon his lips.

"Is not this better," murmured he, "than what we dreamed of in the forest?"

"I know not! I know not!" she hurriedly replied. "Better? Yea; so we may both die, and little Pearl die with us!"

"For thee and Pearl, be it as God shall order," said the minister; "and God is merciful! Let me now do the will which he hath made plain before my sight. For, Hester, I am a dying man. So let me make haste to take my shame upon me."

Partly supported by Hester Prynne, and holding one hand of little Pearl's, the Reverend Mr. Dimmesdale turned to the dignified and venerable rulers; to the holy ministers, who were his brethren; to the people, whose great heart was thoroughly appalled, yet overflowing with tearful sympathy, as knowing that some deep life-matter—which, if full of sin, was full of anguish and repentance likewise—was now to be laid open to them. The sun, but little past its meridian, shone down upon the clergyman, and gave a distinctness to his figure, as he stood out from all the earth to put in his plea of guilty at the bar of Eternal Justice.

"People of New England!" cried he, with a voice that rose over them, high, solemn, and majestic,—yet had always a tremor through it, and sometimes a shriek, struggling up out of a fathomless depth of remorse and woe,—"ye, that have loved me!—ye, that have deemed me holy!—behold me here, the one sinner of the world! At last!—at last!—I stand upon the spot where, seven years since, I should have stood; here, with this woman, whose arm, more than the little strength wherewith I have crept hitherward, sustains me, at this dreadful moment, from grovelling down upon my face! Lo, the scarlet letter which Hester wears! Ye have all shuddered at it! Wherever her walk hath been,—wherever, so miserably burdened, she may have hoped to find repose,—it hath cast a lurid gleam of awe and horrible repugnance roundabout her. But there stood one in the midst of you, at whose brand of sin and infamy ye have not shuddered!"

It seemed, at this point, as if the minister must leave the remainder of his secret undisclosed. But he fought back the bodily weakness,—and, still more, the faintness of heart,—that was striving for the mastery with him. He threw off all assistance, and stepped passionately forward a pace before the woman and the child.

"It was on him!" he continued, with a kind of fierceness; so determined was he to speak out the whole. "God's eye beheld it! The angels were for ever pointing at it! The Devil knew it well, and fretted it continually with the touch of his burning finger! But he hid it cunningly from men, and walked among you with the mien of a spirit, mournful, because so pure in a sinful world!—and sad, because he missed his heavenly kindred! Now, at the death-hour, he stands up before you! He bids you look again at Hester's scarlet letter! He tells you, that, with all its mysterious horror, it is but the shadow of what he bears on his own breast, and that even this, his own red stigma, is no more than the type of what has seared his inmost heart! Stand any here that question God's judgment on a sinner? Behold! Behold a dreadful witness of it!"

With a convulsive motion he tore away the ministerial band from before his breast. It was revealed! But it were irreverent to describe that revelation. For an instant the gaze of the horror-stricken multitude was concentred on the ghastly miracle; while the minister stood with a flush of triumph in his face, as one who, in the crisis of acutest pain, had won a victory. Then, down he sank upon the scaffold! Hester partly raised him, and supported his head against her bosom. Old Roger Chillingworth knelt down beside him, with a blank, dull countenance, out of which the life seemed to have departed.

"Thou hast escaped me!" he repeated more than once. "Thou hast escaped me!"

"May God forgive thee!" said the minister. "Thou, too, hast deeply sinned!"

He withdrew his dying eyes from the old man, and fixed them on the woman and the child.

"My little Pearl," said he feebly,—and there was a sweet and gentle smile over his face, as of a spirit sinking into deep repose; nay, now that the burden was removed, it seemed almost as if he would be sportive with the child,—"dear little

Pearl, wilt thou kiss me now? Thou wouldst not yonder, in the forest! But now thou wilt?"

Pearl kissed his lips. A spell was broken. The great scene of grief, in which the wild infant bore a part, had developed all her sympathies; and as her tears fell upon her father's cheek, they were the pledge that she would grow up amid human joy and sorrow, nor for ever do battle with the world, but be a woman in it. Towards her mother, too, Pearl's errand as a messenger of anguish was all fulfilled.

"Hester," said the clergyman, "farewell!"

"Shall we not meet again?" whispered she, bending her face down close to his. "Shall we not spend our immortal life together? Surely, surely, we have ransomed one another, with all this woe! Thou lookest far into eternity, with those bright dying eyes! Then tell me what thou seest?"

"Hush, Hester, hush!" said he, with tremulous solemnity. "The law we broke!—the sin here so awfully revealed!—let these alone be in thy thoughts! I fear! I fear! It may be, that, when we forgot our God,—when we violated our reverence each for the other's soul,—it was thenceforth vain to hope that we could meet hereafter, in an everlasting and pure re-union. God knows; and He is merciful! He hath proved his mercy, most of all, in my afflictions. By giving me this burning torture to bear upon my breast! By sending yonder dark and terrible old man, to keep the torture always at red-heat! By bringing me hither, to die this death of triumphant ignominy before the people! Had either of these agonies been wanting, I had been lost for ever! Praised be his name! His will be done! Farewell!"

That final word came forth with the minister's expiring breath. The multitude, silent till then, broke out in a strange, deep voice of awe and wonder, which could not as yet find utterance, save in this murmur that rolled so heavily after the departed spirit.

24. Conclusion

AFTER many days, when time sufficed for the people to arrange their thoughts in reference to the foregoing scene, there was more than one account of what had been witnessed on the scaffold.

Most of the spectators testified to having seen, on the breast of the unhappy minister, a SCARLET LETTER—the very semblance of that worn by Hester Prynne—imprinted in the flesh. As regarded its origin, there were various explanations, all of which must necessarily have been conjectural. Some affirmed that the Reverend Mr. Dimmesdale, on the very day when Hester Prynne first wore her ignominious badge, had begun a course of penance,—which he afterwards, in so many futile methods, followed out,—by inflicting a hideous torture on himself. Others contended that the stigma had not been produced until a long time subsequent, when old Roger Chillingworth, being a potent necromancer, had caused it to appear, through the agency of magic and poisonous drugs. Others, again,—and those best able to appreciate the minister's peculiar sensibility, and the wonderful operation of his spirit upon the body,—whispered their belief, that the awful symbol was the effect of the ever active tooth of remorse, gnawing from the inmost heart outwardly, and at last manifesting Heaven's dreadful judgment by the visible presence of the letter. The reader may choose among these theories. We have thrown all the light we could acquire upon the portent, and would gladly, now that it has done its office, erase its deep print out of our own brain; where long meditation has fixed it in very undesirable distinctness.

It is singular, nevertheless, that certain persons, who were spectators of the whole scene, and professed never once to have removed their eyes from the Reverend Mr. Dimmesdale, denied that there was any mark whatever on his breast, more than on a new-born infant's. Neither, by their report, had his dying words acknowledged, nor even remotely implied, any, the slightest connection, on his part, with the guilt for which Hester Prynne had so long worn the scarlet letter. According to these highly respectable witnesses, the minister, conscious that he was dying,—conscious, also, that the reverence of the multitude placed him already among saints and angels,—had desired, by yielding up his breath in the arms of that fallen woman, to express to the world how utterly nugatory is the choicest of man's own righteousness. After exhausting life in his efforts for mankind's spiritual good, he had made the manner of his death a parable, in order to impress on his admirers the mighty and mournful lesson, that, in the view of Infinite Purity, we are sinners all alike. It was to teach them, that the holiest among us has but attained so far above his fellows as to discern more clearly the Mercy which looks down, and repudiate more utterly the phantom of human merit, which would look aspiringly upward. Without disputing a truth so momentous, we must be allowed to consider this version of Mr. Dimmesdale's story as only an instance of that stubborn fidelity with which a man's friends—and especially a clergyman's—will sometimes uphold his character; when proofs, clear as the mid-day sunshine on the scarlet letter, establish him a false and sin-stained creature of the dust.

The authority which we have chiefly followed—a manuscript of old date, drawn up from the verbal testimony of individuals, some of whom had known Hester Prynne, while others had heard the tale from contemporary witnesses—fully confirms the view taken in the foregoing pages. Among many morals which press upon us from the poor minister's miserable experience, we put only this into a sentence:—"Be true! Be true! Be true! Show freely to the world, if not your worst, yet some trait whereby the worst may be inferred!"

Nothing was more remarkable than the change which took place, almost immediately after Mr. Dimmesdale's death, in the appearance and demeanour of the old man known as Roger Chillingworth. All his strength and energy—all his vital and intellectual force—seemed at once to desert him; insomuch

that he positively withered up, shrivelled away, and almost
vanished from mortal sight, like an uprooted weed that lies
wilting in the sun. This unhappy man had made the very principle of his life to consist in the pursuit and systematic exercise
of revenge; and when, by its completest triumph and consum-
mation, that evil principle was left with no further material to
support it,—when, in short, there was no more devil's work on
earth for him to do, it only remained for the unhumanized
mortal to betake himself whither his Master would find him
tasks enough, and pay him his wages duly. But, to all these
shadowy beings, so long our near acquaintances,—as well Roger
Chillingworth as his companions,—we would fain be merciful.
It is a curious subject of observation and inquiry, whether
hatred and love be not the same thing at bottom. Each, in its
utmost development, supposes a high degree of intimacy and
heart-knowledge; each renders one individual dependent for
the food of his affections and spiritual life upon another; each
leaves the passionate lover, or the no less passionate hater, forlorn and desolate by the withdrawal of his object. Philosophi-
cally considered, therefore, the two passions seem essentially
the same, except that one happens to be seen in a celestial
radiance, and the other in a dusky and lurid glow. In the spiritual world, the old physician and the minister—mutual victims
as they have been—may, unawares, have found their earthly
stock of hatred and antipathy transmuted into golden love.

Leaving this discussion apart, we have a matter of business
to communicate to the reader. At old Roger Chillingworth's
decease (which took place within the year), and by his last
will and testament, of which Governor Bellingham and the
Reverend Mr. Wilson were executors, he bequeathed a very
considerable amount of property, both here and in England,
to little Pearl, the daughter of Hester Prynne.

So Pearl—the elf-child,—the demon offspring, as some people,
up to that epoch, persisted in considering her—became the
richest heiress of her day, in the New World. Not improbably, this circumstance wrought a very material change in the
public estimation; and, had the mother and child remained

here, little Pearl, at a marriageable period of life, might have mingled her wild blood with the lineage of the devoutest Puritan among them all. But, in no long time after the physician's death, the wearer of the scarlet letter disappeared, and Pearl along with her. For many years, though a vague report would now and then find its way across the sea,—like a shapeless piece of driftwood tost ashore, with the initials of a name upon it,—yet no tidings of them unquestionably authentic were received. The story of the scarlet letter grew into a legend. Its spell, however, was still potent, and kept the scaffold awful where the poor minister had died, and likewise the cottage by the sea-shore, where Hester Prynne had dwelt. Near this latter spot, one afternoon, some children were at play, when they beheld a tall woman, in a gray robe, approach the cottage-door. In all those years it had never once been opened; but either she unlocked it, or the decaying wood and iron yielded to her hand, or she glided shadow-like through these impediments,—and, at all events, went in.

On the threshold she paused,—turned partly round,—for, perchance, the idea of entering, all alone, and all so changed, the home of so intense a former life, was more dreary and desolate than even she could bear. But her hesitation was only for an instant, though long enough to display a scarlet letter on her breast.

And Hester Prynne had returned, and taken up her long-forsaken shame. But where was little Pearl? If still alive, she must now have been in the flush and bloom of early womanhood. None knew—nor ever learned, with the fulness of perfect certainty—whether the elf-child had gone thus untimely to a maiden grave; or whether her wild, rich nature had been softened and subdued, and made capable of a woman's gentle happiness. But, through the remainder of Hester's life, there were indications that the recluse of the scarlet letter was the object of love and interest with some inhabitant of another land. Letters came, with armorial seals upon them, though of bearings unknown to English heraldry. In the cottage there were articles of comfort and luxury, such as Hester never cared to use, but which only wealth could have purchased, and affection have imagined for her. There were trifles, too, little ornaments, beautiful tokens of a continual remembrance, that must have been wrought by delicate fingers, at the impulse of a fond heart. And, once, Hester was seen embroidering a baby-garment, with such a lavish richness of golden fancy as would have raised a public tumult, had any infant, thus apparelled, been shown to our sombre-hued community.

In fine, the gossips of that day believed,—and Mr. Surveyor Pue, who made investigations a century later, believed,—and one of his recent successors in office, moreover, faithfully believes,—that Pearl was not only alive, but married, and happy, and mindful of her mother; and that she would most joyfully have entertained that sad and lonely mother at her fireside.

But there was a more real life for Hester Prynne, here, in New England, than in that unknown region where Pearl had found a home. Here had been her sin; here, her sorrow; and here was yet to be her penitence. She had returned, therefore, and resumed,—of her own free will, for not the sternest magistrate of that iron period would have imposed it,—resumed the symbol of which we have related so dark a tale. Never afterwards did it quit her bosom. But, in the lapse of the toilsome, thoughtful, and self-devoted years that made up Hester's life, the scarlet letter ceased to be a stigma which attracted the world's scorn and bitterness, and became a type of something to be sorrowed over, and looked upon with awe, yet with reverence too. And, as Hester Prynne had no selfish ends, nor lived in any measure for her own profit and enjoyment, people brought all their sorrows and perplexities, and besought her counsel, as one who had herself gone through a mighty trouble. Women, more especially,—in the continually recurring trials of wounded, wasted, wronged, misplaced, or erring and sinful passion,—or with the dreary burden of a heart unyielded, because unvalued and unsought,—came to Hester's cottage, demanding why they were so wretched, and what the remedy! Hester comforted and counselled them, as best she might. She assured them, too, of her firm belief, that, at some brighter period, when the world should have grown ripe for it, in Heaven's own time, a new truth would be revealed, in order to establish the whole relation between man and woman on a surer ground of mutual happiness. Earlier in life, Hester had vainly imagined that she herself might be the destined prophetess, but had long since recognized the impossibility that any mission of divine and mysterious truth should be confided to a woman stained with sin, bowed down with shame, or even burdened with a life-long sorrow. The angel and apostle of the coming revelation must be a woman, indeed, but lofty, pure, and beautiful; and wise, moreover, not through dusky grief, but the ethereal medium of joy; and showing how sacred love should make us happy, by the truest test of a life successful to such an end!

So said Hester Prynne, and glanced her sad eyes downward at the scarlet letter. And, after many, many years, a new grave was delved, near an old and sunken one, in that burial-ground beside which King's Chapel has since been built. It was near that old and sunken grave, yet with a space between, as if the dust of the two sleepers had no right to mingle. Yet one tombstone served for both. All around, there were monuments carved with armorial bearings; and on this simple slab of slate —as the curious investigator may still discern, and perplex himself with the purport—there appeared the semblance of an engraved escutcheon. It bore a device, a herald's wording of which might serve for a motto and brief description of our now concluded legend; so sombre is it, and relieved only by one ever-glowing point of light gloomier than the shadow:—

"ON A FIELD, SABLE, THE LETTER A, GULES."

THE END.

The Library of Literature

The Library of Liberal Arts

The American Heritage Series